LILY

THE DRAGON AND THE GREAT HORNED OWL

JUDITH ASHLEY

Windtree
Press

CONTENTS

Windtree Press

http://windtreepress.com

Book Cover by Christy Caughie www.gildedheartdesigns.com

Ashley/Judith Ashley – 1st Edition

Print ISBN 978-1940064512

Ebook ISBN 978-1940064529

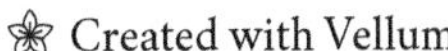 Created with Vellum

ACKNOWLEDGMENTS

No book is born without the help of many people. I've been blessed to have a village of people supporting me for over a decade as I wrote my way through to this date in time.

The Wild Women Writers (Patricia, Becky, Roberta and Michele) read my first draft and were gentle in their feedback. I've reread those first pages and cringe.

I won an hour meeting with Alexis Harrington at a Willamette Writers Conference. She spent over two hours with me, bought my tea and salad, and most important, encouraged me to keep writing and steered me to Romance Writers of America and the Rose City Romance Writers chapter. Alexis was the first person who showed me how generous romance writers are.

My home chapter, Rose City Romance Writers. What's more important? The friends, the support, the shared knowledge – without it all I would not be here. I especially want to acknowledge Sarah Raplee, Paty Jager, Maggie McVey Lynch, Jessa Slade, Deanne Wilsted, Delilah Marvelle, Nancy Lytle, and the #RCRWFTB folks! Romancing the Genres and the Genre-istas are another major group of supporters.

And last but not least, my family and friends. Michele Lauren and

Lois Regn have read every word. My own sacred women's circle: Michele, Kris, and Heather listened to me talk about this journey and always showed interest and excitement no matter how nattering I was.

Yes, this is long! But it is important for you to see that no author can get a book to you without her village.

1 - IN THE BEGINNING

August 1, 1985
Rural Chinook County, Oregon

The acrid smell of hot asphalt burned her nose and throat. The constant slap, slap, slap of the tires hitting the melting surface drummed a beat that reverberated throughout the car. Lily Hughes' sweat-soaked hands slipped on the steering wheel and the back wheels of her dark-green, state-issued car veered toward the ditch. Her heart pounded as adrenalin surged and she fought to keep the car on the road. *What a day to be doing this.*

Disaster avoided, the car under control, Lily swiped a damp hand down the side of her dark purple skirt and breathed a sigh of relief. A glance in the rearview mirror showed John's dark-blue county car still behind her. Slowing at the entrance to the drive, she waved at Merle, the deputy sheriff, waiting as their back-up. *Hopefully, we won't need him.*

Taking even more care due to the condition of the drive, she maneuvered the car into the ruts to more easily steer toward the dilapidated old farm house on a rise in the land. Sweat dripped off her nose and ran in rivulets between her breasts, flowing around the pendant of a lioness she wore around her neck. Her skirt and sleeveless lavender blouse were plastered to her body, her blond hair to her head.

Today was not her first trip to visit the family that lived here. And, as was the case each previous trip, the shadow of something she couldn't define had her heart beating a little faster, her stomach churning with nerves. It didn't happen at every house she visited, but it did happen here.

A glance at the dashboard clock showed the time as two-thirty. Her day, thus far consumed with consults and paperwork had the most important task still ahead.

Parking to the side on a bare patch of ground, Lily got out and watched the unmarked county car following her come to a stop. Tension infused every part of her body and a dose of anxiety coated her stomach. *I'm so glad I'm not doing this alone and grateful the juvenile department sent John.*

"Take care in there, Lily." John's voice was quiet and calm, his steps measured as he approached.

"We both need to," she replied with a slight smile. "Remember, Merle will be showing up in," she looked at her watch, "nine more minutes if we aren't out of here." Turning, Lily took in the scene as she started up the dirt path toward the back door, the only entrance to the house, as the front porch had fallen off. The yard of knee-high-brown grass hid the haphazard holes and scattered junk she'd seen on her first visit.

What struck her most was what was absent, missing. No sounds, no vivid colors, not even bright colored flowering weeds. Nothing but brown grass, a falling down weathered house and the heaviness of despair. She stopped to scratch the ears of the flea-ridden, emaciated mutt chained at the bottom of the steps. "You'll have a new home and a dish filled with food by tonight, Dobbs," she whispered, glad her plan included Merle making sure Dobbs made it to the animal shelter.

Straightening, she grasped the lioness pendant and focused on her goal. She stayed next to the house, her shoulder almost touching the bare siding, the safest way up the rickety stairs. Anxiety churned in her stomach even with John's footsteps behind her. On the landing, she saw two faces peeking shyly through the screen door. "Hi there," Lily said softly. "Is your mommy home?"

"Get the hell back in your room!" a woman's voice shrilled.

The faces quickly disappeared.

"What ya want?" the slim woman snarled, looking out from the kitchen through the hall to the back door.

"Hi, Jane," Lily said with what she hoped was warmth. "May we come in?"

Jane stalked over and shoved the screen door open, nearly knocking it into Lily.

Lily stepped into the hall and followed Jane into the kitchen. Two days ago it had been bad. Today she swallowed rising bile as the smell of urine, feces and rotten food assailed her. Nothing had been cleaned up and more dirty dishes, pots and pans had been added. Jane was wearing the same faded shorts and filthy tank-top, her dirty, stringy brown hair still pulled back in an unkempt ponytail.

"Jane, I'd like you to meet John Jacobson from the Chinook County Juvenile Department." She continued in a calm manner, knowing John's involvement was crucial to her success and the clock was ticking. "I've been out to see you and the children at least twice a week for almost two months now." Lily moved farther into the kitchen. "If you'll recall, I made arrangements for someone to help you take care of your house and children."

"I don't need no help." Jane stomped over to the sink and turned on the water.

Lily continued, pitching her voice to be heard. "The baby's been hospitalized twice now and the doctor says he isn't growing like he should. Your oldest daughter has more responsibility than an eight-year-old should have." She didn't mention the bruises and marks on the middle girl. That was all listed in the papers. "I want you to know this isn't about whether you love your children, Jane. I know you love them and want to do better by them. The truth of the matter is your children need more than you are able to give them."

"Yer not taken my kids," Jane growled, turning from the sink and advancing toward Lily.

Taking papers out of her bag, Lily showed them to Jane. "These are the legal papers that say I will be taking them with me today, Jane. The petition lists the reasons," she said in an even voice, pointing to the top paper.

John stepped between the two women, took the papers from Lily's now outstretched hand. "Jane, let me go over these papers with you so you know what's happening." He blocked Jane's view of Lily and repeated himself, his voice calm, his manner low-key. With one hand he gestured toward the kitchen counter, gently steering Jane so her back was partially turned away from Lily.

Just like I planned. Taking advantage of the opportunity provided by John's distraction, Lily ducked down the hallway to the first bedroom where she found the three children. The oldest, a girl of eight, held her six-month-old baby brother, and half-hidden behind them was the four-year-old sister. A pile of dirty diapers in the corner added to the stench and chaos. A stained mattress on the floor, a ragged filthy blanket strewn on top, a cardboard box for a dresser comprised the furniture; peeling paint, the broken window and screen and holes in the walls the décor.

Digging in her purse, she drew out three large black plastic bags, the kind used for garbage. She reconsidered and stuffed one back.

"Come," Lily said softly to the children. "I'm taking you where you'll be safe."

Both girls' eyes flew open, stark terror showing.

"But," the oldest stammered, glancing toward the door, "she'll find me and hit me."

"No," Lily whispered. "She won't ever hit you again." Holding one bag out to the oldest she asked, "Can you pack your brother's things also?" At the young girl's nod, Lily handed her a bag.

Kneeling beside the four-year-old, Lily held the plastic bag open so the girl could put her things inside. Fighting back tears, she watched the little girl take her meager belongings from the box on the floor. Everything she had didn't cover the bottom of the bag.

She stood, her hand resting on the four-year-old's slim shoulders. The oldest girl was still holding her baby brother, and her black garbage bag showed she'd done her packing.

"Do you have a few diapers for the baby?" Lily asked.

"Only two," she whispered back. "I put his blanket in here," she pointed to the black plastic bag with her foot, and then pointing her foot to a dirty bottle on the floor she added, "We've got that for him if he gets hungry."

Lily stood motionless, lost in the pain of it all. Jane was screaming, her agony and anguish palpable. Fear was etched on the faces of the older children. The baby's eyes were wide. He'd already learned not to cry when startled or scared.

"Yer not takin' my kids!" Jane's strident tone reverberated through the house.

A quick glance at her watch showed she needed to act fast and get the children out of the house.

"You've done such a good job taking care of everything and everyone for so long," she said to the oldest girl. "I can see you've done your best for your baby brother." Her words were met by a solemn face with large brown eyes.

"Now," Lily said bending closer to the three children. "I need you both to be quick and brave for me. Can you be quick?"

Two heads nodded.

"Can you carry your baby brother and one sack of things?" she asked the oldest. Seeing her nod and pick up the sack, she turned to the four-year-old who already had her sack flowing over her spindly arms.

"I see you can carry your sack." She folded it so the ends didn't drape down. "Right now, being quick is more important than being brave." Lily smiled, hoping to reassure them. "You know what my car looks like? The dark-green one?"

Solemn wide eyes gazed at her.

"I want you to go quickly, get in my car and shut the doors. Do not get out unless I tell you to," she said reaching to take the four year old's hand. "Come with me."

Jane's voice rose another octave as Lily led the children down the hall to the back door. She stopped at the doorway to the kitchen, blocking the view into the hallway as she motioned behind her for the children to go on.

"NO ONE is gonna take my kids! NO ONE! They're MINE!" Jane shrieked.

Eyes huge with terror, the children stood as if rooted to the floor.

Lily stepped back into the hall, bent down to the children's level and quietly said, "This is where I need you to be brave. Go quick when I walk into the kitchen. Keep going until you're in my car. Lock the doors and you'll be safe until I get there. Can you do that for me? Get in the car and lock the doors?" Two heads bobbed. She swayed as a wave of relief crashed over her. The hours she'd spent building a relationship with the children during each visit were paying off.

Using her body as a shield to block the view of their exit as best she could, Lily walked into the kitchen. John stood at an angle to the hall door, his focus entirely on Jane. While his demeanor and voice were calm, Lily saw sweat on his brow. Jane, papers grasped in one hand, arms waving, stood in front of him, screeching a litany of complaints and demands.

The screen door slammed.

An unnatural hush fell over the room.

Jane spun away from John and raced to the window in time to see her children scrambling into the back seat of the state car—Lily's car.

"You bitch!" Jane screamed. Her face contorted in rage, she grabbed a butcher knife, raised it over her head, and charging Lily, shrieked, "I'll kill you!"

"Get out Lily! Get the hell out now!" John shouted as he seized Jane's arm and struggled to hold her in place.

And she did.

Lily charged out the door, sprinted down the steps, and ran to her car, just as Merle pulled up the driveway. She ran toward him, waving frantically toward the house. For a big man, Merle could scramble. He was out of his car and racing toward the house in a flash.

Fumbling for her keys, she found them in seconds that felt like minutes. Once in the car, she looked in the back seat to check that the children were buckled in. A few miles down the road she'd stop and double check. Now she had to get them out of here.

"You've done so well," she told them in what she hoped was a reassuring voice.

Starting the car, she began to back out. When she glanced toward the house again, she saw Jane at the top of the stairs, still screaming, pain and outrage etched on her face. Merle's arm around her waist kept her from bolting down the steps and to the car. The butcher knife was nowhere in sight. She didn't see any bloody gashes. Lily prayed the two men were okay as she continued to back the car around. Gravel spewed as she revved the motor and sped out the driveway.

SEVEN HOURS LATER, Lily pulled up to the curb in front of the house in Fremont she shared with her husband, Paul, and her son, Charlie. She was physically, mentally, and emotionally exhausted—drained from a day that seemed like it would never end. From Jane's house, she'd taken the children to a shelter home where she'd stayed while the foster mother made a dash to the store to get them a few essential things.

The children were confused and overwhelmed with all the changes. During the long drive to the shelter home, she'd reassured them over and over that they were safe, that their mother could not come and get them. She saw the middle child's eyes fill with wary hope and the eldest's with disbelief. So she'd stayed through dinner, bath time and tucked them into bed with promises to be back in the morning. Somewhere in the bustle of placement and the children settling in, she'd made a quick call to check on John and Merle. A weight she hadn't realized she carried lifted when she heard John's voice and he told her they were okay. She'd smiled knowing the children would be glad Dobbs was being cared for at the animal shelter.

At her front door, Lily stopped a moment to compose herself. She was depleted, bled dry from the day's events, but knew she had more to face before the night was over. When she'd called Paul to tell him she'd be late, he'd yelled and cussed at her.

Somewhere in the last six months, her fairy-tale marriage had ended. Paul was more upset with her, more critical, more demanding. All of her efforts to talk to him, to explain the importance of her work, to negotiate a peaceful solution made no difference. Somewhere between falling in love and getting married she'd made a horrible mistake.

Opening the door, stepping over the threshold, she was immediately aware of the tension and silence. First thing on her list was to check on her twelve-month-old son, Charlie, the light of her life, the one gift from her marriage. Down the hall on the left, she stopped at his door. With the hall light behind her, she could see the shadow of him. Tiptoeing to his crib, she looked down. He was sleeping quietly, his fist in his mouth. Gently she pulled it away, brushed his hair from his brow and bent over to kiss his forehead.

The light from the hallway dimmed. A dark shadow crossed the carpet.

"Where in the hell have you been!" Paul hurled the words at her in a growl. "Someone else's children are more important than your own?" he said his voice a mix of menace and sarcasm.

Lily turned from the crib and started for the doorway. She just wanted to get out of Charlie's room so he wouldn't wake to their fighting. Another thing that had become more frequent: the fights, the name calling, the barrage of nastiness. "Please let me pass, Paul," she said her voice quiet. "We can go in the other room and you can have your say."

"You're damn right I'll have my say," he hissed.

Behind her, Charlie stirred.

Paul moved slightly in the doorway, but to pass, Lily had to brush against him. Shivers of revulsion turned into a lump of dread in her stomach. She breathed in the musk aftershave he favored. Lungs burning with the heavy scent, she held her breath until she passed him. He followed her down the hall to the family room, his heavy tread echoing in her bones. *What happened to the man I married, the man who laughed and kissed me awake each morning? How could I have gotten it so wrong?*

"Look at me," he demanded as soon as they stepped into the other room. "Look at me and listen, damn you." He grabbed her arm and spun her around.

She hated this. Hated this change in the man she'd loved more than life itself when they married; hated the tears welling in her eyes.

"What's this? Tears? Do you really think I'll fall for that? What kind of a sucker do you take me for?" Paul roared, his hot breath spewing on her, his face contorted in anger.

The second hate-filled face she'd had to deal with today. Steeling herself, Lily locked her knees to keep from buckling and willed the tears to stop. Charlie's whimper escalated to a full-blown cry.

"See what you did? You woke the kid up. Well, you're home now, you go fix it. I'm going out!" He shoved her, stomped past her and slammed out the front door. Moments later she heard tires squealing as he peeled out of the driveway.

Charlie's crying abated.

Lily, sprawled on the couch where she'd landed, grasped the lioness pendant so hard, her palm was marked. Her head swirled with unanswerable questions. *What has happened to us? Why is he so angry and resentful? He didn't use to mind taking care of Charlie. He was happy when I got this job. It doesn't make any sense.*

She was new on the job and unsure of her skills. But her supervisor had stopped by the shelter home to congratulate her on how she'd handled today. 'You're a natural for the job,' she'd been told. While her supervisor's accolades felt good, she had four more months of probation. Four more months when she could be fired without cause. Prickles along her spine warned her to be aware and be cautious. Her marriage was in serious trouble. So far, he hadn't hit her, but he had shoved her: tonight—hard.

Charlie's whimpers brought her back to the present. She strode to his room, lifted him from the crib. Holding him close, she let the intensity and tension from the day ebb from her body.

"Your daddy's changed, Charlie," she whispered. "He isn't the same man I married." She settled into the rocking chair and rubbed his back. "I don't know why he's changed." She felt tears threaten, breathed deeply and tightened her arms around her son. "It doesn't matter why, does it? He appears so reasonable around other people, no one who knows him believes his private side is so dark, that he has such a temper or can be so mean."

Lily shifted in the chair, moved the footstool closer to put up her feet. "I'll find a way," she whispered. "I'll find a way to make things better for us, Charlie. I promise."

2 - TEN YEARS LATER

August 1995
Multnomah County
Fremont, Oregon

Just before five, Lily Hughes pulled her car into the driveway of the little house she and Charlie shared. She grabbed her client notebook from her briefcase, flipping it open, searching through the pages until she reached the one she wanted.

"Yes, Dr. Parker. I appreciate your help with this." Her voice brisk and businesslike, she tucked her cell phone between her shoulder and chin, her pen ready to take notes.

"And I appreciate what you've done to protect Mrs. Chamberlin. The police report portrays you as a force to be reckoned with." He chuckled.

"I'm really not remarkable at all, doctor. All I did was call 911. The police had the task of keeping the son-in-law at bay."

"The way I heard it, you charged the door."

"No. I scooted past when Officer Jacobs's presence gave me the opportunity. I found Margaret on the floor in a back bedroom, cowering. Because her arm looked crooked and her coloring was off, I called 911 for an ambulance and pulled a dresser in front of the door. I wanted Margaret to know she was safe." She paused before adding in a determined voice, "It's so important for the victim to know they are finally safe."

"Sounds like you know a bit about that," Dr. Parker encouraged.

"Actually, I do. I used to work with Child Protective Services," she said.

"When did you move to the other end of the age spectrum?"

"Gradually, over the course of a year. That was… ," she paused. "five or six years ago. When my parents were first ill, it took me hours and hours to figure out the system and how best to get them the care they needed. A family member of another resident overheard my conversation with nursing facility staff and asked if she could pick my brain. I answered her questions and offered to keep an eye on things for her because she lived on the East Coast. I was stunned when I saw the amount she insisted on paying me." Lily shook her head remembering the amount on the check. "My business just sprouted out of that conversation."

"Well, Ms. Hughes, I'm glad you do what you do," he said. "Are you concerned about anything else other than Mrs. Chamberlin's broken arm?"

"Yes, I am. I'd appreciate your ordering what tests are needed to determine if Margaret has some form of dementia or is just traumatized. From another client, the one who told me about Margaret, I learned she's lost some functioning. However, I do know that can be a side-effect of abuse."

"I'll take care of it." He paused. "I'd like to tell Mrs. Chamberlin when she can expect you to visit. She is fearful her family will take her out of the hospital."

"Tell her I've notified Adult Protective Services and I'll be in to see her …" Lily flipped through her organizer. "… in the morning, around ten, if that's all right, doctor?" Lily waited with pen poised to hear his confirmation before writing it down.

"I'll let her know."

"Thank you, Dr. Parker; I really do appreciate all the extras you've done for Margaret."

"Not a problem," he replied as they ended the call.

She'd only heard good things about Mark Parker from the ER staff. Glad he was Margaret's doctor, Lily gathered up her things, tucked them back in her briefcase and headed toward the house. She smiled at the realization Charlie was already there. Last month when he turned eleven, they struck a bargain; he could come home after school if she didn't have a late appointment. There were rules: he had to call and he had chores and none of his friends could come with him. Her heart skipped a beat. Her little boy was growing up.

A spring in her walk, she took the porch steps two at a time. Life was good. She loved seeing other people were safe and cared for and she was good at it. They weren't rich, but they were buying this house, owned everything inside, and had a little bit in the bank.

The main benefit with her case management and guardianship business was the flexibility. And even with a day like today, in comparison to her work protecting children, there was much less stress. All of that meant she had more time with Charlie, who was still the light of her life. A grin flashed across her face as she remembered his flush of embarrassment whenever she called him that even though he knew she took great pains to never do that in front of his friends.

In hindsight, she was grateful for her time working to protect children. There were no regrets. The reality was her work with adults as a private guardian and geriatric case manager brought her a similar sense of accomplishment, a comfortable income and that extra time with her son. Time was a precious commodity and she wanted to spend these years being the best mom she could be.

She lingered on the porch, soaking up the sense of peace and safety that had convinced her this was the house, her haven. Paul's abuse had escalated and she'd been caught up in the cycle – flowers, apologies interspersed with the shoving and just before he left, hitting. Funny, in a not so humorous way, how she'd excused the shoving, told herself it wasn't really hitting, promised herself she'd leave if he ever actually hit her. In the end, he had hit her. Hit her and then packed up and left. Charlie had been two when Paul left. He had been five when her parents had gotten sick not quite six when they died. The small inheritance had been the down payment on this house. *Things have a way of balancing out. This house, my life – I'm so grateful.*

"I'm home," she hollered as she came through the door, dropping her things on a nearby chair. "Charlie?" She sniffed, the scent of chocolate and flour in the air.

"In here, Mom, I'm in the kitchen. Come see what I've done," he said, his voice high-pitched with excitement.

Lily stood transfixed at the kitchen's entrance, the scene before her out of one of those slap-stick comedy movies. Everything was coated with a heavy dusting of flour, the sink full of bowls and pans, and as she stepped through the doorway, sugar grated beneath her shoes.

"I'm fixing dinner," he announced, eyes shining, mouth grinning, his face smeared with an unidentifiable substance, his hair and clothing frosted with flour.

"So I see," she said, proud she didn't shriek upon seeing the mess.

He gestured grandly to where a lopsided cake sat on the counter. "I made it from scratch."

"It looks…delicious." She decided was a safe response. "Cook anything else?" Her glance darted around the kitchen.

"I thought we could grill hamburgers or hot dogs outside." His grin reached from ear-to-ear.

"Let me get changed and we'll roast those hot dogs," she said over her shoulder as she made her way out of the kitchen. "Or do you want hamburgers?" She reached down, taking off her shoes before starting up the carpeted stairway off the dining room.

"Hot dogs are fine, Mom. Should I start the grill?" he said his voice eager.

"Wait until I come down. I'll only be a minute," she called out from her room as she hurriedly changed into a pair of old shorts and top.

～

LILY FINISHED a final wipe-down of the cupboards and counters, straightened and rubbed her aching lower back. Charlie's first solo foray into the culinary arts had turned out rather well. The cake was edible and he hadn't cut himself or burned the house down and for that she was grateful. A smile flashed across her face. *Mom always baked from scratch and that last year we lived with them, guess he picked up more than I realized.* She stretched the kinks out and put the cleaning supplies away. He was so proud of his first endeavor but also somewhat relieved they'd begin cooking meals together.

She cooked, but knowing how and enjoying it were two different things. While she loved having her own home, she didn't love taking care of it. In her dream world she could afford someone to come in and clean every week and in her fantasy dream world, she had a cook.

Shaking her head to rid it of the unrealistic vision, Lily moved to the living room and her favorite chair, picking up her planner from her briefcase along the way. Her nightly routine consisted of reviewing her day and checking on tasks for tomorrow. An inveterate list maker, she took great satisfaction at the end of the day, crossing things off or moving them to the next day. She'd just finished noting her ten o'clock at the hospital with MargaretC when the blinking light on her answering machine caught her eye. Flicking the dials, she pushed "play."

Cold dread encased her bones. Her lungs seized and her heart stuttered as the familiar voice from her past wrapped its hatred around her.

"I've found you, haven't I?" the woman's guttural voice hissed, followed by manic laughter.

Lily struggled to draw oxygen into her starving lungs.

"You took what was mine. Now it's my turn to take something precious from you." The click of the receiver cut off the cackling voice.

The room spun and waves of nausea assailed her. Lily buried her head in her hands, fighting down the panic, willing her unruly body back under her control. It was Jane's voice; Jane, who'd tried to kill her, had finally found her; Jane whose desire to harm her was now an obsession.

Her planner lay open on her lap, the pen fallen to the floor. Numbly she sat in her favorite chair, frozen, staring into the past with unseeing eyes.

3 - A WORLD BROKEN APART

October 1995
Fremont, Oregon

*A*lert and on guard, Lily drove slowly through her neighborhood, past her house, around the block and back again. The call to the police that August night had been devastating. She had no address, no phone number, a ten-year-old description and the threat was vague. Jane hadn't even given her name. It didn't matter that she recognized the voice and told them what Jane was capable of. There was nothing the police could do.

She alerted her neighbors to call 911 if they ever saw a woman matching Jane's description from ten years ago or any woman loitering or lurking in the vicinity. Charlie was never alone. Gone in an instant was the safe life she had built for them.

The most chilling message was the one that came in September, the one that stood out in a string of almost daily calls, the one that galvanized her to do something. "I can kill you and nothin'll happen to me. I'm crazy." Hysterical laughter had followed.

She'd immediately pulled out the phone book, called a security company and had bars on her basement windows and security doors installed. It took another month before she totally capitulated; gave up her insistence that life be fair. Life wasn't fair, this whole situation wasn't fair. Fair had nothing to do with anything. She had the phone number changed, had it unlisted, had it under an assumed name. She hadn't known you could do that until, tears streaming down her cheeks, her words uttered in shaky gulps, she told the telephone customer service person her problem.

The calls stopped.

Gone was the sense of peace and safety, the sense of her house being a refuge from the realities of the day.

Second-guessing herself was the norm. The uncertainty she'd thought she'd surmounted when her marriage disintegrated ten years ago was back full force. Underneath the uncertainty a low-grade fever of panic remained ready to burst forth whenever she saw a slightly built woman with stringy brown hair. She was amazed at how many of them lived in Fremont.

Once inside with the doors locked, it was better, but the joy, the sense of her home as a sanctuary was lost and she didn't know if she'd ever get it back.

The calls stopped, but life had not gone back to what it had been before that August day. Most nights she woke twisted in her sheets from vivid night terrors. Most nights she checked on Charlie at least once if not twice. Most days she startled at shadows and teared up over nothing.

Even the conversation with her friend in Arizona hadn't fixed everything. She'd followed his suggestions: a phone next to her bed, a long stout stick nearby, practice blocking the way to her room at the top of the stairs, prepare herself to be cut most likely on the hands and arms. He'd assured her she wouldn't die from these wounds.

The calls stopped but this house she'd fallen in love with, this house that held her hopes, dreams and desires for a new life was now tainted. She wouldn't let herself think that it might always be. It was too overwhelming to think about starting over again—starting over in a new house, in a new location, building a new business.

Hyper-vigilant was a way of life, distraction its partner. Sleep deprivation was taking its toll. If she could just sleep. Physical work: raking leaves, scrubbing floors, washing walls left her tired, just not tired enough to sleep the night through; left her with too much time to think, to attempt to balance her sense of right and wrong, fair and unfair, to figure out how much of her life she had to give up in order to be safe.

Charlie's safety was even more important than her own. Micro-managing his life was her best effort to keep him safe. Gone were the carefree hours of playing with friends, time at the park or walking the five blocks to the store. She needed to know where he was every minute of the day to know he was safe.

Somewhere in her musing she thought safety a myth, something we tell ourselves that really isn't true. As that thought increased her anxiety, she stopped trying to analyze everything and stick to the basics. It was a work in progress though and she knew her over-protectiveness was driving a wedge between them.

What helped more than anything? Burying herself in her business, focusing on someone else, visiting during the day, telephone calls in the evening, and staying up late into the night writing reports kept the boogeyman-thoughts away. And the reality was everything took longer because of her hyper-vigilant, distraction, second-guessing the simplest decisions.

The key in the lock brought her out of her ruminations. She blinked and looked up from her favorite chair as Charlie came in the door, mail in hand. She noted his wind-blown hair and knew he'd run the half-block from the bus stop to the house. It had been hard but she no longer met him at the bus and walked him home.

"Hi, Mom." He shoved the mail at her, dropped his back-pack on a dining room chair and came to stand before her.

"Yeah, Charlie?" She loved to look at her son. He was almost as tall as she was and took great pride in every inch he gained on her.

"Brody wants to know if I can go trick-or-treating with him and some other guys tomorrow night and then spend the night." He rushed on. "His mom said it was okay and to call her if you wanted to check it out." Charlie stood before her, hands shoved in his back pockets, waiting.

She could feel the pent-up energy in him as he held himself in check. Standing, she put her arm around his shoulder. He no longer welcomed or gave the full hugs she adored.

"I need a little time to think it over." She kissed his cheek, he shied away. She moved in front of him, reached out to put her hands on his shoulders.

He pulled away. "When will you let me do things? I'm not a baby, you know."

She matched his movements and looked him straight on. "No, you aren't and I don't think of you as a baby or even a child. You're growing up so fast and are becoming a wonderful young man."

"Then why don't you trust me? Why don't you let me do things with my friends anymore?"

"This isn't about my trusting you, Charlie. It's about how much I don't trust the woman who wants to hurt us. Actually, that isn't even true. I do trust her. I trust she wants to hurt me however she can." Clearing her throat, she added, "and I trust you, Charlie. But if she hurt you it would ruin everything. I can't let that happen."

"You just don't see, do you?" He jerked away and stomped over to his backpack. Picking it up, he slung it over his shoulder. "She's already taken my mom away."

She heard the frustration and tears in his tone. If she hadn't been listening so hard, she might have missed his next words as he turned away.

"She might as well take me too."

His words cut sharper than Jane's butcher knife. It would be so easy to turn away, so easy to curl into a ball, but easy wasn't the answer. "Charlie," she said, with a firmness she didn't feel.

He stopped. His head bowed, his shoulders slumped. "You just don't see it, do you?

"No, Charlie, I don't see it that way. I don't see she should take you too," she said gently. "But I do see she's taken away how we used to live. I promise, Charlie. I promise it'll get better." She was making a promise she had no idea how to keep. The weight of being a single parent buckled her knees. The knot in her stomach lurched and bile rose in her throat. *If only I....*

"I've got homework." He shrugged, hefting the backpack more firmly on his shoulders, and walked away.

"Charlie? About tomorrow night... ." She was desperate to assure him everything would be all right. *How to do that for him when you didn't know how yourself?*

He stopped but didn't turn around.

"I still need some time to think things over, but I promise I'll call Brody's mom later. That's the best I can offer right now." She refused to wring her hands no matter how much she wanted to. Instead, she stood silent and listened as her son made his way to his room, listened as he quietly shut his door.

4 - A NEW BEGINNING

She needed something to do, anything to fill the void made by Charlie's words. No, not just anything, she needed something productive. The mail still clutched in her fist, she sat at the dining table and began to sort through the day's offerings: the ever-present bills, the solicitations for credit cards, the neighborhood newspaper and miscellaneous flyers.

One of the latter caught her eye. Printed on variegated orange, yellow and red paper, the design featured a border of hummingbirds, dragonflies, eagles, owls, salmon, whales, a lioness and her cub, pandas, elephants and playful puppies and kittens. And while she almost always tossed these flyers in the recycling bin, especially those addressed to "occupant" as this one was, her attention had been captured.

Opening it, Lily found an invitation to learn about and perhaps become part of a sacred women's circle. Her interest piqued, it occurred to her that joining a group of women would be something new, something different, something that might help her move forward. Reading on, she learned that any woman who wanted to know more about sacred women's circles was invited to Sophia Stewart's house on October 31, Halloween, tomorrow night.

If I okay Charlie spending Halloween with Brody and his family, I'm free to go. Why wouldn't she? Brody's parents often included Charlie in their family activities and they were aware of Jane's threats. She'd still make the call because this was the first time the invitation came through Brody and not from one of his parents. With Charlie gone, she could go if she decided to take a chance to see if whatever this was might help her find her footing again.

Sophia Stewart's address, simple directions and a phone number to RSVP were included. Sophia was looking for a like-minded group of women to take this journey with her. But when Lily reached for the phone to RSVP, an internal debate started. *You don't know what you're getting into. It would be something different. It couldn't hurt. I can always leave.*

"Mom?"

"Yes?" She glanced in the direction of Charlie's voice; saw him standing a few feet away, nervously shifting from one foot to the other, his hands jammed in his back pockets.

"Brody wants me to spend the weekend with them. They're going to the beach."

She heard the hope in his voice. He wanted to go. He didn't want to be with her. He might love her but...and that was a big But—a sharp pain stabbed through her chest. If Paul was a part of their lives, Charlie would want to be with him. Charlie with Paul was more than she could bear.

"That sounds like a lot. Halloween trick-or-treating, spending the night and a weekend at the beach?" Lily tried for a bright smile, for a light tone in her voice, but from the look on Charlie's face she hadn't hit the mark. She glanced away. When her gaze rested once again on her son, he was studying his shoes. Standing, she took the few steps to him; her gaze followed his to study his shoes.

"Please come home after school tomorrow so I can see you before you go over to Brody's, okay?" She wanted to reach out to him, take him in her arms, hold him as she had so many times, but she didn't. She was the one who needed comforting but she was the adult, he was the child. It was her job to comfort herself.

"You mean I can go?"

He looked at her as if she'd given him a precious gift and in some ways she had. He didn't have to spend Halloween and the weekend that followed with his hyper-vigilant, anxious, depressed Mom.

"I still need to talk to Brody's parents, but if everything checks out, you can go. Remember, I want to see you after school," she warned, laying her hand on his shoulder. "I just got an invitation to a meeting tomorrow night so this works out really great for me too," she said with growing conviction. "Charlie?"

"Yeah, Mom?"

When he looked up, she caught his eye and held his gaze. "I know I've promised you things will be better. I want you to know I mean to keep that promise. It's just taken me awhile to figure things out, to find a direction to go. This meeting I'm going to tomorrow night?"

"Yeah?"

"I have a feeling it may be just what I need." She took a chance and leaned close to press a brief kiss on his forehead. He was at that stage where he resisted her affection, but she also knew it was important to keep the connection, both the verbal and the physical ones.

"I want my mom back," he said looking at her with serious eyes.

"I want her back, too." She took a chance and put her arms around him, breathed in the scent of growing boy. He didn't resist and instead hugged her back. "How about celebrating and going out for pizza?"

"We're having pizza tomorrow night. How about Mexican take-out?" he countered.

"Mexican take-out it is." She stepped back. "Meet you here in an hour, okay?"

"You bet." He grinned and started back to his room.

Lily picked up her cell phone and the flyer. *Progress? I didn't even hear the home phone ring. Not that it would've rung more than once with Charlie home.* Walking into her office she dialed the number and left a message to count her in.

～

THE DOOR OPENED before Lily even knocked. She was greeted by a woman close to her own age wearing a long skirt in a forest green with a lighter green blouse. Her straight brown hair was waist-length and her warm brown eyes tipped up at the corners.

"Welcome," the woman said, her friendly smile inviting, her hand outstretched in greeting. "I'm Sophia Stewart. I'm so glad you could come."

"I'm Lily Hughes," she said stepping into the front hall and extending her own hand in turn. The aroma of pumpkins and spice filled the air and an arrangement of fall leaves and branches with berries sat on a narrow hall table. "To be honest, I'm not sure why I'm here." Her voice reflected her nervousness and doubts.

"I think you'll be in good company," Sophia said before taking her coat, hanging it in the hall closet and showing her to the living room.

As she was led across the room to the six women making small talk, Lily noted the plethora of candles on every flat surface with different rocks and crystals mixed in. The scents of the different candles blended into a light background fragrance. The doorbell rang and Sophia quickly introduced her to two of the other women before hurrying off to welcome the next person. An underlying current of anxiety—or, putting a more positive spin on things, perhaps anticipation—ran through the room. She wasn't the only person out of her element.

"Ladies? This is Diana Pettybone," Sophia said, introducing the new arrival before turning back to the hall and the already chiming doorbell.

Lily stroked the lioness pendant dangling on the chain around her neck as she looked over at the elegantly dressed brunette, her hair styled in a classic page boy, standing just inside the room.

You can do this, you can do this she chanted to herself as she walked over to introduce herself. They immediately learned they had something in common: sons who were involved in Little League, soccer, and basketball, which meant that as parents, they were involved in car pooling and balancing game schedules with other commitments.

When the doorbell had been silent for a few minutes, Sophia clapped her hands and invited everyone to sit – on the floor if possible.

She and Diana sat next to each other among the seventeen other women of all ages who'd come. They may not know each other but they had sons in common and in this group it was enough to bind them together.

Listening to Sophia talk about *The Millionth Circle* by Jean Shinoda Bolen, Lily knew there was more missing from her life than a place of safety. She didn't really have a group of supportive friends. It wasn't that she had No Friends, but she didn't have friends who just listened and let her talk. She had the 'fixing type' of friends, the ones who tried to fix whatever you were talking about. In this sacred women's circle, Sophia talked about a place where each woman had a chance to say whatever she wanted to say and no one would interrupt or even offer suggestions unless they were asked.

Sophia's vision for this sacred circle included the members developing their own spirituality, this being a safe place to be, to share, to belong, all based upon the power of the Divine Feminine. Listening, Lily's shoulders relaxed and the mild nausea she'd lived with these past couple of months eased. Even when Sophia explained about a 'talking stone' and it started around the room so each woman could say whatever she wanted, the sense of being in the right place remained.

When her turn came, Lily said, "I'm Lily. I've never been to anything like this but the creativity of the flyer drew me." She gripped the talking stone, a nervous laugh escaping. "I'm intrigued by the concepts you've talked about, Sophia, and would like to read Dr. Bolen's book." She handed the talking stone to Diana.

Once the stone had passed from hand to hand around the room, Sophia talked a bit more about a formal opening and closing of a circle to mark their "coming together" she'd called it, thanked them all for being there, and invited them into the great room for pumpkin cookies, coffee and tea.

Lily found herself standing next to Diana again, sipping tea and eating one of the most delicious cookies ever when Sophia approached.

"These cookies are decadent," Lily said, taking another bite.

"I'm glad you're enjoying them. I've made plenty so take a few with you." She gestured to the counter where another plate of cookies sat. "Did the two of you know each other before tonight?"

"No," Diana spoke up, "we didn't but we have sons about the same age. I think a couple of the other women have children but they are either much younger or older."

"Hunter," Sophia called out, motioning a long-legged red-haired woman over. "I'd like you to meet Lily Hughes and Diana Pettybone. I think their sons are close in age to your daughter." And with that she moved off to another group.

"How old are your sons?" Hunter asked an interested smile on her face.

"My son is eleven," Lily answered.

"My son is twelve," Diana added.

Even though her daughter, Logan, was nine, she was involved in sports, so the specter of soccer tournaments in the cold, rainy weather carried the conversation.

A bell rang, bringing conversation to a halt. Sophia stepped up on a stool, holding a notebook in one hand. "Please sign up here if you'd like to come to another Circle. I'll be calling people and organizing a date and time that works best for folks."

"Perhaps those who want to meet again could set a date and time now," Diana suggested.

"Well, that a great idea," Sophia answered. "Who is interested in pursuing this avenue with me?"

Lily tentatively raised her hand, looking around to see who else had raised hers. Diana shrugged and raised hers. Hunter grinned and raised hers. "Should be interesting," she whispered.

"If we've found we aren't interested, is it okay to leave now?" another woman spoke up.

"Of course it is," Sophia responded. "Anyone who isn't interested can leave at any time. I'll get your coats." She stepped off the stool and made her way to the hall closet where she retrieved coats, hats, scarves for the women who were leaving. When she returned to the family room, eleven women remained.

While finding a time that fit for everyone could have been a challenge, in this case it was easy and the group agreed to meet in two weeks. Lily watched as Sophia sent the notebook around for each woman to write out her contact information. Diana offered to type it and mail out the list to everyone.

When the notebook reached Lily, her nausea returned, along with the knot of familiar tension. Those delicious cookies now felt like stones. Who were these women? She couldn't just give out her name, address, and phone number to people she didn't know. Maybe this wasn't the place she was supposed to be. Maybe those earlier feelings of rightness were wrong. Maybe now isn't the time.

"Is there a problem, Lily?" Sophia approached her, brows wrinkled in concern, her warm brown eyes laced with worry.

Her stomach churned, her shoulders had their iron bars back in place. "I can't give you my address. Not now," Lily said, her voice wavering.

"Can you come in two weeks?" Diana, who had joined them, asked in a matter-of-fact tone.

"Yes."

"Then I don't see any problem," Diana added. "The worst that will happen is you'll only have Sophia's contact information. Are you okay with that, Sophia?"

"It isn't a problem for me. I'll expect you in two weeks, Lily, unless I hear otherwise."

A wave of relief flooded through Lily, her knees weakened and she almost staggered. "Thank you," she whispered, fully aware her body was telling her in no uncertain terms how important it was to remain a part of this group.

Sophia, still standing in front of her, placed her hand on Lily's shoulder. "You will always be listened to here and I hope you will always feel safe." She lightly squeezed Lily's shoulder before turning back to mingle with the group.

"I have to go now," Lily said softly to Diana.

"I'll go with you. It's time for me to get home. I don't know if my husband gave out any of the trick-or-treat candy or not. He might have just kept it to eat himself." She turned back to the room, "Good night, ladies. Lily and I'll see you in two weeks."

It was eleven o'clock and raining when Lily approached her house, alert to every parked car and intrepid dog walker. Trick or treaters were nowhere in sight. Driving slowly through the darkened streets of the neighborhood, she circled the block before pulling into her driveway. She sat for a moment, her hands fisted on the steering wheel, taking inventory of what happened this evening. She and Charlie weren't any safer. Her home was not the refuge or haven it once had been. But for the first time since Jane's call in early August, she felt a flicker of light, a glimmer of hope. Maybe, just maybe....

Winter Solstice
Fremont, Oregon

Seven women came together in Sophia's living room after having deposited their contributions for the later potluck in the kitchen.

Lily's bond with Diana was the first to grow stronger. The boys' birthdays were a few days apart in July. Add to that the link of them playing soccer and her initial reserve eroded. Chatting about their sons playing sports and the ever-present school and homework challenge buoyed her spirit. Her home still wasn't her refuge but The Circle's meetings were a safe haven. A few days after she'd shared her address and phone number with Sophia, Lily found a gift of winter squash from Sophia's garden. *I feel closest to Diana and Sophia but I like everyone, even our two youngest, Elizabeth and Gabriella.* She paused realizing just how deep a connection she felt with this diverse group of women.

"I wanted to check in with each of you this evening," Sophia began once everyone was settled in a circle on the floor. "I heard from Elsa yesterday and she is dropping out. So, unless one or more of you are having second thoughts, I think the seven of us will comprise our circle." She took her time, her tipped-brown eyes searching each woman's face, giving everyone a chance to speak. "Does anyone have anything to say before we start tonight?" Her question was met with silence and the shaking of several heads.

"While we have met every other week since our first meeting on Samhain — considered the beginning of the Pagan Year — tonight is the first meeting on another of the Pagan Festivals. We'd talked last time about doing some research so we can create a Winter Solstice or Yule Ceremony for tonight. Is that still everyone's wish?"

"I'm not sure exactly how we'll create a ceremony," Hunter said, waving a hand in the air like royalty. "I did do some reading but..." her voice trailed off.

"In an earlier discussion we decided we did not want to be a formal coven, strictly following the principles of Wicca," Gabriella added. "We liked the 'Harm None, Do As You Will' but weren't sure we wanted the formal casting of a circle and all that."

"Y'all remember we talked about our purpose," Ashley began in her soft-Southern accented voice. She and her husband, Art, had moved to Oregon from Alabama years ago and her two children were born in Fremont but there was no mistaking her roots. "We decided we wanted to create our own spirituality based on the idea of the Divine Feminine and the Sacred Energy that infuses all things."

Murmurs of agreement circulated the room. The challenge for them all, Lily knew, was how to do it. As she listened to each woman speak, a soft smile on her face, she knew her decision to remain a part of this circle was the right one. *I'm so fortunate Charlie can spend meeting nights at Brody's.*

Diana ticked off the decisions they'd already made on her fingers in her formal tone of voice. Hunter added to the list, her lips quirked in a broad smile.

"Prayer," Elizabeth spoke up, her voice serious, her blue eyes solemn. "The subject has been brought up but we've danced around it. Some type of prayer, maybe when we begin and when we end would be nice."

"Since we began, we've tried out several different ways to open and close our ceremonies," Sophia spoke now. "Which did you like best?"

Lily listened carefully to the thoughtful discussion. It was one of the things she was coming to treasure in this circle...everyone contributed, everyone listened, everyone respected each other. She felt a pride of ownership in what they were creating.

She checked her physiology – became aware of what was going on in her body. Relaxed. She was relaxed. No iron bars in her shoulders or spine, no nerves or nausea, no urge to leave or hide. She felt safe.

When the discussion ended, Lily summarized, listing their final agreements. As she spoke she looked around the circle at each woman, looking for signs of agreement or disagreement. She ended with "We've agreed to be respectful of how each of us conducts a Ceremony and to participate with an open heart with what each of us does." Her gaze swept around the circle. "How did I do? Anything to add? Or subtract?"

Sophia was the one to speak up. "As we've had these discussions, I believe we've talked about the traditions of several of the Native American tribes, Buddhists and Wicca as well as some of the pieces of our religious upbringings that have brought comfort to us throughout our lives. We've wanted to include songs and prayer, time to talk and silence, structure but not too much. What's important is we've taken the time to try out various ways to create a sacred circle and we now agree whoever is conducting the ceremony will make the final decisions."

"I'd like to start tonight and see what we come up with," Diana said, tucking her dark-brown hair behind her ears as she leaned forward. "The worst that will happen is we won't like what we've created and we can do it different next year. Let's start and see what happens. And another thing, it's important to take time to talk honestly with one another about our thoughts, feelings and impressions."

They prevailed upon Sophia to be the first to lead them as the idea of the women's circle was hers. Standing, they followed her as she raised her arms over her head, her hands tilted upward, her legs slightly parted.

"Great Spirit, watch over, guide and protect us as together we find our way on this path to the Sacred Feminine and all that is Divine in this world." Sophia glanced over her shoulder, her waist length hair shifting, as she checked in with the other women ranging behind her. "What do you think? Should I end with 'Amen'?"

"Blessed Be," whispered Elizabeth loud enough that everyone heard.

"Blessed Be," Sophia said and turned to face the others. "Anything else someone wants to add?"

Gabriella assumed the same posture as Sophia had, her curly auburn hair tumbled half-way down her back. "May we, on this darkest night, bear witness to the coming light. May we see and honor the cycle of life. May we welcome the darkness as well as the light. Blessed Be."

Silence reigned for several minutes.

"Perhaps this is all we need to do tonight," Lily said, breaking the quiet. She stepped to the side and looked around her. "Does anyone else have something they want to add?"

Her question was greeted with head shakes and murmured, "No's."

"Let's decide what to do to end this, then." Sophia motioned for everyone to move into a circle, took the hand of the woman on each side. Once the circle was formed, she smiled and raised her arms shoulder height. "Thank you, Great Spirit, for being with us this night. Your guidance is always welcome as we start on this path together. Blessed Be." She lowered her arms and dropped her neighbors' hands. "Let's eat." She took the lead, marching into the great room. They'd met here several times so everyone knew where things were. Soon the feast was set out and plates piled high.

"Oh, wait." Ashley's worried tone stopped everyone in their tracks. "What about the Spirit Plate, to thank the plants and animals who've given us this food?"

"You're right, Ashley," Hunter said as she picked up another plate and began arranging tastes of everything on it. "There, it's done," she said as she joined the others at the table.

Everyone stood around Hunter who held the plate chest high. "We are grateful for this bounty. We are grateful for this time together. We thank each of the plants and animals as well as the people who prepared all of this." She looked around the room, a grin splitting her face. "Blessed Be." She lowered the plate to waist high and bowed over it. Straightening, she turned to Sophia. "Where do you want this?"

"In the usual place." Sophia gestured toward the sliding door. "In the usual place will be just fine."

LILY WIPED the sweat from her eyes and rubbed the cold glass of lemonade across her forehead. The heat on this hot August day brought memories from two years ago swirling through her mind. Consciously she took a deep breath, slowly letting it out and concentrated on other memories; memories of happier times, memories of time with her sacred women's circle.

A smile lit her eyes as a picture of everyone at the park this past spring popped into her mind. Charlie and Diana's son, Bill were fast friends now. They acted as big brothers to Hunter's daughter, Logan, and to some extent to Ashley's boys Art, Jr. and Anthony. At five and three, they just couldn't keep up with a fourteen, thirteen, and eleven year old. Thank goodness for Elizabeth. A sip of lemonade, another swipe at the perspiration dripping from her nose. "Why am I out here doing this? I'll probably get heat stroke!" she muttered before moving onto the shaded porch and sitting in her rocking chair.

Waiting for her inside was one of the books she'd purchased on a Saturday last month when they'd all scoured Powell's looking for books on the Pagan Sabbats or Festivals. Samhain, Winter Solstice, Imbolc, Spring Equinox, Beltane, Summer Solstice, Lughnasa and the Fall Equinox were times of creativity and learning. She enjoyed reading about the old traditions, as did Diana and Gabriella who wanted to be a writer.

A squirrel running across the telephone lines, a scrub jay's raucous call, a neighbor walking her dog were all imbued with a new sense of wonder. She was fascinated with the idea of everything having a spiritual energy and loved reading about the attributes given to animals, insects, and reptiles by the various earth-based traditions. That feeling of something being there when she visited certain houses made more sense to her now.

While today she was beset with the devils from her past, overall the panic and fear had lessened and her life was settled into a new routine. Night terrors were not as frequent as they were two years ago and she did not always wake with a scream of terror erupting from her throat, but vivid dreams shattered her sleep several times every week. Even though time had passed, Lily knew Jane was out there, somewhere. Jane's desire to hurt her had not abated. Post-Traumatic Stress Disorder was still alive and well in her world.

Lily rocked and sipped her lemonade remembering what helped her deal with her PTSD symptoms, what helped her be in more control or at least feel as if she was in more control. Just thinking about the night terrors and vivid dreams, her body responded. Heart pounding, lungs seizing, her white knuckled hands clutching the glass of lemonade and rocking chair arm, she forced her mind to focus on her breathing until she relaxed the death-grip on the lemonade and chair arm.

Thankful this reaction wasn't as severe as when the night terrors struck, she went through her safety check to see if it helped outside in the daylight.

Breathe until calm enough to

Relax the death grip then

Move to

Turn on the light

Get up and

Check every door and window to make sure they are locked.

Her breathing slowed. Concentrating on her nighttime routine did help her body even in the light of day.

Sitting on her front porch, her "safety check" seemed so simple but it did the trick; it calmed her pounding heart, eased her desperate need to breathe, and even now her body was settling down. She might not be sitting in her favorite chair, with the figurine of a lioness with her cub in her lap, and a cup of hot tea in hand, but she was more composed and that was what counted.

What in her day triggered the nightmare? A sleepless night was guaranteed if she was involved in actively protecting one of her clients or they needed to talk about abuse in their past. A sure sign it would be a sleepless night was every time Charlie was late getting home from school or a friend's house.

My plan was to weed my front gardens today before I meet up with Diana and Sophia, but I'm only half-way done. It's so hot! Time for a cool refreshing shower and getting ready for a glass of iced tea and a cozy chat. She gathered her gardening tools and put them away.

RINSING off in the cool shower, she thought again of how being a member of The Circle had changed her life in the almost two years they'd been together.

The positives certainly outweighed the negatives. In fact, there was only one negative. What would other people think of her if they knew she practiced earth-based spirituality? Even in these modern times, women were still being persecuted, beaten or stoned sometimes to the point of death because they were believed to be witches. I'm sure that played a part in our decision not to become a coven or focus solely on Wicca. ... And who knows if I'd lose clients if people knew. It made more sense in the broader scheme of things to keep that part of her life to herself.

It had taken over a year of being a member of The Circle before she'd finally swallowed her pride or whatever it was that made it so hard to ask for help and talked about what happened that hot August day seventeen years ago. She asked the other women for ideas on how to deal with her fear for Charlie and herself. She'd known she needed other viewpoints. Hers were locked, stagnating, and she couldn't see past her own barriers.

No one said anything really earth-shattering. And at the end of it all, it boiled down to she was living her life in fear and making Charlie live his from the same position. The reality was, they agreed, no one was ever 'safe'. Safety was a myth. You could be cautious, use common sense, do your best, but it was all out of your control to begin with. Bad things happened to people and that was part of life.

Stepping out of the shower, Lily inhaled the lavender scent of her body wash and shampoo. Towel drying her hair, she pondered how they were open to new ideas, new ways to do things, willing to try new things out. If they didn't like what they'd created, they just did it differently the next time. She'd been their first guinea pig in their energy work, something Diana had read about.

Her prayer floated to her lips. "Please show me the way to easily talk to my son and to find my path so our lives are lived without fear." Everyone had asked for her highest good to be served by the Energy they called in. They'd stood in a circle with her seated on the floor, focusing their thoughts to bring her what she wanted; a life free of the immobilizing fear.

Shortly afterward, she'd had a reasonable conversation with Charlie when he was twenty minutes late getting home from school. She'd been frantic, ready to call the police when he'd walked in the door. "What about a cell phone, Mom?" Charlie'd asked. "I could've called and told you I missed the bus so you wouldn't worry." Charlie having a cell phone was a common sense solution. She'd checked the budget and made it work.

Paul might be ordered to pay child support, but he sent the check when he got around to it. She took pride in being able to support them. *I don't need Paul and neither does Charlie. I know Charlie wonders why his dad doesn't call or come see him or invite him to visit in Ohio but it's better this way.*

Lily slipped her feet into her sandals and trotted down the stairs. Today Charlie was hanging out with Brody and his father. There were other boys' fathers who were constants in his life, who filled the shoes left vacant by an absentee dad who'd moved on and now had another family. She was a good mom and had found a way for him to have solid, positive, caring father-figures in his life. That was enough.

Thoughts for another time. Lily grabbed her car keys and headed out the door. Life might be good but it wasn't always easy.

6 - THE ONLY CONSTANT IS CHANGE

October 3, 2001
Fremont, Oregon

The sharp October air laced with car exhaust nipped Lily's nose as she stomped down the street. Would she ever know true contentment? Would her life ever be without drama and angst? No matter what she did, something always comes up. She never even saw it coming. And what really ticked her off? She encouraged contact. The sound of a car's horn stopped her from stepping off the curb.

Waiting for the light at the corner, she stared off into nothingness, a common occurrence in the last two months. The movement of other pedestrians jogged her back to the present. Her usual passion for and over-indulgence in her work did not ease the emptiness, the sense of betrayal. At the end of this month, she would celebrate seven years in The Circle. And without these women, she'd be even more lost than she was now.

It was hard to admit that her feelings of betrayal by Charlie were even stronger than her anger over Paul's little ruse. But the truth was Charlie was gone. He'd left August 20th for Paul's home in Ohio. He'd left her to spend his senior year with the man who'd paid little or no attention to him until last year; the man who, over the past year, invited, encouraged and tempted him with the image of having a father of his own.

Anger pulsed through her. She paced in the lobby of the office building where she waited for the elevator. She should have forbidden it. Charlie was her son, not Paul's. She had been the one to raise him. She had been the one who carpooled, stood or sat in the rain and cold at the track meets. She had been the one who encouraged him, massaged his sore muscles, and wrapped his strained knee. She had! Not Paul. Not for a minute did she believe Paul really cared. He just wanted to share the spotlight with his star athlete son. Her part in all this? She'd told one of Paul's aunts about Charlie's feats of excellence on the track field. How could she have been so stupid?

The ping of the elevator registered through her rage. She stalked into the car, jabbing the button to the fourth floor. Her fists clenched, her breathing ragged, she fought to calm herself, grateful no one else rode with her.

Stopping outside Dr. Melbourne's office, she plastered a fake smile on her face and stepped inside.

"Hi Lily," Tess, the receptionist said, sliding the window to her desk area open farther. "The doctor is waiting for you, so go on in."

"How are you, Tess?" Lily paused to smile, this one genuine, at the young woman behind the desk.

"Doing well." Tess rubbed her extended belly. "I am ready for this part of becoming a mother to be over though."

"All mothers-to-be reach that point," Lily said and stepped through the door to the hall to the examining rooms. Dr. Melbourne's office was at the back and Lily walked briskly to his door. She knocked softly and opened the door at his greeting.

Dr. Melbourne rose as Lily came into the room. "Thank you for coming, Ms. Hughes." His gruff voice, bushy eyebrows and conservative clothing hid a caring, competent doctor.

"My pleasure, doctor." A slight movement to her right caught Lily's eye. There was another person in this office, an older woman dressed in a fashionable dark charcoal grey pant suit.

"I'd like you to meet Eleanor Montgomery," Dr. Melbourne said, making the introductions and inviting Lily to sit. "She and I've been talking about several things; one in particular has to do with her living alone."

"I do not live alone, doctor," Eleanor Montgomery spoke up in a clipped, accented voice. "My apartment connects to my son's home."

"That may be, Eleanor," Dr. Melbourne said and turned his gaze on his patient. "But we both know there are problems because his work is taking him out of town more and more often. He isn't always home when you need him."

Lily observed Mrs. Montgomery bristle and glare at the doctor before looking away with a sigh. Lily glanced at the doctor, her brow raised.

"The problem today, Ms. Hughes, is that Eleanor's transportation arrangements have fallen through. She came without her checkbook or credit card. Of course, I'd be more than willing to advance her the funds to take a taxi home, but I believe this is more a symptom of the problem. Eleanor relies on her son to make these and other arrangements. When he is working out of town, things can fall apart like they have today."

Dr. Melbourne leaned back in his chair, hands folded on his chest. "I've told her about you and encouraged her to hire you to help her out." He sat forward, pushed up from his desk and walked to the door. "I'll leave you two to sort it out."

Lily saw tears glistening in Mrs. Montgomery's eyes.

"I would be more than happy to give you a ride home today, Mrs. Montgomery. No obligation," Lily said after a few minutes of strained silence.

"I would appreciate that." Mrs. Montgomery said, her gray eyes still a little teary. "I know Dr. Melbourne means well. It is just that... ." She sighed and turned back toward the window. "I moved to Fremont because of my son. He even built an addition onto his house - an apartment for me so I would have my own place and privacy. I am quite comfortable there. He wants to take care of me, see that I have everything I could possibly need, but as Dr. Melbourne said, his work is taking him out of town more and more."

Facing Lily again, she went on. "I used to be so independent. I ran a household, raised children, helped my husband with his business and now?" Her eyes filled again with unshed tears, her voice quavered. "I can't even get myself home from a doctor's appointment."

"Actually, you can." Lily's voice was firm.

"How?" Her voice was incredulous.

"Come with me. I'll take you home; we can talk along the way. If it's true you want to be more independent, take care of your own business, I can help you craft a plan to do that. However, right now, let's just get you home." Lily stood by the door and waited. Outwardly she appeared calm and professional. Inwardly her heart squeezed with sympathy. *Her life is turned upside down and so is mine.* Lily resisted the urge to fidget, to reach out and help Mrs. Montgomery.

"I accept." Eleanor's decisive voice was followed by action. She picked up her purse, pulled her walker out from between her chair and the wall, maneuvered it open and pulled herself upright.

Lily followed the older woman as she slowly made her way to the reception room. As they passed one of the examining rooms, Dr. Melbourne was coming out. "Thank you, Ms. Hughes," he said. "I'll see you next month, Eleanor," he added as he crossed the hall and entered another room.

They stopped so Tess could make a new appointment before making their way to the elevator and out the building. As it was one of those raw, blustery, early October days, Lily asked Mrs. Montgomery to wait in the lobby while she got her car parked a few blocks away. She'd noticed how slowly the other woman moved and worried she'd be chilled to the bone before they reached her automobile.

Lily's mind awhirl, she smiled on the brisk walk to her car, sure there was a story here. Mrs. Montgomery's accent was British and Dr. Melbourne wasn't one to call her on a whim. *I'll find out more as I take her home — or not.*

Now settled in Lily's car, Mrs. Montgomery said, "I'm sure my son is quite worried. He will have called to check on me as I was due home well over an hour ago."

"We'll get you home as quickly as we can, then. Perhaps you can call him when you get there so he'll know you're okay." Lily pulled into traffic and headed in the direction of the Montgomery house. During the drive, they chatted and Lily learned Mrs. Montgomery had moved to Fremont six months ago from the New England area where she had been living with one or the other of her two daughters. Her grandchildren were pre-teen or early teenagers and the hustle and bustle, noise and confusion that naturally went with that age was too much for her. Her son had lobbied and eventually persuaded her to move to Oregon. She'd finally accepted her son's invitation, believing she'd enjoy her own space.

Because she knew approximately where in the West Hills the Montgomery's lived due to another client in the general area, Lily was able to drive within a few blocks before needing Mrs. Montgomery's directions. As she turned into the driveway, a welcoming energy surrounded her. Had she been here before? She blinked and glanced around to assure herself she hadn't.

The house before her was magnificent. More like a Southern-styled mansion, its two-story columns supported a peaked roof over the large porch that protected the double-leaded-glass doors into the house. The triple car garage had high windows with the same leaded glass design as was on the front doors and the door to the single-story wing to the left. The upstairs windows were dull, hollow holes.

Large Asian-influenced pots planted with fall mums, winter pansies, and winter kale led up to the main front door. Smaller pots graced the single-story entrance which mirrored the main entryway. A few early afternoon sun rays caught on the rose trellis peeking over the fence of the side garden illuminating the pale pink colored buds.

"Ms. Hughes, do you have time for a cup of tea?" Mrs. Montgomery's question pulled Lily out of her reverie. "I would like to do something to repay you for all you've done for me today."

"Really, Mrs. Montgomery, I've done nothing much," Lily said.

However, recognizing the importance to Mrs. Montgomery to give something back, she added, "And I'd love a hot cup of tea."

"Excellent." Mrs. Montgomery struggled to unbuckle her seat belt.

"May I?" Lily waited for permission before reaching down and quickly opening the clasp. "There you go," she added as she carefully held the seatbelt away until it released back into its holder.

As they made their way to her front door, Mrs. Montgomery said, "Ms. Hughes, would you mind calling me Eleanor?"

"I don't mind at all, Eleanor, if you will call me, Lily." She could hear the phone ringing in the background as they approached the door.

"Dear me," Eleanor said as she fumbled with her keys, dropping them in her haste. "I'm sure that is my son."

Lily stooped to pick up the keys and held them out to Eleanor. "Do you want me to open the door?"

"Oh, would you?" Eleanor's words rushed out, her mouth pinched, her brow furrowed.

Lily efficiently unlocked the door and stood aside as Eleanor entered with her walker. Once inside, she pushed it to the side, continuing at a slow but measured pace to the counter where her phone sat.

Folding the walker, Lily set it beside the door next to a quad-cane. From her own observations, the equipment and grab bars in the kitchen area; it was apparent the older woman had mobility issues and perhaps even some problems with her balance.

Eleanor stood looking at the phone, most likely willing it to ring, Lily thought, before she shrugged, stepped to the sink to fill the tea kettle and set it on to boil. "Please sit, Lily." Eleanor waved in the direction of the living area of her apartment. "I am getting biscuits to go with our tea."

When Eleanor joined her, she set a plate of cookies on the sofa table and began moving books and magazines around on the low table in front of the couch. Lily's thoughts that British biscuits were American cookies was confirmed. The tea kettle began to sing. She trailed her hostess the few steps to the efficiency kitchen where the kettle's shrill sound pierced the air. Following Eleanor's directions, Lily placed cups and saucers on a tray and carried it back to the low table.

"The tea must steep," Eleanor informed her as she placed the cream and sugar on the table and moved the biscuits next to them.

"I'm afraid I just dunk a tea bag in a cup of hot water or nuke it in the microwave," Lily said as she nibbled on a sugar cookie.

"A travesty, my dear," Eleanor scolded. "Today you will have a proper cup of English tea."

"And biscuits," Lily added. "Don't forget the biscuits."

Every minute or so, Eleanor glanced back at the phone. After another five minutes, during which they continued to chat about a variety of things, Eleanor announced the tea was steeped enough, fetched the tea pot and poured.

As Lily sipped the tea, to which she'd added a generous amount of cream and a teaspoon of sugar, the phone rang. Setting her cup and saucer down, she stood to help Eleanor up.

"Excuse me, Lily, while I answer this call. I believe it will be my son." Eleanor hurried to the ringing phone. "This is Eleanor Montgomery." She smiled and mouthed, 'my son' before turning back to her conversation.

While Eleanor spoke to her son, Lily took in her surroundings in more detail. Her initial impression was of welcoming comfort. The upholstered love seat and two matching chairs in a pastel floral pattern were inviting. The simple, elegant furnishings included a sofa table that held pictures and a vase of fresh flowers whose fragrance filled the small apartment. The tea tray had joined a large crystal bowl in pride of place in the center of the low table in front of the couch.

In the small apartment Lily couldn't help but hear the son's raised voice and, of course, Eleanor's efforts to explain what had happened, to assure him she was just fine. From the tone of his voice, Lily knew he had been frantic about his mother.

Not wanting to intrude more than necessary given the size of the place, Lily took a few steps closer to the front windows, gazing out on the serene view of a small fence-enclosed yard. Mums and asters in red, rust, yellow, white and lavender bloomed but showed the signs of succumbing to winter.

The sun no longer touched the arbor covered with a climbing rose, its few pink blossoms seeming fragile without the sun's light, a small stone bench beneath. Beyond the fence, in the distance, was a grove of Douglas fir. Maple, birch, and oak trees, their leaves bright yellow, red, and orange, were highlighted against the dark green of the fir.

If she sat on the couch, she was too close to Eleanor and felt as if she were intruding on a private conversation. Even here by the front window, she easily heard the frustrated tones of the son's voice. Lily moved to the French doors leading into the main house. Through them, she saw the beginnings of a wide staircase, the corner of the fireplace mantel, and a large gray leather couch with plush pillows in burgundy, cobalt blue, and a dark forest green.

As enticing as that sight was, what drew her forward, so that her nose was almost pressed against the beveled glass, was the wall of floor-to-ceiling windows draped in what looked like dark blue velvet, beyond which rose the view of the distant mountains, especially spectacular now with a new dusting of snow. That sense of welcome, the energy, the feel of the place was stronger here.

She looked through the living room of the main house at the view of the mountains she loved. Eleanor was now engaged in talking with her son about something other than her doctor's appointment. To distract herself from the private conversation, she focused on her favorite, Mt. Hood. The scene reminded her of winter trips she and Charlie took to play in the snow. Her eyes filled with unshed tears. Hurt, loss, betrayal and a twinge of panic or fear welled. Thinking of happy times they shared, once the all-encompassing fear from Jane's threats had lifted, did not ease the pain of today.

It was ironic, really, after a dozen years of Paul being non-existent in their lives, he appears during Charlie's junior year with offers to come and stay with him. Paul, who had never changed his schedule to attend a track or cross country meet, had never rubbed foul-smelling liniment into sore muscles, had never supported any of Charlie's various sports activities all these years; that Paul stepped in and stole her son away. She was missing his senior year of high school, missing his starring in cross country meets, missing his special team's position in football; just plain missing him. Her world turned upside down.

It wasn't that she couldn't understand his acute need to know his father. He'd gone through photo albums from when he was a baby, the pictures of Paul holding him worn to the point of tatters. He looked at bank statements and she knew he saw the amount of child support she'd put aside for his college as a measure of his Dad's caring about him. But Charlie had left her, his mom, the constant in his life. And he'd left his friends, his cross country and football teams, everything he knew, to chase what? The dream, the hope Paul cared about him? Wanted him? Loved him?

Charlie had always joined her in celebrating the full moon, making moon water, putting crystals outside under the Grandmother for cleansing. Together they'd experimented with herbal remedies finding among other things that a dab of essential lavender oil on a mosquito or spider bite did ease the itch. What would happen to him now? What if Paul found out she was a pagan? Would he try to keep Charlie from ever being with her again?

Standing at the French doors, she deliberately forced her mind away from the what ifs, consciously relaxed the iron-clad shoulder and neck muscles, purposefully let the energy of the place enfold her and intentionally released the feelings of hurt, of loss, of betrayal. In the empty space a thought appeared. Perhaps it's time to see what gifts might come my way in the void of Charlie's absence.

Jackson Montgomery paced the Monterrey job site. What had happened to him? *Bloody Hell, I yelled at my own mother!* Guilt swept through him overcoming the all-encompassing fear when he couldn't reach her.

"Damn that doctor and double-damn that transportation. I've aged ten years in the last couple of hours," he muttered as he stalked, scowling at anyone who looked his way. "And who's this 'Lily' person? Someone Dr. Melbourne's office recommends. They don't think I can take care of my own mother?" He fumed, stomping to the edge of the cliff overhanging the Pacific Ocean.

Below, the foaming waves crashed on the fang-like rocks, but rather than the usual sense of peace they invoked, they mirrored his own restlessness. His gut twisted with the overwhelming sense of failure. He watched the surging and retreating water looking for an answer. If he just hadn't lobbied his mother so hard to get her to move out here with him maybe…. He ran a hand through his sable brown hair, his gray eyes moody. "Why didn't Dr. Melbourne call and discuss this with me? I thought he understood that I can and will take care of my mother."

Jackson clenched his hands into fists. "Damn, this project. Damn,

damn, damn." He lifted his face to the sun, purposefully unfisted his hands and willed his unruly thoughts into submission.

"I've got to get a grip, get my head back into this project." He turned back to the site, looking at the forms for the building's foundation with a critical eye. "I'll check things out when I get home and can see mother's face when I talk to her." The image of his grandmother flashed in his mind. "Mother's lonely and could be a prime target for someone taking advantage of her just like grandmother." He continued the muttered conversation with himself.

He kicked a rock, watched it tumble a few feet away, remembered what happened to his grandmother. Even with family close by, that caregiver stole over ten thousand dollars, silver, and had started isolating her from us before we figured things out. He dragged a hand through already rumpled hair, scrubbed the back of his neck and grimaced. His chest tight with guilt and fear, his lungs wouldn't work. "Bloody Hell!" he shouted in his mind. "Hell and damnation," he muttered the curse kicking a rock over the cliff. The rock bounced, picking up a few more rocks along the way. They didn't even make a splash in the ocean but watching them tumble down his lungs released pent-up air. Maybe he could get away from here for a couple of days now instead of next week. He shook his head. The timing on this couldn't be worse. Unless a miracle happened this afternoon, he couldn't leave now.

Jackson saw the contractor, a frown on his face, wave and call to him. He walked slowly back to the site, thoughts about his mother and some unknown female pushed from his consciousness as he forced his thoughts back to the job-at-hand.

8 - A FRIENDSHIP FORMS

"I am sorry, Lily. My son, you see, is most worried about me. When he is like this I've found just listening until he gets it all out is best." Eleanor picked up her teacup and sipped. "Oh dear, our tea is quite cold."

Lily and Eleanor refilled their cups in the kitchen from the teapot covered with a tea cozy. Lily carried the full cups back to the couch. "He must have been very worried about you." She added the cream and sugar to her cup, watching the swirls of cream meld into the darker tea as she stirred.

"Indeed, Jackson tends to worry about me." Eleanor sipped her tea and settled back on the couch. "I am sure when he is home he'll have a lecture to rain all over me. Since it's really a sign of his concern for me, I listen with loving ears and don't let it bother me."

"I'm sure Dr. Melbourne didn't intend for my talking with you to create problems between you and your son," Lily said as she shifted to better observe Eleanor.

"You are correct. Dr. Melbourne called you because he also worries about my being here alone. But both he and Jackson forget I'm a grown woman and have had many responsibilities in my life." Eleanor waved her hand in the air. "I am not helpless. I have this nifty gadget." She pulled out an unobtrusive cord around her neck to which was affixed a device. "All I have to do is push this," she said, demonstrating without putting any pressure on the center, "and help will arrive."

"Those are handy to have." Lily remarked having seen several emergency call systems before. "Have you ever had to use it?"

"No. No I haven't and while I hope never to have to, I am not so dull-witted I don't wear it, just in case."

"Where is the receiver located?" Lily wondered about the range, knowing that if Eleanor was too far away, no help would come.

"Why it is right here in this room." Eleanor smiled and gestured toward the wall dividing the living room and her bedroom.

"Oh my, how clever!" Lily grinned as she finally saw the partially hidden niche in which the receiver was located.

"And it picks up no matter where I am in my own apartment and all the way into Jackson's living room and kitchen. As I have my own laundry equipment here, I never really have to go in there when he is gone." She paused, glancing over her shoulder through the French doors. "I do have to admit I enjoy the view. There are times when I take a cup of tea and sit looking out at the city, the river, and the mountains beyond."

"From the little I could see from your place, it's a spectacular view."

"I would love to show it to you, that is if you have time."

Lily glanced at her watch. "Oh Eleanor, the time has just flown by. I've another appointment to get to so I really do have to go."

"Perhaps another time?"

"I'd enjoy that." Lily rose.

"That would be lovely. I do tend to get lonely when Jackson is out of town on his trips." Eleanor stood, taking the now empty teacups to the kitchen. "What is your schedule like? This isn't really an emergency."

"Next Friday would work well for me. I have an opening at 11:30."

"I would like to invite you for lunch; a simple bowl of homemade soup if that is acceptable?" Eleanor drew back her shoulders. "I don't really know how to go on with something like this."

"Why don't I bring some bread to go with your soup? We'll have a nice lunch, chat, and see what direction you want to go. If you have a chance to talk to your son, you can find out what he thinks you need."

"I certainly will not talk to my son about this," she said bristling. "His work has only recently taken him out of town for longer periods of time and we are just in a period of adjustment. I will continue as I mean to go on. And, while I am very comfortable talking with you, Lily, I'm not sure I need a geriatric case manager. That sounds so formal and official."

"I promise we won't rush into anything," Lily said gathering her things and preparing to leave.

∾

"ELEANOR," Lily said stepping into the small apartment, her voice and expression showing her delight in seeing the older woman, "it smells delicious."

"I believe it will taste delicious too." Eleanor busied herself in the kitchen getting down bowls and plates, seeing that the teacups were warmed. Eyeing the loaf of artisan bread Lily deposited on the counter, she added, "and it will be enhanced with that lovely bread you brought."

Taking off her coat and scarf, Lily extricated a large envelope from her bag. "I brought in one of the assessments I use in seeing what services might be of value. I'm going to leave it here." She placed it on the low table next to the crystal bowl. "You can look it over at your convenience and give me a call if you have any questions."

"I will look it over and we can discuss it when next I see you," Eleanor asserted. "I do hope this is the first of many lunches we'll share."

They chatted as they ate the soup and bread. Lily learned that Eleanor's son was calling every night but had not been able to make it home due to problems on the Monterrey, California job site. It was obvious from the manner in which she talked about her son she was immensely proud of him. And from what little Lily knew about architecture, she was more than a doting mother. He seemed to have a talent for making a space fit the needs of the inhabitant. The small apartment was just the right size with just the right amenities for Eleanor's safety and comfort.

There was something about sitting with Eleanor, her body relaxed and replenished with delicious food, a cup of tea in her hand. The welcoming energy she'd sensed last week enveloped her. Similar yet different from what she'd felt when she'd first seen her little house, the underlying safe, haven-like feeling embraced her.

Eleanor excused herself to use the bathroom.

Lily's thoughts drifted to her previous visit, the moment of anguish, the void, the pain from Charlie's decision had overwhelmed her then. It was still there, but sitting here, in Eleanor's living room, the visceral reaction to her loss was diminished. A place of safety, a haven and, a new friend.

While she'd felt an energy in certain places for a very long time, now images were often superimposed over a landscape. The Circle had discussed this phenomenon at various times and at some length and decided the spirit of the land showed itself to her. If a house was on the land, they called the spirit a House Totem. A soft smile played on her lips. Her morning prayers include being more open to this energy. *No wonder I feel so welcomed in this house.*

Shaking her head to clear her thoughts, Lily turned to see Eleanor had rejoined her and was observing her.

"I do apologize." Lily flushed. "I got lost in my thoughts and didn't hear you return."

"That is fine, my dear, especially since the frown on your face became a lovely smile at the end." Eleanor picked up her teacup from the table. "Would you like to see the main house today? Or we can relax with another cup of tea. Or we can do both."

"I see I have choices to make." Lily laughed and stood. "Let's pick things up first. I'd love a tour, if you think that would be okay with your son."

"I doubt that he cares, as he is quite proud of his work. Although he is an architect, he did the interior decorating himself."

They quickly rinsed the dishes, stowing them in the dishwasher, then put the leftover soup in the refrigerator and wrapped the remaining bread. Eleanor put water on for tea, assuring Lily they would enjoy a bit more sustenance after the tour.

Stepping into the main house, the energy Lily now associated with this place was stronger. The source seemed to come from her left and she noted a statue of a great horned owl on the mantle: the Montgomery House Totem. It was facing the wall of windows as if looking out at the view. Without thinking, she moved to the fireplace and swiveled the statue so it faced the front entrance.

Lily quickened her pace as she crossed the room, stopping when she stood next to Eleanor before one of the floor-to-ceiling windows. A touch of her fingers confirmed the dark blue curtain was raw silk, not velvet. The view overlooking Fremont, bisected by the sun-shimmering Willamette River and snow-capped Cascade mountains towering in the distance, was magnificent.

"It quite takes my breath away," Eleanor murmured and gestured at the panoramic picture before them.

"See the shadow of the clouds crossing the buildings?" Lily was transfixed by the shifting light and shadow dancing among the structures. "I'd never get anything done if I had a view like this," she said with a note of awe in her voice.

"I believe the same could be said of my son, which is why he located his home office facing the other direction. We can get our tea and sit here if you wish," she offered.

Lily saw the smile flicker across her face, heard the gentle teasing in her voice. "Thanks for the offer, but if it's still okay, I'd like the tour."

Gesturing to her right, Eleanor drew Lily's attention to the long cherry wood table, an elegant crystal chandelier overhead and beyond to the gourmet kitchen with cherry wood cabinets, crystal hardware, three sinks, two dishwashers, and a butler's pantry.

Lily stood at the sink with the spectacular view. "I could get used to doing dishes by hand if I could look at this."

Eleanor laughed. "I would think you'd rather be sitting in one of the chairs," she said, gesturing toward the living room, "than doing dishes. I do remember you mentioning that housework wasn't your favorite task."

THE NEXT WEEK, finding a free hour between one appointment and the next, Lily took a chance and dropped by to see Eleanor, who was delighted and immediately put on water for tea. Once the tea was poured, Eleanor and Lily sat on the couch enjoying their hot cup of English Breakfast tea and Scottish shortbread. Eleanor reminisced about how she had met her husband, Archie, when he was in the US Air Force and stationed in England. They'd married there with her family and friends in attendance before coming to The States and building a life together.

Even though he worked long days during the week, he always made time for her and the children on the weekends. Lily thought he sounded like a wonderful husband. Eleanor obviously missed him.

"We loved going to the shore, especially in winter, because the storms were one of our favorite adventures. We found a special place on the beach that looked out over the sea. Archie would take the children for walks along the shore which gave me some time to myself, to soak in the tub, read or watch the waves rolling onto the sand." Her face lit from a smile and the glow of a special memory. "I was showered with gifts when they returned. These are those treasures."

Leaning forward, she dipped her fingers into the crystal bowl, letting the smooth, colorful rocks and sea glass slip through them, creating a soft clicking sound. "Whenever I look at these treasures, I can see my Archie striding up to the house with the children in tow, a big grin on his face. 'Elly,' he'd say. 'We've brought you the treasures of Atlantis.' The children would be dancing with excitement. Of course I would exclaim over every rock and bit of sea glass as if it was truly a precious gem." She turned back toward Lily, her gray eyes soft with the mist of memories. "And, truly they are precious gifts."

~

Lunch on Fridays with Eleanor was now a part of Lily's routine and she looked forward to the break in her day.

The next week as they sat in the living room of the main house, chairs facing the windows, cups of tea in hand, a hint of citrus scent in the air, Lily's thoughts drifted. Each visit the sense of welcome was stronger, the intense energy more inviting. A shiver coursed through her as she opened her eyes and looked around. The statue of the great horned owl seemed to be watching her.

Her glance took in the pictures on the mantle. Pride and longing had infused Eleanor's voice as she talked about the two men in the pictures. In one photograph, an older man had his arm slung over the shoulder of a younger one. In the others, a tall, dark haired man posed in front of various buildings. Archie was the older man as well as the man in front of the different buildings he'd built. He was handsome and from what Eleanor said he was also a wonderful husband and father. She has such wonderful memories of her time with him. *I shouldn't envy her, but I do.*

The younger dark-haired man with intense, brooding good looks was the son, Jackson. Her thoughts flowed to her impressions of the man: handsome, wealthy, very talented, very creative, and from his mother's description, charming, well-mannered, and single. She admitted she was curious about him.

What would it be like to live in a house like this? An image of herself curled up on the couch in front of a crackling fire jigged through her mind, a shiver through her body. Shaking her head, she pushed the image away.

Their tea finished, they rose and returned to Eleanor's apartment.

"Your son's home is amazing, so luxurious and yet comfortable—like a home." A blush heated her face as she heard her own words. "I do mean it as a compliment."

"I know, dear. I feel the same way. It is one of those talents Jackson seems to have and one of the reasons he is so popular. While I believe Jackson got his love of creating and building things from his father,"

Eleanor confided, her gaze straying to the bowl of sea glass and rocks, "I think he brings something special, something from his own heart. He takes the time to really get to know his clients so he can create a home that fits them."

"The connection between your son and his father shows clearly in the picture on the mantle."

"They were very close. Once Jackson was old enough he worked summers and holidays with him. While we all miss Archie," she said a quaver in her voice, "his father's death changed him." Her voice firmed. "It has been almost eight years since Archie's death and it is as if Jackson no longer trusts someone will stay in his life. He was only thirty-two when his father died. It was such a shock. Archie was a young man and had always been in good health. He was sixty-eight when one day his heart just stopped."

"The death of a parent brings up all kinds of issues," Lily acknowledged her voice calm and steady as she listened to Eleanor talk about her family, listened to understand the story, and listened to the message under the words.

Eleanor sipped her tea, her eyes returning again and again to the crystal bowl. "My son dates, but the women do not seem to be any he wants to marry. Not that I have met many of them. But the ones I have? Well, they are physically beautiful women, and some are very intelligent." She paused, cocked her head as she considered what more to say. "Suffice it to say, they seem to be lacking something. I cannot see my son married to any of them and obviously neither can he. Whatever he is looking for in a relationship he has yet to find."

A PATTERN WAS DEVELOPING. When in Eleanor's neighborhood, should she have the time, Lily stopped by for a cup of tea and conversation and on Friday they had lunch. Three weeks after they first met was another week for Eleanor's soup, as Lily had brought deli sandwiches last week. After clearing the table, putting leftovers away, and plates and bowls in the dishwasher, they took their cups of tea to the main house where they sat in the gray suede swivel chairs looking out over Fremont. While the sun shone brightly, highlighting the cityscape, the distant mountains were enveloped in clouds.

"There is something I want to discuss with you." Eleanor swiveled her chair to look more directly at Lily. "I've developed a fondness for you and find that I trust you completely. I do not know if I need a, what is it again? A case manager but I do know I want to stay friends."

"I look forward to our visits, too." Lily smiled and reached out, resting her hand on Eleanor's arm.

"I thought, perhaps, we could go over the paperwork you left here."

Lily saw a hint of anxiety or nervousness and sought to put her at ease. "It may be that you don't really need full services or anything like that. I may be able to give you some ideas, a list of resources that between you and your son... ." Her words dropped off when she caught sight of the frown on Eleanor's face. "You've not said a thing to him, have you?"

A belligerent look on her face, Eleanor responded, "No. No, I have not. Jackson is hovering and over-protective. He hasn't been this way since his father died." She huffed and turned to look out over the city. "I don't particularly like him when he gets this way." Glancing over at Lily she added in a firm voice, "I am able to manage this decision without him."

"Let's go back to your place and take a look at the forms. Then we'll know if any of my services would benefit you."

9 - THE CHALLENGE

That evening Lily opened the computer program to create a new file, completing the face sheet and noting the few services she offered that would benefit Eleanor. Over the past three weeks they'd become friends and that complicated matters. She'd called and talked to Diana about a possible conflict of interest, but since she and Eleanor had discussed their friendship now having a professional element, and because neither saw this as a long-term aspect of their relationship, it wasn't a problem. Eleanor needed a few months of help getting things set up, a little support while she got her proverbial feet under her.

The assessment showed the main problem was being new to Fremont and isolated when her son was out-of-town. Eleanor told her she sometimes became overwhelmed and confused when going to the doctor trying to remember the answers to everything she was asked. Lily mentioned Eleanor's need to protect her son and keep him from worrying about her as well as the strain now in her relationship with Dr. Melbourne. Eleanor agreed that those were things to add to the plan.

Outside her window the rain fell, night crept inexorably in. The days were getting shorter, the nights longer. It might officially still be fall, but winter was knocking, whistling at the corners of her little house.

Her thoughts were interrupted by the ringing of her cell phone.

"This is Lily Hughes. How may I help you?" Lily asked in a warm, professional tone.

"And this is Jackson Montgomery, and you can help me by telling me what you're doing with my mother." His soft voice belied the thread of challenge under the surface.

All of Lily's senses came alert as she replied in a calm, professional voice. "I'm not sure what you're asking, Mr. Montgomery, but I can assure you I run a professional business and my practices are ethical."

"Do you have references?" he demanded, the condescension in his voice unmistakable.

Lily's eyes narrowed at his demanding, condescending tone. "Yes. I gave a list of five current and previous clients to Mrs. Montgomery, as well as my brochure and resume. And, I'm licensed and bonded." Her voice remained professional, but now was tinged with a cool reserve.

"And I'll be checking each and every one of your references," he countered.

"Please do. I prefer that all new clients or prospective clients check my references," her tone of voice while still professional was decidedly frosty. "If you would like to give me an address or fax number, I can send you a copy of the paperwork your mother and I have completed," she added in the same tone, thankful she and Eleanor had talked over what she could and could not discuss with him.

"That won't be necessary. I'll be home tonight and discuss this more thoroughly with my mother," he said, a challenge in his words.

"You have my phone number, Mr. Montgomery. Please feel free to call me if you have questions. I'm more than happy to go over things with you if that will ease your mind," Lily said in a formal and cool professional tone.

"The only thing that will ease my mind is to know you aren't taking advantage of my mother. Good evening, Ms. Hughes," he said, his voice changing from challenge to disdain.

"He hung up! That over-bearing, obnoxious jerk hung up on me," she sputtered as she fought to clear her head of the wisps of anger spiraling through her.

$\sim$

LILY WAS grateful she was staying busy. Saturday she'd spent five hours in the ER with a client who was eventually released home. She'd made arrangements for a neighbor to check on her and take her dinner before meeting Mark Parker for a bite to eat in the hospital cafeteria. She enjoyed spending time with him when their schedules meshed. He was an easy man to be around. Sunday, after catching up on chores around the house, she'd had dinner and spent the evening with Sophia. Weekends without Charlie were the hardest.

Monday as she was in the area, she'd stopped by to see Eleanor.

"I am so very glad you came by today," Eleanor said as soon as she was in the door. "I have water on for tea. Come, sit." She gestured toward the couch. "I'll get our tea."

She noticed Eleanor did not suggest they take their tea into the main house, instead bringing cups and teapot to the low table where cream, sugar and a plate of biscuits already sat. As soon as they were settled, Eleanor handed her an envelope. The handwriting was big and bold. She had an idea who it was from but chose ignorance instead.

"What's this?" Lily accepted the offered envelope.

"Jackson has written you. I do not know what he has said as he would not tell me. But," Eleanor's chin raised, her spine stiffened, "if he's said anything about firing you, just ignore it. I have hired you and I will pay you."

"I take it he isn't happy about our arrangement." Lily hoped her tone was neutral because her feelings certainly weren't. "He did call me last Friday and said he'd be checking references."

"He did. They all said wonderful, glowing things about you. If anything, he grumbled more." Eleanor's upset with her son was obvious as she waved her hand in dismissal of his expressed concerns. "I told him he had nothing to feel guilty about. I know what I am doing." She paused. "Jackson's sense of responsibility for me, his need to see to my welfare since Archie died has created a side of him I've never seen before. I don't know if he'd ever forgive himself if something happened to me especially when he is out of town.

While a part of her smiled at Eleanor's strong defense of her, another part frowned. "I don't want to create a problem between you and your son."

"Oh, you won't do that." Eleanor smiled. "I know how to deal with my son. He's a lot like his father and I dealt well enough with Archie."

"Let's just see how things go for now. We can always make adjustments if he doesn't change his mind. When will Mr. Montgomery be home? Perhaps meeting me in person would help."

"Jackson won't be back for at least a week. It appears there is quite a bit of trouble on one of the job sites; something about a geological study being inaccurate. He may be gone even longer, which is why he is making such a fuss about this." Eleanor smiled at Lily. "I am so glad you could stay for a cup of tea and biscuits."

"How can I resist such an offer?" Lily reached for the plate of biscuits. "I see you have the chocolate dipped ones, but what are these plain ones?"

"Ginger with lemon cream filling."

Before she left, Lily reminded Eleanor about her follow-up appointment with Dr. Melbourne next week. Back in her car, she opened the envelope and read the short note. Mr. Montgomery was definitely not pleased to have her in his mother's life. The note read in part:

I am not convinced my mother requires your services.

If I see any sign that you are taking advantage of her I'll take swift and immediate action.

10 – SAMHAIN

*L*ily rested in her favorite chair, the overstuffed one with the pastel flowered upholstery. A statue of a lioness and her cub sat on the side table. Absently she stroked the carved head and reminisced.

Seven years ago, Charlie'd spent the night and the following weekend with Brody and his family and she'd made the decision to try, yet again, a new way to rebuild her life. A sharp pain stabbed her heart at the memory of her son. He'd be gone seventy days tomorrow and the sense of loss was still acute.

Seven years ago tonight she'd met Diana and Sophia and while she was close to everyone in the The Circle, what the three of them had was special. She saw that same closeness between Elizabeth and Gabriella and between Hunter and Ashley...within the whole of The Circle were smaller arcs of relationships.

Gathering up coat, scarf, contribution for the evening's potluck as well as her bag containing what she'd selected to add to their central altar, Lily locked up and went to pick up Diana before traveling on to Sophia's. They'd tried rotating their meeting at each other's houses but always came back to Sophia's place, especially since the death of Sophia's husband, Jonathan, three years ago.

Her mind flitted with scenarios as she drove to Diana's: how close the children had grown over the years; being there with Ashley when her youngest was born; Sophia's devastation when Jonathan was killed in a senseless traffic accident and yet, even in the depths of despair how she kept her garden going, refusing everyone's help. She'd later confessed that maintaining the garden was her way of making peace with his death, paying a kind of tribute to something they'd created together.

Within fifteen minutes of picking up Diana, they'd arrived. Gabriella and Elizabeth were already there and Hunter and Ashley arrived a few minutes later. With all the food stored away for their celebration, the women stood at the entrance to Sophia's living room, waving sage and cedar smoke around themselves before stepping into this sacred space. One by one they smudged the items they'd brought to place on the altar with cleansing smoke before sitting in a circle on the floor.

At their center a silver bowl on a black cloth was surrounded by contributions from everyone: colorful gourds, oak leaves, apples, stones of snowflake and rainbow obsidian; apache tears for protection on each corner. The air held the scent of sage and cedar smoke as well as the spice of fall-colored carnations arranged in several vases around the room. The soft glow of candles and salt crystal lamps lent an air of sacred spirituality to the room.

"We've been together seven years." Sophia's brown eyes sparkled with happiness. "I never dreamed when I sent that flyer out how important you'd all become to me," she said and brushed a strand of long dark brown hair over her shoulder. "I thought that since there are seven of us and we've been together for seven years, it would be fun to share our favorite memory during our talking circle. What do you think?"

Her question was met with a chorus of agreement.

She picked up a beautiful multi-hued stone. "This is the same piece of Chinese fluorite we used that first night and so many others. Whenever I see it, it reminds me of the beauty and diversity in each of us."

Hunter, the first to take the stone, spoke of their hornet summer and the lessons she'd learned five years ago. Hornet energy was about making manifest your dreams. "Packing up Logan, I moved to LA and tried to break into the choreography and dance industry. And I did try, had some success, but after a year knew it was time to come here, to come home."

"And I focused on building my case management business." An image of a smiling Mark Parker flitted in Lily's mind. What a great doctor and wonderful man. He was one of the reasons her business had grown as he'd referred several patients and other doctors to her. Most important he was good friend.

Ashley, holding the stone in her hands, her gray eyes filled with humor, talked about making drums. Lily laughed with everyone else when Ashley, mimicked Sophia's "You need deer, my dear" in her soft Alabama drawl.

And like Ashley, Lily loved her drum. She beat them in anger, beat them in joy, beat them in celebration. She now had three drums, elk, horse and, the most challenging one to make—buffalo. Buffalo was the one she'd chose to beat when Charlie left. The hide tough; the sound guttural; the exertions of beating it helped but didn't take away the sense of betrayal, the pain she felt at her son's choice. And underneath it all, the niggling fear Paul would find out she'd raised Charlie with pagan spiritual practices. Paul had not been Christian in his behavior when they were married, but he certainly espoused Christian beliefs now. Not for a minute did she believe he'd tolerate another view of the world.

Gabriella's favorite memory was of their first weekend retreat just before Winter Solstice the first year they met. The room filled with feminine giggles as they recalled *The Question* and their answers. "Who was the best lover they'd ever been with?"

While many things had changed over the past seven years, their answers had not. She and Diana shared the experience of cheating husbands. Dennis was more discreet than the women he hooked up with, especially if he stayed involved for several months. She liked to tell herself it would have helped to know at the time Paul had always been involved with someone else but she wasn't so sure. *Diana knows but she stays – for Bill, for appearance sake, for – well, she has her reasons.* There must be something defective in her because she'd never been in a relationship with a man who was respectful, caring, kind, and monogamous.

"While Randy was the best lover I'd ever been with, he also cheated on me," Lily shared the same story she had seven years ago including her stance on monogamy in heterosexual relationships by reframing the child developmental analogy of the 'terrific' twos' when a child sees everything as 'mine'. Then as now, everyone laughed.

The stone made its way from hand-to-hand.

Elizabeth spoke about the magic of being a part of The Circle, the importance of their connection with each other. "There's a special energy, a power, if you will, present when we're all together. I've felt that growing over the years as we've found our spiritual path. Yes, we've come to love each other but we also respect each other, we share a deep abiding faith in the sacred feminine, we have a tolerance, an ability to look at the underlying purpose of the words we use in ceremony." Lily knew the kind of tolerance Elizabeth spoke of. Their Ceremonies were built on a solid foundation. It made no difference whether they called in guides, ancestors, spirits, Gods or Goddesses. There is no wrong way. *And, I'm not seen as crazy or demented when I talk about the spirit of the land. When I'm open, accepting and receptive to this energy, it appears.*

"Jonathan," Sophia's voice choked at the mention of her husband's name. Even after three years, it was obvious how much she missed him. "Without each and every one of you I don't know how I could have made it through that particular hell. It's the connection we have with each other, the fact that we show up not just to celebrate the Divine Feminine but when there is a need."

Lily knew how true that was. Both Sophia and Diana had been waiting for her when she got home from taking Charlie to the airport. They'd fixed tea and sat with her. They'd fixed dinner and sat with her. They would have stayed the night but she assured them she'd be all right and sent them home. She still wasn't all right and knew they knew that because they continued to call and sometimes just show up —Sophia with something from her garden or her kitchen; Diana with a smile and a willingness to let her talk.

Her attention was brought back by Diana's clear voice singing.

"...you're connected to my soul."

As she started the song a second time, Sophia and Lily joined her, with the other women quickly adding their voices. By the time they sang the words for the third time, while smiles were on their lips, emotional tears streamed down their faces. With the dying of the last tone, silence filled the room.

Her head bowed, Lily felt eyes on her. Lifting her head, her gaze traveled the circle resting a moment on each woman's face. She saw acceptance, expectancy...it was her turn.

"I love it all. The power of song, the power of connections, the power of sharing, the power of the various energies we tap into," she said. At that moment she knew in her soul what the words "a full heart" meant. Hers might burst from the turmoil of emotions in her chest. "The power of Ceremony, our ability to create a space where we connect to Source or Spirit or the Sacred Feminine. That is our power —to know there is something greater and be open to it."

Seven women sat on the floor in a circle, skirts flowing around them, an altar of their own making in the center. She would make it through this year without her son. She knew it with a certainty. She knew it would happen because of these women. It was hard for her to ask for help, to admit a weakness but with her circle sisters – well, without her asking, they just seemed to know.

"What about food?" Lily laughed. "No one has mentioned food and I, for one, am starving."

"Does anyone have anything else they want to share?" Sophia asked bringing them back on task. Seeing six heads shaking, she stood, gesturing for the others to stand.

Holding hands, the women raised their arms toward the ceiling, closed their eyes and gave thanks for this time together, for the protection of those who had been called in, letting them go until next time. For a few moments after the last person spoke, they remained as they were. As if someone pushed a button, releasing them: arms descended, hands unclasped, voices chattered.

Lily stood for a moment, looking down on the altar. Their Samhain Ceremony was over. The official beginning of the New Year for pagans was now. Samhain when the veil between the two worlds was thin, when those who had died could be contacted by those still here. She took a deep breath, letting it out slowly as her gaze lifted and traveled around the room.

Time.

In less than two months it would be Winter Solstice. The Wheel was turning and even if she could, she did not want to stop it.

Remembering the question about the best lover, Lily repressed a groan. She hadn't been on a successful date in so long and hadn't had sex in even longer.

It didn't seem to matter what she did or didn't do, she was a magnet for the wrong kind of man. Not just a magnet, she didn't seem able to see a man's true colors. She'd made a mistake with Paul and every other man she'd seriously dated since then. But it was a mistake to say she couldn't see a man's true colors. Mark Parker was a wonderful man. *But there's no spark for either of us.*

She smiled as if holding a secret. Someone like Mark, who respected her and what she did; who she could talk to and someone who listened—a friend. *Someone like Mark and there is a spark.* Lily chuckled. Lost in thought, a sigh of longing from the depths of her soul slipped out. She remained a few minutes more before shaking off the sense of futility, blowing out the candles and joining the others.

11 - THE ENCOUNTER

The Monday after Samhain, Lily, a cup of tea in hand, noticed the sleek black Jaguar pulling into her driveway as she passed through her dining room on her way to her office. Pausing, she admired the classic car, and waited for it to back out, to go on its way. She was surprised when the driver's door opened and a tall, athletic vaguely-familiar looking man with sable brown hair climbed out and started for her porch.

I wonder who that is. Retracing her steps, she left the tea on the kitchen counter, ready to answer the door when she heard the knock. Several heartbeats later, the sound of a firm fist had that part of her body racing. She hesitated in the kitchen doorway, her mind awhirl, trying to figure out who was at her front door.

The solid knocking continued as she crossed her small dining room to the front room and its glass-paned door. Her breath caught in her lungs and fear speared through her when she saw the man's raised fist. She fought the panic with reality: her security screen door was locked and when he saw her, his arm dropped to his side.

Opening the door, she purposefully did not unlock the screen. "May I help you?" she asked in her most formal professional voice.

"Lily Hughes?"

His smooth baritone voice sounded familiar. There was something about his voice that drew her. Her pulse leapt and blood rushed through her veins. He looked familiar but she knew with a certainty they'd never met – and yet…there was something about him. She caught herself before she unlocked the door and invited him in.

"Yes, I'm Lily Hughes." On her side of the screen, she stood poised, making eye contact with the man. His eyebrows matched his hair and framed stormy gray eyes. His set jaw accented his high cheek bones. She said nothing else, endured his scrutiny and waited for him to speak.

"I'm Jackson Montgomery, Eleanor's son. I'd like to talk to you," he said in a tone more demand than request.

Lily noted the smile now on his lips didn't meet his eyes. While he appeared formidable, he didn't emit intimidating energy. From what she knew of him, which was quite a bit because Eleanor was always talking about him, he wasn't dangerous.

She unlocked the door and gestured him in.

When he stepped by her she caught a citrus scent, the same scent she'd noticed when she and Eleanor sat on the couch and took advantage of the fireplace in the main living room.

"May I take your coat?" she offered with hand out-stretched.

He shook his head. "No, thank you. That isn't necessary. I don't expect to be here long."

Lily gestured to the couch. "A seat perhaps?"

He nodded and sat.

Sitting in the chair opposite the couch, Lily waited a few seconds before asking, "What can I do for you?"

"Most likely nothing." Jackson leaned back, crossed one ankle across the opposite knee, studying her.

Lily used her years of experience in child protective service work to keep her expression calm, her gaze steady, giving no outward sign of her inner turmoil. Turmoil not actually caused by his scrutiny but more from his presence as his energy permeated her living room.

The metronome beat of the ticking clock marked the passage of time as the two of them sat regarding each other.

"I've had you thoroughly investigated and I do mean thoroughly." Jackson watched the woman across from him for some sign, for some emotion to flicker across her face, be reflected in her blue eyes. Sky blue, cornflower blue, the color of bluebells, blueberries—he knew color but was having a hard time describing the color of her eyes. While it was true, he had had her thoroughly investigated, with what he knew about her past, he'd expected to find someone harder. *She's a young woman... . No that isn't quite right. She's thirty-eight, two years younger than me.* She looked younger than he'd expected; the pictures the investigator had taken did not do her justice, hadn't prepared him for the reality of her.

"And?"

He heard the calm voice, felt her steady gaze. While he wasn't trying to scare her, he did want her to see him as someone to be reckoned with, someone who was watching out for and would protect his mother.

"It appears, at least on the surface of things," he started in what even to him was a pompous tone of voice, "you run a legitimate business."

"And, I'm sure you are very sorry to have learned that." She remained silent, didn't move, but when he didn't offer a pointed rejoinder she added. "I'm sorry to have disappointed you."

"Sarcasm, Ms. Hughes, doesn't become you," he retorted, arching a brow, his lips quirked in a sardonic smile.

"As I understand it then, you've come by to tell me I run a legitimate business; something you've learned because you've had me thoroughly investigated," she said emphasizing the last two words.

Touché. Jackson found he was enjoying the verbal sparring match with the prissy, prim woman sitting across from him. And, while it was true he wanted to let her know he'd had her checked out by professionals, another truth was he had some things about his mother to discuss with her. Time to stop playing around and get down to business.

"Actually, I do have something to discuss with you, something concerning my mother."

"Oh, is Eleanor all right?"

Jackson watched the unflappable Ms. Hughes become—almost flappable. She was now sitting at attention, her body alert, ready to spring into action.

"Mother is fine," he said, his considering gaze holding Lily's. He saw the tension drain, an underlying level of alertness remained. "I'm finding that the problems on the Monterrey Peninsula construction site are more complex and I need to redesign part of the house. That necessitates my remaining there for several more weeks as I'll be meeting with the owners on the weekends and overseeing the work-site during the week."

He paused and glanced around the room, immediately intrigued with the décor. The two dragons on the porch leading to the front door had caught his eye. And on the antique sideboard across from the door, were more dragons. Rocks and crystals of varying sizes covered virtu-ally every flat surface except for the small table next to an overstuffed chair. That top held an exquisite figurine of a lioness and cub. The detailing of the figures, the artistry of their painting caught his eye. He cleared his throat. "I would appreciate your spending more time with Mother. I'll compensate you as you'll be doing it at my request."

"If that was all you wanted, Mr. Montgomery, you could have called me." She didn't bat an eye as she continued in a syrupy sweet voice, "As I recall, you do have my number."

Ah, she does fight back. Jackson's lips tipped in a slight smile. "True, I do have it. However, I wanted to meet you, see for myself the incomparable Lily Hughes."

"Really, Mr. Montgomery, incomparable? That could even be construed as a compliment." She shifted as if to stand. "Is there anything else then?"

"Other than you answering me? No." He remained where he was.

Lily stood, "Thank you for stopping by," she said as she stepped to the front door. If it hadn't been early November, she'd have opened it wide and stood there waiting for him to exit. As it was, she stood with her hand on the knob, expectations of his eminent departure clear.

Jackson rose and turned to face her but other than that made no move to leave.

They were at an impasse. She, waiting for him to leave, he, waiting for an answer.

Taking charge of the situation, he strode two steps stopping a mere foot away. He invaded her personal space and felt her heat, smelled her lavender scent, and sensed something else he couldn't quite name; something else that made Lily Hughes unique. Hell and damnation! He wanted to pull her tight against him, crush his lips against hers, strip that prissy, prim façade away. When she'd thought something had happened to his mother? He caught a glimpse of the passion banked deep inside, the fervor of energy on the brink of erupting. Normally he prided himself on being able to read people. In that instant he'd known two things: one, she was a fierce protector of his mother and two, there was much more to Ms. Lily Hughes than she let on.

She opened the door, albeit not very far as they were both blocking it. "Again, thank you for stopping by," she used her coolest professional tone to make sure he knew he was no longer welcome.

"Your answer and then I'll leave." He shot back, one hand braced against the door frame.

Lily ducked to the side, slipping out from in front of him. She turned, hands on hips, eyes narrowed.

"It is a breach of ethics to have both you and your mother as my client. Therefore, you need to understand, my client is Eleanor, not you. While I appreciate your letting me know you will be out of town for an extended period of time, it is between Eleanor and me how much time I spend with her."

When she'd made her move, he'd shifted, following her. *My God, she's magnificent.* The urge to kiss her surged.

"For your information, I'll be checking in with her every night," he said, keeping his eyes on her.

"I'm sure she'll be glad to hear from you," Lily responded, arms folded across her chest.

With a nod of his head in her direction, Jackson opened the door and strode out.

Lily locked the security screen, shut the door, moved to the dining room window and watched him fold himself into the car, fasten his seatbelt and check his mirrors before backing out onto the street and driving away. His tail lights flashed as he slowed before crossing the intersection. She let out the pent up air in her lungs but remained at the window. When his car was out of sight, she walked to her kitchen.

"Where is that tea?" She picked up the now-cold tea and put it in the microwave to heat. "I need more than tea," she muttered to herself as she opened a tin and took out two peanut butter cookies, compliments of Sophia's weekend baking.

The ping of the microwave announced her tea was ready. Ignoring the pang of guilt nuking her tea gave her, she took her mug and plate to her office. *Eleanor would be so disappointed if she knew I still heated my tea in the microwave.* Mug and plate on the side of her desk, she sat at the computer.

She'd been in the middle of a report when she'd decided to make a cup of tea. Because she no longer remembered what she was thinking at that point in the report, she began to read it over from the beginning.

A sip of tea, a bite of cookie—Lily swiveled her chair to look out the window at the wintery scene. A cold, gray, dreary day was perfect for report writing. Her mind wandered, impressions of an impressive man, weaving among the thoughts of getting back to work. She shook her head, stood, grabbed her tea and cookies and returned to the living room, sinking down into the comfort of her favorite chair. Holding the lioness and cub on her lap, she sipped her tea and nibbled on her cookie.

There had only been two men who had stirred her like Jackson Montgomery.

Paul Hughes and Randy. And she knew how relationships with those two men had turned out. Both cheated on her and before he left, Paul's verbal and emotional abuse had become physical. Why couldn't she find a man who was nice and who awakened her body? Yes, she admitted to herself, awakened her body. Being in close proximity to Jackson Montgomery created a melting heat low in her abdomen, a tingling in her extremities and an alertness not at all related to hyper-vigilance. The scent of citrus and virile man lingered in the air. She breathed deeply and, for a moment, allowed herself to relish the reality her body was roused. Intellectually she'd known there was a difference between being aware of one's environment but with Jackson Montgomery in her living room, she'd felt that difference in the marrow of her bones.

*N*ovember had flown by. Tomorrow was Thanksgiving. Days she was so busy, she had no time to think much less miss Charlie were, in many ways, her good days. She and Charlie had come to an agreement after the stilted conversation two days after Halloween. Charlie would initiate the calls.

It broke her heart to agree but it hurt even worse to hear his voice when he wouldn't talk to her. She didn't want to put him in the middle by asking if Paul were listening in or how things were going with his Dad. Those topics, anything about his Ohio family, were off-limits.

And underneath the outward concerns, she worried that Paul had learned Charlie had been introduced to the spirituality of the divine feminine and was somehow punishing her son for that. Her fertile mind came up with ideas like having him call her from a friend's house, asking the school counselor, the police or even one dark and lonely night, Child Protective Services to check on him. She smiled. *Dark and lonely night – I'm thinking in clichés. Charlie knows he can call me and knows to call the authorities if Paul becomes abusive. I need to calm down and trust that.*

"How's school?"

"Fine."

"What are you doing in English?

"Not much."

When she replayed their last conversation in her mind, he was right; there wasn't much for them to talk about.

Her plan changed from weekly phone calls to weekly cards. The space was limited so she could only highlight things or events or what was going on with people he knew. She agonized over the cards, spending two hours picking out the eight cards to get her through to January. Once a week, Thursday morning to be exact, she took the time to write. She dropped it off at the post office on her way to appointments and knew he'd receive it on Monday.

Eleanor had been diagnosed with a cold this past week and there was nothing to do except treat the symptoms and let it run its course. Jackson called her every day after he'd talked to his mother to get her take on how Eleanor was doing. Lily heard the worry and guilt in his voice and attempted to ease his concern but despite his now respectful questions and his listening to her answers tension still infused every conversation.

Delivering a few last minute items Eleanor had requested for her Thanksgiving dinner contribution, Lily rounded the last curve in the road. As the house came into view, a taxi backed out of the driveway. Not wanting to see Jackson face-to-face, she slowed, watched him pick up his bags and walk toward the front door. Once she saw he was safely inside, she pulled her car into the far side of the circular driveway and parked.

Lily pulled the two full grocery sacks from the back seat. Her grip precarious, she still thought she could make it to Eleanor's door in one trip. Her head bent, her concentration on keeping a solid hold on the bags, she turned toward the apartment. One step and she ran into something solid, immovable.

She looked up.

Jackson.

"Let me help you with those." His voice was calm and pleasant, his gray eyes flashed.

One of the bags started to slip from her hands. In an instant she decided to accept his offer. "You can take this one," she said as she shifted her body to move the sack between them.

Inadvertently the back of Jackson's hand grazed her abdomen as he grabbed the sack. Where his hand touched, a slight quiver. Her dark blue gaze locked with his silvery grey.

He stepped back.

Although they no longer touched, the connection remained; definitely through their eyes but also through the invisible threads of energy thrumming between them. Their world had shrunk, now encompassing only each other.

A car sped by, music blaring.

The movement and noise startled Jackson. The spell was broken. Spell, he shook his head to clear it. He felt like he'd just been released from a spell. He looked up and down the now empty street, then turned and strode to Eleanor's door.

Discombobulated, a low key thread of panic upping her heart and respiration rates, Lily remained by the car for a moment to gather her thoughts before following him.

"I'm home," she heard him call out as she approached. Coming through Eleanor's front door, she caught a glimpse of him through the French doors into the main house as he picked up his bags and headed upstairs.

"Eleanor?" Lily sounded tentative to her own ears. She ordered herself to get a hold of herself. "I've brought your groceries." She was pleased she sounded stronger.

Eleanor moved with caution as she walked out of her bed-room. "Thank you so much dear." She smiled warmly and watched Lily efficiently put her groceries away. "Are your plans for Thanksgiving taken care of?"

"My friends, Sophia, Elizabeth and Gabriella are coming over for a potluck dinner. I'm doing the turkey and dressing and they're bringing everything else."

"Would you be free to come for dinner on Saturday? It will most likely be leftovers from Thanksgiving Day knowing the way Jackson cooks."

"Eleanor, I really don't want to interfere with your time with Jackson. I know the two of you don't see each other as much as you'd like."

"Oh, you will not be interfering, Lily. I am not even sure Jackson will be able to join us."

"Well, if you're sure I won't be intruding," Lily hesitated, the specter of her first Thanksgiving without Charlie rising before her.

"I am quite sure," Eleanor was firm.

"In that case, I'd love to. What time?"

"Come any time after four. We will be heating things up, so we can eat whenever we want."

"Great, I'll be here between four and four-thirty then." Giving Eleanor a brief hug, Lily left to finish her errands before going home. Her scrambled thoughts overlaying a slight worry coming on Saturday could be a mistake. "My first Thanksgiving Day and weekend without Charlie," she muttered. "It'll be better if I stay busy."

Lost in a romance novel she was reading, Lily didn't hear the knock on her door but she did hear her cell phone ring. When she stood to answer it, she saw her friends' wave to her through her front room window. Changing directions, she let them in.

"The turkey smells wonderful." Sophia set down her box of pies and drew in an exaggerated breath as she took off her red and black plaid wool cape and matching black wool gloves. She ran a hand through her long brown hair, smoothing out the tangles from wearing the hood up.

"Where do you want the veggie platter?" Elizabeth shifted the foil-wrapped plate from one hand to the other as she took off her coat, revealing a casual denim skirt and jacket.

"Let me take it." Lily relieved first Elizabeth of her veggie platter, then Gabriella of her sweet potato dish. Once her hands were free

Gabby shook her ankle length dark green skirt free of wrinkles and tucked in the matching blouse.

"You were really lost in thought, Lily," Gabby said. "You didn't answer our knock so we tried calling to catch your attention."

"It's a really good book, Gabby. You can read it when I'm done," Lily replied, as she bustled around taking care of the food and reminding them to make themselves at home.

She'd been up at seven to make sure the turkey was in the oven in time for them to have an earlier dinner, giving them more time until dessert. Today, Sophia had brought a deep dish apple pie and a pumpkin pie. Yesterday she'd stopped by with a real mincemeat pie with homemade rum hard sauce. Until the turkey started cooking the aroma of the rum sauce permeated the kitchen.

They joked about the amount of food, way too much for just the four of them.

"Since we each brought things in containers, we'll be able to take leftovers home. That's a good thing, isn't it Gabby? Elizabeth?" Sophia looked at them for confirmation.

"I, for one, was counting on leftovers next week." Gabriella's auburn curls danced as she tossed her head and grinned. "I'm not at all worried, Lily. We'll be able to snack for hours before everything is done. Are you worried Elizabeth?"

"Not at all, I don't mind taking a couple of days' worth of leftovers home." Elizabeth sniffed the air, her blue eyes twinkling. "The turkey smells wonderful. When can we eat?"

When the turkey and bacon-onion-apple-sage dressing was ready, the sweet potato dish heated, the veggie platter set out, the apple and mincemeat pies were put in the oven to warm. A small spirit plate was prepared and Elizabeth held it as the four women stood in a circle. Gabriella gave the blessing.

"God, Goddess, Great Spirit we give thanks for the many blessings that have been a part of this day. We are especially grateful for your bounty. Our thanks to all the plants and animals who gave of themselves so we can feast. Blessed Be."

"I'll put the Spirit plate outside so our offering can be easily accessed by the creatures in your neighborhood, Lily." Elizabeth took the plate out the back door, quickly returning to join the others.

As the friends ate they chatted, their conversation liberally sprinkled with laughter. When the main meal came to an end, they quickly cleared the table, loaded the dishwasher, filled the take-home containers and put leftover food away. By mutual accord, dessert was delayed.

"Let's have our tea in the living room where it's more comfortable," Lily invited.

It was Elizabeth who brought up their tradition of sharing what they were thankful for this past year when everyone was settled.

"I've got a great group of students this year." Sophia smiled the warmth of feelings about this group of students clearly communicated in her tone of voice.

"You do know you say that every year." Elizabeth looked at the others. "Well, she does," she said and chuckled. "What is it about this group? Why do you see these students as special?"

"They love learning. Challenge me every day to teach them something new," she answered. "I feel alive when I'm in the classroom."

"Outside of school and students, what else are you thankful for?" Lily posed the question.

"The apples in the pie are from my trees, the pumpkin from my patch, I've beets and carrots for each of you still in the car. All of this comes from my bountiful garden. I've the three of you as friends to spend this special day with. And, then the others. Our women's circle is a source of strength and wisdom for me. I feel blessed to have all of you in my life."

"I'm thankful my day job provides me with the means to support myself, put money in savings and have the time to research the background for my book. My dream is to write a contemporary romance novel. Finding the balance between structure and security and freedom and flexibility, well, it's all been much easier with your support and encouragement." Gabriella's hazel eyes sparkled with excitement.

"I know having security as well as freedom and flexibility is important to you. Do you ever think that being published and having to write to a deadline will decrease the pleasure you get from writing?" Sophia's head tilted to one side, a hand waved vaguely in the air.

"I hope not." Gabriella looked aghast at the suggestion. "Security, freedom and flexibility are important to me but you also know that I work an eight-to-five job now. And while my day job involves research and writing, it doesn't feed my soul. I'm actually looking forward to the opportunity to blend my desire for freedom and flexibility with writing to a deadline," she said, and grinned.

Elizabeth reached over and patted Gabriella's knee. "I can't imagine you failing at something you want, Gabby. You've enough drive and determination to succeed at whatever you set your mind to." She played with the end of a strand of her long curly black hair before tossing it over her shoulder, leaning forward and continuing. "I've been staying busy with work. I love helping children and families find each other. I've had some difficult placements this fall and they're starting to come together, you know settle a bit."

"I see your face light up with an inner joy when you talk about your work." Lily smiled at Elizabeth. "Your dedication to children is a special part of you. It's wonderful seeing you do something you so obviously love and that brings you such happiness."

"It does, it does," Elizabeth bubbled. "I know working with children is one of my passions and so is The Circle. My two brothers and I've lost each other since our parents died. I've no idea where they are. You," she said, pausing, her gaze taking in her circle sisters, her voice filled with determination, "you are my family."

She took another sip of tea before continuing. "I've been saving my vacation time and money and think I'm on track to realize my dream to travel to Ireland next summer. The dream about The Lady, the one where She reaches out and I hear Her calling me, comes almost nightly now. I think it's a sign I need to go. I've started reading about Celtic goddesses and holy places, in part to see if there is any way to identify The Lady and the place I see in the dream. One book talked about sacred groves and that feels right. I believe The Lady is the spirit of a sacred grove. I don't know if I can find Her but I want to see if I can. I'm so very thankful my life is such that I can make this trip." She turned to the only one who hadn't shared. "What about you, Lily?"

"Right now, I'm thankful the three of you are here with me. The almost four months since Charlie left," her voice quavered, "and, yes, I'm aware of exactly how many days it's been, have been so hard. As you know, after Halloween we agreed he'd be the one to initiate the calls. I've not talked to him since. On the one hand, I don't regret the decision because our conversations were so strained. It was like trying to talk something over with Paul."

Lily's throat choked up with emotion. "On the other hand, I miss him terribly and am hurt and disappointed he didn't call me today." Her voice quivered with a mix of agony and anger. Taking a deep breath, she consciously released the pain in her heart with her exhale. A faint smile wavered on her lips as she looked at each of the women. "But with all of you, it's bearable. And, trying to put a more positive spin on things, I tell myself this experience is giving me a chance to see what my life'll be like when he's off to college and the rest of his life."

"Is he coming home for the holidays?" Sophia asked. Her voice laced with concern, her browed furrowed in question.

"I'm not planning on it. If he does, it'll be a bonus. I expect he'll want to stay with Paul. They celebrate Christmas but not Solstice. When I first joined The Circle, Charlie and I celebrated Christmas and Solstice but the last two years, we only celebrated Solstice. I worry about how he's adjusting to a very different perspective on life in general.

"Even though I first raised him as a Christian, I can see now that I always leaned toward the idea of God being in everything and everyone. From some of the things Paul has said, I think his church believes God is separate and we bow to Him and ask Him to save us from our sins.

"It isn't hard for me to understand his wanting to stay there; what's hard is not being able to talk to him about what is actually happening. I just wish he'd talk to me about it. But for now, that isn't going to happen."

"Anything else going on?" Elizabeth asked.

"Not really. I'm thankful my business is going well. I'm spending a lot of time with a new client. We just seem to click. It's like I've known her forever. She and I get to visiting and time just flies by. With her son out-of-town, I've made a point to stop by more frequently. I'm thankful my other clients are stable right now so I can spend the time with her. It won't always be that way I'm sure. Maybe in a month or so her son will be in town more or she won't need my services."

"Aaah, a son?" Sophia interrupted with rapid-fire questions. "Tell us all about this man. Is he gorgeous, sexy, charming? How old? Is he married?"

"He's infuriating, arrogant, domineering. Does that answer your questions?" Lily replied and laughed when Sophia's gleeful expression faded. A moment later she added, "He cares deeply about his mother." Another moment passed, her forehead wrinkled, her tone now serious. "There's something about him I can't quite put my finger on." Her gaze focused on the pumpkin lights twinkling in the window. "We've talked frequently since his mother's illness but I've only met him once. He's used to being in charge and is having a very difficult time working out-of-town and leaving his mother alone. I find him – it's really more his energy than him - disconcerting." She paused. "But I'm handling it so far."

"Of course you're handling it," Sophia spoke with authority, her tone brisk. She paused a moment. "But you haven't said if he's sexy."

"He's not movie star handsome, but handsome enough." Lily's gaze fixed on a far wall. "He can be charming." She shook her head clearing wayward thoughts. "I also find him irritating, frustrating, and, as already mentioned, disconcerting. It's hard to get past all that to see much of anything else."

"Other than he cares deeply about his mother." Sophia's comment hung in the air.

"Yes, he cares about his mother," Lily snapped the words out. "His attitude toward me? His manner? His — oh, I don't know. Whenever we are in close proximity of each other, tension coats the air and I feel my temper rise. Why yesterday I could have just slugged him I was so irritated and frustrated with him."

"Really?" All three women said almost simultaneously.

"Yes, really," Lily sighed. "I know you all see me as having a calm, cool problem-solving manner with clients and their families."

"What happened?" Sophia ordered.

"Yes, tell us," Elizabeth and Gabriella added.

"It isn't really anything," Lily began. "He helped me take groceries into my client's kitchen."

Elizabeth turned to Sophia. "That certainly sounds arrogant, frustrating and irritating to me."

"Obviously, I'm not explaining this very well," Lily's exasperation with the subject tinged her words with coolness. "He trapped me against my car, he demanded." She heard his quiet request in her mind and quickly amended what she was saying. "Well, not demanded really or trapped exactly." The exasperation was back in full force. "He was standing so close and, and he was between me and the house. I couldn't move or I'd brush up against him."

Where is this panicky feeling coming from? Her brain filled with a scenario from just before Paul left. He'd hit her and stomped out leaving her on the floor. She focused on her body, feeling the chair under her buttocks, the floor under her feet, her hands grasping the arms of the chair. The panicky feeling eased.

She took a deep breath and exhaled slowly; let her eyes move to each woman's face. They were watching her, wondering what had happened. "It's hard to explain." She took another steadying breath. "And then, he turned and stomped off, banged the groceries on the counter, and was gone," she trailed off.

"It wouldn't surprise me to learn he likes you." Sophia reached over laying her hand on Lily's knee. "You know, just like the boys in high school picking on a girl they like because they don't know what else to do with the lust."

"Lust! Don't make me laugh," Lily sputtered, the confusion, the panic gone in an instant. "He's a grown man, Sophia. Good looking and rich enough and," she paused for the drama, "from what his mother says or at least implies he certainly isn't celibate."

"It'll be interesting to see what happens next," Sophia baited Lily. "My bet is on this son. I'll bet you he's interested in you and wants you in his bed."

"It's a beautiful bed."

"So, you've had an offer?" Elizabeth sputtered.

"No," Lily said, a big grin on her face, her eyes alight with mischief, "but when I stayed overnight with his mother last week, I could see in the door of the master bedroom. It's stunning with luscious pale blue walls, cream-colored crown molding and cove ceiling with cherry wood furniture. I don't know much about antiques, but I wouldn't be surprised if the armoire with all the carvings isn't one. In the center is a giant four poster bed you practically need a step ladder to get in to. And the duvet? It's so delicious you'd like to eat it. A wonderful variegated red velvet patchwork creation you might think would be too much with the pale blue walls but it's striking."

Mundane comments about master bedroom décor and antiques followed. In the background, the general conversation continued as Lily wondered what they each thought about what she shared and how she'd had shared it. She hadn't told anyone that with Charlie gone the nightmares and her hyper-vigilance had increased. She considered talking to Diana. Bill had chosen to spend Thanksgiving with his roommate's family back east. *She might welcome someone to talk to since Dennis doesn't seem to care.*

Puzzled about her panicky reaction to telling her friends about the encounter with Jackson, she thought back to the actual event. What was it about him that frightened her? What was it about him that drew her? Her heart beat faster, her pulse quickened, a sheen of perspiration coated her upper lip and dampened her palms when her mind dwelled on those questions. She pulled her attention back to the room, determined to put Jackson Montgomery out of her mind.

The women adjourned to the kitchen to fix their dessert of choice — apple, pumpkin or mincemeat pie — returning to the comfort of the living room. Lily brought a tea tray so each woman could replenish her cup. Her dark mood lifted.

"I read somewhere that researchers found that when you eat what you love with people you love you there are no bad effects. It's like the food is healthy and calorie-free." She looked down at her full plate complete with a thin slice of each pie and its attendant topping, and then up at her friends. A forkful of apple pie almost to her mouth, she laughed and added, "I'm eating desserts tonight convinced it's true."

Saturday the weather was crisp and although it was a busy day, Lily had things in order and was driving to Eleanor's on time. Mt. Hood, a brilliant white sentinel, was silhouetted against the clear blue sky. The foothills, nestled around their towering neighbor, had a pale dusting of snow. The view was intoxicating. She relaxed into the car's seat. Adding to her joy was the knowledge the outcome of her morning at the ER with Mr. Cramer was positive. He had not suffered a stroke. His confusion was a combination of dehydration and a reaction to a medication. Scared, Mr. Cramer finally agreed to someone calling him each morning to check on him. Progress!

Eleanor greeted her with a warm hug and hot cup of tea. It wasn't long before they settled on the couch in the apartment's living room, drawn to the stark beauty of a winter garden and beyond the fence, the bare, gnarled branches of distant trees outlined against the dark green of the Douglas firs.

Both of Eleanor's daughters, who lived in Boston, had called Thursday and she'd talked to each family member. Daniel O'Donnell a friend and business colleague of her son's had joined them for dinner. Jackson had fixed the full turkey dinner with cornbread dressing, mashed potatoes and giblet gravy, sweet potatoes, relish plate, and green bean casserole. Even though Jackson had made two mincemeat pies and his own special recipe for a brandy-hard-sauce, Daniel had brought a pumpkin cheese cake and an apple pie from an upscale bakery. Eleanor had added her specialty: lobster bisque. After eating their fill, they'd spent a comfortable evening together watching football. Eleanor leaned toward Lily and said in a confidential tone, "We will not starve tonight, my dear."

"I wasn't worried for a moment." Lily chuckled. "If I'd had any doubts, I've a refrigerator full of scrumptious food I could have brought over." She laughed again as she shared with Eleanor the story about whipped cream covered, calorie-free pie.

"I am sure we can test that theory here today," Eleanor said with a smile. "I love that idea and will use it as my personal eating guide in the future."

From time to time Lily fleetingly looked over her shoulder or checked the large picture window for a reflection. Her back twitched as if she was being watched. Never seeing anything, she shrugged to dislodge the sense of unease.

When she went into the kitchen area to help Eleanor put things together for dinner, she glanced through the French doors into the main house. A tall, model-slim woman with burgundy-red hair worn in an upswept style and who looked like she'd stepped off the pages of a fashion magazine was smiling up at Jackson as he leaned over the back of the gray suede chair saying something obviously amusing.

So that's his type. Eleanor did say the women he was involved with were beautiful.

Dismissing the two of them from her mind, she instead reframed the sense of being watched into an awareness that she and Eleanor were not alone.

With Eleanor regaling her with stories of Thanksgivings past, Lily heated up their dinners.

Later, as they were relaxing in front of the television, again laughing about the magical elves that come in and clean up the kitchen after holiday meals, there was a knock on the door.

"Entrez-vous," Eleanor said without turning.

"Mother, I hope we're not interrupting anything special," Jackson inquired in a formally polite voice.

"Lily and I were just relaxing after a wonderful meal. Would you like to join us for dessert? We have calorie-free-whipped-cream-smothered pumpkin pie." She turned to Lily and winked.

By watching their reflection in the window, Lily could see Jackson escort his companion into the room, his hand curved around her waist. He introduced Susannah to Eleanor as his friend, keeping her close. Susannah leaned into him, certainly defining "friend" as someone special from Lily's perspective.

An odd unsettled feeling twisted her stomach. Clean, comfortable, and presentable were her watchwords when it came to clothes and she seldom wore makeup. But tonight, in the same room with Susannah, she couldn't help but compare herself to Jackson's friend. Susannah could sell a Jaguar or Mercedes Benz. She was dressed to sell a ... well, she couldn't even think of a product she was dressed to sell in her non-descript t-shirt and jeans. She reminded herself she was not in competition here. *So I've been attracted to him. I'm certainly not and never will be his type.*

Eleanor reached over and touched Lily's arm. "Susannah, I would like you to meet my very special friend, Lily." Eleanor paused, her gaze resting on Lily, a bright smile on her face.

"It's a pleasure to meet you, Susannah." Lily rose and turned toward Eleanor. "I'll leave you to visit and start on the kitchen." She smiled. "I don't think those elves are stopping by here today." She moved past everyone into the dining area where she began clearing the table.

Jackson lounged in the chair. He watched Lily as she efficiently cleared the table, put dishes in the dishwasher and washed the pots and pans. *What about her draws me?* He looked closely at the beauty next to him. Susannah was his type. Stunningly beautiful, dressed to the nines, intelligent....

He joined in the conversation between his mother and Susannah who was describing a recent photo shoot she'd been on, name-dropping top industry professionals. Knowing Eleanor didn't have an acute interest in clothing and make-up, he interjected a word or phrase to cue his mother in to who Susannah was talking about.

Time and again his gaze rested on Lily and the question remained. *Why am I so drawn to her?* His mind raced to list all the reasons she was wrong for him. Too short; too fat, well that wasn't right. She just wasn't tall and thin. Her hair wasn't styled, she didn't wear make-up and she wasn't fashionably dressed.

The object of his fascination had finished in the kitchen and now stood to the side of the couch next to Eleanor. His mind betrayed him with another list: softly rounded body; 'natural-look'; silky-looking skin now tinged with a slight flush. He wanted to touch her, to slide his fingers through her hair, tug it out of its pony tail, and arrange it to frame her face. It would be soft, flow through his fingers, release more of the lavender scent he associated with her. Next to him, Susannah shifted; her designer fragrance filled his nostrils. Overpowering. Having the two women in the same room highlighted their differences. Susannah is my type. Intelligent, high-fashion sense, beautiful...the type of woman I like to be seen with. And yet … .

"Does anyone want desert?" Lily asked as soon as there was a lull in the conversation. The answer was unanimous. Jackson invited everyone to have desert in front of the fire in his living room. Pie in hand, they sat and chatted about non-essentials: weather predictions for the rest of the weekend and whether there would be snow for Christmas. Over and over, Jackson found his thoughts straying to the casually dressed woman next to his mother instead of the fashion-plate sitting next to him. "Damn," he muttered to himself. "Why can't I stop thinking of her?"

When Lily and Eleanor got up to leave, his mother reached up and adjusted the owl on the mantle so it faced the front door.

"What are you doing?" he asked, standing to step to the mantle and turn the owl back to face the windows.

"You'll have to ask Lily," Eleanor replied, readjusting it toward the front door. "She is the one with the answer to that question."

"Well?" he asked, eyebrow arched. "I have noticed my owl has been moved. Please, enlighten me," he said in a cool, polite voice.

The light from the crystal sconces on either side of the fireplace bathed the room in their soft, warm glow. The additional brightness from the crackling fire provided enough illumination for Lily to read the expression in his eyes.

Gray eyes, like chips of ice, froze her where she stood. The energy radiating from him engulfed her. One eyebrow remained quirked in question.

"If you understood the purpose of the great horned owl being in your house, you would know it needs to face the front door." Lily's chin went up a notch.

"Are you crazy?"

"In my tradition, this great horned owl embodies the spirit of the land your house is built upon. The purpose of a House Totem is to protect your home and the people within," she said her insides quaking. Worry that he'd try to push her away from Eleanor spiked.

"Really? And you know this how?" What the hell was she talking about?

She ignored the silky disbelieving tone of his voice and her own unease and forged on in a matter-of-fact tone. "I know this because I listen. He told me he could not do his job with his back to the door. So, I turned him as he asked."

"You must be crazy," he muttered darkly, "talking to inanimate objects." He turned to Eleanor, "What do you think, mother? Is a crazy woman here with you?" He tilted his head to the side, a frown on his face.

"Actually, the more Lily talks about the energy around us, the more it makes sense," his mother replied, her own head cocked at a similar angle.

Lily ignored his comment about her sanity. Bolstered by Eleanor's statement, she continued in a soft voice. "In my tradition, everything has spirit and life, even things we consider inanimate. It's a matter of tuning into the spirit of the object to hear its voice. You're entitled to think that's crazy, but I'm telling you this great horned owl is in your home for a reason." Curiosity got the better of caution and she asked, "Where did you get it?"

"I bought it," he shot back sarcasm heavy in each word.

"Why?" She persisted.

"Because I liked it." He raised his chin, peered down his nose and pinned her with his dagger-colored eyes.

"What was going on in your life at the time? Do you remember?" Lily's inquisitiveness won out over her discomfort with the exchange.

He moved closer to the fireplace, settled his shoulder against the mantle. "I'd just moved to Fremont, was finishing the apartment for mother." He turned to Eleanor. "It was a couple of months before you were to move here. Remember, I had that project in Seattle?"

Eleanor nodded.

Jackson's head tipped at a thoughtful angle. "I remember walking along one of the streets wondering how everything was going to work out. I don't even remember the name of the shop, a little hole-in-the-wall kind of place. I just seemed to find myself inside, looking around. As soon as I saw this owl, I knew it had to be in this house, in this room, on this mantle." He scowled and then a puzzled expression spread over his features. *Now why did I tell her all that?*

Her voice gentled as she replied, "You're right. This owl does need to be on this mantle. However, he also needs to be able to see the door. It's the only way he can protect you, your mother, and your home."

"Nonsense, utter nonsense," he muttered staring at the owl that was now neither turned toward the windows nor toward the door.

Lily stood quietly, watching him, waiting, her hands at her side.

Time passed. The room was silent except for the soft pops and sizzles of the fire. He seemed off in a distant place. She took advantage of his distraction to observe him. In the soft light, his hair curled over his ears and shirt collar. *His hair looks darker in this light.* Shadows crossed his face highlighting the angles and planes of his cheek bones, nose and jaw. She waited patiently taking in his wide shoulders, tapered waist, narrow hips and long legs.

With a jerk of his head, Jackson seemed to come back from wherever his thoughts had taken him. "Yes," he said quietly. "You may be right." He moved quickly reaching toward the owl, effectively blocking Lily against the mantle.

Jackson turned the owl toward the front door, pretending to be unaware of the woman trapped between him and the fireplace mantle. However, in this case, appearances were deceiving. He was not only aware of Susannah's intense scrutiny of the scene before her but he was acutely aware of the warm womanly body in front of him, her scent of lavender, the attraction arcing between them and something more he couldn't quite identify.

He'd dismissed it as nothing. Nothing more than the tug of recognition, man to woman, male to female. He wasn't dead and she was attractive in her own way. *Susannah is my type.* But there was something more in that tug, something he could not quite place or name, that disturbed his sense of control.

Lily stifled a shudder when his hard body brushed against her. She hadn't acknowledged he was so big, so male. But as his body touched her she thought he'd be softer, his chest and thighs not so hard. She could see the stubble of his dark beard, smell his scent. A citrus fragrance - sharp and clean.

The current she felt every time he was close was decidedly evident. His heat enveloped her and her body slackened. She locked her knees to keep from wavering, struggled to maintain an outwardly calm façade and hoped he wouldn't guess how he affected her.

For several seconds, they stood there staring at one another. Her look was cool, her breathing irregular. She remained still, watching, waiting for him to make a move. With a shake of his head, he stepped back

Lily let out a pent-up breath.

"Well," he said briskly, "that's that then."

"Thank you," Lily said still shaken from the effect of his nearness.

Jackson's laugh was not one of humor. "I don't know who's crazier, you or me."

She remained in front of the mantle, watched him take a step back his eyes still locked with hers. He blinked and she saw the fierce intensity in his gaze diminish. Her senses expanded and took in Susannah and Eleanor still seated. The animosity in Susannah's glare contrasted with warmth of Eleanor's smile. *OMG what must they think.*

Shrugging, Jackson turned and strode the few steps back to the couch, sat, his arm along the back, oblivious to the two spectators. Susannah scooted next to him, snuggled so her body formed to his, and rested her hand on his thigh. He reached across Susannah and picked up a glass of red wine from the end table, took a deep swallow and stared at the fire.

"It is getting late," Eleanor said a few minutes later. "I think I'll retire for the night."

"Yes, it is getting late," Lily echoed. "Time for me to go."

Jackson put down the wine and quickly rose, taking the few steps to his mother. He bent down to kiss her cheek before helping her to her feet. "I'll be right back," he said over his shoulder to Susannah, who remained on the couch.

Following his mother and Lily into the apartment he said, "I'll see you out."

"That really isn't necessary," Lily replied, hearing the prim tone to her voice, wishing he'd take the hint and back off.

"I'll see you out anyway. It's the polite thing to do," he said his voice cool as he helped her into her coat, reached around her and opened the apartment's front door.

Lily preceded him out the door. She was halfway to her car when she felt his hand on her elbow. He reached out and plucked her key from her hand.

"What are you doing?" she sputtered trying to grab her key back.

Raising it out of her grasp he responded, "Escorting you to your car."

A few steps and they were there. Jackson unlocked the door and gestured for Lily to get in. When she did, he bent over and held out the key. Their hands touched briefly as she took it. The air hummed with vibrant energy.

"Thanks," he said after a moment. "I do appreciate all you do for mother."

"You're welcome, Mr. Montgomery," Lily said hoping that the electricity she felt shoot from her fingers and spread throughout her body didn't show.

He held her gaze. "You could call me Jackson, my friends do," he said softly, seductively.

"We're not friends, Mr. Montgomery," Lily said her diction precise, her manner cool.

Jackson had watched her closely when their hands touched, watched to see if she felt the current raging through his body; watched and saw her eyes widen a fraction, her breath slightly stutter.

Straightening, he shut the door and stepped back a few steps. Lily started her car and backed out of the driveway. As he watched her taillights disappear around the curve, the pull, the arousal he'd experienced since standing close to her by the fireplace ebbed. *I can't believe I told everyone about buying that owl.* He shook his head in disbelief. Turning, he started back to his house still shaking his head. "It's just a basic sexual pull, nothing more," he muttered to himself as he closed his front door behind him.

Once inside he took a deep breath and looked around. He recognized the lavender but not the subtle under layers of Lily's scent. *Hmm, perhaps Ms. Lily Hughes has more to her than meets the eye.* He shook his head. He was tired.

Susannah was waiting. It may be chauvinistic and shallow but he liked having men's heads turn when he walked in the room with her on his arm. She'd traveled all over the world and through her contacts he now had a couple of clients from the Hollywood scene. She was creative in the bedroom. What more could he want?

As soon as Susannah finished her nightcap, Jackson took her home, walked her to the door of her apartment building, declining the invitation to spend the night. He was relieved to be driving home; relieved he was sleeping alone in his bed, relieved to be heading back to the job site on Monday; and doubly relieved the job site was in California.

Distance. That's what he needed.

Distance from both women to sort things out."

14 - THE FALL

Friday
December 6, 2002

"$\mathcal{H}$ello, this is Lily Hughes, how may I help you?"

"Lily Hughes?"

"Yes."

"This is Life Alert dispatcher, William. Eleanor Montgomery reports she's fallen and is unable to get up. We've been unable to reach her son and you are listed as an emergency contact. How far are you from her now?"

"About forty-five minutes away. Please go ahead and call 911. Forty-five minutes is too long for her to be lying on the floor." Her mind clear and precise; her body calm and composed despite the adrenaline surging through it, she was in hyper-vigilant mode.

"What about her son? We've left messages but haven't been able to reach him," William queried.

"What numbers are you calling?"

"The three numbers we have: home, office, and cell."

"He's in California. I'll try him again if you'll call 911. And tell them I'm on my way and please give them my cell phone number, the one you just called."

"Not a problem. I'll let the 911 dispatch know how to reach you. We have voice contact with Mrs. Montgomery through the base unit. I'll let her know we've reached you also."

"Thank you, William." She turned her car around in the Fred Meyer parking lot and started across town. Before she pulled out into traffic, she dialed Jackson's cell number, leaving him a brief message about his mother and asking him to call her.

Thirty-five minutes later, Lily pulled into the Emergency Room parking lot of St. Agatha's Hospital. In a consultation with the paramedics who'd responded to the call, the plan was that Eleanor be seen in the Emergency Room to rule out a broken hip. As she stepped out of her car, her cell phone rang. Jackson's voice boomed.

"Lily? What the hell is going on?"

"Eleanor fell, is in pain, and has been taken to St. Agatha's ER for an assessment. She may have broken her hip. It's hard to tell at this point without x-rays. I've just arrived myself and as soon as I know more, I'll let you know." She trotted through the rain to the ER entrance.

"What do you mean she's at the ER? What's happening?"

Lily heard the panic and fear in his voice. In her most professional manner she responded, "Mr. Montgomery, Eleanor's at the Emergency Room at St. Agatha's. I don't know any of the details about the fall. I've been keeping track of things by phone because I was too far away to get to the house myself. Oh, before I forget, they had to break in the door to Eleanor's apartment to get to her. They did what they could to secure her place but it isn't really secure. And it's very stormy right now."

"I'll take care of the damn door. Tell me about my mother!"

"Mr. Montgomery," she continued in a patient, calm voice as she ducked into a sheltered area. "I don't know much right now. I'll call and let you know when I do. She's getting the best of care at St. Agatha's and I'll make sure everything goes well. I've rearranged my appointments so I can be with her for as long as is needed."

"I'll call you in thirty minutes." Jackson's enunciation was precise.

"I may not be able to answer. Hospitals don't allow cell phone use in the ER. Do you have paper and pencil? I can give you the hospital's main phone number and they can put you through."

"Okay." His exasperation and frustration were clear in the one word.

She gave Jackson the main hospital phone number before running the last few yards in the wind-whipped rain. "I've got to go now, Mr. Montgomery. I'm at the ER and have to turn off my cell phone. I'll call you when I know something."

"I'll get a plane out as soon as I can arrange it."

"Let's see what the problem is first, okay? You may not need to come now."

"Are you telling me not to come home?" Jackson asked his voice low and tinged with ice.

"No, of course not, Mr. Montgomery," Lily said brightly. "I'm just saying that we don't even know what has happened. You may want to wait until you know if it's serious before you change your plans."

"I'll be in touch." Jackson's voice broke on the few words. He hung up.

The noise and odors of the busy ER engulfed Lily's senses as she came through the door. Immediately she was buzzed through to the examination rooms. Locating the right cubicle, Lily was relieved to see Mark Parker examining Eleanor and knew that was why she had quick access to her client. His warm brown eyes watched Eleanor's face for even the slightest sign of discomfort as his long fingers gently probed her limbs. He was a tall man, just over six feet, with a long, lean athletic build. She noticed his medium brown hair was freshly trimmed, not curling over his jacket as it usually did.

"Oh, I am so glad you are here," Eleanor's voice wobbled and she winced as she reached to take Lily's hand. "I don't know what happened actually. I just found myself on the floor with my leg all twisted under me." Her eyes filled with tears. "I couldn't get up."

"It's okay, Eleanor. You have one of the best orthopedists in Fremont taking care of you." Lily said, confidence ringing in her voice. She smiled noting the pale coloring and body tension, signs Eleanor was in pain. Lily gently rested her free hand on the older woman's shoulder.

"Only one of the best?" Dr. Parker's face lit with a grin when he turned to see Lily by his patient's side.

"Well, actually, the only doctor I'd see if I had a broken bone, so I guess that makes you 'the best' in my opinion." Lily grinned back. "I've worked with Dr. Parker a long time, Eleanor. I trust him completely."

"Mrs. Montgomery, I can't finish my diagnosis without x-rays. Someone'll be here to take you down to Radiology in a few minutes. Once that's done, we'll talk again. But, whether your hip is broken or not, I want to keep you overnight for observation. You also have a pretty nasty lump on your head. You hit something when you fell."

"You are not going to put me in a home are you?" Eleanor's voice trembled and her eyes widened with fear.

"Right now it's too soon to know what's best. We need to find out what's wrong before we can come up with a treatment plan." At the cubicle entrance he turned and said, "I'll be back when I've got the results from the x-rays." With a wave of his hand he was gone.

"Eleanor." Lily gently squeezed the older woman's hand, drawing her attention. "Let's do this one step at a time. Dr. Parker knows what he's doing. When we have more information, we can talk more about plans." Changing the subject to distract her client she asked, "Do you want me to go with you or wait here?"

"Can you come with me?"

"I can come with you and wait outside in the hall."

With that, the orderly arrived. A bright and cheerful young man, he and the nurse quickly readied Eleanor. Lily stood back and observed Eleanor's efforts to be stoic. Must be that British stiff upper lip because she's obviously in pain.

"Mrs. Montgomery, my name is Todd. I'm taking you to Radiology." As he took the brake off the gurney, he said, "Well, off you go to have your pictures taken. And you do look lovely, if I do say so myself," he quipped. "Your gown, in particular, sets off the gray in your eyes, don't you think?"

In spite of the pain, Eleanor smiled. "I am glad you noticed my eyes. With the alluring figure I must cut in this gown, I did not think anyone would." Turning to Lily she said, "I will be fine with this young man watching out for me. You do not need to come along." Turning back to the young orderly she said, "You will be looking out for me, will you not?"

"Yes, ma'am. I'll be right there the whole time. Maybe not holding your hand when they take your picture but watching you through the glass. You won't be alone."

Her fear is lessening, her spunk is coming back. Lily smiled to herself. Spying Mark at the counter making notes in a chart, she joined him.

"How bad do you think it is?"

"It isn't a bad break, if it's broken at all. The x-rays will tell us what we need to know. Excuse me, someone is trying to reach me." He reached for his pager and walked away.

Back in Eleanor's cubicle, Lily sat down, got out her notebook and wrote some notes in Eleanor's section. She had other client appointments to reschedule and she wanted to let Sophia know what was going on. They had planned on having dinner together this evening. She paused, glanced at her notes. "I think I can step out and call Mr. Montgomery before Eleanor gets back. Well, it's getting late and I'd better get on it." She tucked her notebook back in her briefcase and began gathering her things to leave. Before she stepped out of the cubicle, Mark confronted her, a scowl on his face.

"Do you know her son?"

"Yes, I do." She heard Mark's clipped tone and saw his clenched jaw. He was barely holding onto his temper.

"Is he always such a jerk?"

"Well, I'm not sure what he's done for you to have diagnosed him with that particular disease," Lily said, her lips twitching, her eyes alight with amusement, "but I do know he's fiercely protective of his mother."

"Well, his opinion of me is much further down the evolutionary ladder than is yours. How did such an elegant lady as Mrs. Montgomery end up with him for a son?"

"Really ruffled your feathers, did he, Doc?" Lily grinned. "I don't know that I've seen you this upset before. What did he say?"

"Besides demanding that I tell him right now what's wrong with his mother? He demanded that I call in *the best person* to oversee her care."

Lily laid her hand on his arm. "Mark, you are the best and you are overseeing her care. You'll know what's wrong when you see the x-rays and the test results come back. I believe Mr. Montgomery gets this way when *his things* are tampered with. I'll go outside and see if I can reach him. Maybe I can talk to him and he'll calm down."

"Oh, he's calm enough right now. As soon as I told him you were here, in the room with his mother, participating in the planning, he backed off."

"I'll go call him anyway," Lily said. "He and I have to work something out in terms of communication and I need to find out how he's managing to get Eleanor's door secured."

Lily chose to go outside rather than try to talk to Jackson in the crowded ER lobby. Finding a corner sheltered from the wind and rain, she dialed his number.

He answered on the first ring.

"What's going on?" he asked.

"Eleanor's down at x-rays which is why I've stepped outside to bring you up-do-date. Your mother's wonderful sense of humor is evident so regardless of final diagnosis, she'll be okay. Mark Parker is the best orthopedic doc in the area. If he hadn't been on call today, I would have asked for him."

"Are you sure he's good?" Jackson asked suspicion in his voice.

"Yes, I'm sure he's good. He's treated some of my clients over the years so I know how good he really is. He takes into account the whole person - so when we're looking at a plan, he'll try to accommodate what'll work best psychologically for Eleanor as well. Oh, that reminds me, what do you know about Eleanor's fear of nursing homes?"

"Damn, she can't go to one of those hell holes." He spoke quickly, his words rushed. "Both her parents died in those homes." He paused before continuing. "I know she feels guilty she couldn't be there to take care of them."

"Well, that was a while back. Care standards here and, I assume, in England have changed dramatically. If it comes to that, I'll see she's in the best one I know."

"Thanks, Lily. I don't know what I'd do if you weren't there. I'm going crazy here worrying about her."

"I'm sure you are, Mr. Montgomery," Lily said softly. "I'll call you as soon as I know what's going on. Oh, there's one other thing. Eleanor is being admitted overnight for observation. Don't worry, I'll stay with her." She glanced at the time. "Well, I'd better get back inside so I'm in her cubicle when she gets back from x-ray."

"Thanks. I'll wait for your call then…Lily?"

"Yes, Mr. Montgomery?" She heard his hesitation, felt a subtle shift in energy.

"Do you think you could bring yourself to call me Jackson?"

A hint of entreaty softened her resolve to keep her distance. "Yes, I think I could." She could only imagine what he was going through, how he was handling his protective instincts when it came to his mother. It was the least she could do she told herself.

"Bye, Lily."

"Bye Jackson." She waited a moment until the call disconnected before she walked back inside. He was a complex man. One minute he was a world class jerk: arrogant, controlling, domineering; the next he was the opposite: considerate, thoughtful, kind, almost boyish. And he trusted her to do what's best for Eleanor.

Approaching the cubicle where Eleanor had been, Lily saw her being returned by Todd. He was leaning over the rail, talking to Eleanor while she watched him with rapt attention.

"Hi there." Lily infused her voice with light energy. "So, we meet again. Did you smile for the camera?"

Todd and Eleanor groaned in unison.

"I know it's a tired old, corny clichéd x-ray joke." Lily smiled. "But, it always works to tell a groaner, doesn't it?"

"I guess it depends on what you want to accomplish," Todd quipped. "If what you want is people groaning, then it certainly does the trick, right Mrs. M?"

"Right-o, Todd," Eleanor said.

"Right-o?" Lily queried.

"Yes, I'm going to be more English as people are mesmerized by accents so I can hypnotize them to do my bidding," Eleanor said straight-faced.

"Really? Mesmerized is it?" Lily's brows arched up. "And who is the fountain of wisdom that pearl came from?"

"My new friend, Todd," Eleanor said in the thickest British accent Lily had ever heard from her.

"I see," Lily said as Dr. Parker entered.

"Well, we have a room all ready for you, Mrs. Montgomery. Todd, can you take her up?"

"Of course, Doctor, I'll get her things together."

"Now, the good news," Dr. Parker leaned over to talk directly to Eleanor. "Your hip isn't broken but you have severely sprained the joint. What that means, Mrs. Montgomery, is that the muscles and ligaments that hold that joint in place have been injured and pain is their way of telling you that. In addition, you have bruises, contusions and the bump on your head. You're lucky you don't have a concussion. Now that we know what's going on, we can give you something for the pain. Let's get you upstairs and settled. I'll be up to see you in a couple of hours and we'll plan from there." His tone turned business-like when he stepped briskly from the cubicle. "Lily, I'd like a word with you."

"Of course, Doctor," she returned in the same professional tone as she followed him out.

"I'd appreciate your calling the son, letting him know what's going on. I'm backed up at the office."

"She and Todd seem to have hit it off so I think it'll be okay for him to take her to her room while I go call Jackson. Do you know where she'll be yet?"

"She'll be in Room 1010."

"Great, I'll just let her know I'll meet her there and I'm calling Jackson. She may have a message she wants me to pass on to him. Hopefully hearing this news and getting a message from his mother will let him know that she will be okay. Really, Mark, that's all he needs. To know his mother will be okay."

STRIDING down the hall to Room 1010, Jackson's head whirled with chaotic thoughts, his chest tight with worry. It was going on midnight and as exhausted as he was, as difficult as it had been to leave the job site right now, the decision to come home and to the hospital tonight was the right one. It wasn't that he didn't trust Lily to see to his mother's care. His suspicions of her over the last two months had proven false. She did want what was best for his mother.

As irrational as it was, he couldn't shake the feeling his mother could have died. The thought of losing her made his heart skip a beat. He knew it wasn't rational. She'd only fallen. Her hip wasn't broken and she didn't have a concussion. He just needed to see her, see she was safe. His shoulders hunched against the weight of guilt. He hadn't been there. She'd fallen and been alone.

Getting the last seat on the last plane out of San Francisco had been a stroke of luck. He ran a hand through his already rumpled hair as he reached the doorway to his mother's room. He stopped and took a steadying breath before looking in the slightly ajar door.

His mother was asleep in the hospital bed. Lily was scrunched in a chair that was neither upright nor reclined. What stopped him in his tracks was the sight of her arm through the bed's railing, holding his mother's hand. She'd said she'd stay and she had. Not just stayed in the hospital or even in the room, she stayed connected to his mother. She stirred, shifted, yet never took her hand off his mother's.

He struggled to breathe. Memories of his father welled up in his mind. The last time he'd felt that sense of being singularly special was with his father. Now the man who'd been the most important person in his life, the man who could look at his blueprint and see the finished building, the man who knew the worth of his work, was gone. His mother loved him and supported him, but he and she didn't have that depth of understanding he'd had with his father. He realized in a new way what he'd lost when his father died.

Jackson refocused on the scene before him: Lily and his mother. He knew their bond was more than client and case manager. A thought hit him in the chest. His hand rubbed over his heart, the pain eased but didn't go away. He wanted to be special to someone again, special like he was with his father. The truth was he wanted what his mother had with Lily.

Scrunched in the chair and rumpled, Lily looked wonderful to his tired eyes.

Shifting, Lily raised her head to check on Eleanor, patting her hand, stroking her arm. Her voice low, he heard her say, "I'm here, Eleanor. You're not alone."

In the dim light he saw his mother's lips move, heard her whisper, "I know."

Had he made a noise? He didn't think so; however, two pairs of eyes focused on him. His mother's face blossomed with a bright smile. "Oh, Jackson! You've come!" she cried out with joy and reached toward him.

Letting go of Eleanor's hand, Lily started to rise.

"Don't get up on my account, Lily." Jackson strode the few steps to his mother's bedside, pushing aside the overwhelming feelings of loss and thoughts of a special relationship with Lily. Bending down, he wrapped his mother in his arms and held her. Feeling her stiffen, he gently laid her back on the pillows. "I'm sorry Mother, I forgot for a moment how bad off you are."

"Nonsense, Jackson," Eleanor said briskly. "You've not hurt me at all. Your hug was just what the doctor would have ordered. It has cheered me immensely."

Stretching, trying to work the kinks out, Lily said, "I'll step out and let the two of you catch up."

"Don't go, Lily," Jackson's gray eyes met dark blue ones, locked and held. "I think we need you here, don't you mother?"

"Of course we do," Eleanor said. "Jackson and I both would like you to stay while we talk about what has happened and what will be."

"All right, I'll stay but if you don't mind, I'll walk around the room a bit." Lily's unease at the intense look she shared with Jackson lessened as she moved stiffly around the room. She bent from side-to-side and stretched back-and-forth working the kinks out of her neck, shoulders and lower back.

Jackson brought his attention back to his mother. "The house is secured, Mother. Daniel brought a crew by before dark and took care of it. He'll be by in the morning with a new door, so by the time you're home; everything will be as it was."

"Well, that was nice of him."

"I hope I can come up with what he wants for payment." Jackson did his best to hide his nerves. He was skating on thin ice.

"What do you mean? I do not believe Daniel would overcharge you, Jackson."

"No, mother, he isn't overcharging me. And, he doesn't want money. He wants something I can't directly give him so I have to ask someone else if they'll do what he has asked of me."

"What is that, dear?"

"He wants a House Totem for his place. I talked to him from the airport last Sunday while I was waiting for my flight. He's been set on the idea of a House Totem ever since he learned the owl on my fireplace mantle is our House Totem." Jackson turned toward Lily who was now standing by the window looking out at the forested hills beyond. "What do you say, Lily? I'll certainly pay you your going rate."

Stunned, Lily turned from the window. She noted the expectant look on Jackson's face as he stood next to Eleanor's bed, holding her hand. She was fairly sure she could sense his friend's House Totem. But payment? The sound of Jackson's voice interrupted her thoughts.

"I'm sorry, Jackson, you took me by surprise. I don't think I quite caught what you were saying after asking if I can tell your friend what his House Totem is."

"I was asking what your usual fee is for doing the House Totem thing," he said, his voice casual.

"I don't have a fee. It isn't something I do." Lily's brow furrowed in confusion.

"You don't? Well, then how did you know about the owl? I don't understand." His questions tumbled one after the other and she noted the bewilderment on his face.

"I don't seek House Totems, I recognize them. So, I probably could identify a House Totem for your friend." Lily hesitated.

"Does $1000.00 sound about right?"

"What?" Her hand pressed against her heart, holding it in. Her mouth flew open, her eyes shocked wide.

"Your fee for doing the House Totem thing. Is $1000.00 dollars right?" he said watching her reaction. "You aren't going to hyperventilate on me, are you?"

Lily took a moment before saying, "I'll have to think about it, Jackson. This is a sudden change in topic and I'm tired."

Turning to Eleanor, Jackson said, "See, I told you the price was steep. It always is when you have no control over the source."

Eleanor held her son's hand. "Give her some time Jackson. Even I am surprised by your request."

Lily left the room and paced the halls, ostensibly to work the kinks out, but in truth she needed some time alone. Was it wrong to take money for using a gift from the Goddess or God? She wasn't sure it was. People who were very good at something often referred to it as a 'gift.' If it was acceptable to receive payment for discovering Daniel's House Totem, she had no idea what a reasonable fee would be. Stopping at the end of the hall, she looked out into the darkness. In a few hours, she could call someone in The Circle and talk this over.

Returning to Eleanor's room, Lily dragged the second chair in the room over to the bed. "Jackson, you look exhausted. I'm more than willing to stay with Eleanor while you go home and get some sleep."

"No thanks, Lily. I'm fine right where I am." He stood, pressing a kiss to his mother's forehead before sitting again. Reaching through the side rails, he held her hand. "Actually, I know I'm right where I'm supposed to be."

The three of them dozed off and on until seven when the hospital came to life. The shift changed, vitals were checked, introductions made.

Thirty minutes later, a soft knock on the door announced yet another visitor. Turning toward the sound, Lily saw Mark. Smiling she rose to greet him, hands outstretched.

"Dr. Mark Parker, I'd like you to meet Jackson Montgomery. Jackson, this is Dr. Parker, the best orthopedist in town." She stood next to Mark, smiling, her hand resting gently on his arm as the men shook hands.

"How are you doing this fine bright morning?" Dr. Parker asked Eleanor. His question belied the reality of the hard rain coming down in sheets of liquid that dulled the light of the new day struggling through the windows.

"I am just fine, Doctor," Eleanor said with forced cheer.

Lily stood back and smiled to herself knowing Mark wouldn't be fooled for a minute.

"Oh, good. Ready to get up and start walking the halls?"

Lily chuckled in spite of herself. Heads turned toward her and she coughed into her hand. "Sorry, something got caught in my throat," she muttered.

Eleanor managed a smile through gritted teeth, shifting as if to move to the side of the bed.

"Don't do that, Eleanor." Mark reached out, his hand on her shoulder. "You're in pain. I need to know the truth about how you feel so I can do what's best for you."

"Please, please not a home. I do not believe I can survive that," Eleanor choked out, tears streamed down her face.

"Let's not jump to conclusions Eleanor. We need to talk about what you need to recover from your fall. Then we'll have a better idea about the services you'll need," Mark said, his voice gentle with understanding.

Lily came to the foot of the bed. "Eleanor," she said calmly, "Dr. Parker is the best. Let's listen to what he has to say, okay?" Her look included Jackson whose face was masked with a night's worth of stubble. After being introduced to Mark, she noted he'd moved to the far corner of the room, hawk-like watched the proceedings, and although he'd remained silent, tension radiated and he seemed ready to pounce.

"I'm going to order physical and occupational therapy consults while you're here in the hospital. Because of the amount of pain you're in as well as the bump on your head and the soft tissue injuries you've sustained, we can justify another day. Once we get the results back from the assessments, we'll go from there." Turning to Lily, he asked, "How does that sound?"

"Good. And, Doctor, don't you agree that we can actually do some planning now that will ease both Eleanor and Jackson's minds a bit?"

"What are your ideas, Lily?" Dr. Parker asked with interest.

"I'm fairly certain both the physical and occupational therapy consults will show that Eleanor would benefit from a program to increase her strength. So, the question is "where's the best place to get that rehabilitation work done?" There are two possibilities: a rehabilitation center or a personally tailored program that'll allow Eleanor to return to her home. I believe Eleanor would benefit from either approach but I'm fairly certain which one she would choose."

"Cost is not an issue here," Jackson strode to the bed opposite Mark Parker and held his mother's hand. "As long as she gets what she needs and wants, expense is not an issue."

"Well, Lily, I'm not surprised at your thinking on this. And, you're right. I do think she needs a strength-building program," Dr. Parker said, ignoring Jackson's comments.

"If there's no need for medical care, we'll be able to put together a home program for you. What do you think about that idea?" Lily smiled at Eleanor, her hand resting on the foot-board of the bed.

"Oh, yes, Lily. A home program. That is what I want." Relief softened her face, the tears abated.

"And what has your fertile imagination come up with for a home program, Lily?"

"A combination of in-home and out-patient physical and occupational therapy in a program that would include Eleanor doing some exercises independently might work. I think she would be motivated to work on her own. And she'd be in a good mental and emotional frame of mind."

"Go ahead and see what you can get set up then for the outside program and I'll take care of the orders for home health. You'll monitor everything, won't you?" Dr. Parker's quizzical gaze was directed at Lily.

"I will, unless Jackson wants to. I can certainly let him know what to ask and what to look for," Lily said looking in Jackson's direction.

"I wouldn't dream of interfering in your work," Jackson said smoothly the smile on his face at odds with the cool look in his eyes.

"That's settled then unless you have some objections," Dr. Parker said looking back at his patient.

"No, it all sounds wonderful to me. Can I go home today?"

"Not today but let's see what the consults come up with. In addition to the consults, Eleanor, I want p.t. to come and work with you while you're here in the hospital.

"Lily, may I speak with you outside?" Dr. Parker said while turning and leaving the room.

"I'll be right back, Eleanor." Lily followed Dr. Parker out of the room and down the hall to a small sitting area.

"So, that's the son, eh?" A wicked glint in his eyes showed the humor behind the question.

Lily nodded.

"What's your relationship with him? I know that's a personal question, Lily, but I do wonder." A grin joined the gleam of humor in his eyes.

"He is the son of a client, Mark. Why?" She frowned.

"Oh, the way he watches you, glares at me. And, speak of the devil." Stepping back from Lily, Dr. Parker's face turned neutral as he watched an approaching Jackson. "Do you have any questions for me, Mr. Montgomery?"

"Not really, I was wondering what'd happened to Lily." He stopped beside her. "We were wondering what was taking you so long so I came looking for you. Mother wants to talk to you and has questions about things I can't answer. We both really do depend on your expertise, Lily," Jackson said putting his hand on her shoulder.

She looked at Jackson's hand on her shoulder and then glanced up into his steely gray eyes. Her brow wrinkled. "Tell Eleanor I'll be there as soon as I finish my conversation with Mark."

"I see," he said, his tone cool, his hand tightening on her shoulder as he spoke. Without further comment, he withdrew his hand, dropping it to his side. Turning he strode back down the hall to his mother's room.

"What was that all about?" Lily looked at Mark for clarification, for help sorting out what had just happened. Something had, she just didn't know what.

"I think you've misjudged that relationship. I don't think Mr. Montgomery sees you as only the case manager for his mother and I definitely don't think he wants you to see him as the son of a client," he added with a rueful look.

"What do you mean?" Lily said, mystified by Mark's statements. "No, don't answer that. There is nothing between Jackson Montgomery and me. I am sooo not his type." Lily's heart pounded as panic swept through her and she wondered if she looked as wild-eyed as she felt.

"Be in denial if you want," Mark offered with a shrug. He turned to leave. "I'll be in touch. Maybe we can have coffee when I make my rounds this evening. I should be back to check on Eleanor and my other patients around six unless an emergency comes up. I'm on call this weekend."

"If you're free around six, I'll treat you to a lovely dinner in the hospital cafeteria. The ambience is stunning! And the food is decent," Lily joked trying to recover her equilibrium.

"I'll take you up on the offer. I've got your cell number and I'll call if I get tied up. Otherwise, I'll meet you in the lobby at six o'clock."

"Great. Now which of the three lobbies at St. Agatha's will you be in?"

"How about the ER lobby? That's where we always seem to meet."

"Good, see you then." Lily started down the hall to Eleanor's room but stopped before she reached the door. Mark must be wrong. She couldn't imagine Jackson Montgomery wanting, thinking – her brain stuttered at the idea Mark had thrown out. *No, Mark is wrong. Jackson is the son of a client and nothing more.*

"Mark, is it?" Jackson's harsh tone of voice hit her full force as she entered Eleanor's room. "Is it very professional to have a personal relationship with my mother's doctor?"

Her voice steely, Lily stood with her chin up and stared him down, ticking the points off one-by-one.

"First, whatever my relationship is or isn't with Mark Parker, is none of your business. Second, I don't appreciate your talking to me in that tone of voice regardless of your perceptions, feelings or misinterpretations. And third, if you don't want my involvement in your mother's care, that's none of your affair either because the agreement is between Eleanor and me."

He glared.

She glared back.

Schooling her features into a smile, Lily stood beside Eleanor's bed, taking her hand in hers. "I'm going now but I'll be back later." She turned toward Jackson who was looking out the window. "I'll let you know when I have an answer about the House Totem, Jackson." Without waiting for any response, Lily grabbed her coat and bag and sailed out the door.

She'd gotten no more than a few feet past the door when a hard hand gripped her arm. Stiffening, she stopped, whirled around, her body pumping adrenaline, on full alert, ready for — her vision filled with a broad, firm masculine chest. Without looking up she knew who it was — Jackson. She waited, taking in his heat, his citrus scent, noting his rapid breathing. She watched as his breathing calmed and he stepped back, putting a little distance between them.

"Please look at me." His voice was soft, the hand on her arm gentled.

She heard his deep sigh, stared into his gray eyes. The adrenalin rush faded.

"I'm sorry, Lily," he began running a hand through his hair, rubbing the back of his neck. "I was way out of line. I don't know what came over me. I know I'm tired and worried about mother, but that's no excuse for speaking to you, for treating you the way I did. Please say you'll forgive me?" he pleaded, a contrite expression on his face. "Don't leave us," he whispered.

"I'm not leaving." Lily pitched her voice just above a whisper. "I've work to do, appointments with clients I had to cancel yesterday that I'm picking up today. I'll be back later. If something comes up you can always reach me on my cell phone.

"Why don't you go home, get a few hours' sleep, and check on the apartment? Eleanor will be busy enough here today and it's the evenings and nights that are hard. Neither of us has had any sleep to speak of. I'll be back around seven and we can talk about plans and things then."

"Okay," he said stepping back. "I know you're right. A shower and a few hours of sleep should fix me right up. Thanks, Lily. I really don't know what I'd do without you."

Lily watched him walk back to Eleanor's room. Something had changed between them. She turned toward the elevators. He trusted her now but it felt like there's something more. Something she couldn't describe. She pushed the down button and sagged against the wall exhausted. One thing she was sure of. Mark was way off base.

15 - THE POWER OF FRIENDSHIP

A few minutes before six, Lily drove into the parking garage at St. Agatha's. No time to sleep today, she mused, pulling into a parking slot. The weight of fatigue slowed her movements as she got out, locked her car and started toward the building. A nap would have been wonderful. Her cell phone rang as she approached the lobby doors.

"Lily?" she could hear the apology in the tone of his voice.

"Yes, Mark?"

"I can't believe I've gotten this close only to be thwarted by an emergency," he said, frustration and exasperation evident in his voice.

"What's happened?

"Got to the ER lobby to meet you just as they were calling me. A four year old boy has been brought in. The police are involved. Don't know exactly what I'll find. They called me in so bones are obviously broken. He's gotta be frightened and in a lot of pain. You've been involved with this type of thing before; any words of wisdom?"

Lily's stomach clenched as she listened to Mark talk about this small child. "I'll hold you both in my prayers. If you'll recall, when I first met you the patient was eighty-four instead of four but the pain, betrayal, and fear are just the same. Just be yourself. You have a wonderful way with people, Mark. Just be you, those are my best words of wisdom."

After a pause she added. "I'll be in Eleanor's room if you need to talk. I know I can leave for a while and meet you somewhere in the hospital if that would be helpful. I'm planning on staying with Eleanor again tonight."

"You'll send her son home?"

"Unless he got a whole lot of sleep today, that's right. I can stay with Eleanor tonight and once home tomorrow sleep until Monday. Take care, Mark. You and that little boy are now in my healing thoughts."

"Thanks, Lily. How about a rain check on that dinner?"

"It's a deal. Bye, Mark." Lily turned off her phone and walked through the lobby to the elevators.

Although it was just after six o'clock, Lily found the tenth floor quiet. They weren't expecting her for another hour. She found a place to sit and regroup. In the sitting area at the end of the hallway, she shifted one of the overstuffed chairs so it faced the window. No stars tonight, she thought as she sat down, looked into the darkness, and prayed for the little boy and Mark.

Focusing on the child, Lily felt his fear. "May you feel safe and know you are in good hands," she prayed whispering to herself like a mantra. Her sense of his fear lessened. Her thoughts now on Mark, she intoned under her breath. "May you follow your path in healing this child." She concentrated on the simple prayer, eventually feeling the tension ease and lightness come over her. Leaning back in the chair, she let her eyes close and her mind drift.

Jackson approached on silent feet. He stopped a short distance away, his gaze intent as he watched Lily. There was something about her. At times he thought he saw a glow, a shimmering light surround her. He was drawn to her --- like the proverbial moth to the flame. He shook his head. *No, not that cliché because the moth dies in the flame. What is it about her?*

At the oddest times he found himself thinking about her. Today, when he was talking to Daniel about the replacement door, was one of them. While it was true Daniel had been the one to bring up her name, she'd already been on his mind, flitting in and out of his consciousness. Shaking himself out of his reverie, he smiled to himself. He was standing there gawking like a lovesick school boy—must be the stress and lack of sleep. A serious, thoughtful look on his face, he turned and walked back down the hall to his mother's room.

Lily roused herself from her half-dreaming state where she'd visualized Mark and the little boy together. Getting up and stretching, she walked slowly to Eleanor's room. Before entering she stopped and centered herself. When she opened the door, her eyes widened at the sight before her.

"Are there any flowers left in the City of Fremont?" She filled her lungs with the floral scented air.

"If there are, not many." Eleanor gestured toward the various bouquets. "These beautiful roses are from Jackson and the arrangement of lilies and carnations and the one of mums on the window sill are from my daughters and their families. The gardenia plant on the night stand is from Daniel. And, while you may think this is an abundance of plants and flowers, I've asked the nurses to take additional ones to their desks or other rooms."

"Wow!" Lily enthused. "They're all beautiful."

"Most of them are from Jackson's friends and clients. I have the benefit of their trying to impress him."

Jackson, who had stood upon Lily's arrival, shifted and made a show of fussing with Eleanor's pillows. "Now, Mother, you know that people love you when they meet you and every one of the plants and flower arrangements are from someone you've met. They are sending them to make your day brighter, not to impress me.

"And how was your day, Lily?" he said, abruptly changing the subject.

"Busy," she said as she shrugged out of her coat and draped it across the back of a chair. Sitting on the edge of the seat, her hands folded in her lap; she looked directly at Eleanor and continued, "I've set things up at Pond's Physical Therapy. I wasn't sure I'd be able to reach anyone on Saturday but, as you can see, I did." She handed

Eleanor a typed sheet of paper she'd removed from her briefcase and gave another one to Jackson. "The details are here. I also checked out Todd, the orderly who took such a liking to you last night." She winked at Eleanor as she went on.

"He's a student at Fremont State, works here Friday night and weekends. I talked to the ER social worker who had good things to say about him so I think he'd be reliable. With your place so close to the Fremont State campus, I thought he might be a resource for you between classes. Until we know if he's available and what his class schedule is, we may have some gaps in coverage which means you'd need to rest in bed for a few hours when someone isn't there. If we can get your home health appointments set up for mornings, I think we've got things covered." She settled back in the chair, a satisfied smile on her face.

"I've also had a chance to make schedule changes." Jackson leaned closer to his mother and held her hand. "I'll be home until Monday night or Tuesday morning and home Friday night. I'm concerned about you being alone at night, Mother." He straightened, his eyes catching Lily's. "What do you think?"

"I've the same concern and have made tentative plans to spend the night." She turned toward Eleanor. "If that's okay with you, that is. And if something comes up with another client and I need to leave, Sophia volunteered to come and stay."

"Does this mean I do not have to go to a nursing home?" Eleanor's anxious face belied the matter-of-fact tone in her voice.

Lily rose and leaned over the bed rail, taking her other hand and looked her straight in the eyes. "You do not have to go anywhere but home when you're released from here." She shifted, turned, and looked out the window to hide the tears in her eyes. *Thank you, Goddess.*

"I do not know what to say," Eleanor's voice quavered, her eyes bright with emotion. "You both have done so much already. I hate to be such a burden." She struggled to sit straighter in bed, her jaw firmed with determination. "I promise to work very hard so this will not be for long."

"Don't worry about it, Eleanor." Lily turned back to the bed. "You may grow tired of me by the time you're on your feet again and be glad to have me gone."

"I doubt that very much," Eleanor's tone was serious. "You've become like another daughter to me and I cannot imagine growing tired of either of the two I already have."

Jackson had been watching the exchange between his mother and Lily. "Looks like you've got everything set up for Mother." He paused. "Thank you. Two simple words that don't come close to conveying what Mother and I feel about what you've done for us in the last thirty hours." He cleared his throat. "My timing probably couldn't be much worse but I was wondering if you've decided about the House Totem for Daniel?"

"Yes," Lily smiled and looked across the bed at him. "You're off the hook. I'll see what I can do about Daniel's House Totem."

"It is nice you can do that for Daniel," Eleanor said.

"I guess I arrived at the right time," joked a male voice. Everyone turned to the door as Daniel came into the room. "So, beautiful," he said, elbowing Jackson aside and giving Eleanor a kiss on the cheek, "What's this all about?"

"Your House Totem, Daniel. Lily has agreed to do that." Eleanor gestured between the two people on either side of her bed. "And as I don't think you two have met, let me do the introductions. Daniel O'Donnell this is Lily Hughes. Lily this is Daniel."

"Wow, that's great! When, where, how?" Daniel, a grin splitting his face, rounded the bed and grabbed Lily's hand, pumping it up and down. "Oh, forgive my manners. I'm pleased to meet you." He rocked back on his heels, his hands now tucked in his back pockets.

"It's a pleasure to meet you too," Lily said an answering smile on her lips.

Daniel's grin was infectious and the atmosphere in the room jovial. When he turned his attention to Eleanor, Lily studied him unobserved. A few inches shorter than Jackson, he wore his dark blond hair short. Brown eyes full of mischief and fine lines around his eyes and mouth showed his grin was an integral part of his character.

When his tan-weathered, callused hands had firmly shaken hers, she'd been drawn to his friendly out-going manner and was totally at ease with him.

A few minutes later, when his attention returned to her, she asked, "When did you want to do this?"

"Right now? Could we leave right now?"

His excitement, his sense of adventure was contagious. Lily found herself looking forward to intuiting his House Totem. "You might notice, right now I'm booked." She paused to heighten the suspense. "I could do it tomorrow, say one o'clock?"

"Perfect!" He pumped his fist in the air and danced a few steps of a jig.

"I'll need your address and directions. And, in case you have other things planned, we should be done within an hour," Lily said and laughed, caught up in his joy.

"Done? I'll have my House Totem?" He was bouncing with excitement, a boyish smile splitting his face.

"No, Daniel, you'll have the name of your House Totem. Then you start on a journey, an adventure to find the right one for you," Lily explained.

"What do you mean by that? I thought this was a package deal?" The rapid fire questions shot out.

"Think about it for a minute, Daniel, what is a totem?"

"A pole with lots of carvings on it?" His forehead furrowed with thought.

"Yes, that's one manifestation of a totem. The animals carved on the pole are representations of the real animals. A totem is just that, not the real object but a replica of it. They take many forms: a rabbit's foot, four leaf clover, or lucky penny. Many people wear religious totems, crosses for example. Depending on a person's tradition they could be wearing a cross, rosary, butterfly, or carrying that lucky penny or stone in their pocket. In my tradition, we all have personal totems," she absently stroked the pendant of the lioness, "as well as House Totems."

"You mean you have a House Totem, too? Can I ask what it is?"

"Of course I do," she said caught up in the moment. "And yes, you can ask. My House Totem is 'dragon'."

Jackson paid surreptitious attention to the conversation between Daniel and Lily. He'd noticed the dragons around her front door when he'd stopped by last month and thought maybe her personal totem was the lioness and cub. Withdrawing from the lively exchanges between Daniel, Lily and his mother, he turned to look out the window as that visit replayed in his mind. *Hell, was I really that pompous? That arrogant?* He continued to stare out at the forested hill, rubbed his hand across the back of his neck, shook his head, a rueful expression on his face. *What is it about her? Why are there times she brings out the worst in me?*

The evening passed quickly with lively conversation. As the hour grew later, the discussion turned toward plans for Eleanor's return home tomorrow or Monday.

"You know you're like a mom to me, Eleanor," Daniel said leaning down to give her a gentle hug. Turning to Lily he added, "When you come by tomorrow, let me know what days I can come and visit with Eleanor. I can work my schedule around a few hours with one of my favorite ladies," he added heading for the door.

"Good night, Jackson." Lily firmly pointed toward the door. "You can go with Daniel. We'll expect you around nine in the morning, won't we Eleanor?"

"And why am I leaving and you staying? She is my mother, after all." His voice was imperious and his eyebrow arched.

"True, she is your mother. When she goes home she'll need you awake and functioning. I won't fight you to stay here tomorrow night if she hasn't gone home by then."

"Children, children," Eleanor interrupted. "I have a better plan." As one, Lily and Jackson turned toward her. "You should both go home and get a good night's sleep. I think I can manage one night without either of you hovering over me."

"Well, I'm more than willing to stay, Eleanor," Lily began.

"So am I," added Jackson.

"And I am honored that both of you are willing to twist yourselves up like pretzels in order to keep me company, but I can assure you, I will be just fine and actually sleep much better not worrying about your comfort."

A sound at the door, Eleanor stopped. "Why Dr. Parker, I did not expect to see you this late."

"I stopped to see Lily for a minute, that's all." Mark was pale, his jaw tight, with dark circles under his eyes. He looked drained, exhausted.

"What is wrong, Dr. Parker?" Eleanor's worried voice asked.

"Mrs. Montgomery, nothing for you to be concerned about. I just wanted to talk to Lily about another patient of mine."

"Well, that settles that." Jackson looked smug and sounded confident. "You run along Lily, I'll stay with mother."

"You will do no such thing," argued Eleanor. "Dr. Parker, if I may ask you one question?"

"Of course."

"Am I capable of spending a night in this room without Lily or my son with me?"

"I'm sure, Mrs. Montgomery, you are capable of much more than that." His tired smile reflected the amusement in his eyes. "If you will all excuse me, I'll wait outside. That is, if you still have time tonight, Lily."

"Of course I do, Doctor. I'll be right there." Picking up her coat and briefcase, Lily leaned over to give Eleanor a hug and kiss. "I'll see you tomorrow," she said turning toward the door.

"Good night, Jackson. I'll touch base with you tomorrow so we can set up an appointment to finalize plans."

"Good night Lily," he said. A frowning puzzled look on his face, he watched her walk out the door.

LILY FOUND MARK AT THE NURSES' station. Taking her arm, they walked toward the staff elevators. "Where do you want to talk, Mark?" Lily asked softly.

"A bar would be a good place," he said dryly.

"Must be pretty bad."

"One of the worst cases I've had." Leaning against the wall by the elevator, Mark looked like he could just slide down and sit on the floor.

Lily pressed the elevator down button. "Any place close by you can think of? You look dead on your feet."

"The doctor's lounge should be pretty quiet this time of night. Let's try there."

"That's fine with me but I don't know where it is."

A ding announced the elevator's arrival.

"I think I have enough energy to make it to the lower level if I can lean on you," Mark put his arm around Lily's shoulders as they got in the elevator.

IN THE QUIET OF THE DOCTORS' lounge Lily and Mark sat on the couch, their bodies touching, hips to thighs. "I'm ready to listen whenever you're ready to talk," Lily's gentle voice coaxed.

They sat side by side in silence. Mark shifted on the couch, a heartfelt sigh escaped. "He's so very small. Not just because he's four, but small for his age. I don't think they fed him very well. And the bruises? Well, there were new ones, old ones and in-between ones." Mark stared blankly at the wall across from where they sat; his hands, loosely clasped, now dangled between his legs.

"It took some time but I finally got a smile out of him. When the bones were set and the casts on and I asked him who he wanted to sign them, I was it. I asked about his mom and dad…" Mark choked up and for a moment was unable to speak. "Oh God, Lily, he literally shrank in front of me." He bowed his head, slowly shaking it; a shudder ran through his body.

When he sat up and turned toward her, Lily's body tensed, her heart stopped for a beat as the desperation in his eyes stabbed her.

The urge to leap up and run was strong.

She stayed seated.

"I tried to assure him he was safe. I told him no one could sign his casts unless he wanted them to. And because I was his doctor, the boss, everyone would do as I said. He asked if his parents were coming to get him and I asked him if he wanted them to. He did that shrinking thing again and shook his head. I told him I would write in his chart that they couldn't see him and the hospital police would make sure they didn't." Mark's words tumbled out, his face etched with horror.

She reached for his hand, gripping hard to get through to him, hoping to comfort him with her touch.

A scream clogged her throat.

She stayed silent.

"I talked briefly with the police who'd responded to the call. The mom and her boyfriend were arrested, child protective services notified. The EMT's who brought him in said the place is bad, drug paraphernalia lying around, filthy, stinks of garbage. One of them also made an abuse report and our ER social worker did too. I don't know if I did the right thing, making promises I might not be able to keep." He leaned back with his head resting on the back of the couch, Lily's hand in his, trying to steady his breathing and control his emotions.

"It's all right to be upset Mark. It's even all right to cry," Lily's calm, soothing voice was the one she used in intense, frightening situations when she wanted the people to know everything would be okay. That was her external posture. Internally she fought for control. Falling apart as she listened to Mark's story was not an option.

"If I thought crying would help, I would," Mark choked out. "It looks like one of them held him by his arm and leg, spun around and then let him fly. He landed against a hard surface, most likely a wall. That's how his arm and leg were broken. He won't talk about it, but that's what the medical evidence points to." His whispered voice seemed haunted with the visions of this small broken child. "He can't ever go back to them."

"The system may not be perfect, but you're describing serious injuries and a dangerous living situation. The police are already involved and so are child protective services. You've written orders in the chart and notified hospital security," her matter-of-fact voice guarded both of them. If she allowed her emotions to show, she'd be lost and of no use to her friend.

"Yeah, I know," Mark said wearily. "He asked me if he could come home with me and he clung to me and cried and didn't want to let go. I held him until he fell asleep. I didn't know what else to do. They're supposed to call me on my cell if he wakes up so I can at least talk to him until I can get back to his room. God, Lily, he's terrified of those people. There's something about him; something that touches my heart."

"I know what you mean. Some of the children I worked with in the past touched my heart also. Even now there are adult clients who touch my heart," Lily said, focusing on keeping her breathing regulated and her voice calm.

"Like Eleanor Montgomery?"

"Eleanor would be a good example. There was something about her that drew me from the beginning." Lily squeezed his hand.

"If we didn't feel pain when we witnessed such deliberate cruelty," she added, "what would that make us? I think we'd be less effective in what we do. The challenge is always to take care of ourselves so that we can take care of them; to keep ourselves separate enough that we don't get sucked into their pain and lose our ability to help them. It's often a fine line to walk." Lily checked her physiology. The underlying tension was there but her heart rate was steady, her breathing even, the urge run from the room, to scream gone.

They sat in silence. Minutes passed before Lily spoke again.

"You know you're not helpless or powerless in all of this, Mark. You'll cooperate with the police and the Child Protective Service worker. You know how you write your report makes a difference in these things. Be proactive, make the calls first."

"I always cooperate!" Energy infused Mark's voice; his head came off the back of the couch as he swiveled to face her.

"I know you always cooperate. You always report suspected abuse." Lily reached up and laid her free hand on his cheek, he still held tightly to her other hand. "But I don't know that after that first phone call, you expedite your report. That's what I'm talking about-be the initiator, the advocate. I know it would've impressed me when I worked with children and it would impress me now in my work with adults. There's a big difference between reporting, cooperating and advocating. This time it seems to me that you need, for many different reasons, to be this little boy's advocate."

"You're right." Mark leaned back, his head resting again on the couch. His voice barely above a whisper he asked. "What do you think the chances are of them letting him come live with me?"

"I don't know," Lily tugged her hand free and turned to face him. "You'd have to become a foster parent. You know, criminal history checks, home study, that sort of thing. But you have many things in your favor. Of course they usually look for family members to keep the continuity of family and traditions, but any family member would have to show they could and would protect him from further abuse. This isn't a decision to make tonight. You've people in your life to talk this over with. It isn't a decision you can make alone. This child will need more than you; he'll need your whole extended family's support to heal from the trauma he's survived."

"I appreciate your honesty. I think it's one of the things I love most about you. I can always trust you'll tell me things straight up, even if they're things I don't want to hear." Mark got slowly to his feet. He turned and pulled Lily up and into his arms. "Thanks for listening to me," he said holding her close. "I really did need someone to talk to; someone who'd understand." Releasing her, he stepped back his tone brisk he said, "Well, I've sure kept you up and out later than I'd antici-pated. You need to go home and get a well-deserved night's sleep."

"I'm going to do just that. I could use a good night's sleep for a change."

Hand in hand, they crossed the room. At the door, he turned to her and gave her a long hug. "Can't do that out in the hall or people will start talking. And your boyfriend would probably pop me in the nose."

"What boyfriend? I don't have a boyfriend, Mark, and you know it," Lily said in a huffy voice as she stepped out of his arms and glared.

"Oh yeah, that's right, you refer to him as the son of a client," he said with a tired chuckle.

"Jackson Montgomery? You've got to be kidding. He's the most insufferable, puzzling man I've ever met. One minute he's impossible and the next he's impossibly charming," Lily said the heat of exasperation in her voice.

"I'm sure that's all true. You shared words of wisdom with me earlier this evening. I'm returning the favor. Just take a look at what you're doing when he's being what you call 'impossible'. He has all the signs of a very confused man—wants you and doesn't know what to do about it."

"Whaaat?" Lily sputtered. "You don't even like him."

"Who said?" Mark grinned down at her as they left the doctors' lounge and started down the hallway. "Where's your car? I'll have security walk you out. I'm going to look in on my kid before I leave or I'd walk you to your car myself."

"I'll be fine, Mark." Lily reached out and took his hand. "Really, I'll be just fine."

"I know you will," Mark said as he waved at a security guard in the distance.

"Hey, Stan, I'd appreciate your seeing Ms. Hughes to her car."

"Not a problem, Doc"

Waving goodbye he headed back to the elevators.

She was fumbling for something. Digging in her bag for what? Panic swelled in her chest. Her breathing disjointed, sweat beaded her brow, she screamed—she had to get away!

Jolting awake, Lily lay tangled in sheets and blankets, her heart pounding, her lungs gasping. Years of waking terrified and her need to quell the fear had helped her develop a plan that still worked.

Turn on the light.

Check and make sure the house was secure.

Make a cup of tea.

Let the memories come (the easy part). Let the memories go (easier now than seventeen years ago). And through it all? Keep breathing.

Calmer now, Lily grabbed her robe, slipped her feet into cold slippers and made her way downstairs. Methodically she turned on all the lights, confirmed the front and back security storm doors were locked, and checked all the windows including the basement ones with bars. On her way back through the kitchen she put on water for tea and got down her favorite mug with the hummingbirds on it.

This part was the easiest. What remained of her routine was the hardest.

Sitting in her favorite chair, sipping her tea, the statue of the lioness and her cub on her lap, she opened her mind and let the memories come. What was important now was to let them go, to release them, to breathe deeply through the worst of them, to find a speck of gratitude for the experience.

The only time she allowed herself to think of that part of her past was when the nightmare came. The remembering, the letting go, finding the blessing of it all worked; denying, dwelling on it and bemoaning the fact that it had happened, didn't.

She stroked the lioness statue. She picked up the piece of porcelain, looked the mother-lion in the eyes. "We've sat like this many times before." No matter where she was in this room, it always felt like the lioness watched. That all-encompassing sense of alertness as the mother lion sheltered her cubs and the painstaking attention to the painted details had drawn her to this piece.

A particularly vivid memory of the three children, huddled in a corner of the dilapidated bedroom—filthy, dressed in tattered clothing, scrawny, hungry, frightened. She breathed through the vision, letting it go, summoning up the blessing. She'd seen them and been able to help them. How many children live hungry, fearful of the anger of the adults in their lives? How many live that way and are never seen, never protected? That was the blessing here, she had borne witness to their plight and because of that their lives were changed.

That was as far as she allowed herself to go. Lives were changed, were different; she hoped for the better but that wasn't anything she could control.

Another inspection of her house, another cup of tea, another memory — this one much later, this one the most terrifying: I've found you. I'll kill you. The gift from the turmoil of that time in her life was The Circle, the group of women who were her friends, her surrogate family. Out of the depths of despair from the series of phone calls, she'd found them.

She focused on each of the women and what she meant to her. Sophia with the generous heart and garden, a nurturer of life and learning; Diana with the formal manner and analytical mind, an angelic voice, who was like her in many ways with a son who'd recently left for college and a dislike of housework. Each of the others, Hunter, Ashley, Gabriella, and Elizabeth brought gifts inherent in themselves to The Circle.

It was comforting to know she could call anyone at any hour of the night and they would listen. But she had her routine and it worked. She'd committed herself to not be a burden to the others; harder with Charlie gone, harder with the empty house—but easier with Eleanor in her life. Spending time with Eleanor filled her hours, filled her heart and with her fall, she'd be spending even more time with Eleanor.

Placing the statue back on the small table, Lily took her cup to the kitchen, rinsed it and set it on the counter. Two hours had passed since she'd struggled awake to escape the horror of the nightmare. Over the past seven years they'd decreased from almost nightly to every couple of months until Charlie left. She paused. Charlie had left for Ohio right about the anniversary of it all. And now the nightmares and vivid dreams were more frequent. *Thank you Goddess for showing me my routine and the way through with gratitude.*

One more sweep through the house to check all was secure.

It was.

She turned lights off, climbed the stairs, and straightened the worst of the covers. Sitting on the edge of the bed, she said a quiet prayer for restful sleep to claim her, to wake energized and ready for her day. Pulling the covers up to her chin, she snuggled down finding a comfortable spot. Listening to Mark talk about the little boy had been the trigger for tonight's nightmare. His distraught face slipped into her mind. In that place half-awake and half-asleep she asked the Goddess to watch over him and the little boy, to guide and protect them, and light the way to their highest good.

17 - THE HOUSE TOTEMS

Squinting against the glare of sun reflected off the newly snow-capped mountains, Lily followed the directions to Daniel's house. Mt. Hood and Mt. St. Helens rose majestically, silhouetted against the bright blue sky. The day was crisp and cold, a hint of snow in the air. As she drove along the winding road, she glimpsed various views of the pristine mountains through the woods. Around another bend, Lily saw a house and knew instinctively it was Daniel's…tall, proud and very Victorian. In her mind's eye she could see the horses and carriage sitting before the wide stairs leading up to the wrap-around porch.

She pulled into the circular drive, got out of her car and stood drinking in the feel, the grandeur of the place. The front door opened and Daniel emerged. "Welcome to my humble home," he said with a sweeping bow.

"Humble?" The house ruled the space with a splendor befitting a castle. She started toward the porch steps as he descended. "It's spectacular." She turned at the bottom of the stairs and gestured out over Fremont to the glorious mountains. "Just spectacular. When I drove up, I expected to see a horse and carriage in the circular drive."

"There's a small carriage house out back. When the house was new, they had horses and a carriage; probably a matched pair. I always like to imagine that they were black with silver harnesses and perhaps black plumes.

"How long have you lived here?" Lily said as she turned to face him.

"Five years but I'd coveted this house for years before that. When it came on the market even though it was in pretty rough shape, I made an offer before the listing ink was dry." He rocked back on his heels, a satisfied smile on his face. "The main house is pretty much done, only a couple of minor projects left to do on the out-buildings. Would you like a tour of the place?"

"I'd love one." Lily started up the steps but Daniel stopped her.

"Let's see the out-buildings first," he said and gestured to the path on her left. Following it around the corner of the house, she saw two buildings.

"The larger one is the original carriage house," Daniel said leading her to the door.

She stepped into a spacious room with three smaller rooms to one side.

"This section," he said pointing to the far side "was where the horses were kept. Upon closer inspection you can see where the stalls were fastened into the floor boards. And here, where we are standing, would have been for the buggy and carriage."

"What about this?" Lily asked, looking in one of the smaller rooms.

"Storage mainly," he answered, "but this larger one would have been the living quarters for the groom and maybe the chauffer when they converted to automobiles. I keep my tools in this room," he said, opening the third door and revealing a well-organized space.

Leading the way back outside, he continued the tour. "I use this other building to store the lawn mower, rakes, and other stuff but I think originally it was an outhouse. Hard to tell as none of the old blueprints I've located include it." They continued along a path leading to a large deck off the back of the house. "One project is to remodel this to match the front porch and tie the two together with French doors out of the main downstairs rooms. I like the outdoor space back here but whoever did this, while doing quality work, missed the point of the architecture."

The outside tour completed, Daniel led the way back to the front porch. He flipped a switch and an outdoor heater warmed the staged outdoor living space well enough that Lily perched on the edge of a chair admiring the view before going inside.

An hour later, the tour complete, she and Daniel relaxed at the kitchen counter, her with a cup of tea and him with coffee. Daniel was regaling her with another restoration tale when they heard the doorbell ring, the front door open, a masculine voice call out followed by footsteps coming down the hall.

"Trust me on this, Lily," Daniel said, his voice pitched low as he took her hand lacing his fingers with hers.

"What?" Lily arched a brow and tugged on her hand.

"Just go along with me on this." He smiled and gently tightened his grip.

Jackson strode into the room, his long loose stride stuttered to a stop. "Well, doesn't this look cozy?" He scowled, his hands fisted on his hips. "How much time does it take to intuit a House Totem?"

"Oh," Lily tugged on her hand in an effort to free it. "That was done long ago. Daniel's just telling me about the many projects he's done on this wonderful old house."

"What did you say?" Daniel stood so quickly his bar stool tipped over. "You already know my House Totem?"

"I knew it when I drove up your drive."

"But you hadn't even seen the whole house or heard all about it," he said setting his stool upright. "How could you do that?" His gaze intense, he leaned across the counter as if being closer allowed him to discern her thoughts.

"Daniel, the House Totem already is." Lily smiled, caught up again in Daniel's enthusiasm. "It's just a matter of sensing it, of finding something that already is. It's not a matter of making it up," Lily explained feeling her own heart rate accelerate.

"Well, I don't care how you do it. Just tell me what it is," he said his voice eager. "Don't keep me in suspense!"

"Horse."

"Horse?" He laughed softly to himself. "Horse. Well, of course it is. That feels so right now that you say it. What kind of horse?"

"That's for you to figure out." She watched the delight flicker across Daniel's face as he straightened. "When you see it, you'll know."

"You know I have an image of a fine horse, proud carriage, prancing, neck arched, a thoroughbred, Arabian perhaps," Daniel said with a faraway look in his eyes. "Maybe the black matched pair with the silver tack that I've always imagined was here."

"That is your task, Daniel," Lily confirmed, "to find the manifestation of your vision, your horse and your house's totem."

"I hate to break up the party," Jackson interrupted in a surly tone that certainly communicated he had no regrets at all. "I need to talk to Lily."

"Me? What about?" Lily was so engrossed in watching Daniel's reaction to the news about his House Totem she'd forgotten Jackson was even there. A glance in his direction revealed his glowering countenance. She didn't blink when he turned toward her and frowned.

"I need you to come to the house and check things out. Mother thinks Dr. Parker may release her this afternoon. And if that's the case, this can't wait until tomorrow."

"I'll get my coat and things then," she said and looked at Daniel. "Thank you for the tour and tea. I've really enjoyed seeing your house."

When Lily moved down the hallway, Jackson stepped in front of Daniel. "What the hell do you think you're doing?" he growled under his breath.

"I was having a cup of tea and talking about my house to someone who's interested." Daniel's expression was one of innocence.

"So why were you two holding hands?" Jackson glared at his friend.

"Is there a reason I shouldn't hold Lily's hand?" Daniel's voice and face were studies in neutrality. "Are you interested in her?"

"Don't be ridiculous. Of course I'm not interested in her," Jackson blustered.

"Then why do you even care if I'm holding her hand?" Daniel clapped his best friend on the shoulder and looked him in the eye. "You know, we've been friends a long time. We've always been honest with each other and never poach. So, if you tell me you're interested in Lily, you know I won't go near her. But," he added a grin now on his face, "I think she'd be a hell of a lot of fun in bed because she's so delightful out of it."

"Keep your goddamn hands off her, do you understand me?" Jackson spit the words out with a snarl. He grabbed for Daniel's shirt front, stopping himself inches from the fabric. Fists clenched he dropped his hands to his side. "Just leave her alone, Daniel," he ran his hand through his hair, rubbed the back of his neck, and shook his head, the arrogant stance gone. "I can't explain it. I just know you've got to leave her alone."

Daniel's gaze thoughtful; his tone of voice serious, he said, "Think about this my friend. Why do you care if I hold her hand? Why do you care if she's involved with Dr. Parker? Don't grimace and glower at me. I listened to your tirade about him for thirty minutes yesterday and the only thing I could come up with is," he paused before continuing, "you suspect he's interested in Lily. If you don't care about her, why're you so upset when she appears to have a man interested in her?"

Friday, December 20th

*D*riving to Eleanor's, Lily reviewed the progress the older woman had made over the last couple of weeks. Her diligence with her physical therapy exercise program was paying off because she moved with more confidence, a sign she was stronger. Although she still saw Eleanor every day when Jackson was out of town, after the first week she no longer stayed at night.

It was growing dark as Lily pulled into the drive. That sense of magic enveloped her as it always did. She was a couple of steps from Eleanor's apartment when the door of the main house opened. "We're in here," Eleanor called out, standing aside, gesturing her in, greeting her with a welcoming hug.

The scents of fir, pine, cedar, bayberry, and cinnamon greeted her. Crossing the gray slate foyer, she stood just inside the great room taking in the scene before her: a lavishly decorated fir tree centered in front of one of the living area windows; cedar, pine and juniper garlands woven through the stair railings and draped across the mantle; bay and holly wreaths dressed up walls and hung in dining area windows. The mixture of fragrances brought the flavor of the holidays alive.

"Lily has arrived," Eleanor called out now standing at the head of the steps downstairs.

"Come on down and see what you think," Jackson invited.

"Go Lily. It is well worth the trip." Eleanor shooed her toward the stairs. "And when you are through there come see my beautiful tree."

As Lily's foot hit the last step, she stopped, transfixed. The downstairs was transformed! The large family room and home theater area was now a wonder-filled room decorated in an old fashioned theme. Her eyes wide, her mouth in a perpetual "O", she moved through the room lingering before each scene.

First were three life-sized figures in vintage costumes with song books in hands; the sounds of the Christmas carols coming as if from their open mouths. Next she gazed at another large Christmas tree topped by an angel with gossamer wings and decorated with cranberry and popcorn garlands, candles, and large red and pink bows, with a train set complete with a small village nestled underneath.

Wandering from one thing to the next, each one took her breath away. Every flat surface had an adornment: the coffee table a frozen lake with skaters of all ages floating across the mirror that served as ice; the top of the bookcase a small village scene. A side table showcasing a miniature manor house, the roof off. She gazed at the lord and lady entertaining staff; bowls of fruit, plates of pastries and kegs of ale set out along the great hall.

"Well, what do you think?" Jackson was hovering, anticipation fizzing through him. His studious efforts to ignore the growing level of excitement at showing Lily his work failing. He wanted her to be impressed and because she celebrated Solstice instead of Christmas he tried to prepare himself to be disappointed.

No closer to understanding what happened to him when Lily was near than he was when Daniel had confronted him, Jackson was confounded by his troublesome feelings for her. There was something about her; something about what she gave to others that he knew was missing from his life. She certainly wasn't his type. Susannah was more his type but he hadn't seen much less talked to her since Thanksgiving weekend. He ran his hands through his hair and rubbed the back of his neck. Hell, he hadn't even returned her calls. *Bet she's really pissed at me now.*

He shook his head dislodging those thoughts, his full attention commandeered by Lily's voice.

"It's wonderful — unbelievable what you've done in less than a week."

A lop-sided, boyish grin spread across his face at Lily's enthusiastic words. He relaxed allowing the excitement at showing off his creation ease any tension. "I've had help putting it all together," he said, stuffing his hands in his back pockets and rocking back on his heels. "Daniel's stopped by and I even got Todd involved."

"I'm almost speechless." Lily circled the room once more, glancing back over her shoulder. "Not quite, you understand, just almost."

"If you sit here on the sofa," he said gesturing to a corner, "you can see everything."

He joined her on the couch, his arm along the back, talking about the behind the scenes part of his displays.

Lily had never been in a relaxed, informal situation with Jackson before. He really was handsome, even with the hint of stubble on his jaw. His baritone voice reverberated through her. She knew the concerned, protective, worried son. She'd seen the evidence of the detail-oriented, professional, successful architect. She'd even felt his intensity and the attraction that zinged between them when they touched. But this was different. She'd never seen this side, the devastatingly handsome, charming, considerate, approachable side of the man.

He'd stopped talking and she'd lost track of what he'd been saying. She rushed to fill in the gap. "How long do you usually leave the decorations up?"

"Until well after New Year's because it takes so long to set everything up. I don't know about this year. I got a late start what with mother's fall and working out of town and all. I always want to have time to enjoy it before putting it away. I already have some ideas to add for next year. Want to hear them?"

"I do." She actually meant that. She did want to hear about his plans, see the enthusiasm for the project in his face, feel his anticipation, see his mind work, experience another side of him. She sat transfixed by his detailed description of the horse and buggy he planned to set up in the front.

"Very impressive," she said looking up into gray eyes, whose sight was blurred with the vision he'd just described. "I don't know how you come up with these ideas."

"Got that idea from listening to you and Daniel. Thought to do a carriage but with parking at a premium, I don't want to lose all possibilities of parking close to the house."

Her gaze traversed the room once again. It was now totally dark outside signaling more time had passed than she'd thought. "I'd better check in with Eleanor and then get going. I've some things to finish up before our Winter Solstice Celebration tomorrow night."

They stood and crossed the room, walking side-by-side. "Do you celebrate New Year's Eve in your religion?" Jackson asked as they reached the bottom of the stairs his tone curious.

"Actually, it's more of a spiritual practice," she said turning to face him. "We've drawn from Wicca, Goddess, Native American and Celtic traditions to form something that is meaningful to the seven of us. But to answer your question, some of the people involved in earth-based spirituality do celebrate New Year's Eve. When my son was younger, we celebrated Christmas and Solstice. But for New Year's I tend to stay home and reflect on the past year and think about what I want to accomplish in the next one. Why?"

"I've always had a New Year's Eve party. Mother won't hear of my cancelling it this year. However, I'm concerned about her. With everyone here, being the host and all, I'm worried I won't be able to see to her and she won't want to be a burden and ask for my help. I know its short notice, but if you don't have anything else planned that night, I was hoping you could come and keep an eye on her...see that she doesn't overdo, gets safely to bed, that sort of thing. Oh, and bring your date as well."

Startled by the invitation and the brief twinge of sadness, Lily stumbled on the bottom step. "I'll think about it Jackson." She didn't have anyone to invite. She and Mark shared coffee or a meal at the hospital, but they weren't personal friends. Lily started up the stairs. "I'll need to check my schedule to make sure that would work for me. Can I give you an answer in a few days?"

"Sure."

A small but elegantly decorated tree nestled in Eleanor's bow window, a bouquet of evergreens, holly, and spiky, sparkly decorations served as a centerpiece on the dining table. "I can't stay," Lily said as she crossed the room to Eleanor who was seated on the couch. "While your decorations are lovely, the downstairs is absolutely amazing! A fantasy land." She bent to kiss her friend on the cheek, "I do hope you make it down to see it," she said before she moved back to the living room, gathering her coat, hat, and gloves from the back of the couch where she'd laid them upon arrival.

Eleanor stepped through the French doors into Jackson's living room as Lily was getting ready to leave. "I expect to because if it is anything like last year, it is quite wonderful." She looked at Jackson, motioning with her head towards Lily. "Jackson has outdone himself this year, haven't you, dear?" Eleanor looked up toward the ceiling at the ball of mistletoe hanging a few feet from him in the foyer while indicating Lily with a nod. "I hear my tea water boiling," Eleanor called out as she returned to her apartment.

Jackson's initial confusion over his mother's eye-rolling and head jerking, disappeared the moment he saw Lily under the mistletoe. She had turned back to the great room for one more look at the tree and the lights of the city. He stepped in front of her, blocking her view. When he slipped his arms around her, uncertainty registered on her face, her eyes widened as she followed his gaze finally taking in the large silver kissing ball filled with mistletoe.

She took a half-step back. He followed, his arms drawing her closer. His eyes locked with hers, his head lowered. His mouth found hers. His whisper of a kiss brushed the corners of her mouth.

Brilliant fireworks of colors flashed in his mind, through his body and anchored his feet to the floor. The sparks whenever he and Lily touched before burned hotter and brighter as he deepened the kiss. A sense of satisfaction settled deep inside him when he felt Lily's arms slide around his neck. Jackson shifted his mouth to more fully capture hers. The hint of creamed tea intoxicated. A sensual darkness enveloped him and he was lost: lost in her taste, her smell, her heat, her softness, her giving. More, more, more…the words were a chant running through his head. He wrapped his arms tighter around her, her softness melted into him and he never wanted to let her go.

The sound of the doorbell brought them back to reality.

The door burst open. Daniel swaggered in with a rush of cold air. "It is brisk out there, folks. Hi there, sweetheart." He gave Eleanor, who'd emerged from her apartment at the sound of the doorbell, a knowing glance as he stepped toward her and offered his arm. "Looks like I've interrupted these two. Why don't I take you into your parlor and regale you with one of my tales. I have a particularly entertaining one to share with you now that I've found my House Totem."

"And I, for one, would like to hear all about that adventure." Eleanor took his offered arm and let Daniel lead her into the apartment.

Jackson, his arms still around Lily, looked searchingly into her eyes. As if someone had hit a release button, he dropped his arms, stepped back, hooking his thumbs in the waistband of his pants. He breathed deeply, inhaled her lavender scent mixed with the holiday aromas and struggled to change his serious look to one of amusement. He cleared his throat. "Lily?"

"Hmm?" her gaze hadn't left his face; mystification still shimmered in her eyes.

"I look forward to seeing you under the mistletoe again," he said and grinned.

Jackson watched mist clear from her eyes as the import of his words register.

"Really?" she snapped out, her fury at herself covering her confusion. "Don't count on it." He'd asked her to bring a date and then he kissed her—like that? Her brain stuttered and the ability to speak was lost in her anger. She stalked to the front door and jerked it open.

Jackson stood in the doorway and watched her stomp to her car, back out, and drive away before quietly closing the front door. Minutes had passed since the kiss had ended yet an impressive arousal still coursed through his veins. He waited by the door as his body calmed before, a tuneless whistle on his lips, he went to join his mother and his best friend to hear about the adventures involved in a House Totem hunt.

ON THE DRIVE HOME, the energy and heat from Jackson's kiss flowed through her filling her core. The feel of his muscled chest pressed against her breasts, his muscled thighs against her legs still real. Her fingers tightened on the steering wheel mimicking his arms tightening around her, moving her an inch and then another inch closer. How her arms ended up around his neck, her fingers tangled in the silky strands of his hair, was still a mystery.

Halfway home she gasped and hit her hand hard against the steering wheel when one critical scene registered through the red haze of arousal. "I can't believe it. Daniel found his House Totem and I just walked out," she cried out in frustration. "Ooohhh, that man!"

*L*ily sat in her car outside Sophia's house, letting the stress from the day seep from her body. She'd had a long talk this morning with Diana and while she didn't mention the incident with Jackson, it had helped to talk over how they felt about their sons growing up and leaving home. She'd also had a long talk with herself about her attraction to Jackson and the reality that she wasn't his type and never would be.

The thought of trying to explain herself to another man or worse yet, try to change into someone else to keep them, made her sick to her stomach. She was more vulnerable now with Charlie gone. It would be so easy to throw caution to the wind and follow him into the flames of desire. She half-heartedly chuckled. She was really in a bad way if she was thinking in romance novel clichés.

She let herself in Sophia's front door. Through the arched opening on her left, Sophia's sacred space glowed with light from dozens of candles and a low-burning fire on the hearth. Black and white netting and a crystal bowl with a black pillar candle set inside, the foundations of their Solstice altar, were in place and drew her.

The scent of pine and bayberry wafted through the air and she paused at the entrance. The murmur of soft voices drifted down the hall and drew her away from the sacred space. She'd be in there soon enough. Continuing along the hallway, she stepped through another arched opening into the kitchen and family room where everyone gathered.

Lily shifted the green salad closer to the apple and berry pies to make room for her contribution, a plate of gourmet cheese and crackers. The aromas of homemade split pea soup, chai tea, and baking bread filled the room and she breathed in the welcoming scent. Seeing the pies, she knew homemade vanilla ice cream was in the freezer. She licked her lips in anticipation of the meal to come.

Even though no announcement was made, they seemed to inexplicably know it was time. As one, they moved to the dimly lighted room, taking their places around the black and white center cloths. One by one they smudged objects that represented the light and placed them on the material.

Lily smiled as the pattern took shape: a pentagram, a star – a sign of light. She placed her wand of crystals, sun and moon stones along the main central line running from East to West. When the five pointed star was complete, it shone with more crystals, replicas of moons, silver and light blue candles represented the dark. A carved robin, miniature porcelain daffodils, sun stones, replicas of suns, crystals, and orange, red, and yellow candles represented the coming light. Our altar is an inspiration.

Arms over their heads, palms up, they called upon the Goddess of Light to bless them this night. Their voices rose as they sung a rousing version of "I am the Light." One-by-one they invited totems, guides, spirits to join them; one-by-one they gave thanks to the darkness, releasing it into the void calling in the light to bring forth a new beginning. And one-by-one, with a sphere of moonstone as their talking stone, they shared their hopes for this time when the light returned to push back the dark.

At this time when the day is short and the night is long, this time of quiet, of death, of hibernation, their voices soft they spoke their truth, what they each wanted to bring forth during this next year. This was the seventh time they'd created a Winter Solstice Ceremony and as had happened every previous year, the light built in her as she listened to the stories of times past when science consisted of observations of the moon and sun cycles, the seasons, the circle of life and death. She smiled imagining the awe people must have felt when, after a night of prayer and ceremony, they bore witness to the sun fighting back the dark, bringing with it warmth, food — life.

Listening to the other's talk, a conversation she'd had with Eleanor popped into her mind. Eleanor asked what religion The Circle espoused. "None," she'd answered. "We're a Sacred Women's Circle, not a religion. We've spiritual practices but no dogma." Eleanor was puzzled by that, having been raised in the Anglican Church but accepted that what Lily did brought her a measure of comfort.

She had a hard time talking to anyone about her spiritual beliefs. She didn't trust she wouldn't experience some repercussions. After all her beliefs, her spiritual practices were outside the mainstream religions. There were still some who would consider her a witch, someone to be feared and persecuted.

Their tradition on Winter Solstice was to pass the talking stone around the circle twice; the first time for thoughts and sharing on a more esoteric level, the second for updates on their personal lives.

Lily listened as Diana talked about Bill not coming home for Christmas. She and Diana had become very close over the years but this year they had even more in common with Charlie in Ohio with Paul and Bill deciding to spend the holidays with classmates. Ashley's struggle to share these traditions with her children without incurring the wrath of her husband, Art, was not something she'd had to deal with since Paul had not been in their lives.

What she had to deal with, wrestle with, was how much to make Charlie even more different than he was being raised by a single mom. Becoming involved with this sacred women's circle had many benefits – women whose company she enjoyed and with whom she felt safe, something that took her outside her rational and irrational fears, creating a spiritual practice that was individual to her while blending various practices into something that fit for the seven of them.

Charlie hadn't been as concerned as she was. He'd seen her relax and change and that was enough for him. Add in a friendship with Bill and "little sister, Logan," and he was sold. But still she worried – what if he was ostracized because of her spiritual path? What if – well, there was a lengthy list. So, in the beginning they celebrated both Solstice and Christmas, although in the case of the latter, much more the secular than the religious event. When Charlie realized decorated trees and other things that were a part of their Christmas rituals were based on pagan practices–well, they'd talked things over and the last two years focused on Solstice foregoing Christmas all together. Stiffness from tension at these thoughts claimed her body. She focused on her breathing and relaxed.

The luminous stone rested in her hands for a second time, the light of love rested in her heart. Lily's gaze traveled the room, pausing a moment on each woman.

"I've several things to share so bear with me. First things first: since Charlie has decided to remain with Paul over the entire Winter Break, I'm alone. Anyone who can join me any evening is invited. This weekend my plan is to fix a pot of chili and a tossed green salad. The way we all do food, there will be enough if you find you can drop by at the last minute." She looked directly at Diana as she said the last because she knew Diana and Dennis were having problems and with Bill gone…well, she wanted her friend to know she didn't have to be alone.

"You also know that I identified a House Totem for Jackson Montgomery's friend, Daniel. I have a check for one thousand dollars and with it I'd like to start a bank account for The Golden Cauldron."

Each face registered varying degrees of astonishment.

"We've had this dream of creating The Golden Cauldron so, if needed, we can draw out funds to support things we want to do," Lily implored, her tone intense. "I want to put this money into making that happen." She raised her hand indicating she had more to say. "In addition, Daniel said he had several clients he thought would be interested in having their House Totems identified. We didn't get much farther than that but we did agree to talk more. I told him I needed to talk it over with all of you because I saw it as an opportunity to manifest one of our dreams."

Ashley was the first to frown. "Is it right to be paid?" she drawled shaking her head, her long platinum blond hair flicking to one side.

"What are your concerns, Ash?" Lily leaned forward. She'd had initial reservations too.

"In the olden days," Ashley's soft voice held an underlying firmness. "These gifts were freely given. The wise women of a village didn't charge for their potions, their skills."

"That's true," Hunter joined the discussion. "But people gave something in exchange: food, clothing, an hour to weed the garden; fix a leak in the roof. These women worked more on a barter system."

"But they wouldn't withhold their skills because a person had nothing to offer is what I'm referring to," Ashley countered.

"I'm looking at our altar." Elizabeth gestured toward the center of the circle. "What on this altar is made from our own hands? I bought the carved robin at a yard sale. I know none of us made the crystals or stones nor did we go out and dig them up with our own hands. While it is true we do make our own smudge wands, I believe the one we used tonight was purchased.

"Who looks at this altar or anything else in Sophia's sacred space and sees it as diminished because money was paid for it?"

In the silence that followed Elizabeth's words, Lily watched her circle sisters withdraw into themselves and seek their own truth.

Sophia spoke first. "I'm grateful for this opportunity to bring our dream of The Golden Cauldron into being. Over the years, we've spent many hours discussing how to manifest it."

"While I too am grateful," Diana paused, her tone formal, her violet eyes serious. She looked around the circle and added, "Before we go further we need to establish some ground rules."

Everyone looked at her expectantly.

"What I mean is, is this something everyone wants to be a part of? Are we going to establish a set fee or sliding scale?"

"We may be getting ahead of ourselves right now," Gabriella advised. "I think Lily needs to talk to Daniel more and see what he thinks about pricing and that sort of stuff. I need more information before I can make a decision."

"I'll talk to Daniel and see what ideas he has about the fee and bring that information back to The Circle. I will admit a part of me is still in shock that anyone would pay for something they could identify for themselves and a thousand dollars seems exorbitant. And then another part of me knows there are things I pay for because it's easier than doing the work myself. Remember a couple of years ago when we made candles? Dip, dip, dip, dip. I was so tired of the process of making candles that I still have mine because I worked so hard to make them, I won't burn them."

"Anything else anyone wants to say about this subject?"

Lily smiled as Diana brought everyone back on topic.

All comments made, the talking stone back in the center of the circle, they stood and joined hands, saying prayers to close the circle, to release the totems, guides and spirits that were initially called in.

"Blessed Be." They ended the Ceremony.

"Blessed Be," Lily whispered. Energy swirled and she sensed a shift. She could feel it; could feel the war between now and the future; could feel the war between excitement and apprehension. In the deepest part of her she knew they would never celebrate Winter Solstice like this again.

20 - NEW YEAR'S EVE

Twinkling lights danced in the naked tree branches, swirled along the roofline and jigged along the fence. Montgomery House was ready for the annual New Year's Eve party. Lily eased her car into the farthest parking slot in order to make room for more cars. Parking was at a premium in this part of town. She walked quickly to Eleanor's door, the crisp air, whipped by a brisk breeze, kicked up under her skirt, and chilled her toes. Knocking once, she opened the door. "It's me, Eleanor," she called out as she stepped inside.

"I'm in here," was the reply.

Peeling her gloves off, Lily stuffed them in her pocket before shrugging out of her coat and scarf and hanging them on the rack by the door.

"I need your assistance," Eleanor called out.

At the door to the bedroom, Lily halted. Eleanor was still in her robe, a few outfits spread on her bed while she sorted through the contents of her closet.

"You are stunning tonight, Lily," Eleanor said her gaze assessing the ankle-length cobalt blue dress with strappy, low-heeled, glittering gold sandals. "That gown is elegant and the color emphasizes your eyes."

Lily caught her reflection in the chevalier mirror in the corner. This dress showed a hint of cleavage in the scoop neck. With her blond hair pulled up and away from her face, a cascade of curls from her crown to her nape she was a familiar stranger to herself. When was the last time she'd donned an evening gown, makeup, and fussed with her hair? A very long time ago.

"Thank you." A blush colored her cheeks and she shifted uncomfortable with the compliment.

"I am trying to decide what to wear," Eleanor turned back to her closet. "I have had no reason to dress up since Thanksgiving."

"Hmmm," Lily came to stand beside her. "You always look so elegant in this black pantsuit. It's so striking with your white hair. But then, this charcoal gray outfit brings out your eyes," she said gesturing to the clothing spread across the bed.

"I want something more in the spirit of the season. What do you think about this one?" Eleanor pulled out a red print dress from the back of the closet and held it up.

"Well, the color is right in the holiday spirit. Ohh, Eleanor, what's this luscious looking green one?" Lily oohed as she tugged a piece of clothing that was tucked away to the front.

"An ankle-length velvet skirt and somewhere in here is a matching jacket and a silk blouse in a lighter green."

"Since you asked for my opinion, the green's the one I'd pick. The color, the fabric…you'll be *tres chic.*"

A flurry of activity and Eleanor was ready. "Thank you, Lily; I could not have managed this without your help. I do so enjoy Jackson's New Year's Eve parties."

It was the first time Jackson had seen her in anything but a professional tailored outfit or jeans and t-shirt. *No wonder my heart rate's kicked up a notch.* He shifted to ease the tightness in the crotch of his pants as his gaze roved over the curve-hugging gown. Striding across the room, he greeted Lily and his mother.

"Mother, you grow more beautiful each day." He kissed her cheek. "Are you sure you are up to it all?" He offered his arm and escorted her to her favorite swivel chair that allowed her to look at the view or the people in the room. When she was settled, he turned his attention to Lily, who had trailed behind. "May I see you over here for a minute?" he said striding back across the room.

"Of course." Lily said puzzlement clear in her voice as she turned and followed him.

Jackson stopped when he reached the foyer and turned to face Lily who had halted a few steps away. His touch gentle, he held her shoulders, looked toward the ceiling and drew her to him.

He glanced down and saw her eyes focus, her lips part, heard her quick intake of breath. "Said I'd look forward to seeing you under the mistletoe again." His words whispered, he lowered his mouth to capture hers. Just a soft brush he told himself as he pulled her more tightly against him and pressed his tongue along the slight opening of her mouth. Just a soft brush and nothing more, he heard in his mind as his arms slid around her waist and he deepened the kiss, sinking into her warmth, and softness. She tasted like minty chocolate and smelled of old-fashioned lavender sachets.

The doorbell rang. Jackson stepped back, steadying himself and Lily before he let go. A smile plastered on his face, he opened the door and greeted the first of his guests.

Lily, her mind awhirl, steadied herself by touching the wall. Where was that sharp retort she'd practiced if Jackson tried to lure her under the mistletoe again? Gone. Her heart raced, her breathing was ragged. Over a simple kiss? But there was nothing simple about being kissed by Jackson Montgomery. In the few moments it took to reach Eleanor's side, she'd pulled herself together — almost.

"Is everything all right?" Eleanor reached out and put her hand on Lily's arm as soon as she'd collapsed in the adjoining chair.

"Oh, yes," she managed. "Everything is just fine." Needing to keep the conversation going, she added, "Are you okay? Can I get you anything?"

"Everything is quite perfect," Eleanor said a tone of satisfaction in her voice. "Quite perfect."

The evening progressed with Jackson bringing friends over to introduce or reintroduce to Eleanor and he included Lily each time. A few of his friend asked her to dance and, at Eleanor's insistence, she had. She was dancing a second time with Daniel, a slow number and with the number of people dancing, they were inching their way along, when she heard him curse.

"What's wrong?" Lily strained to look around her but with the crush she could see nothing.

"I know for a fact, she wasn't invited." Daniel's look was solemn, his tone serious.

And then through an opening of bodies Lily saw who he was referencing. Susannah had arrived and was now draped over Jackson. At least she'd describe it as draped. Was his arm around her? She couldn't tell. Between the crowd of people and the ever-changing view as they moved slowly around the dance floor, she caught glimpses, bits and pieces but that was all.

A flash of heat blazed through her and for a moment she was under the mistletoe, locked in his embrace, her body melding with his. She stumbled, lurched against Daniel's chest, and stepped on his feet.

"Don't, Lily," Daniel's quiet voice was barely heard above the music and chatter. He squeezed her hand. "There's nothing going on there. He hasn't seen her since Thanksgiving. And I know for a fact, she wasn't invited."

Lily glanced over her shoulder at Jackson and Susannah. She saw Susannah's arm around him, saw her reach up and kiss him. She couldn't see if his arm was around her and she couldn't tell if he kissed her back. Her stomach lurched and tightness crept through her body. All along she'd known she wasn't Jackson Montgomery's type. She gave herself a mental kick, reminding herself of her history of being drawn to men who were wrong for her.

However, as she and Daniel danced, her eyes seemed to move of their own accord, capturing vignettes of Susannah and Jackson. As the dance ended, she closed her eyes and immediately, on a visceral level, his lips were on hers, his arms encircled her body; their cocoon of heated energy swirled through her.

She opened her eyes and looked into Daniel's concerned face. As he escorted her to Eleanor's side he leaned toward her and whispered,

"Don't pay any attention to what's going on over there." He gestured with his head in the direction of Susannah's loud, brittle laughter. "She doesn't stand a chance against a class act like you." He kissed her cheek and bent down to do the same to Eleanor.

"I'm the luckiest guy here with you two gorgeous gals for company." He proved that he meant it because he lounged against the window and kept up a running chatter to distract the two women from the scene across the room. Every few minutes, Susannah's shrill laughter pierced the air. After one particularly discordant sound, he leaned down toward Eleanor and pitched his voice low. "She's been drinking. I'm going to see what I can do avert disaster."

Lily and Eleanor had front row seats before the large flat screen television as the clock began striking midnight. "One minute to go." Eleanor's eyes sparkled with excitement. "I love seeing the old year out and the New Year in." She leaned over and confided to Lily, "every year I feel the power of turning away from the old and embracing the new."

Suddenly their view of the screen was blocked. Jackson stood before them. Bending over he put his hand on the outside arm of Lily's chair effectively blocking her from getting up. As the count-down continued he leaned closer to Eleanor, looking at her with such tenderness, saying softly that he was so glad she was with him here in Fremont. As the clock started to strike twelve, he kissed Eleanor on each cheek. His eyes shifted to Lily, his gaze heated and he straightened. While the clock still chimed, he wrapped his hands around hers and pulled her into his arms.

"And, I'm very glad you're a part of my life," he whispered as he bent to kiss her. This time it was soft and brief. Leaning back while not letting her go, he looked deeply into her eyes and then lowered his head for a kiss that was no longer soft and brief but hard and long. Lily found herself clinging to Jackson's broad shoulders, felt his strong arms holding her tightly, pulling her closer until there was nothing between them except fire burning deep inside. She clung to him and as he deepened the kiss, passion's flame leapt within.

"Really, Jackson! How could you!" the shrill voice shrieked. "You bitch! You think you can get him by being nice to his Mommy? Well, I've got news for you!"

Jackson fought his way up from the drugging impact of Lily's kiss. He turned, effectively blocking Lily from Susannah's sight.

"Get out of my house, Susannah. Now," he growled in an ice-tinged voice. When she just stood there, mouth open, staring at him, he pointed toward the door. "Now," his frost-laden voice matched his frigid glare.

"You can't mean that. Surely you don't mean you want me to leave." Susannah tossed her head, her long burgundy-red hair swirling around her, an expression of disbelief etched on her features and mirrored in her leaf-green eyes. "You can't be serious." She moved toward Jackson, a look of seduction on her face, her hips tilted at a suggestive angle, her voice a husky whisper. "Remember how it is between us, Jackson? You know how much I can please you."

"I want you out of my house, Susannah, now." Jackson's finger stabbed toward the door, his voice a dangerously low growl. "Now!" His jaw clenched as he visibly held back seething anger.

Daniel stepped forward, took Susannah by the arm and turned her toward the door. "Come on, Susannah. Let's get out of here. We can find someplace else to party, someplace that's not so stuffy." He looked over his shoulder at Jackson and mouthed, "You owe me," as he led a stunned and uncharacteristically silent Susannah out of the house.

Jackson turned and gathered Lily in his arms. "I'm so sorry, so sorry," he whispered as he caressed her back and rained soft kisses in her hair. "She crashed, Lily. If I'd ever thought anything like this would've happened, I'd have kicked her out when she first showed up."

"I'm all right, Jackson," Lily murmured. His large hands ranged up and down her back leaving warmth and flickers of heat behind. "Really, I'm all right." And, those words were true, she was all right. So lost in their kiss it had taken a minute before she realized what was happening. Staring at his broad shoulders, hearing the steely determination in his voice as he ordered Susannah out of his house was truly a surreal experience. It had always been her job to protect, to put her body between danger and the vulnerable. Safe and frightened. The strange mix of emotions churned through her. In that moment when he'd first taken her in his arms, she had felt safe, safer than she had for almost two decades — truly safe, and — it frightened her.

Susannah's dramatics effectively ended the celebration. Silence followed her exit. People began to quietly talk amongst themselves as Jackson, keeping his arm protectively around Lily's shoulder, walked from group to group. She'd withdrawn but since she did not actively pull from his embrace, he kept her close. Apologizing for the scene, he invited everyone to stay and enjoy themselves. He met the appraising looks and curious stares of his guests with a bland look.

With the party atmosphere gone, people soon took their leave. Jackson and Lily stood at the front door, his arm now around her waist, as he said goodbye to his guests. It was close to one in the morning when the last person left and Jackson closed the front door. He wanted to kiss her again but he noticed her wariness and decided not to press the issue. It must have been difficult for her to have Susannah hurl accusations at her. As they passed under the mistletoe, he bent down and pressed a kiss in her hair breathing deeply of the lavender scent he would always associate with her.

Eleanor had moved to the couch in front of the fire. Lily joined her there. Jackson poured them each a glass of champagne. Refusing Lily's offer to help, he strode into the kitchen and put leftovers away. When he returned, he topped off their glasses, and poured one for himself before sprawling in the big overstuffed chair by the fire.

"A toast," Eleanor said, looking at her son, a slight smile on her lips.

"All right. What's your toast?" Jackson said, rising and taking the few steps to the couch.

"To all things being as they should be with harm to none," she said looking first at Lily and then at Jackson as she said the words. They touched glasses, the ring of crystal sounding clear in the quiet.

"That's a strange toast, mother," he said, returning to his chair. "What does it mean?"

"Think of it literally, Jackson, nothing more and nothing less."

A companionable silence filled the air as they sat, gazing at the fire, sipping the champagne, lost in their thoughts or just entertained by the frolicking flames.

A staccato pinging noise roused Lily from the mesmerizing effects of the fire and mellow mood of the champagne. "It sounds like someone is throwing pebbles at the window." She stood and walked toward them. Icy fantasy patterns were forming on the glass. Her gasp of dismay filled the air, "Oh no! I've got to go."

Turning back toward Eleanor, urgency in her voice, she said, "Come Eleanor, let me help you into your night clothes so I can get home before the roads close."

The two women crossed the living room to Eleanor's apartment. Jackson trailed behind them veering toward the front door. He opened it and looked out. She wouldn't be going anywhere tonight. He softly closed the door, locked it, a smile of satisfaction on his face.

At the doorway to Eleanor's apartment he called out, "Lily, I think you need to plan on spending the night. I don't think you'll be able to make it from the front door to your car much less drive home."

"Oh no," Lily protested, "I have to go home!" Leaving Eleanor alone in her bedroom, she hurried to the apartment's front door, opened it, and peered out.

Jackson joined her. "From the looks of it, I'd be surprised if the city isn't totally shut down tomorrow," he said.

The scene that greeted Lily when she looked out Eleanor's front door lent truth to Jackson's statement. The ground was a sheet of ice, her car coated. A sense of foreboding overwhelmed her. She locked her knees and pushed the accompanying panic away. Disconcerted by her predicament, she turned, ramming into Jackson's hard chest. His hands grasped her arms to steady her. She raised her head and her eyes met his intense gaze. She sternly told herself she could do this, could be in close proximity to this man and not lose her way, could stay calm and composed around him.

"You're right," she sighed. "I'm iced in." She shrugged to dislodge his hands. "No need to rush, Eleanor.

"You've stayed before, so I think you know where most everything is. Let me know if you need anything," he said over his shoulder as he walked into his living room toward the fireplace.

She heard the clang as he picked up the poker, the hiss of flames as he stirred the embers back to life.

Eleanor safely in bed, Lily stood at the bottom of the stairs, exhausted physically and emotionally. Jackson sat on the couch staring into the flames, appearing deep in thought. After a moment's hesitation, her foot resting on the bottom step, her hand on the rail, she said, "Good night," and started up.

He nodded an acknowledgement, his gaze never leaving the fire.

The room she used when she spent the night with Eleanor was at the top of the stairs. A swath of dark color in stark contrast to the pale cream of the comforter caught her eye. She padded to the bed, her hand skimmed the shimmering fabric. Silk. Cobalt blue silk…like my dress. A thrill of energy rippled through her when she picked the pajamas up. Resisting the temptation, she tossed them over the back of the bedside chair and began to undress. I'd sleep in her bra and panties. Lily's gaze returned again and again. The lure of the blue silk was constant.

She succumbed to the call. It wouldn't hurt to hold them up. The material caressed her skin; she shivered with an awareness of something she refused to identify.

The top fell to mid-thigh. She slipped it on and looked in the full length mirror. The luxurious fabric shimmied down her body.

In the bathroom, she brushed her teeth with an extra toothbrush kept in the cabinet. She caught her own gaze in the mirror. Her eyes were luminous, made darker by the reflection of the cobalt blue of the top. She shifted one way and then another, the silk moving against her skin creating flickering sensations as it glided over her body. She felt decadent. Her feet grew colder on the bare tile floors. She was here for the night and whether it was wise or not, she was sleeping in the elegant cobalt blue silk top.

She slipped into bed and snuggled under the goose down comforter. She needed to sort out what was going on? *I can't remember ever feeling so safe with a man. Even my Dad had a temper and I was wary around him. What a dangerous combination for me. Safety and seduction. How can I ...* the question never finished, never answered, Lily slept, lost in vivid dreams.

"You're so beautiful," she heard him say and felt the brush of his lips over her forehead, cheek and finally her lips.

21 - NEW YEAR'S DAY

Subdued gray light and the absolute quiet of a snow-covered world filtered into Lily's awareness. Wrapped in warm silk, deliciously relaxed, the idea to laze the day away beckoned. She resisted, instead cracking open her eyes ready for another day.

She splashed her face with cool water; finger combed her hair and dressed in her gown. As much as she loved the pajama top there was no way she'd wear that downstairs.

Jackson was puttering in the kitchen and Eleanor was seated at the dining table.

"I've a fresh pot of tea, Lily," Eleanor said and gestured to her to come and sit. "Jackson is making Eggs Benedict for us."

"Thank you. A cup of tea sounds perfect." Lily crossed the room to the table. "Is there something I can do to help, Jackson?"

"I've got everything under control," he said without looking up.

"I think, my dear, you need to keep a change of clothes here just in case something like this happens in the future. While you do look lovely in that gown, it isn't very practical under the circumstances." Eleanor patted Lily's arm.

"Come on upstairs. I think I can put something together to get you by until the roads clear." Jackson started across the room without waiting for Lily to follow.

She was halfway up the stairs when Jackson appeared at the top.

"Here. Try these." He shoved a bundle of clothes in her arms when she reached the top and continued on his way down.

Shivers of awareness tingled her skin where his hand brushed her arm. His scent of citrus heightened her sense of his aura. He was definitely male and he called to everything female within her. She gripped the handrail to keep from swaying, took a steadying breath and continued to her room.

The giggle became a full-bodied laugh when she looked in the mirror. Her outfit, courtesy of Jackson Montgomery, consisted of pair of shorts made from sweat shirt material that reached below her knees, a pair of socks that reached above her knees, a piece of cording to keep the pants from falling off, and a heavy cotton T-Shirt that fell past her hips and covered her arms to her elbows. There was also a cardigan she could pull around her shoulders. She was covered and warm and that was what mattered.

There'd be no attraction between them. "A no brainer" Charlie would call it. One look at her in this getup and Jackson would forget the mistletoe, kissing or anything along that line. With that thought in mind, she carefully made her way down the stairs making sure her feet didn't slip out from under her with the wool socks.

Wrong. Pinned by the intensity of his gaze, she stopped at the bottom of the stairs unable to continue across the room. How could he look at her as if he wanted to leap across the room and ravish her on the spot?

Worse. He was striding toward her, his hand outstretched. How could she avoid him?

Worst. He stopped before her, took her hand and placed a chaste kiss on her palm. No, it wasn't a chaste kiss. Chaste kisses weren't placed on palms. Her mind fragmented. Was she leaning toward him like a heat seeking missile, guided to his warmth?

"I hope you slept well," he murmured a wicked gleam in his eye. He kept her hand in his and escorted her across to the dining table. Pulling a chair out, he waited until she sat before pushing her up to the table. "Breakfast will be served in fifteen minutes."

Jackson was a wonderful cook. The Eggs Benedict were perfect with a generous amount of Hollandaise sauce. An even better host, he refused both Eleanor and Lily's offers to help clean up, limiting them to putting their dishes on the kitchen counter.

A fire burned in the fireplace all day, more for ambiance than heat as they never lost power. They decided to surf the football games because no one had a favorite team playing. At one point they pulled out a Monopoly Game but Jackson's skill was such that Lily and Eleanor soon capitulated. He crowed in victory, they made comments about sportsmanship.

As soon as Eleanor went to bed, Lily did also. She remained in her room the next day until she heard voices downstairs. It was important to her not to be alone with Jackson. He frightened her and she knew she didn't want to chance any more kisses under the mistletoe. Trying to sort out why his attentions evoked such a strong reaction all she could come up with was the crazy answer that it scared her to feel safe in his arms. Why it scared her to feel safe she didn't know.

AFTER BREAKFAST on this second day of being iced in, Jackson began to take down some of the decorations. The spirit of the season was gone. All that work to set everything up was now being undone. Smaller pieces were wrapped in bubble wrap. Figurines returned to their original boxes. Smaller boxes in larger boxes all neatly labeled.

With three of them working, by afternoon all the smaller displays were packed and the trees were bare. At Jackson's direction, Lily had packed the artificial wreathes but left the fresh ones up.

Surveying the great room, she noticed the mistletoe ball still hung in the foyer. She lugged the small step ladder she'd used to take down the wreathes to the entryway positioning it just to the right of the large ball. At the top of the step ladder, she stretched to grab the decoration, lifting it up in order to disengage it from the ceiling hook.

"Here, let me help you with that."

Jackson's voice resonated through her.

His hands clasped her waist.

His touch reverberated in her bones. Heat streaked through her body and she gasped a sharp intake of breath.

Hands shaking, she lowered the ornate aluminum ball filled with Styrofoam, half-turning so Jackson could more easily help her. It was heavier than it looked and with the fresh mistletoe tucked in the carved openings, awkward to handle. Their hands brushed, electric charges shot through her, she wobbled.

In an instant Jackson had the ball firmly in one hand, the other on Lily's back to steady her. As soon as she had both hands on the ladder, he stepped back and placed the ball on the floor.

"Thank you, Jackson." Lily's voice was formal as she scurried down the six steps to the floor.

"You're welcome." Jackson wrapped his arms around her slim body and pulled her back against his chest. They were spooned together, his chin resting on her head.

She was torn between a longing to sink into his heat and let him hold her and a rising panic and need to escape.

His grasp firm, preventing her easy escape, he turned so he faced her.

"What do you want," she whispered.

"You," he said softly, resting his forehead on hers. "You," he whispered caressing her arms from shoulder to elbow and back again. "You," he kissed her lightly on the lips, pulling her close. "I can't believe how good it feels holding you like this," he murmured into her hair. "I could hold you like this for a very long time," he said flowing kisses over her face.

The panic won. Her heart raced, her palms perspired, her breathing stuttered. "Jackson, please stop. I-I can't…. Please stop, please," her whispered voice desperate, her eyes locked on his chest.

The tip of one finger lifted her chin and his intense gaze devoured her face. He saw the effects of his kisses in her flushed cheeks and swollen lips. He looked in her eyes, blue eyes that were dazed with passion but darted away in panic.

What the hell! He stepped back and dropped his hands to his sides. The fevered delight of mere moments ago gone. The urge to reach out, to touch, to hold was strong but he forced himself to take another step back and then another, never breaking the connection he had with her through their eyes. Why one minute she was a willing participant in their kiss and the next not? He was smart enough to know she'd been badly hurt. But what was more important was right now she felt panicked in his arms.

"As you wish." He stared at her for another long minute before picking up the mistletoe ball and, without looking back, strode to the stairs and disappeared below.

Still shaken, Lily took a steadying breath, the fingers of one hand touching her lips while the other pressed her abdomen. She was honest enough with herself to admit the quivering was from both unsatisfied desire and a sense of loss. Would she ever feel safe in the arms of a man she's attracted to?

A noise outside interrupted her thoughts. Opening the front door she saw a blessed sight—the plow followed by a sanding truck.

She could leave.

She ran upstairs, changed into her gown and heels, slipped on her coat and stopped downstairs to say good-bye and remind Eleanor of the doctor's appointment in two weeks. "Let me know if Jackson leaves and you need me to come and stay with you," she said brightly giving Eleanor a quick hug and running out the door.

Safe in her car, Lily gingerly drove down the winding roads, following the flashing yellow lights of the sand truck. At the bottom of the hill, the roads were in fairly good shape and her drive home passed quickly. Parking in her driveway she made her way through the ice and snow to her front door.

"Home, I made it home." Lily closed the door, leaned against it, and hugged herself. Memories of kisses, vivid dreams and how it felt in his arms washed through her. "Oh Goddess, I'm so frightened, so confused." She shook her head as if doing so would erase the pictures she didn't want to see. "He protected me from Susannah's attack and no one's ever protected me like that before. It scares me to feel so safe with him. Am I crazy?"

22 - AND THE WORLD CAME TUMBLING DOWN

Construction on the Monterrey jobsite was on hold due to the winter rains. Jackson remained in Fremont. It was two weeks since Lily had dashed out the Montgomery House door and followed the sanding truck to safety. Two weeks since she'd seen Eleanor. Even though they'd kept in touch by telephone and she knew how diligent Eleanor was about her exercises, Lily was surprised at how well Eleanor was doing when she picked her up for a follow-up appointment with Dr. Melbourne.

"You're making amazing progress." Lily watched Eleanor walk around her apartment unaided.

"I do use my cane when outside, but here I'm easily able to get around safely," Eleanor said picking up her cane and starting out the door.

ON THIS COLD BLUSTERY DAY, Eleanor was very deliberate, concentrating on each step as they made their way back to Lily's car. Eleanor's steps slowed further as they approached the car. Lily clicked off the alarm and unlocked the doors.

"Here we are," she said to Eleanor.

Holding Eleanor's free arm, she steadied her as Eleanor stepped off the curb. Parked on the one-way street, the passenger's door was street-side. Lily assisted Eleanor around the car and into her seat.

"Are you settled?" Lily asked as she finagled the seat belt buckle into place.

"Quite settled," Eleanor replied and patted Lily's arm. "I've missed our visits and am very much looking forward to having lunch with you today. Split pea soup will hit the spot on a wintery day like this."

"Yes, it will." Lily straightened, stepped back and closed the door.

TIRES SQUEALED, the car shuddered, a flash of dark blue bounced once on the hood and disappeared. Air bags inflated. Eleanor's mind whirled, trying to make sense out of what happened. Stunned, she sat strapped in the car's seat, a deflated air bag now in her lap. Violent shivers wracked her.

Those first few minutes seemed like an eternity.

Her voice wouldn't work. She couldn't scream. She couldn't call for help. She couldn't...she was numb. *Lily, where is Lily? Lily, where is Lily? Lily, where is Lily?*

The blast of a siren, the car's windshield reflected flashing lights. On-lookers parted. A police officer approached.

Her door jerked opened.

"Are you hurt, ma'am?" the masculine voice was gentle.

"Lily, oh my God, Lily." Eleanor whispered.

"Is Lily the name of the young lady?" The officer leaned into the car.

The sight of the uniform penetrated her terror.

"Lily, oh my God, Lily? Ohhh," she whimpered. "Jackson, where are you?"

"Who is Jackson?"

"My son."

"Where is he?"

"At the office."

"If you have the number, I'll call him for you," the officer spoke in a calm comforting voice.

Her hands shaking, Eleanor fumbled in her purse for the small appointment book.

"It's under "M" for "Montgomery," she said in a shaky voice that matched her trembling hands.

"Who is Lily?" he asked while dialing the number.

"She's my friend. She was helping me." Her voice rising with hysteria, she reached out and grabbed his arm. "Is she okay? Where is she?"

"My partner's with her now, ma'am," he squeezed her arm to reassure while listening to the phone ring. "Help is on the way."

Eleanor was floating, looking down at the scene except she couldn't really see. She heard the police officer's voice.

"Is this Jackson Montgomery?"

He must have reached Jackson. She gripped the officer's arm and concentrated on his words.

"Officer Davidson, Fremont Police. Mr. Montgomery, there's been an accident. Your mother appears to have sustained no injuries but her friend, Lily, has been injured. The ambulance is on its way. Do you know what hospital? Who her doctor is?

Eleanor couldn't make out Jackson's response but she knew - St Agatha's. Dr. Parker.

The nice officer was peering at her, his lips moving. With effort, Eleanor focused on him. "Mrs. Montgomery, your son's on his way. I'm going to check on your friend. I'll be right back," Officer Davidson promised.

His partner, Kelly, was kneeling beside the still form, talking into her shoulder microphone. A cacophony of sirens: Fremont's fire department and ambulance. He stopped just behind Kelly, looking at the woman on the ground for any signs of life. She was breathing. Otherwise she was motionless.

"Damn! I hate it when we can't stop something like this from happening." Officer Davidson squatted beside his partner. "How's she doing, Kelly?"

"She's hanging in there. Could've been worse." Kelly's eyes never left Lily's face as her hands gently probed her neck for a pulse. "She's still unconscious. They'll want to know how long." She glanced over her shoulder at Davidson. "What do you think? Two, three minutes? Maybe five?"

EMTs surrounded them. The fire truck had arrived. While the others went to work, the leader stopped.

"Hey, Davidson. What happened here?" the fire lieutenant asked.

"Hit and run. Looked like she was clipped by the fender when she stepped back from the car. Thought she'd been thrown over the hood but the dent in the top indicates she hit there before landing on the pavement. We were calling for backup as it was happening."

"Good thing. She's pretty beat up. Skin doesn't fair well with pavement. And she's a prime case for shock."

Another police car arrived on the scene. Jones and Parson: Jones on traffic control, Parson coming to check in.

"So far … nothing. Driver may have gone into one of the parking garages. You'd think we'd be able to find 'em," Parson's voice was harsh. "Looks like you've got things under control here. The older lady okay?" At Davidson's nod, he glanced towards the EMTs. "What about her?"

"Too soon to tell anything," Davidson's tone was grim, his eyes watched the EMTs work: an IV line started; a neck brace; a back board in place; in constant contact with the ER. Not taking any chances, I see. He started back to see how Mrs. Montgomery was doing while Parsons stepped to his car talking into his shoulder microphone about the search for the other car.

A black Jaguar screeched to a stop almost a block away. A man who looked to be in his early forties jumped out and forged his way through the on-lookers. Bet that's the son. Jones was trying to deter him and the man wasn't handling it well. His steps brisk, Davidson stepped over to intercede.

"Hey, Jones, he's all right. Let him through."

"Okay, Davidson."

"Mr. Montgomery?"

"Yeah," Jackson's voice came out like a growl. The last fifteen minutes had been the longest in his life. It had seemed to take forever to forward his phone to his service, grab his coat, lock his office up, get to his car, and drive the ten blocks to get here. He only knew there'd been an accident. He didn't know what had happened, only that the police were involved. And if the police were calling that meant something serious. But what?

His mind had raced with scenarios of blood, crumpled metal, a lifeless body.

As he'd driven up, other than the emergency vehicles, it hadn't looked like anything had happened. But as he strode toward Lily's car, he could see the side view mirror was gone; a long scrape marred the front fender. As he reached the car he could see the dent in the hood and an air bag had been deployed and now lay deflated in his mother's lap.

He bent down.

"Mother, how are you? Are you okay?" His voice soothed. His mind grappled with the reality that something had happened and someone was missing. Lily.

"Oh, Jackson." Eleanor grabbed his coat and clung. "It's horrible. Lily," her voice trembled, "I do not know what happened to her. Please, Jackson. You must find out for me. I must know." She slumped against him, tears streaming down her face. "It is all so terrible. I don't," her voice broke. "Please, Jackson," her agonized whisper muffled against his chest. "Please find out what's happened to Lily."

Jackson hugged his mother, his quiet voice hiding the emotions engulfing him. "I'm here mother," he soothed. "I'll take care of everything. Don't worry. I'm here."

A shudder rippled through Eleanor. "Please find out what happened to Lily for me," she choked out.

"I will," Jackson promised, straightening. His hand rested on his mother's shoulder. His eyes, roving over the scene around him, zeroed in on the group of EMTs.

Immobilized, he couldn't move. A wave of fear crashed through him. His jaw clenched and he shook his head to banish the fear-driven images. *I need...* He stopped short. What did he need? He needed to be clear-headed. He needed to take care of things. He needed to take care of his mother. And he needed to take care of Lily.

The voice of Officer Davidson talking into his shoulder mic penetrated his thoughts.

"What happened here?" Jackson asked, stepping away from the car after giving a light squeeze to his mother's shoulder.

"Hit and run." Davidson gestured to the hood of the car. "Fender clipped her. She hit the hood of her car and landed over there." He nodded to where Lily lay on the pavement. "We've patrols out but nothing so far."

Jackson stalked the few feet to the team of EMTs. Davidson followed explaining in more detail what had happened.

"Several people had called 911 about a pick-up truck, ricocheting off parked cars, driving up on the sidewalk. My partner and I were on our way to intercept, about a block away when we saw it career around the corner, swerve, the fender just clipping her. We called for fire, ambulance and back-up: to pick up the chase and for traffic control."

"How is she?" Jackson asked. His chest was wrapped in bands of iron. He needed to get closer, to see her. A hand on his arm kept him where he stood.

"We need to stay back so they can take care of business." Davidson's grip on Jackson's arm tightened. "Let's see if my partner can tell us anything." With his free hand he gestured to Officer Kelly who was off to one side talking to one of the EMTs.

From the vantage point by Officer Kelly, Jackson could see her—strapped to a back board, neck immobilized, IV in her left arm. The fear he'd held at bay lunged to the fore.

"We're about ready to transport," the EMT on the phone with the hospital said, glancing over at Jackson and Officer Davidson. "Mercy General's expecting us."

"No!" Jackson shouted. "No," he repeated more quietly. "She can't go there. Her doctor is at St. Agatha's. She has to go there."

"Mercy General's expecting us," the EMT repeated.

"I don't give a good God damn who's expecting her." He turned to Davidson. "I said she needed to go to St. Agatha's."

"Mercy General is closest," the EMT said.

"She's going to St. Agatha's if I have to take her myself," Jackson roared, using every ounce of his control to keep from punching the guy. *She's so small, so vulnerable. I have to get her to St. Agatha's to Parker.*

The EMT radioed, "Mercy General they want her transported to St. Agatha's. I'll check with them and if they're on divert, I'll get back to you. Otherwise, we'll transport her to St. Agatha's as requested."

"Okay, 492. Patient is being transported to St. Agatha's unless they're on divert."

"Yep, that's it Mercy General"

"St. A's? This is 492. We have a female, in her 30s, unconscious from a MVA. We have her on a back board, neck restraint, and an IV started through Mercy General's ER. Family's requesting she be transported to St. Agatha's due to her being a known patient and her doctor being on your staff."

Turning to Jackson, he asked for Lily's information and who her doctor was.

Jackson spoke tersely taking a step toward the EMT. "Lily, Lily Langdon Hughes is her name. She's about 38 years old. Mark Parker, Dr. Parker is her physician. Why the delay? Why can't you just take her?"

The grip on his arm tightened bringing Jackson back to Officer Davidson's side. "Let'em do what they do, Mr. Montgomery. I know you're worried about her but they're a good crew. See, they're already moving her onto their stretcher. From here they'll take her to the ER."

"Good to go, Davidson," said the EMT. "They're expecting her and are already notifying Dr. Parker."

"Thank you, guys," Jackson blurted out. "Nothing personal. Just damn frustrating is all."

"Don't worry about it. Happens all the time. She'll be in good hands," the EMT called back over his shoulder as he finished gathering gear and putting it in the ambulance.

Jackson turned back toward Lily's car. "Damn, can't just leave it here. It could be vandalized or towed." He strode back to the car and his mother while he pulled out his cell phone and hit speed dial.

"Daniel? Thank God I caught you. I need you to come to Alameda and 5th and take care of Lily's car. There's been an accident. If you can, take all of her things out of her car and get it towed somewhere for repairs.

"You can?" Jackson's shoulders sagged in relief. "Great. I'm taking mother to St. Agatha's to be checked out." He glanced over his shoulder. "The ambulance is just leaving with her now," he said struggling over the words.

"Daniel's on his way." Jackson heaved the air from his lungs and forced himself to deal with the business at hand. "He should be here within fifteen minutes and can take care of whatever needs to be done." His dispassionate recitation of the damage "side view mirror broken, front fender scratched and the dent in the hood," faltered as an image of Lily's body landing on the hood became all too real.

"A tow truck's already standing by," said Officer Davidson. "I'll remain with the vehicle until things are cleared out. Who's coming to take care of that?"

Jackson quickly gave Officer Davidson Daniel's name and contact information.

"Do you have a repair shop in mind?" Officer Davidson asked, notebook in hand.

"No, Daniel will take care of that." Jackson added this favor to the debt he still owed his friend for taking Susannah away on New Year's. Turning toward the car, he bent down and told his mother that Lily was hurt and needed to be seen at the hospital.

"I have got Lily's purse and cell phone, Jackson. So, if you can help me maneuver out of this seat, I'll be all set." Eleanor's jaw was firm, her spine straight, as she moved in the seat to get out.

"I'm having you checked out also, mother, so don't fuss about it when we get there." Jackson was firm but gentle as he helped Eleanor to stand. He reached back into the front seat for her cane. Exchanging her cane for both purses, he took her arm and walked her to his car. Settling her inside, he turned to Officer Davidson. "Officer, I appreciate your taking care of things here and your reassurance. I don't know what mother and I would do without Lily." He reached out to shake his hand.

"She seems to be a special person in your lives," Officer Davidson reciprocated.

"Yes, yes she is." Jackson strode to the driver's side of the car. Before getting in, he called out over the roof, "Thanks again for all your help, Davidson. Mother and I appreciate it."

"You're welcome, Montgomery. We're just doing our job. Good luck."

WALKING into St. Agatha's busy ER provided Jackson with another lesson in frustration. Of course they wouldn't tell him anything about Lily because he wasn't her husband. He was tempted to lie and instead of that thought being distressing, it comforted. Worried he would miss learning about Lily, he chose to wait rather than check in his mother. He figured once they knew how Lily was, he'd have her seen by an ER doctor. An hour filled of impatiently pacing, sitting with his mother and hounding the receptionists passed. He still knew nothing.

"Montgomery." He heard his name and almost ran to the receptionist.

"You can go back now. She's in B5."

Gathering purses and Eleanor, Jackson walked through the automated doors into a white, sterile area that smelled of disinfectant.

"We're looking for B5, mother. Aah, over this way I see some "B's. Yes, B5," the words whispered out between dry lips and an even drier mouth.

Eleanor's muted voice chanted, "Please, God; please God; please God."

At the curtain-draped door, he paused before pulling back the cloth screen and escorting Eleanor inside. The scene before them: Mark Parker bending over Lily, her eyes closed, bruises already forming, her vibrancy scraped away by the unforgiving pavement.

Dr. Parker's voice continued as a soft murmur before he straightened and looked over at them. He bent down again saying something to Lily and Jackson thought he saw her hand move in the doctor's. A strong feeling of protectiveness flared and for an instant he saw himself leaning over the bedrail, her hand tucked in his own. Steady now, he repeated to himself until his heart rate and breathing leveled.

"How is she, doctor? Will she be all right?" Eleanor whispered.

"She has a severe concussion, contusions and lacerations." Mark studied Lily's face as he talked. "Her left rotator cuff has a small tear and her right shoulder separated. She also has a cracked collarbone. What that means is she can't raise her arms. She's drifting in and out of consciousness because of the pain."

"What's going to happen?" Jackson's eyes were riveted on the still, pale figure before him.

"We're keeping her, at least overnight, for observation. We'll know more in the morning. I'd be surprised if she didn't have sprains and strains we haven't fully diagnosed. The report stated she was clipped by the fender of a pick-up, the force of which threw her across the hood of her car to the pavement about six feet away." He turned towards Jackson, Lily's hand still in his. "I don't mind telling you, if she hadn't been so warmly dressed, it would've been worse." He looked back at Lily, studied their interlocked hands. "Thanks for making sure she was brought here, Montgomery. I really appreciate it."

"She trusts you, Parker." Four words that wounded; wounded his guarded heart. Every time he and Lily touched, every time they kissed, a spark arced connecting them in a fundamental way. The attraction was elemental but underneath the attraction, she didn't trust him.

She trusted Parker's gentle touch, his expertise; she listened to his soft voice. He knew she was listening to every word. He felt it. Maybe she could learn to trust me. Maybe there could be something more. He shook off the thoughts with a shake of his head. Parker was speaking.

"I'm going to make arrangements for you to be our guest for at least tonight." He kept her hand in his and spoke over his shoulder.

"Eleanor, will stay with you." Straightening, he turned toward Jackson, "Montgomery, come with me. I need you to get Eleanor checked in with reception so I can take a look at her."

Jackson nodded.

"Just so you know, she hears and understands," Mark said to Eleanor. "Due to the concussion we can't give her much for pain. Right now everything hurts." He left the room with Jackson on his heels.

"I am here, Lily," Eleanor said, her English accent thick with emotion. She patted Lily's hand. "I am so very, very sorry this happened." Her voice broke, tears trailed down her cheeks. A light pressure on her hand, Lily was watching her.

"Oh, do not mind me. I am just a watering pot and crying with relief that you are alive and will be okay. I was so worried you had died...so, these are tears of joy and you should just ignore them. Please do not worry about me. I am fine." Standing beside the gurney, she held Lily's hand and whispered prayers for her swift recovery. "Goddess, please help your daughter. She needs you desperately now and in the days to come. Amen."

The curtain parted and Jackson entered, stopping on the opposite side of the gurney from his mother. He slipped his hand under Lily's watching her face for any signs of additional pain.

"Hi there, Lily. Yep, it's that miserable arrogant, insufferable bore, Jackson, here to make your life a living hell as well as make sure Parker does his job." Jackson stopped. His voice quavered; the light easy-going tone gone. He cleared his throat, his tone now serious. "Mother, you're checked in and they said you can wait here with Lily and me until Parker can see you."

Their efforts to engage in casual conversation floundered so for the most part they remained silent, lost in their own thoughts. A long and tense ten minutes passed before Mark returned.

"You're going to 9B-12, Lily. I expect some gratitude from you because I made special arrangements to get you into the vitamin room," he quipped, bending over his patient, laying his hand along her cheek. "No more jokes," he said. "That's right, take shallow breaths for the pain," he coached.

In a nearby cubicle Mark checked Eleanor out. Other than an elevated blood pressure and heart rate, she was okay. "If you notice any problems with ambulation, severe headaches, chest pains, that sort of thing, make sure she gets to the ER right away," he instructed Jackson.

"With your permission," Eleanor said once she was back in Lily's cubicle. "I will call your women's circle. I believe they are all programmed into your cell phone." She slipped her fingers into Lily's hand. "Do you want me to call Charlie? Oh, let me say that again. Squeeze my hand if you want me to call Charlie." It was a moment before Eleanor realized there wasn't going to be a squeeze. "Well, I am sure it is a call you want to make yourself."

More waiting before everything was in order: Lily was formally admitted; the gurney to take her to her room arrived as well as a wheelchair for Eleanor's use. The gurney rolled out of the cubicle, Mark walked beside it.

"Until we are sure complications from the concussion are past, rest is the best thing for her. Complications show up in how the brain functions and because they can come on suddenly, she can't sleep for more than an hour or so at a time and when she's awake we need to talk to her, make sure she can follow a simple conversation. Hopefully tomorrow we can give her some pain medication." The gurney stopped at the elevator. Mark held her hand. "I left patients in my examining and waiting rooms, so I've got to go. As soon as I clear things up, I'll check in on you."

The only sign she heard? A slight squeeze of his hand.

Any movement other than shallow breathing and sharp pain stabbed through Lily's body. Even opening her eyes hurt. Distracting herself from the pain, even for short periods of time was exhausting. As her gurney was pushed through the halls, every bump in the floor jarred her senses. Her mantra as they made their way through the hospital? Goddess, be with me through this time. Goddess, be with me through this time. Goddess, be with me through this time.

Excruciating pain lanced every cell when she was moved to the bed. Her will to remain silent shattered. A moan escaped. Eyes closed, she drifted in and out of consciousness. Time passed. When alert, she listened, easily recognizing Eleanor and Jackson's voices. One, if not both of them, always held her hand. Eleanor's smaller softer one was comforting. In a very different way so was Jackson's larger rougher one. In the deep recesses of her mind she remembered he'd fought to have her brought here, brought to Mark. *The second time he's protected me.*

"What the hell?" a male voice exclaimed. "Jesus, what happened to you, Lily?"

I know that voice … but ….

"Daniel, she can't talk…she's in too much pain." Jackson's voice.

Someone else is here…Mark.

"Too many people for Lily to have the quiet and rest she needs," Mark said firmly.

"I just came by to let everyone know the car is secure," Daniel rushed on. "Had the car towed to Mario's Body Shop. It'll be fixed up good as new for you in no time at all. They'll do a great job and deal with the insurance company and everything. Oh yeah, Officer Davidson said don't worry about the time frame for completing the accident report. Just attach his report to the official accident form, sign it, and be done with it. He sure seems like a nice guy."

"Breathe, Daniel," Jackson ordered. "You're rattling on here."

"I know," Daniel replied taking a deep breath. "Lily, you take it easy and don't worry about anything other than getting better. Jackson and I'll make sure everything is okay, won't we, Jackson?"

"Of course we will," Jackson replied. "I'd appreciate it if you'd take mother home, Daniel. I'm staying with Lily. I'll let both of you know if there're any changes. Now, don't argue, mother. You know you're exhausted."

She heard rustling and imagined Jackson helping Eleanor to her feet and into her coat; seeing her settled in the wheelchair; handing her the cane and her purse, maybe even pushing the chair to the doorway or out to the elevator.

A gentle touch brushed her hair back off her forehead and she heard Mark's voice. "You are certainly my most colorful patient today, Lily." He seemed closer, maybe leaning over the bed, holding her hand. "Daniel is taking Eleanor home. Montgomery's staying to keep you company." He whispered in her ear, "From what I've seen, I think he just realized how much he cares about you."

His voice further away, Mark said, "Glad you can stay with her a bit, Montgomery. The nurses here check in frequently but it isn't the same as someone being right here with her. She's a special lady and I want the best for her."

"I know. That's why I made sure the ambulance brought her here, Parker. I knew she'd feel better knowing you were taking care of her. She can be a bit suspicious about doctors."

"Yeah, I know. She sure has her standards for herself and everyone else."

"Yeah, I know," Jackson mumbled.

What's happening? It's so quiet. With a supreme effort and searing pain, she opened her eyes a slit. In her line of vision: two men standing side-by-side watching her, seemingly at ease with each other.

"Ah," Mark said his face split in a grin. "It's curiosity in the face of silence. That's a good sign."

"Add to that, she knew the two of us were in the same room." Jackson's face showed a mirroring grin.

"I think you're right on that count," he said. "I've got rounds to make now," Lily felt the air from his words as Mark talked. He'd bent over her. "I'll check back before I leave the hospital. Get some rest now."

In the silence, she listened to the sounds around her. Muted sounds from the hallway meant her door was closed. A chair scraped the floor; the creak of someone sitting down. Quiet. No, a sigh, a shift and a warm rough hand covering hers, the thumb moving rhythmically across her palm. The mesmerizing movement lulled. She slept.

Jackson sat in the chair with a view of the forested hillside. Superimposed on the dark green stately trees were staccato images of Lily strapped to the backboard, neck collar and IV in place; EMTs working over her; police, fire, and ambulance lights flashing. Waves of emotions: fear, loss, protectiveness and possessiveness surged.

He shook his head to clear the disturbing pictures, exhaled the excess of feeling and glanced over at the still figure on the bed. Beneath the scrapes and bruises was his Lily. *My Lily?* A pang of unease spiked through him. The reality that he could have lost her forever slammed his gut. Time had passed since Daniel had challenged him about his feelings for Lily and he'd done some soul searching. In the early hours of the New Year, after the debacle with Susannah, he'd come to the conclusion Lily was important to him.

In the darkness of the not-quite-quiet hospital room, Jackson confronted himself. Lily was more than important to him. Yes, he was attracted to her but that was nothing new. He'd been attracted to women since his teens. He was attracted to her physically and intellectually but also in other ways. What she gave to others drew him. Remembering her commitment to his mother when she fell just last month, a pang of jealousy pulsed through him. He wanted that. He wanted her. In the quiet room, in a moment of self-reflection and honesty, he admitted he was damn close to falling in love with her.

Jackson ran his free hand through his hair and rubbed the back of his neck, a rueful smile settled on his lips. His eyes never left her face, his hand never left hers as he shifted in the chair. He'd never had to convince a woman to be with him; in fact quite the opposite. But Lily, he knew, was different. He understood she desired him, but also acknowledged she was resolved to resist him. Well-enough acquainted with women, he knew at least one man in her past had hurt her. *If I'm going to convince her to give me a chance, I need a plan.* He grinned. *And, I've hours to come up with one.*

23 - REBUILDING A LIFE

Stabbing pain lanced through every inch of her body as Lily struggled to shift in the bed. Tears welled but she fought them back. Now was not the time to cry. She'd save that for when it was dark and she was alone.

The last three days had been horrific; she'd lost every battle she'd engaged in. Perhaps she shouldn't call them battles. That wasn't exactly fair to everyone else. It was just that her hard won independence had been shattered in the seconds it took for the fender of a truck to clip her. Not that she remembered anything after seeing Eleanor settled in the car until she was in the ER with Mark Parker. Vague pain-filled images but no real memories. From the stories she'd heard, she should be grateful.

She wasn't grateful. She could do nothing for herself...not dress herself, feed herself, not even go to the bathroom herself. Well, the last wasn't exactly true. She was fortunate the bathroom had a bidet and she had gained the privilege of taking care of that personal business. Something she was more than willing to do despite the excruciating pain.

Lily wanted to curse, throw something, scream – anything to release the mountain of frustration trapped inside her chest. Instead she smiled at Diana and Elizabeth who had accompanied her from the hospital and were helping her settle into her room at the top of the stairs of Jackson Montgomery's house. It wasn't as if she'd never been here before – of course she had. This was the room where she stayed when he was out-of-town and someone needed to be with Eleanor.

Her efforts to convince Mark Parker she should go home fell on deaf ears. Even with their varied schedules, the six women could not cover her 24/7 and Mark was insistent she needed someone with her 24/7.

Her choice?

A rehabilitation center or here.

She should be grateful she had a choice, she should be thankful for the support The Circle could provide, she should…

Dragging her mind away from those unhelpful thoughts, Lily focused on what was going on around her. She tried not to glower as her few items of clothing were folded and placed in drawers or hung in the closet. The bedside table held lotion, lip balm and a CD player. The shelf below contained several CDs.

Because of the double immobilizers she couldn't lift her arms/hands to her face so talking on the phone was out, which gave her an excuse for not calling Charlie. Thank goodness she had the cards for January and February purchased. How humbling to ask one of her circle sisters to write the note. Diana will understand and she can add a bit about what Bill is doing. *How am I ever going to tell him? What will Paul do? Will he try to take full custody?* Tears leaked trickling down her face, catching at the corner of her mouth, dribbling past her ear and down her neck.

Why couldn't she be more appreciative of what everyone is doing for her? Fear… .

The energy it took to beat back the "what ifs" exhausted, leeching out anything left from battling the pain.

Logic finally inserted itself into the rambling panic running through her mind. Charlie would make the decision regarding custody and she wouldn't entertain the thought he'd shut her out. Diana and Elizabeth had the most freedom in terms of their schedules and they were overseeing her clients. They'd already called and visited everyone. At that moment, everything was stable so there really wasn't much to do except monitor things…both women were more than capable of doing that.

Recovering and healing was now her job and while some of it was in the Goddess's hands, much of it was up to her. Hunter and Gabriella were checking on her house, mail, etc. Sophia and Ashley were fixing food for the Montgomery kitchen so Eleanor only had to unwrap or heat something up for them at lunch.

Grateful, thankful, appreciative, pleased – not her. She growled her thanks leaving no question she didn't really mean it. Sitting in bed, she glared daggers at her friends who were only trying to help and snapped answers to their questions. Indebted, obligated, ungrateful, selfish, mean-spirited. Stop! She shouted in her head. Stop! A deep breath brought searing pain; a welcome relief to the negative stream of thoughts and feelings rushing through her.

She breathed through the pain with shallow breaths finally relaxing against the pillows. When she opened her eyes, Diana was standing beside her, a cool cloth in her hand. A weak smile, not even a nod but Diana knew and gently wiped her forehead, cheeks and chin. Her eyes closed blocking out the unwelcomed sight.

"Try this," Diana's soft voice urged.

Lily felt a straw at her lips. Her eyes still closed she took it into her mouth and sucked. The tart lemony liquid trickled into her mouth, down her throat.

"Ash?"

"Her special treat for you." Diana's voice held the hint of a smile. "She thought you could use a special treat once you were settled in."

"I love her lemonade." Lily sipped through the straw, savoring every tingly burst of flavor. She could be grateful for friends like these women. The thought soothed. Eyes still closed she concentrated on the play of light against her eyelids. Light fractured by the tree limbs jigging in the wind.

Vignettes from the past couple of days drifted through her mind: Jackson remaining by her bedside, holding her hand, his thumb rhythmically stroking her palm; Jackson arguing with the nurse and calling Mark so she had pain medication before her work with the physical therapist; Jackson just being there so she wasn't alone. There were other scenes – Diana and Elizabeth were the first to come. Before she was discharged this morning, everyone had stopped by, brought flowers or chocolate, taken charge of some part of her life and assured her it was "no problem at all."

Ha! Even that thought had her wince. 'No problem' what a crock. Of course it was a problem – everyone had busy, full lives. Her efforts to become outraged failed. Yes, everyone had busy lives but they were a sacred women's circle and their commitment to be there for each other was solid. Over the years they'd been there for each other: for Sophia when Jonathan died; for Ashley when she underwent treatment for breast cancer; for Hunter when she moved to Los Angeles to follow her dream to be a choreographer – cheering her on when she left and welcoming her back on her return.

The sigh came from her soul. *My turn, I guess.* Tears threatened. She hated to be dependent on anyone for anything…so much better to be the giver than the receiver. There was the concept that receiving was a gift to the giver. *No, that isn't quite right. More like being a gracious receiver or something along those lines.* Another sigh indicative of the amount of work she had to do if she was going to become gracious in the face of this adversity. Today, her goal was to not be totally ungrateful or ungracious.

The day finally passed, Sophia came by and fed her dinner and helped her wash up for bed. Sophia rubbing lotion on her back before the immobilizers went back on was a bit of heaven. While she had to keep them on, she was allowed a few minutes out of them during the day. Someone had to be with her and she could not move her arms while they were off. Now she was lying in bed, no desire to watch television, the CD had finished playing; there was an hour before she could take her pain medication and slip into the nothingness of a medicated sleep.

A knock on her door brought her out of her reverie. Jackson lounged against the jamb, his arms and ankles crossed.

"How's your day been?" His voice was friendly, his gray eyes watchful.

"As good as can be expected, I guess," Lily said and squirmed to sit up more. A wrenching spasm seared her back, she gasped for breath.

In an instant Jackson was beside her, his faced etched with concern.

"Damn," he muttered, "I'm sorry. Didn't mean to cause a problem. Just stopped to see how you were, if you needed anything or not." He gingerly perched on the side of the bed and gently stroked her back.

She didn't know if it was the heat from his hand or the gentle rubbing motion on her back, but something penetrated the webbing and Velcro of the immobilizer and the spasms eased.

Jackson moved to the chair beside the bed, when the corded muscles in Lily's back relaxed. "Anything I can do for you? Or is that the worst question I can ask you right now?"

"Pretty much the worst question anyone can ask," she said, a small smile tilting the corners of her mouth.

"Must be tough having everyone hanging around."

A small sigh escaped. "I'm taking a crash course in being transformed. Being gracious instead of surly, seeing the people around me as being helpful instead of hovering."

"Ahhh." A chuckle escaped. "I can see how that might be a challenge for someone as independent as you."

"As if you wouldn't be a bear with people hovering around, feeding you, wiping your nose, brushing your teeth." Her words caught in her throat.

Jackson leaned forward, caught and held her gaze. "By this time, no one would be around me. I'd have driven them all off." He sat back and grinned. "You must not be as bad as you think. You've a small army ready to do your bidding."

"Actually, they try to anticipate my 'bidding' as you call it and that makes it worse. It's hard enough for me to ask but to have someone think I want something when I don't," she said, her voice tinged with a blend of helplessness and irritation. She paused before continuing, wanting her voice steady and calm. "I know they want to help, to make things better so saying 'no' at that point is hard too," she confessed.

"I know you have pain medication to take at ten. I can stay and we can talk or I can go and come back. Which do you prefer?"

"Can we talk about something other than how I'm feeling, if I need anything, or how I'm doing?" Her raised brow mirrored the question in her voice.

"We can talk about anything you want: the weather, sports, favorite places we've been. You name it."

"Tell me about one of your projects." Lily rested her head against the pillows and closed her eyes imagining the house Jackson described. She wondered what it would be like to be there, to walk through the doors, look out the windows, to see it in person. It sounded wonderful, open, airy, full of light, views from every window. Magnificent.

The room was quiet. Lily opened her eyes to see what had happened. She'd been so drawn into his description she'd lost track of this room and this bed.

He appeared in her line of vision holding a glass and the bottle of her pain pills.

"It's almost ten." He fished two pills from the bottle and bent over her. "Open up," he encouraged.

As soon as her lips parted, he eased the two pills into her mouth. He held the glass tipped at just the right angle for her to take sippy drinks. The pills finally swallowed, he gently wiped her mouth with a washcloth she hadn't even noticed.

"Sleep well." His voice low he gazed into her eyes while he brushed a lock of her hair away from her face. "If you need anything, I'm right next door." He straightened and before she could thank him he was gone, pulling her door closed, just short of latching.

Lily stared at the door for a moment before closing her eyes and whispering. "Oh, Goddess, please help me deal with this with grace. I really am blessed to have so many good people in my life. Please stay with me, let me feel your presence. Blessed Be." Another layer of tension ebbed.

OVER THE NEXT FOUR DAYS, a routine developed. Soon after Lily woke either Diana or Elizabeth was there to help her start her day. Home health physical therapy or a trip to Pond's left her drained, too tired to eat, too despondent to care. Jackson or Sophia fixed dinner. By nine o'clock, her nerve endings twitching, her mind fixated on ten o'clock, pain pills and the oblivion of sleep, Jackson settling into the chair by her bed became a welcomed sight.

IT WAS SATURDAY NIGHT, just over a week since the accident. Lily was exhausted. Everyone in The Circle had been by to see her. Every flat surface in the room had flowers or plants. Her beloved lioness and cub on her night stand, a few special crystals within view on the dresser top, a bowl of river rock in the bathroom added a touch of home. Her favorite picture, a fantasy painting of a maiden and her knight on a horse, all done in silver, white and grays, now hung on the wall across from her bed. The first thing she saw in the morning and the last thing she saw at night.

Jackson slumped in the chair, one ankle resting on the opposite knee. She sat upright, pillows plumped behind her.

"How's it going?" A deceptively simple question asked in a moderate tone with his left brow quirked.

"It's been a tough week. I'm pushing myself because I know Mark won't let me go home until I have some use of my arms. I'm hoping he'll let me have my client book and case notes as well as my lap top in a couple of days."

"And if Mark doesn't okay that, what'll you do with the four to six weeks until you are fully healed?"

"Don't even," she gasped as she twisted to glare at him. "Don't even talk like that." She sighed and sank back against the pillows, her breathing shallow until the pain subsided. "Please, Jackson, I can't even begin to deal with that possibility right now.

"It isn't like I'm on vacation, touring, seeing the sights, watching people. I have four walls surrounding me," she snapped. "It isn't like...," her voice trailed off. "I'm sorry. I know I sound ungrateful." She paused. "And the view out the window is lovely," she added in a syrupy voice.

Jackson suppressed a chuckle. "Don't apologize. You're right; you're not on vacation and doing fun things. Recovering isn't fun at all. But it's something to think about. If Mark doesn't okay your working, I don't know anyone who'll override him."

"I know you're right," Lily said on a long exhale. "My only hope is to push myself as hard as I can. I want to go home. I want to get back to work."

"Mark did say something about having a setback if you pushed yourself too hard," Jackson reminded her.

"Don't Jackson. Just don't. I can't even begin to think about everything taking more time than at least six weeks or maybe more. The fog of despair looms when I let myself think like that."

"What if there was something else you could do to help occupy your time?"

"I've no idea what it could be. I'm just not able to read and watch television for hours on end. I'm used to being busy, on the move, you know, in charge."

"I know you wouldn't be satisfied just sitting around reading and watching TV. Mother comes up once a day, but says she doesn't want to stay too long and tire you out. I expect that will change as you get better. However, there's another idea I've had for a while and since you've almost an hour before your ten o'clock meds, want to hear about it?"

He was leaning towards her, enthusiasm reflected in his face.

"Just don't make it too exciting," she cautioned.

"Actually, it's about that House Totem thing you do. Daniel mentioned he'd talked to you about doing them for his clients but you hadn't firmed anything up yet. You know Daniel and I refer business to one another. He and I were talking about the idea of adding House

Totems to the list of options we give our clients. You'd be working with both of us. What do you think about that?"

"I'm not sure I understand what you're talking about." Lily's brow wrinkled, her eyes filled with questions. She remembered talking with Daniel about the possibility of her intuiting House Totems for his clients; but that was all. What Jackson was talking about sounded much more formal.

"You know I design houses. But I also oversee them being built for my high-end clients. In Fremont, Daniel's usually the builder plus he has his own customers. My clients come to me because they want something that sets their house apart from the ordinary. Don't you see? It's a great fit, my design and your House Totem."

"You want me to look at one of your designs, like a blue print and pick a House Totem?" Her voice and eyebrows rose with incredulity.

"Can you do it that easily?" Jackson's eyes lit with excitement, a grin split his features.

"No!" Her voice was edged with exasperation.

"Well, what do you need to make it work? You know, to come up with a House Totem?"

"Jackson, I don't 'come up with' a House Totem. I sense the spirit that has chosen this place to protect, guard or influence. I can't just look at a drawing or picture here in Fremont to know what is needed in San Francisco or wherever you're working. You can't even sense a House Totem across town. You have to be there, it's about the energy of the land."

"Okay, so if I'm understanding you right, you'd need to travel to the house, walk the land, spend some time there and then you'd know what the House Totem should be. Right?"

"Close." She looked thoughtful before she attempted to explain more. "And I don't know what the House Totem 'should be', I know what it is. There's a difference that's obviously hard to explain to someone else."

"Okay, sure there's a difference," Jackson interjected. "If all this can be set up, will you do it? Will you do the House Totem thing with me?"

"I don't know that I'll work with you, Jackson. House Totems are not frivolous things, something you add to the house like- like crown molding in the kitchen. House Totems are already there, invisible perhaps, not set up or energized to do their job, but still they are there. Here in your house, you had the owl and he was visible. There already was a fair amount of energy around him, but he wasn't 'set up', you know, positioned to do his job. I just tweaked it."

"But what about Daniel's horses?"

"The old carriage house, the remains of the stable, the feel of the place all evoked the era of the horse drawn carriage. His is a stately Victorian house. I could almost hear the neighing and hoof beats as I drove up to the house. That's what I mean, Jackson. It's already there; you just need to be open to sensing or intuiting it. It isn't made up. It's not something I'm choosing for them or for the house. It's already there. I'm just identifying it."

"You really believe this, don't you?" He relaxed back in the chair, still alert, still intent, still listening, knowing that understanding this part of her was crucial to his plan to win her for his own.

"Yes, I really do believe everything has a spirit or energy...trees, plants, animals, rocks, even dirt. Everything in nature and everything from nature has a living energy. We're all connected through this energy. When one part of the Universe is hurt, we're all affected.

"This bed is made from oak," Lily said. She nodded toward the bed post. "Put your hand on the wood of the post and just feel it. The textures, the temperature, the words that come to your mind while you touch the bed post are the words of the spirit of the tree the wood came from."

"It's a really old bed," Jackson said. "It came from England with my Mother. Been in her family for generations. Handmade. If you look closely you can see the markings of the tools."

"Go ahead. Put your hand on the post. Sometimes it helps to close your eyes. Take a deep breath. Relax, breathe," Lily soothed.

Jackson found himself standing up and taking the few steps to the bed. This is silly. Doing as Lily instructed, he put his hands on the bed post. In the silence, Jackson could feel the subtle texture of the old oak wood, thousands of strokes of someone's hand and tools had made the wood warm silk beneath his hand. "Solid," "warm," "strong," "protective" ... words. No, not really words, more like 'feeling words' that swirled through him. *What the hell!*

He jerked his hand away.

Lily saw emotions flicker across his face, ending with profound disbelief. How disquieting to sense the spirit of things when you don't believe they exist. He felt something now just like he did with the owl on his mantle. Her mood lifted, a small smile formed. He feels the spirits around him and it's confounding him.

"What happened?" She looked amused.

"Not much," he muttered.

"Define 'not much' for me," she asked, an intent look on her face as she watched him sort his thoughts.

"There's not much to say. I did as you instructed." His irritation grew at her infernal probing.

"And?"

"And what? What do you want me to say, Lily? I'm out of my element here. This mumbo jumbo stuff is way out there for me." Jackson strode away from the bed, his hands shoved in his back pockets, irritation radiated from him.

"You felt or heard or sensed something and you don't know what to do about it because you don't believe it's possible, right?" Lily's voice was calm, reassuring, as she watched Jackson struggle with his comprehension of something he didn't accept as real.

"Yeah, something like that." Jackson turned, paced back and collapsed in the chair. He sighed and leaned forward, elbows on knees, hands clasped, an earnest look on his face. "Doesn't it scare the wits out of you? How do you not hear all the, what do you call them, messages or whatever?"

Lily looked into his eyes. "Jackson, the 'messages,' as you refer to them, are always there. The change is in us, in our willingness to tune in, hear, sense what's always been. It's up to us - we can tune out or tune in. What's important is to remember that the spirit of life surrounds us at all times." She paused, "I tuned out my pain while you and I were talking about House Totems. I know I've the ability to do that. The energy and focus it takes is more challenging when I'm in pain. Talking with you about House Totems distracts me from the pain and I feel better.

"Let me think about your idea, Jackson. I won't say 'no' for now, but I'm also not saying 'yes.' There's a lot to think about: ethical and moral issues."

"What are they?"

"Not tonight, Jackson. I need to think about this and then talk it over with The Circle. We had a general discussion when Daniel first brought it up but, whatever is agreed upon would involve them too. And, are you sure Daniel doesn't want to be more fully involved? After all, it was his idea."

"Okay, I'll check it out more fully with Daniel and you can discuss everything with your circle friends. We can revisit this topic another evening, okay?" Seeing her nod of agreement, he stood. "Looks like it's time for your next pain pills." Walking into the bathroom to get her fresh water, he called over his shoulder, "Do you know what the oak post said to me?"

"No."

"Want to know?" he asked as he came back into the room.

"Only if you want to tell me."

Jackson's grin along with a devilish gleam in his eyes still didn't prepare her for his answer. "There's been a lot of loving in this bed but you haven't been part of that. I told it that might change."

"I-I-I don't think so," she sputtered, straightening to catch her breath, stiffening as spasms rippled down her spine.

He put the water and pills on the bedside table. "My timing on that was bad, I'm sorry," Jackson apologized, gently stroking her back. "I shouldn't have teased you like that."

"It isn't just your timing, Jackson." Lily sank back into the pillows. "I don't believe that's the message you got at all." She gave him a stern look to cover her mixed emotions. *He's being so nice. It's hard to keep my guard up when he's like this.* "It isn't nice to fool with the spirits. They might get back at you."

"I'll take my chances." Jackson grinned at her as he picked up the pills and glass of water. She opened her mouth and he popped the pills in one at a time. Holding the straw to her lips, he stood quietly while she swallowed the last pill down. Bending down, he tucked her hair behind her ears and kissed her forehead. "I'll wish you a good night's rest." He turned at the door. "I'm leaving the door open a crack so you can call if you need something. Remember, I'm right next door and can be here in a few seconds."

24 - FIRST COMES FRIENDSHIP THEN...

$\mathcal{L}$ily looked forward to the time she spent with Jackson each evening. Whichever of her circle sisters came to help her with dinner and getting ready for the night left the bedroom door open. She heard his lower masculine tones and Eleanor's higher feminine ones as they said their "good nights." His footsteps on the stairs announced his visit.

She'd been here ten days. When she'd seen Mark earlier today, his cheerful statement that she was doing well, right on target, and "no" she was not released to work or go home, left her in a dark and brooding mood.

The expectancy and hope that Jackson would provide a distraction from her black thoughts was wiped away in an instant when she saw him at her door.

"Given the look on your face, I'd say your day was worse than mine," Lily infused her voice with a cheery note.

"I'll come back later. No need to darken your day," he said in a grumpy voice. He stood in the doorway, propped against the door jamb, arms folded across his chest, the frown on his face mirroring the moodiness of his voice.

"Come and tell me about it. It'll take my mind off my whiny self," she offered.

"Are you sure?" He hesitated. "I'm not very good company. I can just come back at ten."

"I'm sure." She nodded toward the chair, her professional interested look on her face. Her full attention on him, she relaxed back against the pillows as he told her about a customer who continually changed her mind only to change it back again after he'd spent an hour talking her back around to the original design.

"Her ideas are crazy!" he exclaimed running the fingers of one hand through his hair. "There's no way in hell I'd have my name attached to them."

She asked some questions, learned the client was a woman, divorced by her husband of twenty-plus years so he could marry a twenty-something woman.

"She's interested in you," Lily declared. She winced as a sharp jagged bolt of pain stabbed her chest when a bubble of laughter erupted at the look of horror on his face.

"You're wrong!" He was on his feet, pacing around the room, gesticulating as he explained why she was wrong, itemizing all the ways he made sure things like that didn't happen.

Fascinated, Lily listened to him list at least six strategies he had for nipping in the bud anything even close to a personal relationship with a client.

He stopped at the foot of the bed, an arm wrapped around the post and leaned in. "What words of wisdom do you have, assuming you're right, which I don't think you are." He looked and sounded like a belligerent little boy.

"My advice is to go along with her. Thank her for coming by, repeat back the changes she's asked for and show her out. My guess is she'll change her mind back to your original design. Just be professional, charming, agreeable and see her out.

"And, I'd ask her a couple of questions such as what her goals are for herself or what direction she sees her life taking at this point. You mentioned she volunteers. You could ask her why and why she doesn't do more. My guess is she's lonely and having you design and oversee the building of this house gives her something to do and you to focus on."

The belligerent little boy look faded. His eyes lost their focus, his head tilted in a thoughtful considering pose. "A part of me hopes you're right and another part of me hopes you're wrong. I've always been good at picking up on things like this," he murmured. He shifted, brought his attention back to Lily, and said, "I really hope you're wrong."

Back in the chair he asked about her day and watched emotions flicker across her face, deepen the blue of her eyes, as she told him what Parker had said. He wasn't surprised by either Parker's restrictions or Lily's disappointment. Even though she could have a new Blue tooth headset that allowed her to talk to friends who called, it wasn't enough to lift her spirits.

"In other words, if someone calls you, Mark said you can talk to them but you aren't released to make calls?" Jackson clarified.

"He doesn't trust me." Her face contorted in a combination of hurt and indignation. "Can you believe it?"

"Actually, I can. All I hear you talk about is getting back to work. I can understand why Mark is reluctant to let you have access to anything you can use to sneak behind his back and do it anyway."

"Sneak!" she shrieked. "You think I'd sneak? You think I'm dishonest?" She gasped as the spasms clenched in her back.

"Calm down," Jackson's voice was calm and pitched lower to soothe. "I think you are normally a very honest, above-board person but you are in a difficult place right now. You believe if you can just go back to work in some way that will mean you're okay." He paused, waited for her denial. She glowered but said nothing. "Maybe you need to figure out how to be 'okay' just the way you are?" Standing, he walked to the bathroom, returning moments later with her pills and water.

"Here, take these." He held the pills out.

Lily opened her mouth, let him drop the pills inside and then took the offered straw and sucked. The pills slid down and she knew in a few minutes the effect of the sedation would wipe out the frustration and depression. She was so tired, so very tired of it all and by all accounts she still had at least four weeks ahead of her. Today she'd failed at her goal to be gracious and grateful. Lying back against the pillows she let her eyes slip closed. Tears pressed against her shut lids, a kiss was pressed against her forehead.

"It may be trite, but it is true. Tomorrow is another day. Good-night, Lily."

She felt him move away and thought he may have stopped in the doorway. "I'm leaving the door open a crack. Call if you need something. I'm right next door."

The days passed as she knew they would, her routine varied on the weekend when she did modified exercises at home, her circle sisters came to visit, and Jackson checked in on her throughout the day.

Saturday she'd had a long talk with Diana and Sophia about what to tell Charlie. Diana had written the last couple of cards explaining in the first one that Lily had hurt her hand and Dr. Parker said she wasn't supposed to write. The decision she made was to tell him nothing more. Why worry him when there wasn't anything he could do. Even if he offered to come home and stay with her, it wouldn't work because he would be in school during the day. She had been uncomfortable at first, but that had changed. She had settled in and was at ease now.

What had hurt was waiting for his phone call, a Get Well card, or note—one never came or at least had yet to come. Her sigh was one of resignation. He'd known for over a week now. If he was going to contact her, he would have. While it hurt to know he wasn't calling or writing, he did think it was a minor accident. If he knew how badly she'd been hurt and still hadn't responded? Tears welled and a sharp pain tore her gut. That would be devastating.

Yesterday, her appointment with Mark had gone a little better and he'd released her to do stairs once a day if someone was with her. Instead of elation, she was leery about the stairs. What if she fell? She'd be flat on her back again. Another lifted restriction? She could get up and sit in the chair on her own. The third gift from Mark was being allowed out of the Immobilizers for ten to fifteen minutes four times a day. But like the stairs, there was a catch. Someone had to be there because she was unable to get herself out of them or put them back on. The idea she'd made gains and had those bits of freedom was heady.

Now, two and a half weeks since the accident, Lily hoped she was at the half-way point. The sense she'd never get back on her feet was lessened but had not entirely disappeared. Overall her mood was better. When Eleanor visited earlier in the day, they made a plan for her to have a dinner of ham and cheese sandwiches downstairs. Waiting for Eleanor to call her to come down, she heard Jackson's voice boom a jovial, "I'm home."

He seemed to be taking the steps two at a time, she thought just before he burst into her room. "You're incredible, Lily-love." His face split by a huge grin, his arms thrown open wide, he strode into the room.

"You were right," he exclaimed, dropping into the chair next to the bed. "Amazing I didn't have a clue." He stopped, noting the blank look on Lily's face. "The client? You know the one you gave me the advice on?"

"Oh." She nodded and smiled as she remembered the conversation. "I was right?"

"And it doesn't even bother me to tell you that." He chuckled and then became serious as he leaned forward in the chair. "I did as you suggested and as you know it's been pure hell. She came in today and we talked, really cleared the air. She admitted she'd hoped something would develop between us and I told her I thought something had – a firm friendship. I asked her those questions you mentioned and learned she only volunteers during the holidays because it's just too depressing to do more. She's always wanted to be a parent, a mom, she said but her husband didn't want children. Of course he's having one with wife #2 which hurts a lot."

"She could always look into adoption," Lily said.

"She's in her forties, too old to adopt."

"Not necessarily. She may not be able to adopt a baby, but she could certainly adopt an older child. If she's interested, give her Elizabeth's name and phone number. I know E'd be more than willing to talk to her."

"I'll do that." Jackson relaxed into the chair. "She's really a great lady. I think you'd like her." His eyes remained on Lily.

"What? What is it?" Lily demanded.

A slow smile spread over his face. "Nothing. Nothing at all." He stood and started toward the door hoping she didn't notice his body's reaction to the incredibly sexy way she licked her lips. She may have been sitting in her sweats, her hair mussed and no makeup but he felt his attraction to her growing stronger. No superficial airs, no false front, she was herself — just genuine Lily. "Going to change now and then escort you downstairs for dinner."

"Eleanor and I are having ham and cheese sandwiches."

"Nope, you, mother and I are having Thai. Pad Thai Noodles, Chicken Satay, Mussaman Curry, fresh Spring Rolls and I've some homemade coconut ice cream for dessert. Get yourself ready. I'll be back in five." Heading to his room, Jackson contemplated how his view of relationships had changed since meeting Lily. The idea of hooking up again with Susannah or another woman like her no longer appealed.

The man he'd become looked back at him from the mirror. Pamela, his first wife, had left him for an older, wealthier man because he would not settle for a life in an architectural firm. He wanted to build his own business, grow his reputation, and reap the rewards of the work it took to do so. They'd married right out of college, too young to know better – and then she'd told him she was pregnant. In the devastation that followed her duplicity, he made a promise he'd kept until now. Until Lily. Until he'd come to understand a truth about himself. Having someone in his life who was committed to him, who saw his value not as a successful architect but as a man, as a person – that's what he sought, what he wanted with Lily.

LILY COULDN'T REMEMBER anyone other than a client or the women in her circle being so appreciative of something she'd done. Dinner was fabulous. Jackson's homemade ice cream was divine and the table conversation lively. She averted her head as a large yawn claimed her mouth. A brief respite from the immobilizers during dinner allowed her to feed herself, but she'd paid a painful price. Welcoming them back on, she sat on the couch with Eleanor. Jackson sat in his chair as the three of them continued to visit in front of the fire.

"I believe I'll ready myself for bed," Eleanor announced as she rose and started toward her apartment. "Toodles."

"Good night, Mother."

"Good night, Eleanor," Lily said as she scooted to the edge of the couch. Positioning herself to stand, her way was blocked when Jackson moved in front of her and placed his hands on her waist.

"On the count of three," he said firming his grip. "One, two, three."

She scrambled her feet under her to help rise up to a standing position when she felt him begin to lift her.

"There." A self-satisfied voice said into her hair. "Ready to head upstairs?"

She nodded and stepped away. Pausing at the bottom, Lily took a second to make sure she was balanced before starting up. Jackson followed one step behind. It was distracting, the sense that his hand was at the small of her back, not touching --- just there. At the top, she stopped. She'd made it without faltering. One challenge down, so many more ahead of me.

"Are you up for a little company?"

Her skin prickled as Jackson's breath feathered across her neck, ear and cheek. "Uh, sure, come on in," she invited.

"I've grown accustomed to our nightly talks," Jackson said as he sprawled in the chair he always sat in. "Do you need anything?"

Lily settled into the chair on the other side of the bed, disgruntled that his tone indicated no real interest in her. "I'm fine for now." A few minutes passed before she noticed him shift, sigh, and glance in her direction

"About those House Totems," he started.

Is that an edge to his voice?

He cleared his throat and assumed the posture she recognized when he had something on his mind: leaning forward, elbows on knees, clasped hands dangling between his legs.

She waited.

"I talked to Daniel and he wants to have access to you doing the House Totems but he doesn't care about being a formal part of any business arrangements." He stared at his hands before looking up and meeting her gaze. "So, what about it? Will you do the House Totems with me?"

Lily, surprised that Jackson appeared nervous, unsure of himself, relaxed in her chair. "I've talked individually with my circle sisters. Our main reservation has to do with our concern about the honoring of the spirit of the House Totem. We know there isn't a way to ensure it isn't demeaned or devalued but we want to do our best to see the totems are treated with respect, are in a place of honor – for example, not used as a hat rack. Overall it's a great idea and we're thrilled to have the opportunity to bring forth, from invisible to visible, more of the spirits that surround us.

"Our ideas include having a Contract, writing a guidebook focused on the purpose of the House Totem. We already have a title: The Care and Feeding of Your House Totem. And then to have a Certificate of some kind – something in writing that would say what the House Totem is, it's purpose, range of influence – that kind of thing." Lily paused looking at Jackson to gauge his reaction. He was listening, alert and not frowning.

"Gabriella, Ashley, and Sophia are collaborating on the Guide-book; Hunter and Elizabeth are working on a format for the Certifi-cate; and Diana is working on the contract."

"It's a place to start," Jackson said as he shifted in the chair his hands now resting on his knees. "I can appreciate your reservations as I know this is serious business to you. Respect—respect for what can be seen but more than that, respect for what can't be seen. It's a big part of who you are. I think I understand where you're coming from.

I'd be interested in seeing what you all come up with. I know my clients so I have a good idea of what they'll buy into, or not."

"Our plan is to have you look things over so if we're way off base we can talk and see if we can work out something that fits your clients but still keeps within our principles," Lily said. "Everyone's bringing something for a potluck on Sunday and bringing what they've put together so far. You don't really have to do anything," she added. "I don't want to impose more than I'm already doing but we couldn't figure anything else out. Mark did say I could do stairs once a day as long as someone is with me, so this seemed to be the best plan."

Muscles he didn't realize were clenched, relaxed. A grin on his face, he sat back in the chair. "Nope, that isn't how it's going to be at all."

"What do you mean?" Her brows scrunched and she squinted as if what he said made no sense.

"What's going to happen is I'm going to fix dinner for everyone and you can use the living room. No need to take that additional flight of stairs. How about spaghetti with my homemade sauce, a great bread, a tossed salad with a couple of my dressings, maybe a bit of antipasto as an appetizer and a selection of my ice creams for dessert?"

"Really? You'd do all of that for us?" Lily was stupefied at the offer but her mouth watered at the thought. Jackson was a fantastic cook.

He nodded. "I want this Lily and I'll play hardball to get it. I'm hoping my cooking will sway votes my way."

"It just might work," she said her head tilted at a thoughtful angle. "I think Ashley and Diana's husbands may grill something now and then but I doubt any of them have had a full home cooked meal prepared by a man before." Her eyes met his and held. "What I don't understand is why this is so important to you. It isn't as if you don't have clients. From what Eleanor says, you've more work than you can possibly do. Why add this?"

The thought to tell her this was part of his plan to woo her flashed through his mind and was immediately extinguished. Not the time and not the place. Although she'd softened toward him and he even thought they'd become friendly over the past couple of weeks, what he wanted was much more than being friends. Instinctively he knew Lily was not ready to be his partner in life.

"I've built my reputation on being different, tailoring every design to the special needs and personalities of my clients. House Totems are a perfect fit. It sets me further apart from the hordes of architects out there. That's part of what I want, exclusive rights. You don't work with anyone else."

"Then it's a good idea you'll be there on Sunday so you can speak up – share your vision. You've obviously done a lot more contemplating the various aspects of this than any of the rest of us."

Jackson rose, went into the bathroom and returned with pills and water in hand. The nightly ritual: popping the pills in her mouth, holding the straw for her to sip, a quick kiss on her forehead and his parting words at the door "I'm leaving the door open a crack. Call if you need something. I'm right next door."

25 - HOUSE TOTEMS OR NOT

On Sunday, Lily still wore the immobilizers but they were looser and she could take her right arm out to eat. As she guardedly made her way down the stairs, she was accompanied by Giovanni Migliori, Jackson's colleague from Italy. He'd arrived last night and been invited to join everyone for dinner. She'd hoped Daniel would join them but he'd declined, having another commitment.

From her place on the couch, she could hear the men working in the kitchen. Two masculine voices with different tones, cadences, inflections bantered in a friendly rivalry as noodles for spaghetti were made, meatballs and two different from-scratch marinara sauces cooked.

Eleanor joined her and the two women sat in companionable silence, watching the flames flickering, enjoying the aroma of sauce and freshly baking bread.

The doorbell rang.

"I'll get it," Jackson called out as he strode to the front door, opened it, and greeted the women and children who were gathered en masse at his door.

"We carpooled," Sophia said as she stepped inside.

"Come in, come in." Jackson stepped back and gestured for everyone to enter.

"We know where everything is, Jackson." Gabriella gently shoved him toward the kitchen. "You keep on cooking for us. We'll take care of our coats and make sure Lily doesn't over-do."

"What do you mean by that, Gabby?" Lily challenged good-naturedly from the couch. "Are you accusing me of over-doing?"

"If the shoe fits." Gabby put her arms around Lily in a gentle hug. "It's good to see you up. I'd heard you were able to do the stairs on occasion."

"Slowly but surely wins the race, I'm told." Lily chuckled. "At the rate I'm going a snail could beat me." She shifted until her feet and legs were under her and she could stand. Eleanor stood by in case she needed steadying. She was thankful she was strong enough to get up on my own.

Coats hung in the foyer closet, the women moved toward the dining room. At the kitchen island, Jackson was setting out two heaping platters of spaghetti and meatballs, each featuring its own special sauce, along with an enormous bowl of salad, and three baskets of bread, one plain and two garlic. Giovanni opened three bottles of wine. Plates, silverware and sparkling crystal glasses were ready for people to help themselves. Not forgetting the children, Jackson set out smaller plates as well as milk and lemonade.

"Help yourself, everyone," he waved his hand toward the feast. "We're eating casually," he added gesturing to the dining room table. "Between the dining room table and the seating here in the kitchen, I think there's room for everyone.

"But, before we go any further and my mother chides me on my manners, I want to introduce my friend and colleague from Italy, Giovanni Migliori." Jackson nodded toward the dark-haired man casually leaning against the kitchen counter. Giovanni straightened and stepped forward with a sweeping bow toward the women.

"Ahh, my pleasure, Jackson, to meet such lovely ladies." His wide grin showed straight white teeth. His brown almond-shaped eyes sparked with mischief and an unruly lock of dark brown hair almost obliterated his right eye as he bowed, winked, and flirted outrageously with each of the women as Jackson introduced them.

Once the meal was over, Eleanor and Lily were banished from the kitchen. Sophia led the others in putting away left-overs and loading the dishwasher while Hunter and Ashley took the children downstairs. Jackson and Giovanni were delegated the task of wine stewards and made sure glasses were filled.

Lily and Eleanor sat in chairs that flanked the fireplace, sipped their wine, and watched the busyness around them. Jackson joined them, leaning against the mantle.

"It's time to begin this meeting." Jackson said. As the women moved to the living room area taking seats on the couch and chairs, he added, "If you don't mind, Giovanni would like to sit in because he has some interest in House Totems. If that isn't all right, please speak up. This is really your meeting and neither he nor I want to intrude."

Diana looked around the room silently checking for objections to the two men remaining. "Your staying seems to be okay with everyone." She smiled at both men before she reached into her briefcase and pulled out some papers. "This is the contract I put together. As you can see, it is simple and straightforward."

It was true her work with House Totems was the reason for this meeting and Lily listened closely to the conversations with mixed feelings. On the one hand she was so proud of The Circle for their creative ideas and designs. On the other hand, it felt like her life was shifting into another phase. Was this what Jackson meant when he suggested she learn to be okay with her life as it was?

Everyone looked over Diana's one-page form. Hunter and Elizabeth passed around their draft for the Certificate. Again, it was simple and straightforward with a space for the name of the House Totem as well as the person who would get the certificate and a place for the woman who intuited the totem to sign it. "We thought we could do some graphic art work on it to personalize the Certificate for each House Totem. For example," Hunter stood and strolled to where Jackson stood, "we made one up for your House Totem. See, we've added a border of owls."

"This is very creative." Jackson looked closely at the certificate. "Although I think some of my clients might see it as frivolous with the little animal border. That's something to think about if you want people to be more serious about their House Totem."

"That's good information for us," Elizabeth toyed with the ends of a lock of hair as she looked at the copy of the Certificate in her hand. "We need to find the line between being whimsical and frivolous. And for some clients, it may be we just stick to a more formal Certificate."

"Is it possible to have different types of certificates for different clients?" Hunter asked. "That way we can tailor the certificate to the personality of the home owner."

"That's something to consider," Jackson replied.

"We've come up with the first entries in The Guide Book." Sophia gestured to the pages now being passed around by Ashley and Gabriella. "We started with Jackson's Great Horned Owl and Daniel's Horse. We have the Great Blue Heron which is my House Totem and as you can see, we've included a few more."

"Our layout features a picture of the totem on the left and information about its attributes on the right. In addition, we're considering room on the back page for the home owner to write down their own thoughts and ideas, perhaps their search, where they found it, etc.," Gabriella added. "We aren't sure whether to have a whole book that would go to each client or to create an individualized document with just that particular client's House Totem information."

"And we want to have some sort of a presentation folder that will hold the Certificate, Contract, and The Guide Book but haven't worked on that yet," Ashley finished.

The room was quiet except for the rustle of paper as everyone looked through the pages being passed around. Jackson was the first to speak.

"I'm impressed with the work you've done. It's obvious you've put a lot of thought into your projects. Other than the bit about the borders on the certificates and a reminder that you want the final product to be of the highest quality, I don't have anything else to say. Any of my clients who want a House Totem will be very pleased."

Giovanni, who had remained silent during the presentations, grinned at Lily, his dark eyes dancing mischief. "I must have you come do this for me. These House Totems are intriguing." He winked. "You can come stay at my villa, find my totem, make me the envy of every other architect in Italy." His teeth flashed as he grinned.

Lily laughed. "However, Giovanni," her expression became more serious but there was a twinkle in her eyes, "we've agreed to only work with people Jackson recommends. I don't remember seeing your name on Jackson's list."

"I don't remember seeing any list," Gabriella interjected. "Is there a secret list somewhere?"

"No, Gabby, there's no list." Lily met Gabriella's direct hazel gaze. "Right now, if there was one, only Jackson and Daniel's names would be on it."

"Ahh, my friend," Giovanni smiled, walking over to stand in front of Jackson, putting his hand on his shoulder in a friendly gesture. "You would put my name on the list so Lily can come home with me, *si*. It is only right as we are friends and share so many things between us."

"Ahh, my friend," Jackson's drawl was a poor imitation of Giovanni's accent, "it is true we share so many things, a bottle of excellent wine, a good meal, but to have your name on this list? No, Giovanni, for now that will not happen." Jackson looked around the room at the women before him. "There are reasons beyond a friendly rivalry with Giovanni for my answer. This is a new project and while Lily has identified my House Totem and that of my friend, Daniel, we haven't really formalized things. I'm suggesting we go slow and make sure everything is in place, before we expand."

"That seems reasonable," Sophia interjected, "the children will need attention before too long. Is there anything else we need to discuss?"

The remainder of the meeting went well. Two other architects had approached Jackson about House Totems having heard about them through Daniel. The women decided to accept Jackson's suggestion that they take their time, make sure everything was in place before adding other architects to their list. They also decided, when the time came, to only work with people Jackson recommended.

"I'd like to thank you for your confidence in me. It means a lot to know I have your trust. And, once we have things up and running, should one of you want to travel to Italy to work with Giovanni, I think you'd find his buildings inspired. Just remember," he grinned at his friend, "to be on your guard. He is truly an Italian to the tips of his fingers."

~

Two days later Giovanni left for home. While he was entertaining, his seemingly endless energy and vitality at times was draining. Lily was relieved to have him gone. Over the next three days she settled into a routine that kept her upstairs until early afternoon. She did fifty minutes of lower body strengthening exercises, took a shower followed by a nap before getting dressed and descending the stairs for a light lunch with Eleanor.

Friday, four weeks after the accident, the exercises and shower exhausted her. The nap gave her enough rest and energy to make it through until evening. No longer was she strapped into the immobilizers twenty-four hours a day, but the list of restrictions was long.

It was also Valentine's Day and Jackson marked the occasion with cooking dinner and gifts. She was uncomfortable with the pendant necklace he'd bought her, but it was the same design he'd purchased for Eleanor so she swallowed her unease and accepted it.

Another week passed and her impatience was palpable. Mark still wouldn't release her to work, not even a little bit. Nothing she said, nothing she promised budged him. She now could raise her arms to feed herself, brush her hair and teeth, and wash her own hair, but lifting, pushing, shoving and driving were not allowed. *Why won't my body heal faster? Why is my progress so slow? Why can't I just relax and let it be as it is?* She knew she didn't help herself when she was like this.

Another Friday and she was bored and bordering on depressed. She didn't want to read, watch television, call someone on the phone or contemplate anything. Glowering in the bathroom mirror she scowled muttering how very unreasonable Mark was being. She couldn't believe he tossed her own advice back at her. So unfair! Tears threatened. Frowning she turned away from the mirror. She needed something to do.

She carefully made her way down the stairs and knocked on Eleanor's door.

"*Entrez-vous, s'il vous plait.*"

A smile on her face, her spirits raised, Lily entered.

Eleanor sat at a card table set up in front of her windows bent over a jigsaw puzzle.

"Ohh, Eleanor, I didn't know you did jigsaw puzzles." Lily crossed the room, her eyes lit with excitement.

"It is a family tradition to do one large puzzle after Christmas. This one has 2000 pieces." Eleanor kept her eyes focused on the puzzle. "With all that has been going on, I have not gotten around to doing one until now. I could certainly use some help if you are available."

"I'd love to help," Lily said slipping into a chair. Her mouth a perfect 'O', a laugh bubbled forth when she saw the scene on the box. "This is an awful puzzle! A winter scene of bare trees and lots of snow?" She scrutinized the picture on the box and the puzzle on the table. "I see you've got the cabin in the woods almost done."

"I'm not sure I will finish this one before I go to my daughters. It may be too much for me." Eleanor's gaze remained on the puzzle a wry smile on her lips. "It reminded me of a place in the country near where I grew up. There was a small wood with a cabin similar to this one. I couldn't resist purchasing this puzzle when I saw it."

"This scene reminded you of your youth?"

"Of a lovely place from my youth. A walk in the woods on warm days was always delightful."

"Well, it's a challenging puzzle, that's for sure," Lily said as she leaned slightly to the side to see the puzzle from a different angle. "I'd love to come and help out...if that's okay." She plucked a piece of puzzle from the table and tried it in a part of a branch. It didn't fit.

"I would welcome your help. Jackson just took one look at the picture on the box, muttered something, and walked out. With his eye for design, shape and his ability to conceptualize, he should be wonderful with puzzles. But, that is just not true. He doesn't have the patience it takes, that stick-to-itiveness needed to finish them off." Eleanor reached for a piece and slipped it into place.

"My family also had the tradition of putting together a jigsaw puzzle the week between Christmas and New Year's. I lost that tradition after the divorce when Charlie and I were on our own." Lily tried a piece in several different places. It didn't fit.

Eleanor glanced at Lily, patting her hand, her voice soft, "It must have been difficult for you, dear, to have your parents die so close to one another."

"Yes," Lily allowed. "My Dad died within six months of Mom. I was still reeling from Paul's leaving me and the divorce. It was during that time, I decided I needed a new career direction for myself. I knew I couldn't keep doing Child Protective Service work and be the kind of Mom to Charlie I wanted to be. It took me a couple of years to make the transition but I've never regretted it." She reached for another piece and tried it in several places. It didn't fit.

"And I am very glad you do what you do. I hate to think what my life would be like without you in it." Eleanor picked up a piece and fit it into the web of stark tree limbs that framed the cabin.

"I don't want to think about life without you in it either," Lily said reaching out and squeezing the older woman's hand. The moment passed. The sense of loss with her parents' deaths and now Charlie spending the school year with his dad eased. She had a home now, friends to support and encourage her, and who knew what would happen with the House Totems. Taking a deep breath she focused on the puzzle and chatted easily with Eleanor, putting everything else firmly out of her mind.

They took a short break and Eleanor made Tetley's English tea before they resumed working on the puzzle. Just as Eleanor slipped another piece of puzzle in place, Lily heard Jackson come in from the garage.

A few minutes later he walked through the French doors. "I brought steaks for dinner and pieces of Tiramisu from Carlo's. I've bread warming in the oven and all that's left is chopping up the lettuce for a tossed salad." He looked expectantly at Lily and his mother, waiting for a reply. Neither woman glanced up from the puzzle.

"Ladies?" Jackson stalked from the doorway to the card table. "Is this any way to treat the man who is feeding you? Don't I deserve some recognition for all the work I've done to put food on your table?" Hands on his hips, Jackson glared at the two women who studiously ignored him. He opened his mouth to rain another deluge of words on their heads when he saw Lily's shoulders moving. A closer look at his mother's back revealed her pent up mirth. Another step and he was almost touching them. He leaned down and whispered in Lily's ear, "Gotcha" his breath feathered over her ear and down her neck.

Lily startled as the shiver of arousal slipped through her. She looked up into Jackson's laughing eyes. Before she could speak, Jackson shifted and kissed his mother's cheek. Eleanor absently reached up and patted his arm, her eyes never leaving the puzzle.

"That's it," Jackson muttered as he turned and walked to his mother's kitchen. He picked up a dish towel, returned to the table, flicked it open and let it drift down over the puzzle.

Eleanor turned to her son. "That was uncalled for, Jackson," she sputtered. "Whatever do you think you are doing?"

"Getting your attention, Mother. Dinner will be on the table in ten minutes, just enough time for you to wash up." Neither woman looked up. "Have it your way. It'll be cold if you wait too long," he said as he turned and left the room.

Lily and Eleanor looked at each other and smiled as they stood moving slowly to work out the kinks from sitting and working on the puzzle. Side by side they left Eleanor's apartment for Jackson's dining room, the smells of steaks grilling drawing them forth.

SATURDAY LILY'S day was spent exercising, visiting with the women from her circle who stopped by and helping Eleanor work on the puzzle. Jackson fixed dinner. Settled in front of the fire, she, Eleanor, and Jackson interspersed conversation and silent contemplation.

At nine-thirty Eleanor said "good night." Jackson escorted her to her door, kissing her on the cheek, leaning against the door jamb as she made her way through her apartment to her bedroom and turned on the light. Lily remained nestled on the couch watching the coals shimmer gold, red, orange, and blue. She loved sitting in front of a fire and even though she had a fireplace at her own home, she seldom took the time for one. Another thing Jackson did for Eleanor and her. Dinner, fires, talking with us.

"I'm off to bed, Lily. Can I get you anything before I go up?"

Lily shook her head. "I'm fine. I won't be long and I'll make sure the fireplace doors are closed."

"Thanks."

Lily heard his steady steps on the stairs. For a moment she thought to call out to him to wait so she could climb the stairs with him, feel his arm around her waist, lean into his strength enveloped by his scent. She shook her head to dispel that image. No longer did she sense the magic of being in this house. She felt at home.

Stunned with this realization, Lily staggered to her feet, took the few steps to the fireplace, bent to make sure the doors were tightly closed. As she straightened, she noticed the great horned owl on the mantle turned toward the front door. She'd met Eleanor in early October. It was late February — almost five months. So much has happened. A tremor passed through her, a premonition — something was about to change.

At the stairs, she stopped and centered herself before starting up to her room. She could get herself ready for bed and even though she still had to wear the Immobilizers at night, because they didn't have to be so tight so she could wriggle her way in to them on her own.

Once ready for bed, she crossed to the window and searched the night sky for Grandmother Moon. Spying her rising just above the horizon, Lily watched as she rose higher into the darkness. A shadow dimmed Grandmother's brightness, distorting her features. Lily shivered at the sight. The sense of change was strong as she turned to the bed and climbed in. It took longer than usual before she found 'her spot' and was comfortable. As she drifted off to sleep, the shadows from the moon slid across her face.

26 - WHEN DEMONS COME

A scream of terror jolted Jackson awake; the hairs on the back of his neck on end. Lily. Grabbing his pants, he stumbled into them, cursed as he stubbed his toes and rammed his shoulder into his four poster bed.

At the door to Lily's room, he paused. The moonlight streamed in the window illuminating her tightly curled body, the immobilizers' crisscrossing her body. In three long strides he was by her bed, leaning over, touching her forehead as if taking her temperature. Shudders wracked her body, harsh breathing filled the silence. His sense of impotency heightened when the moan of despair escaped from her lips. The heart-rending sound of her scream was indelibly etched in his mind but this sound of anguish tore at his soul.

His heart beat so hard it was a wonder Lily didn't hear it. "Lily. It's me. Jackson. What's wrong Lily?"

"Oh Goddess, no. Please no," she whimpered, turning her face into her pillow.

"Lily?" Jackson spoke softly as he sat on the edge of the bed.

"The dream," Lily whispered. "The dream … Oh Goddess, please no, no more, please," she choked out the words.

He reached out touching her shoulder to comfort, felt her body startle and recoil from his touch. What the hell was wrong? He reached out again. "Lily. It's me. Jackson." Confused at her response, needing to see what was wrong; he reached over and turned on the bedside lamp. With its stronger light he could see her eyes — open but still caught in the terror of her dream.

With his stomach in revolt, his throat dry and his shoulders tense, he fought for control so his voice would sound calm. "Lily, it's me. Jackson." He spoke a little louder, "I'm sitting on the bed and I'm going to touch you. Lily, I'm putting my hand on your shoulder. Can you feel my hand? Wake up, Lily. It's me, Jackson," he soothed as he gently shook her shoulder and tenderly brushed hair back from her face.

"Where?" Lily's eyes flashed around the room, panic twisting her features.

"Lily, it's me, Jackson. Jackson Montgomery. You know me, Lily." He continued talking in a quiet, calm tone, tamping down his concern, instinctively knowing he had to appear in control for her.

"Jackson? Oh Jackson, it's you. Please," Lily's voice trembled as she leaned toward him. "Please," she whispered as her shivers grew more violent.

"I'm here Lily. I'm not leaving you." He kept his tone composed as he gathered her in his arms shifting on the bed so he held her as one would a child. Her head nestled in the curve of his shoulder; he rocked and pressed soft kisses in her hair, on her forehead. And as he stroked her back with his free hand, he whispered the litany, "You're safe. I'm here. I'll take care of you."

Lily burrowed against his broad chest finding comfort in his arms. Even after the trembling stopped, she remained in his arms, still and quiet, grateful for the sense of peace and safety, grateful for the sanctuary, grateful for a safe haven from the terror of her dream.

"Thank you," she said, her voice a mere whisper, starting to move away. "I'm better now, Jackson. You don't have to hold me anymore."

"I know," he whispered, not letting go at all.

Lily sighed and settled back against his chest, the beat of his heart, like the sound of a drum, brought comfort and ease to her troubled mind.

"Tell me about the dream. I want to understand."

While the grandfather clock at the foot of the stairs chimed three, Lily began to talk about her life protecting children who were bruised, burned and battered; how she worked to keep them safe; and how Paul left her, not understanding or maybe not even caring about these children. And, she told him about the death threats years later.

"In the nightmare, I'm not there and the mother stabs the children. They're lying in pools of their blood, the oldest girl holding the baby, trying to shield him with her own child's body. I can't save them because I'm not there. I'm home fixing Paul's dinner, like a good wife. The children die because I'm not there," she said without inflection. She shifted in an attempt to move away but when his arms held fast, she relented and settled back.

"It didn't happen that way in real life. None of the children on my case load died. I always got to them in time." She turned and looked at him the determination to finish the story clear in her eyes. "But my marriage died. I never could make Paul understand. I couldn't leave the children. I just couldn't leave the children." Her eyes glistened with unshed tears. "And then, I had to leave. They were everywhere: the predators, the abusers. I saw evil better than I saw good. It was then I knew I needed to get out or my soul would die and I'd be lost."

Jackson listened to Lily's monotone recitation of her life as a child protective service worker and tried to comprehend the job she'd done and the price she'd paid. As she talked about her work, all he saw was the danger she'd put herself in to protect the children. Anger, frustration, protectiveness and tenderness rumbled within him as he held her. Every word she spoke solidified his decision to win this soft, gentle, kind, passionate woman. He shook his head in amazement as feelings he'd never felt for any one woman claimed him.

"Asshole," he muttered to himself.

"What'd you say?"

"Paul was an asshole. A colossal jerk."

"No, he wanted a wife and mother, not a career woman."

"No," Jackson countered. "He wanted a convenience, not a wife and a mother."

"A convenience?"

"Someone who was what he wanted when he wanted and how he wanted. A convenience," he finished gruffly.

"Oh," Lily said softly. "Not entirely. He liked the added income."

"Like I said, he was an asshole, a colossal jerk"

"Jackson?" her voice drowsy, her body relaxed, she fought against the hovering sleep. "One more…" her voice trailed off.

"Yeah?" He held her, rubbed her back, stroked his fingers through her hair the rhythms mimicking what he'd done in the hospital.

"Thank you." Her eyes closed and her breathing deepened.

"Go to sleep, Lily." He pressed soft kisses in her hair, breathing lavender and the subtle something else that was uniquely her.

"Jackson?" She roused herself, struggling to say something more.

"Yeah?"

"I.…." her voice faded.

"Go to sleep, Lily. You're tired and need your rest. I'm here. We can talk more in the morning."

THE BRIGHT WINTER sun streaming through the window created a halo of light behind Lily's eyes. A thumping in her ear, the rough texture of hair on her cheek, the smell of citrus and soap, strong arms holding her. She was under the covers in Jackson's embrace.

"Good morning, Lily," his voice rumbled in his chest beneath her ear. He'd been watching her sleep for some time, her face relaxed, her body pressed against his. A slight smile on his face, he pressed a light kiss on the top of her head. She wants to bolt. He kept her enfolded in his arms.

"Good morning, Jackson." Lily's voice matched her stiffening body as she tried to pull away.

Jackson, not ready to let her go, held her lightly against his chest and simultaneously distracted her by asking, "Do you feel different?"

"What do you mean? Do I feel different?" Lily squirmed to look up at him. She saw his face, altered with the stubble of a night's growth of beard, his eyes alight with amusement.

"Well, we've spent the night in bed together. I thought maybe you'd feel different," he said in a gravelly voice.

"We didn't really do anything but sleep." Her eyes searched his to confirm this statement. "Do you feel different?"

"Yeah, I do," his voice deepened. "Yeah I do," he shifted caging her with one arm while raising himself to rest on the other's elbow.

As he moved, Lily tried to wriggle further away. Her effort failed. She stilled. The hard length of his body pressed against her was both comforting and confining. "How do you feel different?" she asked.

Jackson saw the puzzlement, the questions in her eyes, felt her softness nestled against him. His answer to her question? A kiss. A thorough and complete kiss. He pulled the Velcro strap on the immobilizer, loosening it.

"Ohhh, Jackson," Lily sighed as she kissed him back. "We can't do this." She released the Velcro straps and gingerly moved her arms free of the constraints.

"Okay, we won't do anything more than lie here and talk." He ran his hands over her now bare arms. Her body was responding but her mind was resisting. When they were lovers he wanted all of her, mind and body. "How's that for a deal?"

"You won't kiss me again?" Lily heard the thread of disappointment in her voice.

"Not unless you want me to." Jackson tried for a more business-like tone. But mere moments later, his voice rough with checked passion, he added, "Then I'd be glad to oblige."

"You're a bit scratchy-faced this morning. If you kiss me like that again, everyone who sees me will know. I'll have a red face." Lily was astounded that she now sounded grumpy.

"That's easily handled." Jackson grinned. "Don't see anyone today except me. I won't mind at all if you have a red face."

"Jackson." A look of horror spread over her face. "We can't spend the day in bed together."

"Why not? We spent most of the night in bed together. What difference does it make?" His grin widened as he teased, "Or are you one of those women who only takes a lover in the dark?"

"We are not lovers. I'd know if we'd done anything like that last night. I know I'd know," she said indignation ripe in her voice, temper flashing in her eyes.

"You'd not only know, you'd remember," he bantered. "I'll make sure you remember every kiss, every place I touch you with my hands and mouth. When we're lovers, I promise that you'll remember every minute, every detail."

"We won't be lovers, Jackson," she said through clenched jaws.

"Yes, we will Lily. Yes, we will," he said kissing her on the top of her head again. "Tonight I'll be sure to shave before I come and say "goodnight." No scratchy beard then."

"Jackson, there's no need to shave because we aren't going to be lovers tonight." She saw no humor in his teasing. At least she thought he was teasing, and then she moved to look him in the eyes and saw he was not.

"Okay, I'll go shave now," he offered.

Lily shifted in his arms. "Jackson, listen to me. Listen to me carefully." Her expression deadly serious, she enunciated, "We. Can't. Be. Lovers."

"Why can't we?"

"We just can't," she fretted as she realized how serious he truly was.

"I know you have a reason. If you're so sure we're not going to be lovers, at least tell me why," he countered.

"I can't, Jackson. I'm just not able to tell you."

An idea crept into his mind. While there was much he didn't know about Lily, he did know there was always a reason, an explanation for everything she did. If she wouldn't tell him and considering the subject matter, he figured she'd resist, he might as well forge ahead.

Instinctively he knew this was the time to get out in the open the reason for her reluctance. If not now, he didn't know when another opportunity would present itself. She may be determined to shut him out, but he was even more determined to work his way through her defenses. Whenever they touched, kissed, or were in close proximity to each other, sparks arced and smoldered. He was selfish enough to want to see the fire, the flames of passion leaping between them but he'd go slow because he didn't want to harm their fragile friendship.

Jackson strove for calm and in a neutral voice asked, "How many lovers have you had since you and Paul divorced?"

"It doesn't matter." She snapped the words out.

"It does to me," he said in a mild tone adding, "More or less than ten?"

"More or less what?" Lily tried to wriggle away but his hold firmed.

"More or less lovers than ten?" he asked in a gentle voice.

Exasperation suffused her tone, "Less than ten. Are you satisfied?"

"I'll be satisfied when I know why you think we're not going to be lovers."

"Because I can't," Lily whispered, hiding her face in the curve of his shoulder.

"You can't make love with me? Did I hear you right?" It was his turn to sound incredulous.

"I've not been with anyone for a long time," her voice was muffled against his chest. "I don't want to be with anyone in that way again."

Jackson tilted her chin so he could look at her face. Misery, shame, guilt were etched in her features. She averted her gaze, not looking him in the eye.

"It's hard to be so vulnerable, Jackson. You already know I'm not good at being vulnerable and being lovers with someone is being very vulnerable." Her misery echoed in her words. "And," she caught him off guard and ducked her head, "I'm not sure I'd be very satisfying for you anyway."

"And you learned this from whom?"

"By the end of our marriage from Paul, and then there were two others who said I was frigid. When I tried to show them I wasn't, I couldn't really, I didn't..." she stammered the words out and then just stopped as the tears began to flow. "I'm sorry, Jackson. There's only been one man I was really responsive with and he slept around. I'm just not good at relationships with men. So, I just can't, that's all."

Jackson heard not only her words but her pain. His jaw clenched and he inwardly cursed his sex for cheating on her, playing the 'cold, frigid game,' and blaming her for it all. Rocking her in his arms, he said nothing as he battled his anger back. He held her close, absorbed her tears, let his body relax. By the time her tears abated; when she lay quiet and still in his arms he had a plan.

"I have a proposition for you."

She started to struggle.

"Now hear me out before you object, okay?" He was relieved when she settled back in his arms. "This is the deal. I'm going to kiss you and as soon as you are no longer responding, I'll stop."

"I don't understand." She looked confused.

"I'll kiss you and you'll kiss me back. If we both enjoy that, we'll see where that leads. You're in total control. Just stop responding when you don't want to go further." He pulled the immobilizers out from around her.

"I don't know," Lily said hesitantly. "I don't think this is a good idea."

"I think it's an excellent one." He grinned. "Of course, it is my idea." He waggled his eyebrows and looked in her eyes. A serious look on his face and in a serious voice he said, "If it isn't a good idea, there's only one way to find out. Try it and see what happens. Okay?" He bent down and placed a light kiss on her mouth. "Oh Lord, Lily, can't you feel it? The heat flowing between us? Kiss me back, Lily." His voice grew hoarse with desire as he once again claimed her mouth with his.

Jackson cautioned his racing heart. *Go slow or lose it all.* His body hardened, his breathing stuttered, his heart pounded when Lily's hands grabbed and held him close. She pressed against him, relaxed into him. *She's mine.* His hands began a slow journey to learn her body's secrets: where she was sensitive to his touch, what aroused her, what made her arch into him seeking her release...with him. He kissed her neck and noted her shift to give him better access to where her neck and shoulder joined. His hand cupped her breast, his fingers teased her nipple and she pressed against his hand. He shifted, his body tangling with hers. His own arousal evident as his turgid flesh pressed into her thigh. *Cold? Frigid? I don't think so.* Then all thought stopped as he gave himself up to the glory of loving.

27 - TO LOVE OR NOT TO LOVE

Jackson's heartbeat slowed, his breathing calmed. He wasn't an inexperienced man and he'd been emotionally involved with women before but this time? His release with Lily was far more than physical. Intellectually he'd known she was different, known he wanted her in his life. Now, in the aftermath of love-making, he was convinced it was more than want - he needed her.

Sexually sated, still careful of her body, he cradled Lily in his arms and thought about his next move, what he needed to do to convince her to remain here with him. He wasn't so naïve as to think she had capitulated and surrendered to him based on the past few hours. In fact, he was fairly certain the opposite was true. In for a penny, in for a pound was now his motto - make that English pound sterling.

He nuzzled her neck reveling in the feel of her relaxed in his arms. When she moved as if pulling away, he was disappointed but not surprised. An edge of panic infiltrated his thoughts as he continued to sift, sort, and discard options, searching for the perfect strategy to keep her with him.

Lily struggled past the lulling effects of an orgasm still rippling through her body, struggled past the desperation welling in her heart, struggled past the satiating fog in her mind. She tried to put some space between them but when his strong arms didn't budge, she quieted.

"Lily, we," Jackson started, his voice gentle, one hand stroking her back, the other relaxing its hold.

"There is no *we*," Lily interrupted her voice certain. "There is definitely no *we*."

"I know you felt something just now – with me. Deny it with your voice but you can't deny it with your body." Hell, he sounded arrogant to his own ears. "Look, Lily, that didn't come out the way I meant it. What I want you to know is that," he heaved a deep sigh. "The truth is I've never felt like this before."

"Please don't lie to me," she ground out. "You've had plenty of women in your life. Now let me go." She pushed against him.

He eased his grasp but didn't totally release her afraid she'd bolt and be gone for good. "Listen. I'm telling you the truth. I admit I've not lived a celibate life but I can tell you, I felt something very different just now with you. Please, Lily, give us a chance," he said, a note of pleading in his voice.

"Aren't you listening? There is no we, Jackson. There is no us. This was a mistake, a big, huge, gigantic mistake." She shook her head emphasizing her point and squirmed to put more distance between them. Conflict swirled in her stomach. How could she feel so safe, so protected in his arms and yet feel such turmoil? What if this was a mistake? What if she was wrong about him? What if he was just like Paul? like Randy?

"It wasn't a mistake," he countered. "We fit together, you and me. I'm not Paul or that other guy who cheated on you." He knew he was grasping at straws, using his powers of persuasion to keep her, hoping his words resonated with her heart. For a moment when fear won out, he blurted, "I haven't been with another woman since I stopped by your house."

"Wha? What do you mean? What about Susannah? At Thanksgiving?" She tilted her head to look at his face, stunned to see the truth in his eyes.

"I had dinner with her. The three 'D's: dinner, drinks and discussion. No sex. I told her when I took her home I wouldn't be calling again and I didn't. Other than when she crashed the party on New Year's Eve I haven't seen or talked to her. Seeing you and her together…well, there just wasn't… ." He stopped and exhaled his frustration. "Hell, I don't even know what I'm saying right now."

Stormy gray eyes locked with dark blue ones. He forced himself to relax, to ease the tension in his body and his tone this last interchanged evoked. Another sigh escaped as he dipped his head, resting his forehead against hers. "I only know you can't leave. I know we have something here … something special."

"I'm not your type, Jackson," Lily said in a practical voice.

"No, you're not and I'm not your type either. Have you thought maybe that's what's so special? That we fit together in a different, unique way? You know I care about you, trust and respect you. You commit yourself every day to living your beliefs. I may not know them all, but I do know you respect and honor all forms of life and live by the motto "And harm to none." Please give this a chance, Lily. Give us a chance," he urged afraid he was babbling in a desperate need to have her understand what she meant to him.

With his arms now loose around her, Jackson looked deeply into Lily's dark blue eyes searching for some sign she felt the same way. He wanted to steal a glimpse into her heart, into her very soul. Underneath the cool regard she leveled in return he sensed panic, under control, but there nonetheless. That wasn't a good sign. *Please believe me. Please believe in 'us'* he chanted to himself to ward off his own desperation.

Every ounce of self-control was brought to bear as he watched the range of emotions fly across her face. A cross, stubborn look came last and he didn't know whether to be relieved or worried. At least the terror had passed and he thought that a good sign.

Jackson's gray eyes, dark with boiling emotions, held his truth.

Lily, faced with his reality, panicked. He believes in 'us' in a 'we'. *Oh Goddess, what have I done?*

"I told you, Jackson. I'm not very good at male/female relationships. I've never been very good at them," she grumbled.

"I'm forty years old and other than being married for a year or so in my early twenties, I've never stayed with a woman longer than a few weeks or so — you know like going on a vacation together. I don't know that anyone who knew my track record would say I'm very good at relationships either." Earnestness infused his voice, "I do know I've never felt with anyone else what I feel for and with you." He held her gaze, instinctively knowing he was fighting for a life, a future with her.

"I don't think I can be what you want. I need to be myself, my independent self. I think you want more." Lily's mind searched for more arguments fighting the impulse to rest in his arms.

"Right now, all I want is you. Just as you are. I want to come home and tell you about my day and hear about yours. I want to walk up the stairs at night with my arm around you. I want to wake up in the morning and make love with you." Even though her expression remained neutral, he sensed her withdrawal and stopped. His voice almost a whisper he said, "If you could structure our re...scratch that...If you could, I don't know exactly how to say this, but if you could structure our time together, what would you be okay with? Having dinner, watching television with Mother, talking? And, just to keep things out in the open, I really hope sharing the same bed is on your list."

"I don't know, Jackson. I've spent a lot of time making sure I didn't see us together doing anything. It's hard to change that," Lily muttered and glared.

"Ahh, so you have thought of me, of there being an *us*?" Jackson's voice held a touch of satisfaction.

"No!" exploded from her lips as panic slammed through her. She fought for calm before she continued in her normal, logical voice. "Not an *us*...just being with you, doing something together."

"Like what?"

"Like…oh, Jackson, just leave it be. This is foolish, ridiculous," she tried to pull away again, gave up again and settled back against his body.

"Really? Why is it foolish and ridiculous to want to know what you've thought about me in the past?" Jackson teased.

Lily paused before answering. She knew he wanted to hear her opinion of him. "You are domineering, arrogant, overbearing!" She watched him listen to her, his face remaining passive. But that isn't all of who he is. "And, you can also be caring, generous, funny, compassionate and creative," she murmured, "but usually in an arrogant, bossy way," she huffed.

"How about loving? Can I be loving, Lily?" Jackson pressed soft kisses on her hair, forehead and cheek.

"You have, on one very recent notable occasion, been very loving." Lily looked up at him, her voice a whisper. "I'm so scared, Jackson. So very, very scared."

"So am I," his voice was soft; a note of tenderness ran deep. "But I'm willing to risk the possibility of pain for the glory of loving you now and for as long as I can." The breath from Jackson's last words fell softly on her face as he closed his eyes and lowered his lips to hers in a gentle kiss. His hands moved slowly to her breasts where he cupped their fullness. He rolled her nipples between his fingers. One hand played with her soft, full breast while the other drew lazy circles down her abdomen. Her muscles quivered under his touch. Continuing his exploration, his hand stroked down one leg and up the other. He stopped playing with her breast to pull her closer. His own arousal surged. She was responding, kissing him back, running her hands down his back and then up to tangle with the ends of hair curling at his nape. Slowly, he reminded himself, he needed to go slowly for both of their sakes.

"Jackson," Lily gasped as his mouth nibbled around her breast. He worried her nipple with his tongue. "Oh Jackson…I don't know…we can't." How did she refuse him when her body ignored her mind? She arched into him, desire coursing through her. Her conflicted mind gave voice in a throaty whisper, "I don't know what to do."

"Just let me love you," he said one hand still playing with her breasts the other tangled in the curls at the apex of her legs. "That's all you have to do for now. Just let me love you."

She gave herself up to the torrent of feelings rushing through her: on fire one second, floating in a sensual haze the next.

"Jackson?"

"Hmm?" He didn't stop kissing a particularly sensitive place on the side of her breast, smiling to himself as she shifted and pressed closer.

"Jackson, don't stop. I don't want you to stop now," Lily gasped, her body aching and burning from his kisses and touch.

"I won't," he promised.

And he didn't. Not until they had collapsed in a tangle of limbs, sated to the bone lying limp almost lifeless in each other's arms.

"I don't know what happens to me when you kiss me like that," Lily whispered, a touch of embarrassment in her voice.

"Well, I like what happens to you when I kiss you like that," Jackson's contented voice caressed her ear. He grinned. "I like it very much."

"I sort of melt and my mind stops working. I can't think, Jackson. It scares me when I can't think. It's like I've lost control. I don't feel safe when I lose control." Lily's voice held a note of vexation.

"Hmmm, you don't feel vulnerable being naked in bed with me? You only feel vulnerable when I kiss you?" he said in an amused voice.

"I know it sounds strange."

"Well, next time, we'll just have to see what happens if I don't kiss you 'that way'. Of course, you'll probably have to kiss me instead but maybe that will work better for you," he mused.

"You're making fun of me!" Lily said struggling to sit up and move away from him.

"Not really, Lily, not making fun of you, teasing perhaps but not making fun." Jackson pulled her back to cuddle against him. "I get carried away myself when I kiss you."

"You sort of lose it too?"

"Yeah, I more than sort of lose it. I'm way off somewhere, lost myself, but sure enjoying the journey," he said with a chuckle.

"That sounds like something I'd say Jackson."

"You must be rubbing off on me. I've always believed in setting goals and enjoying the process of reaching them. That's another way of talking about the journey and the destination. What is that saying?"

"Life is a journey, not a destination."

"Maybe that can be our motto. We'll enjoy the journey and not worry, at least for now, about the destination. Maybe I can work on that arrogant, overbearing and whatever it is."

"Domineering is the other word, Jackson. Domineering as in deciding what we will do instead of discussing it and both of us coming to a decision."

"Okay, what do you want?" Jackson asked softly. "I'm listening."

"I don't know. Well, that's not entirely true. What I do know is I don't want to make a mistake with you. The price is just too big for me to pay. I'd lose too much. Eleanor is important to me and, in spite of everything, you've become a friend. I'm excited about being able to teach people about House Totems."

Jackson listened to Lily's rational talk. He knew there were risks, but he was willing to take them. Was she not? He felt the raw edge of fear deep in his gut. "I'm a bit scared too, Lily. Well, actually, I'm terrified right now. Terrified you'll leave me, terrified I'll lose you. I don't think we can sort things out between us if we're both scared. I've been told I'm more overbearing when I'm afraid I'll lose," he confessed, a wry smile on his face.

"I agree we aren't in the best place to make any real decisions." Lily gazed into Jackson's dark gray eyes. "Perhaps we can let it go for now and talk about all of this at another time?" she asked tentatively.

"Okay, I'll go along with that as long as we talk about it later today. I want you in my bed tonight, Lily. I want to wake up with you beside me in the morning."

"After dinner, then?" Lily quivered as nerves and emotions tripped up and down her spine. "Jackson, please don't be angry with me. Please don't take this personally. It's more about me than you, honest."

"I'm not angry," Jackson said as he sat up and swung his legs over the side of the bed. "I'm anxious, nervous, frustrated, but not angry. And underneath it all, I'm scared. I'm trying to be honest here, Lily, not overbearing. I don't know that it's more about you than me, and I don't know that it isn't personal. But, if we can talk tonight, I'll deal with it."

"I'm sorry, Jackson," Lily whispered. "I'm so sorry."

"For what?" Jackson asked in frustration. "For having feelings? For being scared? For not wanting to be hurt? Dammit, Lily! I don't need nor do I want someone who tries to appease me, to please me. I may not like everything you're saying, but," his voice softened as he reached out, took her chin in his hand and lifted her face to his, "I can deal with my own feelings and I'd rather you be honest with me, have your doubts, take your time, than have you change into someone you're not in order to make me feel better, okay?"

"Okay."

He kissed her, slow and tender, before he stood, turned back and bent to kiss her again. He straightened, grabbed his trousers from the bedside chair and strode out the door.

"Okay, Jackson," she whispered to herself. "We'll see what happens. I'm not sure you meant what you said, but I did like hearing it." Her hand brushed her kiss-swollen lips. "I liked it too much, I think. I could get used to having someone like you in my life and that frightens me into a mindless mass of nerves. I don't know how I'd survive then when you left."

Getting out of bed, she crossed the room to the dresser and her cell phone. It was time to check in with someone wiser than her in the ways of the world. She dialed Sophia's number.

At the sound of her friend's welcoming voice, Lily felt the tension ease. "Sophia," her voice reflected the comfort of her friend's voice. "Do you have time to spend with a friend who needs someone to talk with?"

"Of course," came the lively reply.

"Great! I'm going to call Diana to see if she's available," Lily said.

"She and I had already planned to stop by and see you today. So plan on both of us being there, say around three o'clock, okay?"

"Perfect. See you both at three." Lily felt much better when she hung up the phone. Having someone as a sounding board helped her figure out the answer. She paused and thought about her schedule. Shower next. A soft secret smile graced her lips. *I think I got enough exercise this morning.*

28 - THE BEST LAID PLANS

Because she was sore from her earlier activities with Jackson, Lily wore the immobilizers. They supported her arms and shoulders and eased her discomfort. While she waited for Diana and Sophia, she cautiously made her way down the stairs to visit with Eleanor. Knocking, she smiled and opened the door when she heard Eleanor's *"Entrez-vous, s'il vous plait."*

Eleanor was sitting on the couch, a photo album in her lap, the incomplete puzzle on the table in front of the window. "Come in Lily and see what I have," she invited.

"It looks like a photo album," Lily said as she settled on the couch. "Your family?"

"Actually, it is an album I put together of Jackson's childhood. I've already completed the ones for my daughters. I start them with pictures of Archie and me as children." She turned the pages back to the beginning. "Here is our wedding picture."

"You were a beautiful bride, Eleanor and Archie a handsome groom." Lily saw the glow of love emanating from the old photograph.

"My wedding day was one of the happiest days of my life and also one of the scariest." Eleanor traced Archie's features on the picture.

"It sounds as if there's a story in that statement," Lily encouraged.

"Oh yes, quite a grand story. I loved him with all my heart. You may think it strange or maybe that I'm touched, but he is still with me. There are times I hear his voice. 'Ellie' he says before telling me something to help me find my way. When I fell, he was with me."

"I don't think that's strange at all," Lily reassured. "You aren't the only one who's experienced that. But, I do believe there is more to this grand story."

"Oh yes," Eleanor said as she turned the page. "Here we are on our honeymoon."

Lily saw a picture of Eleanor and Archie standing at the rail of a large steamship. "Your honeymoon was spent crossing the Atlantic?"

"Yes. It was a lovely trip. Archie and I had hours each day to ourselves. I was so enthralled with my new husband, being on a ship crossing the Atlantic the reality of leaving my family, friends, all I'd ever known was tempered."

Eleanor turned another page. "Here we are in front of Archie's family's house. We lived with them for one year while we saved to buy our own home. Archie was always good with his hands, with building things. He knew he wanted to be in construction. He told me if I would help him, he thought he could build a business." She pointed to other pictures on the page. "I worked as a clerk in a department store on weekends and took an accounting class at night so I could take care of the books. During the day, while Archie worked, I helped my in-laws by taking care of the house. They owned a neighborhood grocery store and both worked there."

"You got along well with them, it seems," Lily said, noting a picture of Eleanor and Archie with an older couple.

"Not really," Eleanor confided. "They had their hearts set on him marrying a girl from the neighborhood. Archie had written them he wanted to marry me but they didn't expect him to do so before he came home. Indeed, it was quite a shock to them when we arrived on their doorstep...together." Eleanor paused and looked with unseeing eyes out the window. "He never considered they would not accept me. They never did, you know. Not really. They managed to be polite toward me but that year was very awkward. If not for Archie's love and the promise of our own home, I don't think I would have survived."

"And your love for him? That must have helped." Lily offered.

"Oh yes, my love for Archie and knowing it was returned in full—that is what got us through that first year. Archie was always the optimist; always saw the good in everyone and everything. I'm not sure he even saw the strain between his parents and me." Eleanor pointed to another picture. "Our first house. You can see I'm with child. Evelynn."

Two pages later, the object of this album was introduced: Jackson as a baby: curly dark hair, chubby cheeks, a big toothless grin. Lily was totally engaged in seeing the pictures of Jackson as an infant, as a toddler, as a little boy, in school, growing up before her eyes. Pictures of him with his father on various work sites when he was a teenager foretold the man he'd become. At some point the pictures changed from black and white to color and she could see the rich sable brown of his hair, the gray of his eyes, the tan of his skin. Eleanor told her stories, vignettes of Jackson's life, as she turned the pages of the album.

"I do hope Jackson mentioned he'd been married before." Eleanor said in a neutral voice. She half-turned and studied her friend, a frown between her eyes.

"Yes, he's mentioned it," Lily replied inordinately thankful he had, if only this morning. In some ways she was grateful he was divorced. It made more sense now that he wasn't married – actually hadn't remarried. Pamela leaving him because he wasn't willing to settle for less than he dreamed of must have been devastating.

Eleanor turned the page.

Jackson in a tuxedo next to a woman in a wedding dress filled the page. She was almost as tall as he, with dark hair and eyes, a trim figure. Lily thought they looked formal, serious. The love so evident in Eleanor and Archie's wedding picture was missing. "She's really quite beautiful," Lily said to fill the silence.

"She was," Eleanor acknowledged. "However, she wanted more than Jackson could give her at the time. If she'd waited, helped him build his business, she'd be happy with his success. But as brilliant as I think my son is, it did take time for him to build his reputation. She wasn't willing to wait, found an older rich man and walked out on Jackson. He wasn't enough for her as he was."

Lily's personal knowledge of being dismissed as not good enough cramped her stomach. It was shattering to be shoved aside. If you rose above it, others often saw you as cool or cold or even arrogant. Is that what happened to Jackson?

There were a few more pages in the album. Photos of Jackson with his sisters, niece, nephews and Eleanor at various family gatherings followed his maturation as a man. Lily noted the last picture was of Jackson, his arm around Eleanor, in front of this house. He looked content if not happy.

"What does Jackson think of this album?" Lily's curiosity got the better of her.

"Oh, he has not seen it yet," Eleanor said and smiled secretively. "I've a few more pages to fill before it is done." She closed the album and placed it on the table. "What are your plans for the afternoon?"

"Sophia and Diana are stopping by to visit." The words were barely spoken when the door chimes rang.

"I'll get it, Eleanor," Lily said looking at the clock. "I'm sure it's them now." She stood and walked to Eleanor's front door. Slipping one hand from the immobilizer, she opened it, looked out at Jackson's front door and called, "I'm in here with Eleanor."

"Go ahead and visit with your friends, Lily." Eleanor said as she smiled and looked up from the couch. "Good afternoon Sophia and Diana. It's good to see you again."

Both women took off their coats, scarves, tucking gloves into pockets as they exchanged greetings. "It's good to see you again, Eleanor." Diana draped her coat over her arm. "My, it's brisk out there!"

"You're looking good, Eleanor," Sophia commented as she followed suit.

"I am feeling wonderful," Eleanor replied standing to accept their hugs of greeting.

"We're going to have herbal tea. Would you like a cup?" Lily asked Eleanor as she and her friends walked toward the French doors into the main house.

"That would be lovely, dear." Eleanor sat back down on the couch, picked up the album and started looking through it again.

~

Sophia, Diana, and Lily were settled around the fire in the living room, chamomile-peach tea and cookies on their laps. Lily had loosened the immobilizers so her hands and arms were free. Looking through the glass doors into Eleanor's apartment, she saw her friend still on the couch, appearing to gaze out her window, her cup of tea and cookies apparently forgotten.

"Thank you so much for bringing these delicious cookies, Soph. Your peanut butter chocolate chip cookies are sooo sinful!" Lily moaned as she savored one of the moist chewy treats.

"I thought you could use something sinful if you're having problems," Sophia said, her brown eyes searched her friend's face as she reached over to gently touch Lily's arm.

"So," Diana tucked her hair behind her ears and leaned forward, "what's going on?"

"Right to the point as always, D." Lily's face reflected a rueful smile.

"Just let us know if you've changed your mind about talking something out and we'll enjoy the tea and cookies," Diana added in a practical tone of voice. "If you haven't changed your mind, then tell us what's going on."

Lily sighed. "I'm on a very slippery slope and am afraid I'll tumble into a deep, dark abyss." She sat staring into the bottom of her tea cup as if the answer to all her problems could be found if she just looked hard enough.

"You and Jackson?" Sophia glanced over at Diana.

"Sort of," Lily blushed. "Oh Goddess! I hate this stumbling about with words." She took a deep breath; her words tumbled out, "Jackson wants me to stay here. I know I need to leave and go home."

"Why?" chorused Sophia and Diana.

"Because I'm afraid to be hurt and of hurting him," Lily said softly.

"Are you letting the ghost of Paul, of other men in your past into this, Lily?" Sophia reached out to lay her hand on Lily's arm.

Lily just stared at her hands folded around her tea cup, holding it as if it were a life line.

"What does Jackson do or say that looks or sounds like Paul?" Diana asked her tone soft and soothing.

The three women sat in silence. The clock chimed the half hour. The sound seemed to bring Lily out of her trance. "I guess I am letting Paul's ghost, the fear of the awful pain in that marriage, frighten me," Lily whispered.

"Are you saying there's nothing about Jackson that reminds you of Paul then?" The question came from Diana whose voice was still soft but the question took the soothing out of it.

"No, there're things that remind me of Paul - the arrogance, the testosterone swagger, the over-bearing, steamroller–run-right-over-you attitude - but they also remind me of other men I know. The 'I know better than you what you need' male domineering attitude that I see in Jackson, I saw it in Paul and in some form or another in lots of men. Even Mark Parker gets into that place at times."

"I know it's been a long time since you've done more than casual dating, but from my observation, you and Jackson seem to have a connection. A sizzle between you," Sophia commented quietly, her hand still resting on Lily's arm.

"Fire burns, Soph. I don't want to get burned and I don't want to burn anyone either," her voice shook with emotions, her hands still clutched the cup, her insides were in revolt with her stomach the general.

"You know, Lily, Jonathan and I were very happy in our marriage," Sophia spoke softly, a slight smile of reminiscence on her face. "I feel very blessed to have had him in my life. But, do you really think we didn't have problems? That every day was bliss?"

"No, I don't think that. But, you were never really unhappy, were you?"

"Yes, Lily. I was," Sophia's voice was quiet but her tone was firm. "Early on in our marriage I found myself thinking of leaving him. He seemed so possessive. He never wanted to do anything without me. Remember, we taught at the same school. We were together from morning to night. I began to feel smothered, like I was losing something important. Losing me."

"What did you do?" Lily asked, her eyes never straying from the cup in her hands.

"I had decisions to make," Sophia continued. "The first one? Decide what I wanted in my marriage to Jonathan. Second? Talk to him. I really hadn't up to then. Not a real heart-to-heart honest talk. It wasn't easy. As soon as he realized I was thinking about leaving, he panicked and became even more possessive."

"We all tend to do that, don't we." Diana's comment hung in the air. "Our fears tend to bring more of what we fear into our lives. We know that you and Jonathan worked it out, Soph. What did you do?"

"Kept breathing. Kept focused on how much I loved him. Kept talking. Jonathan and I both learned many things during those months that made our marriage something we both trusted and treasured." Sophia gave Lily's arm a slight squeeze. "That was the gift of not giving in to doubt or retaliation but staying focused on love when things got tough."

"Trusting someone is hard to do when trust has been broken."

"That's true. But the challenge is to keep in trust with someone in our present even when things happen that remind us of someone who broke our trust in the past."

Lily took a deep breath and looked at her friends with eyes full of emotion. Her smile wavered.

"Wise words, Soph, but not easy words."

"No, Lily, they're not easy words. Fear is Trust's greatest enemy. Love is Trust's greatest friend."

"But I don't love Jackson," Lily protested. "How can I focus on love when I don't love him?"

"You do love Jackson, Lily. Perhaps not in a romantic way," Diana's eyebrow raised slightly as she observed the blush spread across Lily's face. "But as you love all life, all people, Jackson is included."

"Do you think I'll ever heal from my time with Paul?" Lily's voice quavered. "I keep thinking I'm over something and then realize I'm not."

"You're more over him now than you were fourteen or even ten years ago," Sophia pointed out.

"Yes, I guess I am when you say it that way. This is probably one of those life lessons spiraling around again." She set her cup of tea on the coffee table and gazed into the fire.

"I think you're right." Diana leaned over and put her arm around her friend. Looking at her profile she went on, "Things got pretty bad between you and Paul by the end. He hit you, he cheated on you, he humiliated and demeaned you. And while all of that was bad, the worst thing he did was destroy your confidence in yourself when it comes to men. And Randy didn't help either when he cheated on you."

"I know," Lily whispered. "I don't trust myself when it comes to men. I don't trust I can keep myself safe in a relationship with them."

"That is a truth from your relationship with Paul. In order to complete the healing, that is the piece that needs to heal."

"I know you're right, D. I know you're right and it scares me to death," Lily whispered taking Diana's hand and holding it tight.

"Do you need or want to talk about this anymore, Lily? We certainly can if that would be helpful. I just want to check in with you so we don't overwhelm you with kindness here." Sophia took Lily's other hand in hers and held it firmly.

"No, I don't want to talk about this anymore. I need to think. You've both given me lots to think about," Lily's smile belied the somber tone of her voice.

"Did you hear Elizabeth's news?" Diana, her violet eyes twinkling, changed the subject.

"I'm not sure."

"She's flying into Shannon instead of Dublin and starting out in the West counties. She's renting a car and driving herself. Our Elizabeth is going to have a wonderful adventure!"

Conversation turned to other matters as tea was sipped and cookies devoured. The next hour passed quickly and soon Diana and Sophia were leaving with hugs and promises to be there if she still needed to talk.

After saying goodbye to them, Lily walked slowly up the stairs to her room. When did she start thinking of this room as hers? Sitting in the chair by the bed, her mind grappled with questions. She needed to sort this through. She owed it to Jackson to talk to him.

"I'm home," Jackson called out, coming in the door from the garage. "I've brought dinner."

"What did you bring for dinner?" Eleanor asked coming through the doors from her apartment.

"Chinese, all our favorites: sweet and sour pork, fried shrimp, orange chicken, mandarin beef, house special lo mein." After setting the bags of take-out on the kitchen counter, he strode over to the bottom of the stairs. "Lily, I'm home with Chinese. Come and get it!"

"I'll be right down."

Jackson set things up buffet-style on the kitchen island. The aroma of Chinese food greeted Lily as she came into the kitchen. She battled nerves by busying herself dishing up her plate.

"There is enough food here for a regiment, Jackson," Eleanor said as she added some of everything to her plate.

"I know, Mother. I got carried away. Just wanted to make sure everyone got what they wanted," he said. *Something's wrong. She looks like she's seen a ghost she's so pale.*

He pushed her chair to the table, noted how rigid she sat and took care not to touch her. If he wanted her, I couldn't pressure her. *Guess I need a change in plans.*

Conversation during dinner was stilted; the tension palpable. Eleanor observed two people she loved and cared for withdrawing from one another, and her efforts to draw them into conversation failing.

Finally dinner was over.

"I'm going back to help Daniel with a project," Jackson announced, putting his jacket on. "I'll be back in a few hours," he added going out the door.

Eleanor turned to see Lily looking stunned, frozen in place. "Come my dear," she said reaching out for Lily's hand. "While you are here, we can watch Jeopardy and Wheel of Fortune."

He's left me! Lily grasped Eleanor's hand as if it was a lifeline. Pain wrenched through her. "I'm not feeling up to that right now," Lily whispered, releasing her hand. "It's been a long day and I'm really very tired."

"Then you need to take yourself to bed and get a good night's sleep." Eleanor slipped her arm around Lily's waist and gave her a hug. "Whatever is bothering you, tomorrow will be better."

In a daze, she gave Eleanor a hug and a good night kiss on the cheek before she slowly ascended the stairs. He's left me stalked through her mind.

PANIC RUSHED through Lily as she fought her way out of the depths of darkness.

Had she screamed? What woke her?

The unrelenting terror.

Her bedding showed signs of her struggles, her nightgown was wet and her hair damp. *Breathe, Breathe, Breathe* she chanted in her mind. She sat up in bed and looked around the dark room.

"Maybe I didn't scream," she whispered creeping out of bed and crossing the room. She looked out at the open door to Jackson's bedroom. Quietly she tiptoed to his door and looked in. Nothing. His bed neat, untouched.

A sharp insistent stabbing pain in her stomach, the dull pounding at the base of her skull, the quivering of her legs - pain from learning Jackson had not come home. The remnants of the nightmare faded.

She returned to her room, loosened the immobilizers and picked up her lioness statue. Curled up in the chair, she hugged herself and tried to find comfort. If she'd been home, she'd have her routine of getting up, checking doors and windows, but here it was different. Last night she'd had Jackson's presence to help ward off the dream. The cold seeped into her bones, her feet frozen … a metaphor for the numbness in her mind. She sat huddled in the chair unaware of her surroundings.

Something happened. A noise? And she was aware of her surroundings, back in the room and this chair, aware of the feelings of loss. Three feet away was the bed where she and Jackson had slept last night; where they'd made love this morning. She stood and crossed the room to the closet gathering a small basket. She wrapped the lioness statue in the middle of a pair of sweat pants and top. *I've got to go.*

Quickly she dressed and packed her medications, toothpaste, comb and brush from the bathroom. She tightened the immobilizers before hefting the basket, making sure it was light enough to carry. That done she stopped at the bedroom door, turned back, and looked at this room where she'd experienced excruciating pain and exhilarating pleasure. Tears filled her eyes. It hurt to swallow. "I wish … ." Pain washed through her. The pain of regret, the pain of what might have been, the pain of what almost was.

Using her cell phone, she called for a taxi. A few minutes later she'd retrieved her basket of belongings, descended the stairs, and let herself out into the darkness.

29 - HOME AT LAST

The sunlight filtered through the bare branches of the small leaf maple outside her window. Patterned shadows flitted across the white comforter on her bed as the wind danced through the tree. Enveloped in the comfort of her own bed, she relished the feeling of being in her own home, her own bed, looking out at the familiar view. She was really there, in her own bed.

Intending to get up, she turned away from the window and slowly moved to the edge of the mattress. The joy of being home was compromised by a different emotion - sadness. "I've worked so hard to be here, to regain my independence," she whispered to the empty room. "I thought I'd feel happier."

Eleanor's image rose in her mind's eye. She'd left with no note, no message of any kind for her friend, she curled back onto the bed. Emptiness seeped into every pore, eliminating whatever her feelings of accomplishment were. She remained curled on her side struggling to find an answer to her dilemma regarding Eleanor. She had to do it, had to call and talk to her – but not now, she'd do it later.

Her decision made, Lily moved tentatively to the side of the bed. Her feet dangling, momentarily overwhelmed with the choice she'd made, she grappled with the enormity of it all. She was home before she was fully healed. Both of her shoulders ached, even with the immobilizers on. She'd stressed them by coming home last night. Add to that, the list of restrictions on what she could and couldn't do was still long. Worst? She had yet to be released to drive and wouldn't be for several weeks.

What had she done? She'd have to ask people for help, lots of help. *I can't even drive to the store to get groceries.* Unshed tears burned, her nose began to drip and with her hands confined by the straps, she couldn't even wipe it. She stifled the tears that threatened, loosened one strap enough to grab a tissue and wipe her nose. Her choices were to deal with it or return to Jackson's. The idea of going back to live in Jackson's house…well, she'd made her decision and left. Going back was not an option. Facing Jackson when the pain of his abandonment was so great – she prided herself on her courage but it was all just too much.

"First things first," she muttered. Her clothes lay where she'd tossed them, haphazardly draped on and around the chair. She removed the immobilizers, crossed the room and slowly dressed. As she made her way down her narrow steps, an image of the wide staircase and treads from the Montgomery House rose. She shook her head erasing the erstwhile memory of Jackson walking with her up the stairs. A sad smile lurked at the corners of her mouth. There wasn't enough room on her stairs for two people to pass much less walk up side-by-side.

In the kitchen she put water on to boil for tea and searched the cupboards, freezer and refrigerator for something to eat. She put the immobilizers back on, leaving the right one a bit loose. While the tea steeped she started 'To Do' and 'Grocery' lists on the refrigerator notepad.

"One of the first things on my 'To Do List' is to get to the store for groceries. And then there're my clients to contact, appointments to set up and physical therapy exercises to do." The sound of her voice kept her company as she wrote on the pad. "It'll be a busy day. Just what I need," she spoke aloud, determination in her voice.

Two muffins had been in the freezer and she thawed them in the microwave. Waiting for the familiar 'ding', she looked around. Something wasn't quite right but she couldn't figure out what it was.

Two trips and she'd moved her tea and muffins to the dining room. She took a sip of her tea and a bite of a muffin. That same feeling of something being out of place was here too. What isn't right here? She got up and started through her house. In the middle of the living room it dawned on her. A big grin on her face, she continued into her office. "Yes, that's it! Everything is in its place, everything is neat, and everything is clean. I've been gone for almost six weeks. Not only isn't there a speck of dust, the energy is fresh!" She returned to the living room and slowly spun around confirming her earlier impression.

She moved her tea and muffin to the small table next to the statue of the lioness and her cub and settled in her favorite chair. Taking in the sight of a clean, organized living room, she reveled in the delight of being home surrounded by things she loved and cherished. While she knew who was going to check on her house, mail, etc., this was so much more. She picked up the phone and dialed.

"What a wonderful gift!" Lily's enthusiasm flowed through the phone line. "An absolutely spectacular gift!"

"You know I'm not very good with illness and injury," Hunter grumbled, "but I kept you strong in my prayers and healing light."

"I know, I knew," Lily replied softly. "This is such a wonderful gift, Hunter. You know how much I love housework," she said and laughed.

"I know," Hunter said and chuckled. "You and Diana would rather go without new shoes or clothes in order to have someone come in to clean."

"Yes, we would. There's just something about us that's defective. Thank goodness there are normal people like you, Sophia, and Ashley." Her voice was soft and serious when she added, "Hunter, I don't think my house has ever looked this good. Thank you so very much."

"I didn't do it all myself you know. Logan came with me every time. She did the plants and dusting. I sorted the mail and vacuumed. With no one living there it really wasn't that big a deal."

"Well, I know it was at first because I hadn't done anything to keep the place up other than the basics for a few weeks or longer."

"I just needed to do something special for you, Lily, and I knew you were being well taken care of by the others. It's what Logan and I wanted to do for you, that's all."

"You have my gratitude, both you and Logan. Please tell her how much I appreciate it." Tears were threatening to spill and her voice quavered, "It's a really emotional time for me, Hunter. I've made it back home."

"I know, you worked hard and it paid off." Hunter paused. "But while you do sound emotional, I don't hear the joy. What's going on?"

"I guess the reality of being home doesn't quite meet the fantasy in my mind."

"You're home a little earlier than any of us thought you'd be," Hunter started out. "We were going to see your kitchen was stocked and there were fresh flowers in each room. You know, make it a real celebration. So how come you came home without letting any of us know?"

"I had to leave," her voice cracked and she swallowed hard around the lump in her throat.

"I'm on my way, Lily. I'll be there in ten minutes."

The dial tone buzzed in her ear.

The earlier sense of emptiness crept back. Threatening tears won silently slipping down her cheeks. She struggled to regain her composure, taking a sip of tea. She couldn't face Eleanor yet. *I'll have to call her later.* Lily wandered through her small house and forced her mind to think about what she needed to do, anything to stay away from thoughts of Jackson and Eleanor.

Ten minutes later a knock on the door announced Hunter's arrival. Without saying a word, she took Lily in her arms and held her. The tears no longer slipped quietly down her cheeks but flowed in a torrent as Hunter held her while the storm of emotions took its course. When Lily's tears stopped and she no longer clung as if she were on a life raft, Hunter stepped back, still keeping her arms around her. "So, what's really going on, Lily."

"Nothing really. I thought things were one way and they weren't. Now I'm home and it just isn't what I thought it would be. That's all."

"It's okay if you don't want to talk about it," Hunter said, her voice gentle, her turquoise-blue eyes concerned. She released her and took another step back. "It'll be okay. I'm here. You're not alone."

"Thanks, Hunter. Right now I don't want to be alone."

"Well, you aren't and won't be. I can stay until noon because I don't have students until one. We can hang out, get some grocery shopping done, whatever you want," her tone was brisk.

"Let me fix you a cup of tea and we can make plans," Lily smiled and felt the sadness and emptiness begin to ease.

"No, sit down and I'll fix my own. I do know where everything is." Hunter was already gliding toward the kitchen. At the door she turned back and smiled reassuringly saying, "We'll have a grand time of it this morning."

"I'm sure we will." Lily moved to one end of the couch. "I'll take you up on the grocery shopping offer. There really isn't much here."

ELEANOR AWOKE and went about her morning routine. As she drank her tea and ate her toast, she saw the dark purple flowers of the blanket of violets along the fence and maybe some buds on her primroses. She looked forward to the pink tulips, yellow King Alfred daffodils and dark purple, pink, white, and blue hyacinths that would soon be in bloom. Across the fence, the bare branches of the red leaf maple and dogwood trees were in stark contrast to the lush dark green of the fir behind them.

Her thoughts drifted. I wonder what is going on between those two. There was so much tension last night. She took a sip of tea and nibbled on her toast. She'd heard Jackson come in at seven and leave almost immediately. Did he do more than shower and shave? Well, they will have to work things out between themselves. Indeed they will if they are to have a future together.

After breakfast she called Evelynn to discuss final arrangements. She was due to fly out Friday for her March visit and then on to see Mary Beth the month of April. She mentioned the possibility of postponing her annual trip. She didn't want to be away while something was wrong between Lily and Jackson.

The grandfather clock in the living room chimed eleven. She wondered where Lily was this morning. She usually heard her up and about by now. Eleanor walked through the French doors into the main house. At the bottom of the stairs, she stopped and listened.

"Lily, Lily, are you all right? Lily?" There was no answer; no sounds of anyone upstairs at all. Turning she looked around the open space of the great room but didn't notice anything missing or out of place. The sense something was wrong grew. She couldn't believe Lily would leave in the middle of the night, without saying something to her but nothing else accounted for the silence. She called Lily's cell phone. It rang once and went to voice mail. She left a message asking Lily to call her, telling her she was worried.

"But, what if she's fallen, hurt herself," she worried. Trepidation in every step, Eleanor trudged up the stairs, a prayer on her lips.

She knocked lightly on the bedroom door before turning the knob and pushing it open.

The room was empty.

Shook with the realization Lily had left, she was extra cautious as she returned downstairs and called Jackson.

Her call went to voice mail. Remembering he'd mentioned a meeting with clients today, she left a message for him to call her. *I have quite done what I can. Something has happened between them and my worrying about it will not help a thing.* Moving around her apartment, Eleanor straightened a few things, tried to keep busy, anything to keep her worries at bay. With nothing left to do, she decided to write out birthday cards for the next month and pen a note to her daughters.

❧

JACKSON EMERGED around 4:30 from a meeting with clients that consumed most of his day. He was exhausted and still had Lily to face when he got home. Although his message light blinked, it indicated only one message had been left. He continued out the door, he'd deal better with whatever it was tomorrow when he was fresh.

Commute time, normally ten to fifteen minutes took almost an hour due to construction and its attendant traffic snarl. He used the drive time to shake off the intensity of the meeting with his new clients and think of ways to approach Lily. He knew if he wanted a future with her, he needed to face up to his own fears and uncertainties.

It was five-forty-five when he walked in the door.

Eleanor, who had been watching for him, met him as he came in from the garage. "Oh, Jackson, Lily is gone. I checked her room and she isn't there. I rang her cell phone and left messages but I have not heard from her. What has happened? Do you know?"

"Let me check upstairs." He took the stairs two at a time.

He knew she was gone the second he stepped over the threshold to her room. How? The sense of life and vibrancy she brought into his home was missing.

Faced with the reality she'd left, he collapsed in the chair. The irony was it was the same chair he'd sat in every evening discussing his day and listening to what she'd achieved. The vacuum left by her absence struck him anew, and he sat, elbows on knees, head heavy in his hands, a sense of desolation creeping into his heart.

We had an agreement. We agreed to talk. Determination replaced desolation. He charged out of the room down the hall to his office while calling Lily's cell phone. The message indicated her phone was turned off. "Damn you, Lily, turn the blasted thing on!" he muttered in frustration. In front of his desk, he shuffled through notes and papers finally locating Sophia's phone number. Dialing the number he listened to it ring. After what felt like twenty rings but was most likely only five, her voice mail clicked on. He left a short message asking her to call him when she could; he turned back to the desk to search for Diana's phone number.

On the fourth ring, a man answered.

"This is Jackson Montgomery, is Diana available?" Resolve infused every word and every step as he paced back and forth across his office.

"No, she isn't," a cold male voice said. "And what business do you have with her?"

"My name is Jackson Montgomery. I'm trying to reach Lily Hughes and thought Diana would know where she is," Jackson replied, his tone deceptively calm. He'd thought something wasn't right in her marriage but he hadn't realize she was married to such an ass.

"My wife isn't here," the male voice said, the cold tone now dismissive, and hung up.

Since they are her best friends and neither is home, that narrows my options. Jackson strode down the hall and stairs where his mother waited. He put his arms around her, walked her into her apartment, to her couch.

"No need to worry, Mother. I'm sure Lily is just fine. We'd've heard if something had happened. Just sit here for a minute. I'll be right back."

Once she was settled, he headed for the kitchen, his strides long and assured. Who the hell did she think she was, leaving them like this, leaving him like this? When he reached the kitchen he rummaged through the refrigerator finding what he wanted, something to eat. With things gathered in his arms he headed back to Eleanor's apartment.

"Okay, Mother, I've got dinner for us," he called out as he came through her door.

"I do not think I am very hungry, dear."

"That's all right, we'll just have a bite to eat," he said over his shoulder as he started assembling a plate of vegetables, crackers, cheese and some dip. "Just something light. You know you need something." He turned, plate in hand, napkins tucked under his arm and two glasses of Perrier in his other hand. "This will tide us over until we get things sorted out."

Sitting beside his mother on the couch he added, "I'll get to the bottom of this before the night is over, Mother. But right now we need some sustenance and I know you love this French, double creamed Brie with these English biscuits."

They ate in near silence, neither with much of an appetite. Once the small helping they'd each taken was consumed, Jackson rose and rested his hand on his mother's shoulder giving it a light squeeze.

"My instinct tells me she's gone back to her house. And, I couldn't reach Sophia or Diana and she's closest to them. I'm going over to her place. I'll call you and let you know what's going on." He leaned down to give her a reassuring hug.

Grabbing his car keys, he stalked to the garage and his car.

Thoughts filled his head as he drove across town to Lily's.

The twenty-five minute drive felt like an hour but eventually he pulled to the curb across the street. Cars were parked in front of her house and the place was ablaze with lights. For a few minutes he sat, a mixture of relief and frustration warred with another mixture of relief and anger. "What the hell is she doing, throwing a party?" Jackson muttered to himself as he parked his car. Getting out, he set the alarm and strode to the house, a glower on his face.

From the front door he could see Sophia and Diana through the glass. Lily was nowhere in sight. However, it looked like the two women were talking to someone in the kitchen.

They turned at the sound of a knock on the front door.

"He's obviously not giving up," Sophia remarked to Diana in a low-pitched voice as she turned and walked to the front door.

Diana turned back to the kitchen door. "You've got company."

Lily appeared in the doorway. "Who's selling what now?"

"Come in, Jackson," Sophia's voice and gesture invited Jackson into the house.

A thin smile on his face, his gray eyes staring icicles, Jackson nodded an acknowledgement to Sophia and stepped into the living room. His chest constricted, his shoulders tensed, he held himself rigid. He was brittle and about to break. His eyes swept her form, noting she wore the immobilizers loose, before settling on her face. In a stiff voice, he said, "Thank you, Sophia. It's good to see you. Good evening to you also, Diana."

"We just got here ourselves," chattered Sophia. "We're surprised to see Lily home."

"As am I," Jackson said icily.

"I'm sure there's enough food for you to join us for dinner, Jackson. That is if you want to," Diana added in a warm yet formal tone.

"I'd love to," Jackson replied still not taking his eyes off Lily.

"Well, let's eat then," Sophia said lightly. "Jackson, there's another chair you can bring to the table," she gestured toward the other room and I'll get another place setting out," she continued. "It's a simple meal---spaghetti, salad, garlic bread although not as grand as what you fix."

With everyone seated and served, the conversation turned to safe topics --- the weather, spring, gardening, traffic snarls, the start-up of construction season.

Throughout the meal Lily's mind whirled. The dominant questions: Why was he here? What did he want? Nothing in the way Jackson behaved or his conversation gave her any hint, any inkling as to what the answers were.

"Imagine" by John Lennon — everyone turned to locate where the sound was coming from as Jackson reached into his jacket pocket to retrieve his cell phone. "If you'll excuse me, I'll take this in the other room." He stood and walked away talking quietly to the caller. Once in Lily's office he closed the door.

"Mother, I'm still at Lily's. I apologize for not calling sooner." He paced in the room, running his free hand through already rumpled hair. "She's fine. Diana and Sophia are here and we've just had dinner. Lily and I need to talk before I come home. … Yes, I'll give her your love. Don't worry, Lily's all right. We'll talk more when I get home, okay." Ending the call, he stood looking around Lily's office appreciating the touches that personalized this room. I know all these things have meaning to her…the flowers, birds and animals. You've got a lot to learn, buddy, if you want this woman.

As soon as Jackson left the room, Lily struggled to get both hands free of the immobilizers and grasped the nearest of Sophia and Diana's hands. "Please don't leave me alone with him. I don't think I can deal with him right now."

"How did your talk with him last night turn out?" Diana gently squeezed Lily's hand and leaned toward her.

"We didn't actually talk," Lily mumbled.

"Perhaps that's the problem." Sophia leaned in from the other side. "Remember our conversation? Who's in control here, the ghost of Paul, your fear?"

"If he meant nothing to you," Diana pointed out, "you wouldn't be so upset. You know we love you and support you, but you also know there are some things you have to do for yourself. I think this is one of them."

SOPHIA STOOD and took the few steps to stand by Lily's chair. She leaned down to give her a hug and looked her friend in the eyes. "You know you remain in our hearts and prayers. Diana is right about Jackson. This is something you need to do for yourself. There's something between you two, something that's wondrous to see. The question is, do you have the courage to see it yourself or will you let your fear of making a mistake, of being hurt, your fear of a failed relationship, your fear of possible abuse — the ghost of Paul, shadow your eyes and blind you to what could be."

30 - THE COUCH

The sight greeting Jackson when he returned to the dining room? Sophia hugging Lily and Diana holding her hand. Out numbered. Or was he? The other women had invited him in, invited him to dinner and included him in the conversation. Maybe they weren't against him. He stopped a few steps from the table. "That was Mother. She sends her love."

"I'll call her tomorrow." Lily said averting her eyes, unwilling to give him any opening, any advantage.

"I'm sure she'll appreciate hearing from you. She's been very worried about you."

"I'll call her and apologize tomorrow, Jackson," she said, a blush of discomfort coloring her cheeks.

"With the four of us, I'm sure we can make short order of this mess," Sophia's brisk voice interrupted the stilted atmosphere. She straightened from her crouch next to Lily and began stacking dishes. "Are you ready to hit the hot soapy dishwater with me, Diana?"

"I'll wash, you dry, Lily can put silverware away and Jackson can entertain us." Diana picked up a few dishes, gave Lily a knowing look and started into the kitchen.

"Do you want jokes, songs, or stories, Diana?" Jackson, grinning, cleared a few dishes away. "I'm a multi-talented man you know."

"Of that I have no doubt," Diana said running water into the sink and adding soap. "My mother always said nothing hit the spot like having your hands in hot soapy dishwater. From her point of view, hand washing dishes cured anything." She laughed and said, "I much prefer my dishwasher."

Lily was unsettled and irritated as she watched her friends laugh and joke with Jackson. They were enjoying his company and that wasn't right. Her jaw clenched at the idea she might be jealous or even more horrific, pouting. It was her house. Soph and D. were Her friends. He's was... . She stopped herself in mid-thought refusing to complete it. Tamping down her temper, she carefully put silverware away. She wouldn't be jealous! It was just that, well, it was just that ... well, maybe she was a little jealous. He'd been so furious when he got here and now it was like nothing had happened. Turning her attention back to the talk around her, Lily watched Sophia give the pots to Jackson. Her eyes were drawn to his muscled arms and flat abs as he reached above his head to put them in the cupboard above the stove.

"Anything else?" Jackson asked as he shut the cabinet door.

"I think that's it," Diana replied, shaking out the dishcloth and draping it on the faucet.

"There's one more thing," Lily said turning to her friends. "This place looks as good as it did this morning." She gestured around her kitchen, looking everywhere but at Jackson. "I can't thank you enough. You know Hunter and Logan came by every day to check on things and made sure everything was kept up." Lily chattered away as if her life depended upon it, pointing out the details of Logan and Hunter's work, as she led everyone out of the kitchen and to the living room.

"She wanted to do something and in the beginning it was so hard for her to see you struggling. This was something she wanted and could do for you," Sophia said.

Diana grinned, "She truly did know you would adore what she gave you while barely tolerating the rest of us and our hovering."

"Your hovering wasn't that bad," Lily retorted. She stood arms folded at her waist but without the immobilizers and watched the grins on her friends' faces. "Well, it wasn't always bad." The grins got bigger. "Okay, you win; I hated every minute of the hovering and worked to turn it into loving care. Of course, it was loving care in…in…the form of…of…hovering," she stammered. "We need to change the subject as I keep digging myself a deeper hole," she finished.

"Speaking of changing subjects, I need to get going. I've a busy day tomorrow with the kiddos." Sophia walked to where her coat was draped over the back of a chair.

"Me too. I'm putting together another proposal for the community college." Diana reached for her coat and slipped it on.

Lily held out her hands and Diana and Sophia wrapped her in a hug. She looked at her friends, her voice earnest. "Thank you for all you've done for me. You are both such blessings in my life. The Goddess is good."

"Thanks for the entertainment, Jackson." Sophia walked to where he was leaning nonchalantly against the archway and put out her hand.

Straightening, Jackson took her hand and instead of shaking it, raised it to his lips, brushing a light kiss along the back of her hand. "It was my pleasure."

"My turn next," Diana stood to the side of Sophia and held her hand out. "I can't remember the last time I had my hand kissed by a handsome gentleman." She batted her violet eyes in outrageous flirtation.

"It's my pleasure," Jackson murmured, raising her hand and kissing her fingers. He winked when he released her hand and resumed leaning against the archway.

Lily watched the scene unfold before her. *I'm not jealous, I'm not jealous, I'm not jealous.* She stiffened her spine and raised her chin as she walked her friends to the door and accompanied them onto the porch.

"You know if we thought Jackson would do anything more than talk, we wouldn't leave, don't you," Sophia said.

"He's been very protective of you since the accident," Diana added.

"I know," Lily whispered. "He can be so charming around others, just like Paul."

"From what you've said about your ex, that's true. But you also said people never saw his dark side. While Jackson can be charming, we've also seen him frustrated, upset, and tonight I think he was furious when he got here," Sophia said.

"Remember how angry we've been with our sons when underneath it all we were worried to death?" Diana said. "That's what it felt like to me. As soon as he came in and saw you were okay, he settled down. He may be frustrated, maybe even upset, but he isn't angry much less furious."

Lily hugged her friends again and watched them walk to their cars. They looked back and waved. Diana gave her a "thumbs up" and Sophia blew her a kiss before they got in their cars and drove away.

Minutes ticked by as she stared into the night wrestling with her thoughts. What Sophia and Diana said made sense but did not erase her fears. Trepidation at what she faced when she went inside kept her standing on the porch in the cold night air. A resigned groan escaped. The longer she stood out there, the longer he'd be here. She turned and went back inside.

Jackson sat in a chair waiting for her. His eyes, dark with emotion, watched her. What was he thinking? Emotions clouded his eyes but his face was impassive.

"What's going on, Lily?" Jackson asked in a quiet voice, his eyes never left hers.

"I couldn't stay at your place," Lily whispered, too drained to move.

"When did you leave?" Jackson asked, the bone-weariness weighting his voice.

"Two or three. I was okay. I took a cab. Really, you needn't have worried," she rattled on, her arms banded around her waist.

Silence filled the room.

"Jackson, this won't work." Desperation clawed its way through her, shredded her stomach, shredded her nerves.

"No, no it won't if you take off in the middle of the night with no note, no word, nothing. Why, Lily, why did you leave?" He said struggling to keep his tone mild, his voice low-keyed.

"I-I-I-," Lily stammered. "It just won't work."

"You came to that realization after midnight and just left without any word to anyone, not even Mother? I'm surprised you were awake at that hour; you looked exhausted at dinner. I figured you'd go to bed early." His brow quirked a question.

Sometimes, driving at night, her lights caught a deer, standing eerily still in the middle of the road. Here in her living room, she was the deer, his eyes the headlights. The idea of moving, of having his eyes follow her overwhelmed. Like the deer, she remained still, her gaze locked with his.

"I did," she said.

He didn't blink.

"I woke up."

Something flickered across her face. If he hadn't been scrutinizing her so intently, he might have missed it.

"The nightmare?"

"Yes." The word was whispered.

"Same one?"

"Yes."

"And I wasn't there."

"Yes."

"So you left."

"Yes."

"Maybe you're right Lily. Maybe it won't work between us…maybe there isn't really anything there to…" Jackson looked away. The need to protect himself strong. Raw emotions seethed just under the surface, tightened his biceps, fisted his hands, clenched his jaw.

With his eyes averted, the spell was broken. Lily moved the few steps to the couch. Sitting, she tucked her feet up and wrapped her arms around herself. What were they doing to each other? What were they doing to themselves? She shuddered when thoughts of life without Jackson, a life she admitted appeared terrifyingly empty crossed her mind. A veil of tears blurred him in her sight. As bad as this was, it would be worse if she stayed. How could she get him to understand? She sat and rocked in that age old way of comforting oneself. "I couldn't stay, Jackson. It's hard for me to explain it all to you. But at the end of any explanation, it boils down to—I just couldn't stay."

Jackson's breathing, constricted by tight steel-like bands, reminded him of his grief when his father died. He shook his head trying to clear his mind of the painful thoughts of that loss. The ticking of the wall clock echoed in the silence. Across the room he saw Lily, lost in her own thoughts, gently rocking herself. Maybe he hadn't lost her. Maybe there was still a chance. Maybe if they kept on talking. ... *It's worked for me in business. Keep talking until we find common ground and can work out an agreement.*

"I'm sorry I wasn't there last night, Lily," quiet intensity permeated his voice. "You looked so tense, so stressed at dinner I thought if I insisted we talk, I'd lose you for sure." He laughed a strangled, bitter sound. "I went to Daniel's because I thought you needed more time. Oh hell, I don't know exactly, I just thought if I tried to talk about us, about a future ..." His voice trailed off. He leaned his head against the back of the chair and looked at the ceiling. "I thought if you had some space you wouldn't feel pressured and my chances of keeping you with me would be better. Guess I really made a mess of things," he said in a sad, regretful voice.

Lily stopped rocking, her gaze resting on Jackson. The arrogant domineering man was gone and in his place sat another who was less sure of himself, more approachable and much easier to talk with.

"I thought you left because you'd changed your mind about me, about a future together," she said softly.

Jackson was in front of her in two long strides. Squatting he took her hands and gently kissed them. "Never, Lily, I'll never change my mind about you, wanting you in my life, in my bed. But having said that, I do think we've things to work out between us. I very much want to carry you off to bed and love you until dawn, but I know we need to talk."

"Talk about how to talk to each other when things are hard?" She searched his face and looked deep into his intense gray eyes for a sign he saw a future for them.

"That's the crux of the matter if part of that includes how to argue and disagree with each other." He held her gaze and her hands.

"You mean fight?" Lily's eyes widened, her forehead wrinkled in concern and her mouth pursed.

Before the words of protest were said, Jackson added with a smile, "Any word you want to use is fine with me. I know it won't always be easy because I'm an arrogant, domineering male and you're an independent-thinking female." He brought her hands to his lips, kissed the backs one by one, turned them over and planted another slow lingering kiss in the middle of each palm. Closing her hands over his kiss, he looked into her eyes. "If we want it, want us enough, we can work something out. Of that I'm sure."

He stood, settled his hands on her waist and pulled her to her feet. "I'm not decrepit but I'm not so young I can manage this discussion in that position. Here's an idea. How about starting in our respective corners of the couch and see if we can make it to the middle?"

"Like when we work something out, we move closer together?" she asked. His face brightened with a smile that reached his eyes drawing her smile in return. Her breath caught as the vision of an adventure with him spread before her.

"Something like that. And Lily," he said catching her gently in his arms, "when we get to the middle you are mine," he paused to place a soft kiss on her lips, "and I am yours. I want you, Lily. I want you in my life and I'm willing to fight for us."

The look in his eyes smoldered. She shivered from the intensity of it.

"I want you. Not just in my bed," he said and grinned wickedly, "or me in your bed, but in our bed wherever that may be. Lady's choice - pick your corner." Jackson stepped back and gestured to the couch with a flourish."

"In that case, I'll pick the right corner." Lily sat, her hands folded primly in her lap, wedged into her corner, thankful he couldn't see the turmoil crashing through her body. Her hands were damp and a T-shaped steel-rod ran across her shoulders and down her back.

Jackson lounged at the other end of the couch, his long legs stretched out before him, and one arm along the back. He wanted her and was willing to do something different to win her. Through lidded eyes he watched her. He waited.

"I guess, I'm afraid of being hurt, Jackson," she said worrying her fingers in her lap. "Well, no, I don't guess," she huffed. "I know how devastating it was when my marriage to Paul fell apart. It wasn't just the affairs, the neglect, being shoved around, and eventually hit, it was the feeling that I didn't matter, what I did wasn't important. I promised myself I'd never do that to myself again."

"Understandable." His eyes never left her face.

"But that's not all, Jackson," she said and turned to face him head on. "I thought I loved Paul, that we were right for each other, that he was 'The One.' Do you understand? Now I don't know if I can trust my own judgment in these things." She sat ramrod straight, her hands twisted together in her lap and looked off in the distance.

"Are you saying you love me then?" Jackson asked a slight tremor in his voice. A sense of lightness filled him. He prided himself on self-control and he used all those years of self-mastery to keep himself from leaping across the space and gathering her in his arms.

"I don't know if I'm all the way there but probably pretty close."

Her irritable look, the defiant tilt to her chin told him he'd made a good choice to remain in his corner.

Lily saw a flash of emotion flit across his features. Possessiveness? Triumph? She pressed further into her corner of the couch, her hand up, palm out. "No, Jackson, no. Love doesn't really mean anything. I've seen love leave welts, burns, scars on children's bodies and warp a child's mind. I've seen love kill. I need to know, Jackson, to truly believe and trust that if we love each other and are together, we won't do that to each other."

Silence.

Taking a deep breath, Jackson leapt into the stillness. "Why do you think I'd do those things? Do I do them now?"

"You are you, Jackson. Strong willed, domineering … ." Her voice trailed off.

He restrained the impulse to move but not to speak. "And that's all you see in me?" His voice was harsh, his eyes narrowed, anger etched his features although he'd hid the worst of it, the pain searing his heart.

"No, Jackson, that isn't all I see in you. But I thought Paul was a loving man. I thought he was gentle. He was when we were dating and first married, but later, when I didn't please him or do exactly what he wanted, he began to change."

"What do you see in me beyond arrogant, domineering, strong willed?" He waved his hand in a dismissive gesture even though he'd needed to ask the question; even though he inwardly cringed to hear her answer.

"You are very generous, Jackson. You always leave big tips, compliment people, give your full attention and your respect to someone when talking to them. You are loyal to family, friends and clients, I think. I find myself smiling when I'm with you."

He interrupted. "Did you smile and laugh with Paul?"

"Yes, but as I think about it, it was different."

"How?" Puzzlement furrowed his brow.

"Paul told jokes and made fun of people and situations. Sometimes it was funny but often it was uncomfortable too. He'd tickle me to gain my agreement. I would will myself not to be ticklish but he bullied his way through my defenses, in the end I always agreed." The steel beam in her back gave way and her rigid posture eased.

"Is that how you see smiling and laughing with me?" Jackson's gut clenched but he needed to know how she saw him.

"No, I smile and laugh when I'm with you because I'm happy or find your posturing endearing."

"My posturing endearing?" Jackson's brow arched haughtily. "That doesn't sound very respectful to me."

"Perhaps an example would be better." Lily's gaze drifted to a spot over his shoulder. A smile quirked her lips and she looked him in the eye. It was hard to talk looking straight at him but she soldiered on.

"Remember when Daniel was over last week and you were teasing him about the teenage daughter of that account he has?"

"I remember," Jackson said warily.

"Well, there was a time during that exchange when Daniel denied the daughter was flirting with him and you rolled your eyes and arched your brows in an exaggerated way. That's what I mean…yes, that would be a perfect example of what I mean."

"And you find that endearing?" His eyebrow arched in a similar manner.

Lily tried but failed to stifle her giggles. "Well, that may also not be my best word. But it is so like you." Her giggles subsided and her soft voice was serious when she continued. "To tease in a gentle way so that everyone knows you are teasing and meaning no harm. Paul's teasing was almost always a way to hurt me or someone else without them being able to get back at him because he could always say 'what's wrong with you, I'm only teasing. You can't believe I really mean that.' but underneath it all, you knew he really did."

"Paul and I both tease but not in the same way if I understand you correctly."

"That's true, your teasing is just that, teasing and nothing more." She smiled.

"Does that mean we can move a bit closer on the couch?" His voice was hopeful.

"No, because that was never a problem. And you aren't really mean to me."

"Really?" only one eyebrow rose; there was steel in his voice. "Tell me more."

"Oh, Jackson." Lily looked away, took a deep breath and exhaled slowly. Her eyes returned to his as she continued quietly. "When you look at me like that, when you talk to me with that tone of voice, it scares me. I think you're mad and upset and you'll yell at me, say hurtful things, and maybe shove me or hit me."

"Just like Paul?" Pain was evident in his soft voice.

She looked away again. "Yes, just like Paul," her voice whispered.

"Are you asking me to never be upset or angry?" Jackson struggled internally to keep his posture open and his voice calm. "Because if you are, I know I can't do that. I've too much emotion, too much passion in me to be able to bottle it up," the calmness evaporated, distress colored his tone, "even for you, Lily," he whispered as he removed his arm from the back of the couch, drew his knees up, his feet now flat on the floor.

"No, it's me Jackson, not you." Lily noticed him change from the more open, casual posture to one that telegraphed he was shutting down. Panicking she quickly added, "The problem is within me."

"But it's also my problem," he leaned slightly toward her, earnestness in his voice and posture, "if my being who I am keeps us apart."

"I just don't know what to do about it," she said in a choked voice. Nausea and tears threatened. The urge to bolt – to run to the bathroom and lock the door surged. She hated feeling small, defeated, vulnerable. Hated those feelings threatened to swallow her. Those feelings were her enemy. She fought them back.

"Do you think I'm trying to intimidate you?" he queried.

She hesitated before answering; looked over at him. "Sometimes."

He sighed deeply. "I suppose, at times, I am. There's something I want you to do so I put my will and my powers of persuasion to work on you. But, Lily, when you compare me to Paul, that hurts. I don't think you really know me or see me." He ran his hand through his hair in frustration. Hell, what was he doing here?

"Sometimes that's probably true," Lily acknowledged. "Last night at dinner I kept expecting you to say something to embarrass me in front of Eleanor. I didn't know exactly how to say any of the thousands of thoughts flying around in my mind. And then when I woke up and you weren't there to hold me and tell me everything would be all right, I thought you shouldn't have to be burdened with me." Her watery eyes and sardonic laugh mirrored the pain from her core. "No one would think the competent Lily Hughes, the Lily Hughes who can create miracles for her clients, would be so incompetent in her personal life."

"I don't think you're incompetent in your personal life," he said softly. "I think you're doing your best, just like I'm doing my best not to get hurt or to hurt someone else in the process." He decided to be bold, to reach for something he could hang on to. "Do you trust me in anything at all?"

Lily stared at her hands and took her time in finding the words to answer his question. She didn't see the myriad of emotions crossing his face or the distress darkening the color of his eyes. *She doesn't even trust me.* He saw her mouth moving before he heard her words so caught up in his thoughts of losing her.

"Trusting is difficult," he heard her say.

"You find trusting me difficult?" shocked and offended he rose to leave.

She grabbed his arm. "NO! Jackson, you didn't hear me. I do trust you although trusting is difficult for me. There aren't many people I do trust. But, you Jackson, you are one of them. I couldn't love you if I didn't trust you. Not after what I've been through. Not after what I've survived."

He sat back in his corner, relief coursing through him. He felt exhausted, drained. "Will we ever move closer to the middle of the couch, Lily? All this talk and we don't seem to be closer at all."

"We may not be closer yet, but we have cleared up some things. For example, I hadn't really thought that I sometimes wrapped you in Paul's ghost, expecting from you the same kinds of reactions when you aren't Paul. I understand better why that is: your passion and intensity are not anger and if I stop and think about it, I know that. And I know I do love you and I do trust you. I've not allowed myself to admit that to myself or to you." She paused to look searchingly at him. "Has anything been cleared up for you, anything at all?"

"I think I know what you're thinking or feeling and sometimes I'm right and sometimes I'm wrong, like last night. I'm quick to wrap Paul's ghost around myself as the reason for your discontent instead of seeing how I might be contributing to the problem." He also paused then reached toward Lily. His smiling face was in contrast to his serious tone of voice. "I'd certainly be willing to move toward the middle of the couch with that. What about you?"

Lily's tone mirrored his and she moved away from her corner. "I'm comfortable about here, what about you?"

Jackson mirrored Lily's place on the couch.

"Is that where you think you should be? Does that feel right to you, Jackson?" she asked.

"No, it doesn't feel right but it's where I think I should be."

"Where would feel right?"

Grinning, he scooted until he was next to her. His arms gathered her close and he kissed her thoroughly. "Here next to you feels right to me," he whispered nuzzling the side of her neck nibbling the sensitive spot where her neck and shoulder met.

His warmth, his citrus scent enveloped her. She relaxed and melted against him. He hadn't told her he loved her, but he was here talking to her. He cared about her, she mattered or he wouldn't have come after her, stayed for dinner, talked. It intrigued her, the idea of talking things out on her couch. She remembered Sophia telling her she and Jonathan had kept talking and made their marriage into what they both wanted. His breath stirred her hair, curled around her ear, sent shivers to her toes.

"Let me love you, Lily. Let me love you tonight. We can mark our places on the couch and talk some more but I need you with me tonight, all night," his voice was husky with a growing passion, his arms tightened around her and he pulled her onto his lap.

"Do you think we've finished, Jackson?" Her words were tentative.

"No, but we've made a start, a good one I think." He brushed light kisses into her hair, inhaled the lavender scent and felt her warm curves press against him. "It's getting late and I'm figuring you're going to try to work tomorrow so a good night's rest is a priority for you."

"Yes, I do want to work tomorrow, but having you in my bed all night doesn't promise much rest." She snuggled closer.

"I can control myself, Lily. I'm no hormone-driven adolescent." Indignation tinged his words.

Lily laughed and wriggled on his lap, feeling the evidence rising to the contrary.

"I may not be able to control Mercury here, but I can control what I do with him," Jackson's voice rang with dignity.

"Mercury?" Lily snorted in a failed attempt to camouflage her laughter.

"It isn't uncommon for a man to name his penis," Jackson's voice reeked of righteousness.

"It isn't that I've never heard of it before. I've just never known someone who had, or at least they've never shared that with me," she said stifling her laughter.

"Much more likely the latter." He could feel her shaking trying to suppress her laughter; the heaviness and tightness within him eased.

"Is this something you all talk about?" She leaned back looking up at him the air of innocence she tried to project marred by the laughter dancing in her eyes.

"Damn it, Lily, this isn't..." Flustered, Jackson stopped. She's teasing me about this. She's having fun teasing me.

"It isn't what, Jackson? Proper to talk with me about these things? Or for me to be curious? Or what?" Laughter bubbled up and spilled out.

"No, none of that," he grinned. He tried to pull her close but her hands, now on his chest, kept some distance between them. "It's just off the point ... er ... topic." He let her go. "Invite me to your bed tonight Lily. Just invite me to your bed."

She stood, reached out and took his hands. He surged to his feet and she wrapped her arms around his waist. Leaning into him, his arms slipped around her waist when she rose on her toes. Her voice a whisper, she gently sucked his lobe. "Come to bed, Jackson, come to bed and love me."

31 - WORKING THINGS OUT

It was the fourteenth of March, almost three weeks since she'd returned home. Yesterday marked the eight-week anniversary of the accident. Mark Parker had lifted a few more restrictions—ones to celebrate.

"I never thought driving to the grocery store would be a highlight of my day," Lily muttered to herself. "If I hadn't been so worried about falling, I think I might have leapt in the air and clicked my heels together." Laughing at the image, the milk carton in her arms, she walked into the house. "Who knew I'd feel so shaky driving five blocks and back. My plan to jump in my car and speed off to see all of my clients isn't realistic." She grimaced fighting the black cloud that accompanied those thoughts and straightened with determination. "I'm good at making realistic plans; I just need to use my skills on myself."

Sitting in her favorite chair, sipping a cup of tea, the couch was in her direct line of sight. "Taking it slowly. Our friendship is important to both of us." She moved across the room to sit on 'her spot' on the couch, the piece of tape indicating 'his spot' just out of reach. "We've moved a few inches... ," she mused, "but there's still much that separates us. I love that we meet every week to work things out. Who knew Thursday would become such a special day."

Here she was, talking out loud to herself. She missed spending time each day with Eleanor who was now back East visiting her daughters and their families. "I felt so awkward when I called her the next day. Realizing how worried she'd been was another damper. I didn't handle coming home very well." Rubbing her hand on the tightness between her breasts did not banish the lingering guilt. "I'm grateful Eleanor accepted my apology. Another reason to work things out with Jackson. At the very least I want to remain friends so Eleanor is in my life."

Warmth tugged her belly. Jackson'd been lobbying her to spend the night with him since Eleanor left. "Tonight's the night." Envisioning herself sprawled on his luscious duvet the warmth spread lower and intensified. "I may not get much sleep but I'll be very relaxed in the morning."

She finished her tea and headed for her office. The neatly stacked notes for the Court Report due next week sat untouched, her mind wandered as she gazed out her office window. Early spring flowers stretched and turned to the sun. She leaned forward to better observe the birds at the feeder and bird bath in her yard. Idly she watched the robins playing in the water. Robins are a sign of spring when things come to life. *I wonder what they herald for me?*

The smaller birds scattered from the main bird feeder when a flicker landed. What message did the flicker have for her? Only a few feet separated the flicker from her – a few feet of space, a thin piece of glass – a totally different world.

A shiver shuddered through her. Turning away from her window, she shook off her reverie and wandered into the kitchen to fix a cup of tea. *What am I doing trying to work when my mind is so full of Jackson?* She puttered around the kitchen, putting water on to heat, getting out the half and half, opening the sugar bowl. He was so respectful. Not like Paul at all. He didn't just listen to her, he tried to understand.

Their talk last night came to mind. While they'd touched on the topic of her feeling intimidated by him, there was more. There were times when she felt he was pushing her so hard it bordered on bully-ing. *It went better than I thought it might.* A smile lit up her face. *Well, he's an arrogant male, used to having his own way by charming or intimi-dating, whichever works.* It felt good to challenge him, tell him how she felt and see what he did about it. *Paul never thought things over the way Jackson does.*

Underneath the warm feelings a sinister thread of doubt threaded its way into her consciousness. Jackson's willingness to listen, to try to understand her point of view was frightening. Her parents loved her and sometimes listened but they'd never understood her. Paul was too busy bending her to fit his notion of a good wife to even listen to her. Having a man really care about her, really try to under-stand what she was saying and how she felt about what was going on in her life was like sailing in uncharted waters, not knowing where the reefs and underwater rocks were---only knowing they were there.

Returning to her office and sipping her tea, thoughts on the work they'd done to build a relationship they both wanted surfaced. *He obviously thinks things over after we talk because when we're next together he always has something to add.* "But what if, no matter how much we talk, listen and compromise it isn't enough?" she dared ask the question she most feared. Her head pounded, her jaw clenched. Her hands fisted around her cup. *Losing him would be even more devastating if we've tried so hard.* Forcing her focus to the blank computer screen before her, she shook the disturbing thoughts away and started writing reports.

The phone's ring was a welcome intrusion. She stretched the kinks from her neck and picked up.

"This is Lily Hughes," she answered, her tone professional.

"Hi," a deep voice whispered in her ear. "It's me"

"Hi you." She leaned back in her chair, her voice warm and soft, "What're you doing?"

"Inviting you to Carmel for a few days," his voice was full of promises of a most intimate nature.

"Jackson, I can't take time off now. I'm just getting back into some type of a routine." She straightened in her chair, her voice laced with exasperation.

"A few days won't hurt, Lily. And, it'll be work, not just play," his tone shifted from light and easy-going to determined and professional.

"What do you mean? I don't have clients in California." She stiffened at the tone of his voice, shook it off. He isn't Paul.

"You do now," he said satisfaction in every syllable. "I just got off the phone with two of my clients. They want House Totems for their homes. Since I have to go down to check on things in ten days, it makes sense for you to go with me. Scope things out."

"Really? Someone wants a House Totem? I never really thought it'd happen...not really. I'm blithering, aren't I?" The stiffness dissolved, joy soared in her heart. She stood and began to pace. "Tell me more, Jackson. I want to hear everything."

"We can discuss the details tonight over dinner. I've a meeting to get to." His dictatorial professional tone was back. "I'll pick you up at 5:30 p.m. We'll stop at that little Thai place on the way home; pick up some take out, so I can nibble on you along with Spring rolls, Pad Thai noodles, the chicken and broccoli in peanut sauce, chicken satay. I'll call ahead with our order."

"That's enough food for four people! Are you inviting anyone to join us?" she asked, fighting the unease his tone of voice elicited, reminding herself of their talks.

"No, but we'll have enough for lunch or snacks tomorrow. We both could use a little down time, a lazy day. Saturday will be our day of rest. And Lily?"

"Yes, Jackson?"

"Give the Carmel trip some serious thought, okay?"

"Yes, Jackson, I'll give it some serious thought. I'll see you at 5:30," she said briskly and hung up the phone. Energy surged through her. Maybe a walk around the block will burn some of it off.

"No," she muttered to herself as she took herself to task, sat herself down, and picked up where she left off on the Court Report. As diligent as she tried to be, her thoughts veered to the idea of going to

Carmel, to sense the Spirit of the Land, to identify the House's Totem. *Oh my, this is so exciting!* Failing at keeping herself focused on the report, she reached for her phone and dialed the familiar number.

"D? I'm so glad I've reached you. Such news! I couldn't wait until we have lunch on Monday," she bubbled with excitement. "I just got off the phone with Jackson and he has two clients who want House Totems. Isn't that wonderful?" Unable to sit, she paced through her house. "He wants me to go to Carmel with him in ten days. I don't know if I will or can, but it's exciting to know someone is interested."

"That's great news!" Diana's voice reflected Lily's enthusiasm. "The Goddess is good. Remember, She'll watch over, guide, and protect you."

"Yes, She always does." Those words resonated in a deeper part of her being than ever before. "However, I won't have the option of saying 'yes', if I don't get this and three other Court Reports done, D. So, on that note, I'll hang up. May your day be full of love and light."

"May your day be filled with grace and gratitude."

"Blessed Be," they said in unison.

JACKSON ARRIVED AT 5:30 SHARP. Lily insisted on carrying her small bag to his car, overriding his objections that it was too heavy; all it contained was a change of clothes. She did allow him to carry her purse which was much heavier because it contained her organizer and phone.

Sliding into the passenger seat of the sleek black Jaguar, she settled her bag between her feet.

"Humor me," he said grabbing her bag and tossing it into the back seat next to her purse. He grinned at her scowl, gave her a quick kiss, and turned the key. The quiet engine purred to life. After shifting, Jackson reached over and pulled her hand from her lap. He raised it to his lips, kissing the back, one by one sucking her fingers, licking her palm. "I love the taste of you," he breathed over her knuckles, his thumb stroking her palm.

Lungs seizing, heart stuttering, waves of heat coursed through her. Resigned, she leaned back into the leather seat, closed her eyes and let the sensations of his mouth, his tongue, his lips, his breath fill her.

Reluctantly Jackson released her hand. Traffic was heavy and needed his full attention. He changed lanes again to take the exit to the Thai restaurant. Pulling into the Take Out space, he jumped out of the car and disappeared inside.

Alone in the luxurious car, Lily struggled to collect herself, her mind swirled. He stirred her up with seemingly little effort. He knew she preferred a quiet dinner at home to a restaurant. Or maybe it was a trait they shared. Her body had barely settled down when he reappeared, tucked two bags of food on the floor between her feet.

The aroma filled the car and Lily's stomach growled in anticipation.

"We'll be home in five minutes and have dinner on the table in ten. Can you wait that long?" Jackson teased.

"It'll be a test of my endurance, but I believe I can," Lily rejoined. She looked over at Jackson's profile as he steered the car out of the restaurant parking lot and toward the house. She could see his lips quirked in a smile. "A penny for your thoughts." She watched his smile deepened.

Jackson reached for her hand, brought it briefly to his lips before returning it to her lap, "I've waited a long time to have you in my bed, love. Tonight is the first of many nights to come…having you…in a variety of ways," he chuckled.

"I'm not moving back in, Jackson. So if that's what you're thinking, you can stop," Lily clarified in her no-nonsense voice. "Don't plan on my being here the remaining nights Eleanor is back East. That won't happen, no matter how charming you are." Not only was her tone of voice firm, there was the determined set to her jaw.

"I know, Lily. At least every Thursday we'll be at your house because our places are marked on your couch but I want more than tonight with you here, with me, in my home, in my bed."

"I'll be here with you more than tonight, Jackson, but most likely not as often as you want."

"Did you bring your calendar?" Jackson was already thinking of a plan as he pulled into the garage.

"Yes, I have it in my purse. Why?" Lily got out of the car. Jackson loaded her arms with one sack of food before grabbing the other along with her bag and purse from the back seat. He maneuvered to open the door, held it with his foot as Lily scooted in around him.

"We can look at each other's schedule and make a plan." He set her bag and purse on the floor inside the door. "I know I'm scheduled to be out of town and I know you have time you'll spend with your women's circle. I thought we could coordinate our calendars, figure out which evenings, other than Thursday, will be ours," he added retrieving plates and cups from the cupboard while Lily placed the food on the counter.

"I like that idea," Lily said getting out the silverware and serving pieces from a drawer. "Do you want tea or wine?"

"Tea'll be fine," he said taking containers from the sack, readying them with serving spoons beside them while Lily started the water for tea.

They dined on their favorite Thai foods, drank jasmine tea, relaxed and chatted about their days and scheduled their time together. Once dishes were cleared and leftovers put away, they lounged on the couch in front of the cheery fire.

"We have all day tomorrow to spend together." Jackson nuzzled Lily's neck seeking the sensitive spot that made her shiver. "I wonder what we'll find to do." He smiled as he hit the right spot. "Hmmm, do you have any ideas?" He nibbled on her ear lobe. "If not, I've got a few." He drew her lobe into his mouth and gently suckled feeling her sigh and melt in his arms.

Lily's arms, now wrapped around his waist, were heavy, responding to the sensuous pull of his seduction. His heat enveloped her and she shifted, entwining her legs with his. Closer, she needed to be closer. She pressed against him seeking comfort from his touch. Comfort was not what he was giving her. Heat, arousal, sparks, tension followed his questing fingers. She was catching on fire, burning brighter than the fire in the grate and only the man in her arms could ease her need, bring her relief. She reached for his burgeoning erection, stroked him, and worked the zipper down.

Jackson moved his hand to stop her caress, his voice a guttural whisper, "Let's go to bed before I can't stop."

She leaned back, pressing her breasts, abdomen, and legs against him. She smiled a siren's smile, her eyes glazed with passion. "I thought you'd never ask," she murmured as she leaned forward to nibble on his chin.

"Now, Lily." Jackson took charge, shifting her so he could stand. "We need to go upstairs now." He tucked himself back into his pants, made sure the glass doors on the fireplace were tightly closed, slipped his arm around her waist, and led her to the stairs. "We may have all night and tomorrow to make love, but I'm about to burst with wanting you right now."

Her arm around his waist, she leaned into him as they went up the stairs. Her heart filled with the rightness of being here – on her way to his bed, to a night she ached for. Ached for and feared. Could she do this, be with him like this, and not be hurt? His kiss at the top of the stairs chased all questions and doubts from her mind.

It was their Thursday night to work on the issues they'd identified. Jackson had come over early to make dinner since Lily had a late appointment. Having dinner fixed for her was a huge plus in their relationship and no big deal for him because he loved to cook. During one of their long talks when she was recovering at his house, she'd shared that having a cook and housekeeper was a fantasy of hers.

Dinner over, Lily sat on the couch on her mark from last week in what he thought of as her 'professional pose', both feet on the floor, hands folded in her lap, an attentive look on her face. Brow raised, he lounged on the couch on his mark, attempting to dismiss what he'd come to call 'the tight-ass Thursday ache' because it wasn't really a headache. He resisted the impulse to rub the back of his neck. No, not a headache, it was much more. The tightness ran along his spine from his head to his ass. He woke up with it every Thursday morning, even if he'd spent Wednesday night with Lily. It remained with him all day its intensity varying depending on what he was doing, finally disappearing once this Thursday night torture was over and Lily was in his arms.

"Well, where do we go from here, Lily?"

"I've been doing some thinking." Lily looked cautiously at him, her voice prim. She turned at the sound of a soft chuckle and bristled even seeing the warm smile on his lips reflected in his eyes. "Don't laugh at me, Jackson."

"I'm not laughing at you. I was chuckling because I would've been disappointed if you hadn't been thinking." Leaning toward her, a serious look on his face he added, "If we're going to work this out, we both have to think things through."

"You've been thinking too?" The note of surprise in her voice was answered by an instant arching of his right brow. "Well, of course you have," she hastened to add. "You always have some additional comments to make. I'm sorry, Jackson. I didn't mean to sound so incredulous."

"That's all right. I didn't put Paul's ghost on. However, I have plans for later that includes you," both his eye brows rose and slightly wiggled, "if you catch my drift here," he added with a drawl. "Why don't you tell me what's on your mind?"

She took a deep breath, the words rushing out on the exhale. "I worry that we're too different, we don't have enough in common." Taking another breath, she hurried on. "You have money, a big house, a fancy car, tailored clothes; I don't have any of those things, Jackson, and I never will. There's an enormous gap in our lifestyles." She gestured in emphasis as she said, "Why you practically bash your head every time you come to my bed because the ceiling is so low."

"So, if you had more money, a bigger house, tailored clothes, and a fancy car, we'd have a better chance of making it?" Jackson said, in a languid tone.

Not looking up, Lily missed the searing look Jackson sent her way. "Well, I think that people who are from the same background usually do better together, so yes, I do think we'd have a better chance," Lily added glancing up to see Jackson's intense look.

"Good," was his brisk reply, "because if I've anything to do with it, you'll have more money. You'll earn a hefty fee for the House Totems and these two are just the beginning. Then if you marry me, you'll live in a big house and can drive a fancy car and if you want, you'll have tailored clothes. So, that takes care of that."

"Don't you take that highhanded manner with me, Jack-son Montgomery. It'll be your house, your car and your money. It'll change nothing."

"I'm not being 'highhanded'," Jackson said. The urge to get up and pace consumed him; exasperation rang in his voice. "It'll be our house, our car and your money. I'll transfer everything into our joint names. I can contact the attorney tomorrow and have things drawn up."

"You will not! You will not transfer anything into my name tomorrow. IF we were to get married, there would be a prenuptial agreement and what's yours would remain yours and what's mine would remain mine. You are not giving me anything. I'm perfectly capable of taking care of myself!" Fire and fear flashed through her.

"Not even my heart?" Jackson settled back on the couch, struggled to maintain an outward façade of calm.

"What are you talking about, Jackson? I'm trying to be serious here," her own frustration was clear in her expression and tone.

"I can tell that. And I am being serious. You just said that I'm not to give you anything. Does that mean you won't accept my heart?" His gaze locked with hers.

Time stood still.

Lily looked away, looked down at hands now clasped again in her lap. "Please don't, Jackson. Don't make fun of me," she said softly.

"I'm not making fun of you," his voice softened also. "I'm being serious. You don't seem to want anything that is already mine. What will you accept from me?"

The ticking of the clock on the mantle filled the silence as Jackson sat and watched the woman he had come to know and love, struggle with her thoughts and feelings. A sense of despair crept over him.

Watching the fading sunlight play on the walls, Lily said a quiet prayer to herself. Please Goddess, let my words tell my truth in such a way that Jackson can hear me. In love and light. Blessed be.

She shifted on the couch to face him, lifted her chin, and looked directly into his turbulent gray eyes. "I want your love, your respect, your friendship. I want you to cheer me when I'm down, take care of me when I'm sick and comfort me when I'm sad. Maybe in time I can accept more tangible things, Jackson, but not yet."

"All right. I can do that. Give you those things you've said you want." His posture straightened, his voice was clear and firm.

Lily noticed these changes but did not feel alarm. She saw clarity and intent in his manner and knew he wanted her. In a quiet yet certain voice, she countered, "What do you want from me?"

"Everything. Your heart, your body, your laughter, your wit, your compassion, your energy, your passion. I want it all, Lily. I want it all." His voice husky, he leaned toward her.

His hands rose from the couch, his biceps tightened, he was going to reach for her, pull her into his arms. She waited with bated breath. His hands relaxed back on the couch. He remained on his spot.

"You have my heart, Jackson." Because she was watching him so closely she saw the desire flare, saw the struggle to control, saw him win. "I hope I don't disappoint you when it comes to the rest. I'm not sure I can be all those things for you."

"I'm not asking you to be anything except yourself. That's what I see, what I love about you. I can't remember laughing so much or feeling this happy. Even now when we are struggling to work things out, underneath the frustration, I am happy because I'm working this out with you." Jackson reached the few feet between them and took Lily's hand in his. "Your passion, your commitment to your clients is awesome. If I get a tenth of what you give to them, I'll have more than I've ever had with anyone else." He'd leaned forward, close enough to kiss her but he didn't reach for her. She felt the tug, the pull of longing and knew it would only take a slight indication of her willingness for him to take her in his arms, hold and kiss her.

Lily broke eye contact. She looked to her left and then let her gaze drift so she was looking straight ahead. "Thank you for talking with me like this. I've hoped things will work out between us if we just keep talking." She slid toward him and moved her piece of tape along the back of the couch to mark her new spot.

He mirrored her movement. A sense of elation swept through him. He pulled her to him, cupped her neck in his hand and pulled her into a soul searching kiss. She surrendered, melting into him. Breaking the kiss without releasing her, not letting her move an inch from him, his whispered breath feathered across her cheek to her ear. "Talking and other things, Lily. The other things are important to."

32 - CARMEL

The lobby with its intricate Moorish-influenced-tile floor, the large vase of fragrant fresh flowers on the marble top table, the comfortable looking sofas and chairs in shades of blue upholstery gave the small elegant hotel a sense of timeless luxury. Lily took a small vial from her purse and inhaled the invigorating scent of bergamot and eucalyptus. She was exhausted. That middle of the night trip to the ER with Edna really did her in.

Turning from the inviting sitting area, she watched Jackson talk to the desk clerk. After another breath of the special blend of oils, she capped the vial and returned it to her purse while observing their interaction. *Everyone from the limo driver to this desk clerk knows and likes him.* She smiled to herself. He's even won over all of my circle sisters.

Finished at the front desk, Jackson walked toward her. His eyes held an invitation that echoed in his smile. His hand on her elbow, he whispered "Just a few more minutes and we'll be there." She shivered.

A young man in a hotel uniform approached.

"Hi, Turner, how's it going?"

"Great, Mr. Montgomery. I've got your things and we're ready to go." Turner started toward the elevator, pushing the luggage cart in front of him.

"Looks like the weather's been pretty fair recently," Jackson said, sliding his arm around Lily's waist and pulling her closer. She leaned into him.

"Yes, it has." Turner looked over his shoulder and grinned. "Expect it to stay that way until the weekend that is. Probably'll rain 'cause I've got those days off." He stopped and pushed the 'up' button.

"Still going to school?"

"Yep, just finished my first semester in Hospitality. Hope to get a promotion here to Desk Clerk or maybe Bell Captain," he said as he stepped aside to let Jackson and Lily enter first before following with the luggage cart.

"Good for you. Let me know if you need a letter of reference. I'd be glad to write you one."

"Thanks, Mr. Montgomery!" Turner looked sheepishly down at his feet while the elevator moved swiftly upward, a blush flaming across his face. "That would be great! You're one of our best customers. A reference letter from you? Wow! That'd be something else!"

"Consider it done, Turner. I'll have it for you before I leave Wednesday," Jackson said in a matter-of-fact manner.

"Well, here we are, Mr. Montgomery." Turner held the 'open' button while Jackson and Lily disembarked.

"This way, Miss." Turner gestured to the right. "Mr. Montgomery's suite is down this way."

"It's Lily, Lily Hughes, Turner. You can call me Lily or Ms. Hughes, whichever is most comfortable for you."

"Ms. Hughes it is, then."

As they started down the corridor, Jackson said in a loud whisper, "Turner here is magical in his own way. He knows before I do what I might want or need."

"I see." Lily nodded looking again at the young man.

"Here we are," Turner said as he opened the door and stood to one side so Lily and Jackson could precede him into the room. Coming in behind them, he propped the door open and continued across the room to open the sheer curtains. The large window showcased a view of water and grass, trees bent from weathering storms and wild flowers. He took Jackson's luggage into the bedroom and Lily could hear the suitcase being opened, the closet door sliding.

"He's putting my things away. Told you he was magical. He knows just how I want everything."

A few minutes later Turner returned. He gave Jackson a questioning look while tilting his head to the suitcase still on the cart.

"Turner, if you would get the ice now, I'll take care of Ms. Hughes suitcase."

"Sure thing, Mr. Montgomery," Turner replied as he picked up the ice bucket and left.

Jackson walked over to the cart, picked up Lily's suitcase and carried it into the bedroom placing it on the bench at the end of the king-size bed.

Lily stood transfixed in front of the window, lost to what was going on around her. Her initial impression of the view had expanded as she approached the window and saw the rolling waves crashing on the cliffs beyond the dancing grass and flowers. He walked toward her, his progress replicated in the window, hands rested on her shoulders, his head bent, his lips kissed her neck. Her head tilted in a silent invitation to continue. Desire flashed.

"Ahem," sounded behind them.

"There you are, Turner." Jackson dropped his hands and turned back into the room. "Just put the ice on the counter." He strode over to Turner, shook his hand, and she knew pressed a generous tip into his palm. "That'll be all for now. We're expecting clients at one but will meet them in the bar."

"I'll let the kitchen know you may want a few appetizers about then."

"Good idea," Jackson added. "Just shut the door behind you."

"Right. You got it," Turner replied as he got the luggage cart and left.

Lily watched this exchange through the reflection in the window.

As the door closed she turned and watched Jackson, a smile on his face, stroll across the room. He really was the most handsome man.

He pulled her into his embrace, his mouth hungry on hers, his hands roaming over her body effortlessly finding every sensitive spot. Pulling him closer, her hands in his hair, she deepened the kiss and pressed her body against his hardness as the heat of him sank into her every pore. The exhaustion vanished.

Pulling back from the kiss, Jackson turned Lily to look out the window, spooning them together. Shimmering, silvered water blended with the blue sky at the horizon. Gnarled trees permanently bowed to invisible winds, the grass and wild flowers pranced.

"What do you think of all this?" he whispered against her hair.

"It's magnificent," she whispered leaning back into him.

"You haven't seen the view from the bedroom yet." He began to walk backward, Lily still encircled in his arms.

She turned in his arms, looked up at him and smiled, slowly shaking her head. Her arms slipped around his neck, she pulled him to her and met his lips in a slow passionate kiss. "How much time do we have before we meet your clients?"

"It depends," he nuzzled her ear.

"On what?"

"On what you want?"

"You, a shower, a nap."

"We've about an hour and a half before we meet Ted and Amelia Waltman."

"Hmmm. A nap now and then we can take a shower together. I think that's a good plan."

"Okay. Nap first." Jackson put his arms around her waist and danced her slowly toward the bedroom and the bed. Leaving her by its side, he walked to the window and pulled the drapes. The room darkened.

Lily was already curled up on the bed when he turned back. Grabbing the cozy throw from the chair, he crossed the room, leaned down and kissed her gently on the cheek. "Here." He tucked the throw around her. "This will keep you warm while you nap."

Snuggling down, she yawned. "Thanks." Her eyes fluttered closed. A slight smile on her face, her breathing evened.

Jackson watched her sleep. He knew she'd been up most of the night dealing with a client's medical issues and was prepared for her to cancel. He'd asked her to give him a tenth of what she gave her clients. Her being here was indicative she was doing that if not more. Sleep was what she needed and sleep was what she'd get. He quietly returned to the living room, pulling the bedroom door shut as he went. At the window he stood looking out, lost in the view, lost in his thoughts. With a sigh, he shook himself out of his reverie and walked to the small desk. He took his laptop out of his briefcase, set it on the desk, plugged it in and began to check emails. *Oh yeah, I've that reference letter to do for Turner. Might as well get that done now.*

A half hour later, Jackson checked on Lily from the bedroom door. She was sleeping soundly. He gazed at her relaxed form. She needed sleep and they'd have all night together. He entered the bedroom, remained by the bed observing her sleep for a few minutes before he selected a change of clothes and went into the bathroom to shower and get ready.

"Wake up sleepy head. Wake up."

Lily's sleep-fogged mind finally registered the words.

"Wake up, Lily. It's time to get up."

Slowly stretching, Lily opened her eyes and saw Jackson bending over her, a smile on his face, love in his eyes. "Oh, how long have I been asleep?" Her voice was husky, her hair tousled, a crease from the pillow on her cheek.

"About an hour," was his casual answer.

"An hour," Lily screeched jolting up in bed. "Oh, Jackson, I don't know if I can get ready in time." She scrambled out of bed, located her suitcase at the end of the bed and hurriedly opened it searching for the green flowered dress she planned on wearing. Pulling it out, she groaned. It was wrinkled. *Take a deep breath, Lily. Just keep breathing and you can get through this.*

Seeing her distress, Jackson gently took the dress. "Go take your shower, Lily. I'll have the dress ready for you when you get out. Really, go on. Let me take care of this," he said nudging her toward the bathroom door. "I can have this dress ready for you in twenty minutes. Can you be ready to put it on in that time?"

"Yes, of course I can," she said in a haughty tone as she grabbed her cosmetic case and headed for the bathroom. "It just would be easier if I didn't feel so rushed."

"I'm sure that's true. Go along now. Get your shower. I'll take care of the dress."

YESTERDAY'S AFTERNOON meeting with Ted and Amelia Waltman had gone well. So well in fact, they were driving up the winding road in a sporty red rental car; Jackson, who was in race-car-driver-mode, at the wheel. *They are an interesting couple.* She remembered both Ted and Amelia. He was so quiet and unassuming and she so vibrant. But they seemed to suit...to complement each other. She looked out the window, a slight smile on her face, memories and emotions reflected in her eyes. She let out a long breath.

Hearing her, Jackson glanced her way. "Why the sigh?"

"Just thinking." A light blush infused color on her cheeks.

"About what?" Jackson grinned when he saw the flush of color.

"Oh, nothing." Her cheeks turned a brighter pink. "Nothing at all - really."

"Nothing? Then why the blush?" He chuckled and added, "Could it be a memory about our activities last night? Or this morning?"

Her cheeks flushed a bright red. Words of denial sprang to her lips. Why would she deny something so wonderful between them? He was a tender, thorough, thoughtful lover. She shouldn't be embarrassed. She shifted in her seat. As her gaze settled on his profile, a rush of love, lust and longing flowed through her.

"Actually, I was thinking more about the activities we'll indulge in later," she said in her primmest voice.

"Ah, Lily," Jackson said and laughed, "I love you, sweetheart, I really do love you." He reached across the front seat, found her hand, brushing the side of her breast in the process. Bringing it to his lips, he licked the palm and squeezed lightly.

"Good, because I love you too," Lily continued, her prim voice had a breathless quality to it. "I'm glad you're keeping your eyes on the road, paying attention to your driving because there are lots of curves through here."

"And here as well." Jackson deliberately grazed the side of her breast with the back of his hand as he reluctantly returned her hand to her lap. "We're almost there," he said. Both hands on the steering wheel, he accelerated through the curves on the road his mind on the curves of the woman beside him.

The beast rose from its burrow. Nose, eyes, head silhouetted, framed by the sea. Lily closed her eyes and her inner vision was filled with the face of Badger emerging from its burrow. *What can I remember about Badger? Stories, Healer, Keeper of Light. Bits and pieces.*

Opening her eyes and looking around, Lily saw the partially finished house. What had been nose, eyes, and head were actually the portico, windows and gabled roof line.

Amelia hurried up, her face flushed with excitement. "Well, Lily, what do you think? Can you do it? Can you figure out our House Totem?"

Once out of the car, Lily caught Amelia's hands and looked deep into her eyes. She voiced a quiet, "Yes."

"We're so excited about this, aren't we Ted?" Amelia said looking over her shoulder at her husband who was just joining them. "We want this house to be our home, our haven. A special place where we reconnect with each other." She tucked her arm in Lily's and turned toward the house. "It does get a bit strained living the LA/Hollywood lifestyle."

"Don't forget that downtime for the creative process to regener-ate," Ted added, looking younger and more boyish than he had yesterday afternoon. "Well, Lily, what've you got for us? Or do you need some time?"

"No, I don't need any time. Your House Totem is Badger." She paused checking their reaction, seeing a frown on Amelia's face, curiosity on Ted's. "Badger is the keeper of knowledge, of stories. It represents bold self-expression and self-reliance."

"Badger? Isn't a badger a kind of weasel?" asked Amelia.

"Yes, it is," Lily responded matter-of-factly.

"Ohh." Disappointment echoed in that small quiet word.

"Amelia, this is your House Totem. Badger spirit is here on this land," Lily's voice was gentle. "What you said you wanted this house to be for you and Ted? A haven, a place where stories can come on a breath of air? That is supported by badger."

"Jackson has designed a great office for me. My imagination already soars and stories flow and it isn't even done yet. Why just standing in the space waiting for you to arrive, I got a couple of ideas. If Badger is about storytelling, it feels right to me." Ted's stance relaxed, hands shoved in the back pockets of his casual pants, an affectionate grin on his face.

"But if we are to have a badger here at our front door," Amelia said, gesturing widely in the direction of the house, concern furrowing her forehead, "where on earth does one find one?"

"It means shopping, Amelia; looking in shops, galleries, checking out websites. Badger will show up. Right now it's a matter of faith that you'll find it."

Jackson had remained somewhat apart, observing these interactions. He stepped closer, slipped his arm around Lily's waist. "How about a tour of the place, Lily? You've never really seen my work before, have you?"

"No, not really. The setting is magical and from here the house is impressive. I'd love to see more."

"This way then," Jackson said with a wave of his hand that encompassed the site. His arm slid from her waist to take her hand, his finger twined through hers. Leading the way across what would be a lawn and walk, he guided Lily up the steps and through massive double front doors.

Lily gasped, her feet froze in place. "It's breathtaking," she said in an awe-filled soft voice. A shiver skimmed from her feet to her head.

Before her the Pacific Ocean sparkled in the sunlight, its waves moving relentlessly toward shore. But what had her moving tentatively forward was the sense of being suspended over the water. "Jackson, where's the land? It feels like I'm floating above the water," she said, excitement and joy bubbled in her words. Closer to the windows she slowed unable to take her eyes off the water flowing toward her wave after wave after wave: waves that disappeared under the house.

Jackson grinned like a pleased little boy. "It's the land, Lily. The house is built flowing down the side of the hill. It falls away more steeply and we've cantilevered this level of the house so that it juts out. Come on out on the deck here," he said pulling her along.

"How do you even get to a deck through the windows? I don't see a door." Lily voice was full of wonder.

Sliding open a panel on the wall, he pushed a button.

Lily watched in amazement while a wall of windows, moved back on tracks in the floor and ceiling. Within minutes the whole window wall was tucked away and the space was open to the outside. "This is absolutely amazing!" Lily's voice filled with admiration. Turning, she saw the beaming faces of Jackson, Ted and Amelia.

"He's really something, isn't he?" Ted said, pounding Jackson on the back. "We fell in love with this lot and thank our lucky stars we heard of Montgomery here. The setting may be magical but the house is even more so. Right, Melia?"

"You are so right." Amelia came to stand next to her husband, her arm sliding around his waist. Leaning into him, she looked up and smiled. "It hasn't been easy. Last fall there were lots of problems but Jackson worked with the engineers, the contractor, well, with everyone. He's given us our dream home, our very own magical space."

To the left of where they stood in what would become the main living area, were stairs going down to the other levels of the house. To the right was an open area already plumbed for a gourmet kitchen.

The next level housed the home theater and two en suite bedrooms. The lowest level was the master suite, Ted and Amelia's personal spaces. Decking enhanced the indoor-outdoor feel on all three levels.

"Your home is wonderful," Lily enthused as Amelia finished the tour. "Ted is right about his office space. There does seem to be a different energy there. And, in your special space too. What do you feel when you're in it?"

"Joy." The word burst forth with the energy that marked her personality. "Yes, joy…a great deal of joy."

"Hmm, you feel joy in your space and Ted feels creative in his. I'm sure you'll be very happy here." Lily glanced behind them. "Somewhere along the way, we lost Ted and Jackson. Where do you think they are?"

"I think they're on the main level looking at blue prints with the contractor. Let's go find them and then we can be off to the shops!" Amelia said with enthusiasm.

Finding Jackson, Ted, and the contractor, Murray, was easy. They were on the main floor going over blue prints, discussing some minor changes and one major one. Ted wanted a couple of niches by the front door for the badger he was sure Amelia would find. The discussion was animated as the front door columns were finished.

"What do you think, Lily? Shouldn't there be a place for the totem outside the house?" Ted questioned.

"Jackson's is in his house, on his mantle but within sight of the front door. Mine are both in and outside. It's really up to you and Amelia, Ted," Lily responded, a bright smile on her face. She could hardly believe she was having this conversation. She felt so incredibly at ease! Maybe she didn't have to hide her spirituality from everyone.

"Maybe we can wait and see what the ladies come up with before we go further on this." Murray's brow was furrowed. "Once we see it, we can build whatever is needed."

"I'm sure that'll work just fine, Murray," Jackson said reassuringly. "You've done a great job here." He reached over and squeezed the older man's shoulder. "You've handled tougher changes than this."

"Yeah, I know. Just feeling a bit pressured with this other house I bid on. Don't know right now if I want to win it or not. The architect has a reputation for being difficult to work with," he said grinning at Jackson.

"Really, so you're one of the bidders on that house?" Jackson said, feigning concern.

"Yep, I think I've got a good chance of getting it as I've assured them I can handle difficult architects." Murray rolled up the blue prints, turned, and walked away whistling, a jaunty step in his stride.

"I think he got you good," Ted laughed as he watched the look of mild disgust pass over Jackson's face. "Yessiree, I think he did."

"I hate to break up this male bonding moment," Amelia said walking up to Ted and Jackson, "but Lily and I are going shopping for a badger. Do you and Jackson want to come?"

Ted drew his bubbling wife into a loose embrace. "You want to know if I want to spend hours poking around in little shops looking for a badger?" He kissed the tip of her nose and laughed. "Thanks for the offer, but I think Jackson and I'll go hang out for a while. You know, do guy stuff. Call me on my cell and we'll meet you two when you're done."

"Okay, then," Amelia said with a faked pout in her voice. Rising on her toes, she kissed her husband lightly before turning to Lily. "Well, I guess we girls are going to do the hunting while our menfolk tend the home fires."

"What a day! I'm exhausted, Jackson. But what a day!" Lily flopped on the bed laughing.

"No badgers, not even a sign of one?" Jackson lounged casually against the door frame at a slight angle to the bed the better to keep his arousal hidden from the object of his desire.

"No, but several leads on them." She wriggled on the bed finding a comfortable spot. "At the pottery place, the owner said she'd look through her sources and the galleries we stopped at also said they'd keep an eye open." She stretched her arms over her head and touched the headboard with her hands. "Amelia and Ted will have such fun searching for Badger! You do know, Jackson, that this is rather perfect. Badger's a loner, keeps to himself. Even though the fathers sometimes help raise the young, in the fall, father and babies leave and the mother badger is on her own. Burrows are like the haven Amelia wants for them. That's the piece that finally won Amelia over – the bit about haven and when we drove away, we stopped and looked back at the house. She saw the face.

"Her disappointment in having Badger as her House Totem is still there but I think she'll come to terms with it. Ted sees the badger protecting his home where he is creative. He saw that right away. And, I learned that while she and Ted have a close relationship, she's left for days and weeks at a time on her own because of the demands of his job. Melia's become very self-reliant and is able to entertain herself."

"You're amazing, Lily love," Jackson said, his eyes scouring her body stretched out before him. One by one he undid his buttons and leisurely took off his shirt. "I love looking at you sprawled on the bed." He toed off his shoes. "You look good enough to eat," he said, arching an eyebrow and removing the belt to his pants.

"So do you, Jackson." Lily scooted to the middle of the bed and patted the place beside her. Her heart raced, her mouth dry, sizzles of passion licked her insides.

He pushed his pants and briefs down over his hips. They fell to the floor. He stood silhouetted in the doorway.

Lily's breath caught as the evidence of his desire for her swelled before her eyes.

He sauntered toward the bed his eyes never leaving her. "Hmm, looks like I'm a bit ahead of you." He climbed on the bed and lay on his side next to her.

"I'm so tired from such a busy day, I don't think I have the strength to do anything more than just lie here," Lily said coyly, a smiling pouty look on her lips. "I just don't think I have the energy to do anything at all."

"Hmm, you look like you have lots of energy, my dear." Jackson wiggled his eyebrows and took her shoes off with his feet. "This dress looks a bit warm though," he remarked with laughter in his eyes as he reached for the buttons, slowly, carefully undoing each one, sensuously touching her all the way down the front. "Great dress," he said as he opened the front, exposing all of her warm feminine charms to his view. "I love it that you don't wear anything under your clothes except your bra and," chuckling, he moved his hand to her breasts, "it opens in front. Hmm, how did this happen? You now appear to be in almost the same condition as I."

Turning toward him, Lily wiggled and snuggled in his arms. "You might as well finish what you've begun, Jackson." She pressed light kisses along his jaw line.

"Oh, I intend to. I intend to thoroughly finish what I've begun," he whispered, kissing her softly while removing her dress and bra. Tossing them to the floor, he turned back to her, hands roaming the warm softness of her, breathing in the scent of lavender and that certain essence that was uniquely her. Loving her slowly, meticulously, completely with his hands, mouth and heart, feeling her languid, flowing response turn into a passionate joining of their bodies, minds, hearts and souls.

In the aftermath of their loving, quiet and fulfilled, they lay in each other's arms, legs tangled. "I love you, Jackson," she whispered.

"I love you too, Lily," he whispered back.

THE NEXT DAY found Jackson and Lily with Bert and Tammy Mallory. The couple met them for breakfast at a local diner close to where their new home was being built. After breakfast, they followed the Mallorys to the building site. Like night and day, the couples were very different as were the houses. While Ted and Amelia's house was set on a hill and overlooked the Pacific, Bert and Tammy's was set into a hill surrounded by trees. The light reflecting off the bank of windows across the front of the house gave the appearance of a wide opening. Almost like a cave. No sense of an animal came to greet Lily as it had at Daniel's and the Waltmans'.

At breakfast, Lily had spent time talking to both Bert and Tammy about the house, their hopes and dreams for it, and why they had picked that particular spot to build. It felt so right to talk to them like this. They weren't mocking her but instead were truly involved in this process. The Circle would be so glad to learn of this.

Bert and Tammy both worked in high octane jobs dealing with people almost twenty-four hours a day, seven-days a week. Both said, in different ways, that when they were alone, the energy came flowing back. They didn't do anything different other than get a little more sleep as they kept to their routines of exercises, eating, etc. Meetings with clients were replaced with time for each other, catching up on paperwork, or researching projects. They didn't describe anything like hibernating, just time away either alone or with a few close friends.

Going into the house, Lily was surprised at the amount of light and space. Other than the fact that both the Waltmans' and Mallorys' homes had open-concept kitchen and living areas the houses were as different as night and day. The view out into the woods was soothing but still energizing...just a very different energy than looking out over the ocean. The private rooms were on the other side of the kitchen, accessed through a hallway on the right of the house. Although dimly lit, there was still light even though the electricity was off due to needed adjustments to the power lines on the outside.

"Look up," Jackson coached.

A series of tube-like structures going from the ceiling through the earth to let light in from above were spaced along the hall.

"There'll be lights along the hallway floor as well as higher on the walls." Bert told her.

Off the hall was a bathroom, replete with a multi-head shower, double sink vanity with an off-white granite countertop and white tiled floor. The shower had a pattern of glass tiles that sparkled from the illumination from the skylight. Lily smiled as the sense of whimsy, of fairy lights touched her fancy.

The hall turned and she saw doors leading to a series of rooms along it.

"We don't intend to become total recluses when we're here," Tammy explained. "So, we have three en suite guest rooms."

Lily noted that not only did each guest room have its own bathroom but they also had their own skylights.

At the end of the hall the double doors opened to a large room: the master suite. Three skylights in the main room as well as one in the large master bathroom provided enough light to see for basic activities. This bathroom not only had the multi-head shower but a soaking tub with Jacuzzi jets, a vanity with double glass bowled sinks and overhead recessed lighting as well as lighting over the long mirror that extended the length of one wall.

"We've chosen to use the same granite and tile in all the bathrooms but we've varied the color of the glass tiles in the showers. It's important to have things light in color and texture in order to downplay the sense of being underground, which we really are in this space," Bert noted as he showed Lily the master bath.

I'm in awe of his creativity! Lily looked again around the master bedroom. How does he do this? It's so very different than the Waltmans' house but seems to be exactly what the Mallory's want. In this house you could be invisible! She gasped. *Of course, Fox! The master of invisibility.* Chuckling to herself, she followed Bert, Tammy, and Jackson back to the front of the house. How perfect was this! Fox lived in a den, a shallow cave. *My first impression was that this was a cave.*

On the wide deck across the front of the house, Bert and Tammy turned to Lily. "Well?" they chorused.

"Fox," Lily replied instantly. "Foxes live on the edge of the forest, and blend into their environment. Some people see an air of mystery about them and surmise they live between the seen and unseen worlds. I believe Fox will be able to guard and protect your home providing you with the invisibility you want when you are here."

"Fox," Tammy said with an expectant look at Bert. "Well, we'll have to go find one."

"Yes, we will," Bert replied looking fondly at his wife. Turning toward Lily, he asked, "Can we do this on our own or do you need to be with us."

"Finding the House Totem you both want to have here at your

retreat is something you can certainly do on your own. And, if you need me, you can always reach me through Jackson."

"Well, break must be over," Bert shouted over the sound of construction roaring back to life. "A necessary part of having the place built, but unless we need to stay, I'd rather leave now." His voice rose over the noise.

"That's fine with me," Jackson yelled above the din as he took Lily's arm. The four of them walked quickly, stepping around construction debris toward where the cars were parked. "You know where we're staying," Jackson shouted leaning near Bert. "Our flight leaves later tonight but you still know how to reach me when I'm in Fremont." Jackson and Lily stopped by the Mallory's car. The men shook hands as did the women.

"Thank you so much, Lily." Tammy's hand shake was brief, her eyes lit with excitement. "Bert and I love to go on adventures and this will be a wonderful one. I'm hoping we don't find a fox at the first place we stop."

"If you do," Lily leaned closer so she needn't scream to be heard, "you can always keep looking to make sure it is the 'right' fox."

"Very true." Tammy smiled and turned to Bert who stood holding her door open. She gracefully got in, he closed her door and with a wave toward Jackson and Lily, strode around the car and climbed inside. Moments later their car sped off.

Jackson made sure Lily was safely in the car before he walked around to the driver's side. He stopped for a moment, looked back at the house with a critical eye, observing the buzz of activity of the construction crew. It's coming along nicely. Very different from what I usually do. On the road back to the hotel, Jackson broke the silence. "It seemed this one was different, Lily. What happened?"

"Well, I didn't sense the totem at first. It finally showed itself in the master bedroom," she chuckled.

"Weren't you worried?"

"No, I wasn't. The House Totem already is. It shows itself in its own time and its own way. When you think about it, it would be so unlike Fox to be standing at the door waiting for us. If a House Totem had been there, it wouldn't have been Fox."

"Guess we get some time to ourselves since you aren't going fox hunting with them. What do you want to do?" he asked as they approached the hotel.

"Just be, Jackson. That's all. Just be."

"And can I 'just be' with you?"

"Of course you can." She reached for his hand, turned toward him and smiled. "It will be ever so much better if you are."

PUTTING the last of her things in her suitcase, Lily thought over their relaxing afternoon: a quiet lunch on the balcony of their room, a romantic interlude followed by a shared shower. A blush stole across her face at those memories. Music, flowers, champagne and excellent food – the setting for their dinner was magical in its own way. Another image of the priceless look on Turner's face as he read the reference letter Jackson had written brought a smile to her face. It's the little things he did that let you know you were important in the world, in his world. *Oh my, I really am in deep, I'm so in love!*

The sound of a knock on the door to their rooms brought Lily out of her reverie. The sound of muted voices came next. Curious she walked to the bedroom door, opened it, and stood looking at the living room bathed in candlelight. The small table, moved in front of one of the large picture windows, held a pair of sparkling glasses, and a new bouquet of flowers filled the room with their sweet perfume. Next to the table nestled in a bucket of ice was an open bottle of champagne. She felt his presence, turned to see him standing by the hall door observing her as she took everything in.

He strolled toward her, one hand reached out to her, drew her effortlessly into his arms. A soft tender kiss pressed on her lips, a soothing caress down her back. She felt special, cherished, safe. His arm around her, he walked them toward the table.

A small box of Moonstruck chocolate truffles was tucked between the two stemmed champagne flutes. How can it be more perfect than this? She sighed.

"Our last chance to celebrate on this trip," Jackson said pulling her back into his embrace. "Champagne, chocolate and you, an unbeatable combination in my book."

"Oh, Jackson, this is like a dream. I keep thinking I'll wake up and everything will be gone. This whole trip — everyone, everything, you — has been perfect. How can I ever thank you for this time to restore my soul, to bring a vision, a dream of mine and my circle sisters to fruition?" she whispered circling her arms around his neck and kissing him with a well-spring of emotion.

"Marry me, Lily, marry me, be my wife, my love, my comfort, my companion. Just marry me."

"Marry you? You want to marry me, Jackson?" Lily pulled back and stared deep into his gray eyes. Heart wildly beating, blood pumped through her veins. He wanted to marry her. Stunned, wrapped in his arms, she searched his face looking for something. He wouldn't joke about something this important but ... He loved her. That statement alone shook. The double whammy was adding a proposal. She opened her mouth but words wouldn't come. Still stunned, still staring, still looking for an indefinable something, she closed her eyes to see more clearly.

His arms banded around her. He didn't move. He didn't speak. She opened her eyes and looked, saw him waiting, saw his truth, his vulnerability.

"With all my heart," he said with a fervent intensity in his soft voice as soon as she looked at him again.

"Oh, Jackson, I don't know what to say." Her eyes filled with unshed tears, she wavered, leaned into him, and grasped his arms.

"Yes would be a good answer." Jackson's heart beat faster, doubt crept into his mind. He resisted the urge to tighten his hold, knowing he had to wait, knowing it had to be her choice, her decision. *Just say yes, damn it, just say yes.* Relief flooded through him when an instant later her arms flew around his neck and her lips brushed dozens of little butterfly kisses all over his face.

"Yes, Jackson. Yes, I'll marry you." The words tumbled out and she laughed.

One arm still firmly around her, Jackson guided her closer to the table. "I'm not ready to let you go yet." He poured the glinting bubbles into the glasses, handed one to her and gently clinked them. "I'd like to propose a toast."

She raised her eyes to his, smiled, and nodded.

"May our life be sustained by the love and joy we feel tonight."

"Blessed Be, Jackson. Blessed Be." Lily sipped her champagne and leaned into him, resting her head on his chest. The feeling of being untethered, floating, flying free abated. The sound of his steady heartbeat, the safe haven of his arms: this was where she belonged.

THEY ARRIVED in Fremont well after midnight, and without any real discussion, went to her home for the rest of the night. Morning was time enough to share this wonder with others flittered through her mind as she drifted off to sleep in Jackson's arms.

"Well, sleepy head, its nine o'clock and you are just beginning to stir. Does this mean you're going to be a slug-a-bed now we're marrying?" Jackson chuckled, leaned over and placed light kisses all over her face.

"You look like a pirate. A patch over one eye will complete the look," Lily retorted, reaching up to stroke his stubble-roughened cheek. "A rather disreputable pirate at that," she added with a forced frown.

"Are you my wench, then?" he asked his best leering piratical look on his face as his hand started a leisurely journey down her body in stroking, circling, smoothing but not soothing movements.

"Hmm, I might be," Lily said with a laugh, her hand now moving under the covers to stroke him. "I see you're in need of a wench."

"A saucy wench. I'm in need of a saucy wench, that's for sure." He grinned, his hand now moving back up her body to cup her breast. Thumb teasing her nipple, he lowered his head replacing thumb with mouth and suckled, his tongue teasing the sensitive tip. He relished the feel of her body arching up to him before he surrendered to the passion that was Lily.

Well over an hour later, they were showered, dressed and had eaten a light breakfast. As they were cleaning up, Jackson stopped and leaned back against the kitchen counter.

"Let's call mother before we go ring shopping. You know she'll be in seventh heaven. First thing she'll ask is 'when'. Let's set a date," he urged reaching for her as she passed by him with the last of the dishes.

"Okay, we can call from the speaker phone in my office." Lily avoided his hands, got the dishwasher door open, and put the dishes in. "A date? Well, Jackson, I don't know. How long will it take to have the pre-nuptial agreement drawn up? That needs to be in place first." Lily was still smiling as she straightened and turned, saw the happiness in his eyes, the joy on his face disappear replaced by hurt and anger.

The sense of lightness and joy of a second ago was gone.

"A pre-nup?" His voice vibrated with chilling anger. "You still think we need a pre-nuptial agreement? With all that's between us? I'm not enough? Why? Don't you trust me? Do you think I'll take everything of yours and leave you with nothing?" His voice growled with incredulity.

"Of course I trust you." Lily reached out and touched his arm. His muscles clenched and he pulled away from her touch. "I thought we'd already discussed this. I told you how I felt about everything you've worked for becoming mine. I don't need your money, Jackson. I'll still be working. I can contribute to the household expenses. I know we need to sort this out first, put it in writing, make it legal...so we both know where we stand in this. And then there's Eleanor. You'll want to make provision for her."

"So, you're saying I can't trust you? That you'd take advantage of mother?" Jackson's voice was a graveled whisper, his eyes bored into hers.

"No, I'm not saying that," Lily's voice was gentle, her eyes stayed locked with his. Over the years, her work had exposed her to difficult and dangerous situations. She'd learned to keep an outward façade of calm. In that moment in time, she was grateful for those challenging situations. "It's just better to have our affairs, our business affairs I mean, in order. You never know what the future will bring. People in love, planning on marriage always think everything will work out. I guess I'm more realistic and know sometimes it doesn't."

"Are you saying you doubt my love for you?" Jackson's jaw clenched, pain infused every word.

An inner voice started screaming at her to stop talking but the urge to explain, to make him see how she viewed this situation won out. "No, Jackson. No, I don't doubt your love for me. This really doesn't have anything to do with love. It's all about we need to work this out, come to some sort of an agreement before we set the date." Even though her eyes never left his and her voice was calm and reasonable, inside she was terrified, terrified she would lose him if she gave in and even more terrified she would lose herself and all she'd worked for if she didn't.

"And that's your final word on it?" He bit out the challenge in his eyes.

"No, no it's not. I'll think it over and ask that you do also." Visibly calm, she never flinched, never looked away while she gently touched his cheek. "We love each other. I know in my heart and soul that's the truth. We can find a way through this problem. I know that in my heart and soul too."

"Are we telling people we're getting married?"

She heard his pain in that short question. Her eyes still locked with his, she sensed his withdrawal. Her inner turmoil increased yet she hung on to the external layer of reason. "Yes, unless you'd rather not." She broke eye contact, stepped back and began pacing. "I need some time to figure this out for myself. Right now it's a raw, frightening feeling to think of being married without a pre-nuptial agreement."

Her stance determined, her face reflected her worry when she stopped in front of him. "From what you've said, for you it's a matter of trust and a pre-nuptial agreement says to you that we don't have trust in our relationship. So, if I heard you right, we're really at apples and oranges. I don't know the way forward, I only know there is a way forward if we take the time to find it." Stepping toward Jackson she reached up to touch his cheek with her fingertips. "I'll do whatever you want about telling people or not, Jackson. It's up to you," she said softly.

"I guess this is one of those situations that require faith, not something I'm particularly strong in," he said exhaling heavily. Capturing her hand, he pressed it against his cheek. "But we've worked out other things." His eyes caught hers in an intense gaze. "We can work this one out also if we can keep the faith. I'll trust that we can," he said resting his forehead against hers.

"We both want this to work out. That's a good start." She leaned into him and felt the comfort of his presence, the rightness of being with him like this. "You're right; we've come a long way as we've sorted things out. This is just one more thing to work through." She wrapped her arms around his waist. "I know you aren't Paul so I don't think this is about him. There is something I need to sort out for myself before I can explain it better to you."

"Okay," he said his fear of losing her, his panic in not really having her eased. "Maybe we need to keep this to ourselves until we work this out." Slipping his arms around her, he pulled her closer. "I think we need to hold off telling Mother. When we have a date set, then we'll tell her. I don't want her to cut short her visit with my sisters. I figure you'll tell your circle sisters. I'll most likely tell Daniel. Maybe … ." his voice trailed off, the sentence incomplete.

They stood together, his head bent with his forehead resting on hers, their arms around each other.

THE NEXT TWO weeks flew by as Lily continued to regain her strength and range of motion. Mark released her to drive more than a mile or two and on the freeway, which meant she saw all her clients. Because she was pacing herself with client appointments, she caught up on her documentation and filed four more guardianship reports.

While getting back into an almost normal swing of things regarding her work was good, what fed her soul was resuming spending individual time with each of her circle sisters outside of The Circle's gatherings. She had missed the casual lunch or supper, going for walks or to a movie.

Because they'd had such success discussing serious matters using Lily's couch, moving closer together when they worked something out, that easily became the foundation to sort out the pre-nuptial issue. However, the reality that many things had been discussed and resolved including her keeeping her professional name (Hughes) while assuming Montgomery outside work, her house would become her office and thus remain in her professional name, household duties, yard upkeep, engagement and wedding rings which they'd shop for when it felt right. They even agreed to have a judge they both knew and liked officiate but they were still at an impasse when it came to the main issue: the pre-nuptial agreement.

The business of House Totems was flourishing and she'd traveled with Jackson on two more trips to California. Short, one day, one night jaunts but all together she'd worked with seven clients. Having returned from the last trip three days ago, Lily was now on her way to Sophia's for the first meeting everyone would attend in a month. After parking in front of the house, she picked up the salad she'd brought for the potluck. A floating lightness in her step, she walked to the house.

Barely in the door, Lily was surrounded by her circle sisters' excited voices, warm wishes, and comforting hugs. As they stepped back, Lily saw the joy and happiness on their faces and knew it was for her. Over the last two weeks she told them individually that Jackson had proposed and she'd accepted, but this was the first time since that momentous event they'd all been together.

"We're all so happy for you," Sophia said, linking her arm in hers and leading Lily into the living room while Hunter took her salad to the kitchen and Diana collected her coat and purse. "Come." Sophia gestured Lily toward the East, the symbol of new beginnings. The other women took their places around the circle.

A piece of rainbow-color-watered silk was draped over the green glass bowl in the center of their altar. Diana picked it up and placed a small cloisonné hummingbird in the center. One hand on Lily's arm, she said, "May you find the joy you so richly deserve with Jackson."

"May you find peace and understanding," Elizabeth said in a soft voice as she added a cabochon of moonstone to the silk now in her lap.

"May you find a safe haven," Ashley whispered as she set a small box with a two inch wand of fragile selenite on the material.

"May your heart be full of gladness." Hunter reached over and touched Lily's knee. She held a piece of shimmering sun-stone in the palm of her hand. Gently she added the gem to the growing bundle and passed it to her left.

"May your nights, and perhaps your days, be full of loving," Gabriella said with a wink and a laugh. "I can't imagine it being otherwise with a hunk like Jackson around." She rested a piece of rose quartz intricately engraved with entwining hearts with the other items.

Lily's cheeks flushed with a blush at Gabby's bawdy remark.

"May the Goddess bless you and Jackson and may your years together be filled with Her love." Sophia took the silk, adding her contribution of a soul mate crystal before pulling the sides together. After tying it with a red ribbon symbolizing love, she handed the rainbow silk pouch to Lily.

The silk bag pressed to her heart, her smile tremulous, her eyes watery, Lily's voice wavered with overflowing emotion. "I'm so very blessed to have you all in my life." Energy from each gift seeped through the thin fabric and warmed her. "I'll remember your prayers for me," she said and met the steady gaze of each of her circle sisters. Her cheeks pink, she added, "Well, really they are for us – you know, Jackson and me. Words can't really express how I feel right now, what this means to me. Thank you."

"Let's continue with prayers, ceremony and our talking circle,"

Sophia said looking around the room. "Is everyone in agreement?" Heads nodded. She stood, lit the sage smudge and began.

Prayers were said with everyone contributing. Their ceremony called upon the Goddess to bless them and lead them forth to their highest good in the relationships in their lives. At the conclusion of the Ceremony, they sat in a circle on the floor. Tonight's talking stone was a large rose quartz representing unconditional love. Although Lily was asked to start, she demurred, requesting to speak last.

"Okay, then, I'll go first," Elizabeth bubbled, her sky-blue eyes sparkling. "I've got my ticket for Ireland. I'll leave the day after summer solstice so I can celebrate it with you. The Lady comes to me almost every night in my dreams. It's really quite wonderful." Elizabeth paused, a curl of her black hair wrapped around a finger, her blue eyes searching the faces of the other women. "I have a feeling, like a premonition, that something life-changing will happen on this trip. But, I know I must go. I've felt the draw for too long to let this feeling stop me." She paused. "Flying into Shannon, renting a car, spending five weeks driving around, I'm pinching myself every day," she said and laughed while stroking the rose quartz. Her tone was serious when she next spoke.

"This is so unlike me, all fluttery and flighty. I do have a couple of families who are expecting to travel while I'm away and a part of me can't believe I'm saying this, but someone else will have to support them if they need it. I won't be available at all." Elizabeth inhaled deeply and exhaled slowly. "Such a freeing thought in so many ways," she added more quietly. Smiling softly she passed the stone to Gabriella on her left.

E. just glowed when she talked about Ireland. Lily too felt something life-changing would happen for her circle sister while there. *I'd love to go to Ireland, to be with her but I know she needs to do this on her own.*

Gabriella's auburn hair flowed down her back; her hazel eyes glowed as she took the stone. "Work is work and I'm glad I'm employed. However, I must confess writing is more challenging than I originally thought. While I love my story, the writing workshop I went to last weekend has me doubting I have what it takes to pull this off. I know I have a great story, it's learning how to tell it that's the struggle. And, some days I'm just so tired when I get home I don't have the energy to write. I'm open to a pep-talk."

"You have the drive and determination to succeed in whatever you do, Gabby. It may take more time than you figured but I am confident you'll succeed," Diana said, turning to give her friend a hug.

"Here are stones you can use for grounding," Sophia said and pulled a piece of Hematite and another of Carnelian from her pocket. "And here is a crystal for communication." She reached across the circle and placed the stones including a small crystal on the floor in front of Gabriella.

"Thanks, Soph. I can use all the help I can get." She leaned forward and picked up the stones. Turning to her left, she smiled at Diana. "Your turn, D."

"My contract to teach my two favorite classes has been picked up for another year by Fremont Community College," Diana's quiet well-modulated voice still conveyed her delight. "And in addition, some of my class participants have been hiring me to consult or work with them on projects.

"Bill is planning on working this summer with one of his room-mates, so other than stopping by for a long weekend or two; I doubt I'll see much of him. I'm glad my business is picking up."

Lily noticed Diana looking at her hands clasped in her lap, her head bowed. She had to lean forward to hear what she said next her voice was so low.

"Dennis doesn't know how much I'm paid or how well I'm doing. I've opened a savings account in a different bank in my name only so I can save all my consulting income and a large chunk of my teaching income. Knowing I've a little money set aside that is in my name...." The rose quartz remained in her hands. "I hope I'm doing the right thing," she said softly looking up and around at the other women, a question in her eyes.

"Perhaps it's time to name your business and become officially a trainer and consultant. I can give you the name of my accountant, D,"

Lily offered. "She's great and can give you the names of whomever else you need to talk to.

"Perhaps it is." Diana sat straighter, brushed her hair back behind her ears. Her chin raised and her voice firm, she added, "I'll call her Monday. Thanks, Lily. I know you think highly of her."

"I do. She saved my life this year with the accident and everything. I didn't know if I'd ever get my taxes done and filed."

"I thought you could file an extension. Can't you take until June or August 15th or even October 15th?" Hunter interjected.

"I could have but I hated having it hanging over my head so I just sat myself down and did it," Lily said and grimaced.

"So like you, Lily. You have more determination and perseverance than most of us put together." Hunter grinned.

"Don't get me started. I can tell a tale or two about everyone in The Circle and her determination, perseverance, commitment, courage, spunk...whatever you want to call it. We all have an abundance of it," Lily's voice was stern but there was a smile on her face.

Laughing, Diana agreed and passed the stone to Ashley.

"The children're all doing well," she said in her soft drawl. "I've another mammogram coming up next week, but," she sat a little straighter and spoke up, "I've my list of 'rules' for the technician all written out 'cause it helps me keep myself from going into a panic. I know panic won't help but sometimes it's so hard not to go there." Her brow wrinkled, her lips pursed, her shoulders slumped. "My neighbor, Betty, will watch the kids."

"If you want someone to go with you, I can go," Elizabeth said, in a solemn voice.

Lily watched Ashley's concern shift to hope, her brow smoothed, her lips relaxed, her shoulders straightened. This was one of the things she loved about them. Ashley would never have to go to another mammogram or oncology doctor appointment alone. One of them would find a way to be there with her.

"It's next Thursday at ten a.m.... "

"That's not a problem at all for me." Elizabeth smiled warmly. "It's my morning to write reports. You'll be doing me a favor as I'd much rather spend it with you than in front of the computer --- we'll figure out the details before we leave tonight, okay?"

"It's more than okay, Elizabeth." Ashley sat straighter, brushed her pale blond hair over her shoulder, bone-deep relief flashed across her face.

The rose quartz in hand, Hunter started, "Business is booming and Logan and I are doing very well, teenager though she is. The wise women in this circle who suggested that I enjoy her, nurture and support her rather than try to mold her, may have been on to something." She chuckled. "She has several guy-friends interested in her. They hang out at our place, walk to and from school with her, all those teenage kinds of things. I'm grateful she doesn't seem interested in them beyond a friendship." Her mouth tipped in a wide smile. "If all goes as planned, she'll help me more around the dance studio this summer but," she said turning toward Ashley, "she loves your kids and I know would delight in taking them on outings to the park, zoo, you know those kinds of kid things."

"They love her too, Hunter. That'd be great if she wants to. Otherwise, I'm sure we'll manage," she said softly.

"Of course you will," Hunter agreed. "You manage very well, Ash. Always remember, though, if you need us, we're here for you and your children." One hand reached out to take Ashley's while the other hand passed the stone on to Sophia.

"Garden is almost in. Some plants are already showing their perky little heads. Peas are climbing the fence and poles. I love spring and all its reminders of life. So, you are all forewarned that the garden will be plentiful as always," Sophia said as she slowly looked at each woman. "This year, however, I'm doing things a bit differently. With this friend I'm helping out, I don't have quite the time I've had in the past. I've decided to host a garden party once a month and you're all invited to attend in your work clothes. We'll weed, trim, prune and do whatever is needed in the main garden. I'll keep the smaller ones up on my own." Her look was expectant. "Well, what do you all think?"

"You, Sophia, not only asking for our help but inviting us into your garden? Into the sacrosanct?" Diana said, a bemused tone in her voice.

"I think it's a wonderful idea. When's the first garden party to be?" Ashley chimed in.

"I thought we'd do it the first Saturday of the month so people could plan on it. We may need an extra day in July and August, but I think with your help I can manage between times." She went on, "You see, helping this friend is taking up more time than I'd anticipated. Although he's very ill and dying, it doesn't seem to be a very quick process in his case. Well, actually I guess when someone has emphysema it can be a very long, drawn out process."

"Never fear, Soph, your gardening circle sisters will appear!" Elizabeth said, raising and waving her fisted hand as if it were a wand. "I can hardly wait. Living in an apartment doesn't give me much chance to nurture life." Looking around at the aghast looks on her sister's faces, she hastily amended, "Well, to nurture plant life, you know, from the ground. Well, I'm only digging a deeper hole." She looked around as the giggles erupted. "Sophia has the stone and perhaps has more to add?"

"Actually I don't have anything more to add and so turn the stone over to Lily."

Holding the rose quartz, now warm from the heat from her circle sisters' hands, she said, "Life has been so eventful since we were all together. I know I've talked to each of you individually or in small groups but I love the energy when we're all together. When I get caught up in the busyness of my life it's even more important to be here like this with you.

"I feel so blessed at your reception to my news." Lily found herself floundering, words failing to come easily. Her tongue tangled with telling everyone about the problem she and Jackson had. The weight of the rainbow silk bag in her lap strengthened her resolve. "However, what I haven't shared is we've hit a stumbling block. While I want a pre-nuptial agreement Jackson does not," her voice wavered on the last words, her eyes glistened with unshed tears, her chest constricted and her heart stuttered as steel bands wrapped around her body. "We've worked many other things out so we're both hopeful we'll work this out also." Staring at the green bowl in the middle of the altar, she sat quietly, her attention on her breathing until the steel bands eased and her heart beat its normal rhythm. Letting each breath out slowly, her body settled.

Focusing on her other news, moments later, a big grin split her face. "On to other things: I bring tidings of great joy," she said with relish. "Tidings I've not shared in any detail with any of you so I could tell you all at the same time." She paused, her gaze sweeping around the circle. "You know I've traveled to California with Jackson to identify House Totems for some of his clients. What you don't know is that we now have twenty thousand dollars for our fund. With that money we can afford to have ideas and act on them! So, what's your pleasure? What're your ideas? How do you see these funds being used for our highest good?"

"Wow! That's an awesome amount of money. So that's what's left over after your fees?" asked Diana.

"Oh, all my expenses are paid separately," Lily responded blithely, "and since I've stayed with Jackson, other than my airfare and meals, there haven't been extra expenses even for him. The total for the House Totems I've done is twenty thousand dollars."

"So, what you're saying is that you go and do the work for time with Jackson?"

"Well, D, it hasn't really been work."

"It's using your gift, Lily. It may not be work, but it certainly isn't *nothing*."

"Oh, I know Soph, I know it isn't *nothing*. But I so want these monies to be ours. Can you understand that?" she asked looking at each woman. No one's head nodded in agreement. "Okay, then," she sighed in exasperation. "What do you all suggest? That's really what this is all about; for us to come to some agreement on this work, the fees, and their use."

"Well, I think the person who does the work should get something in addition to her expenses being paid," said Gabriella. "Maybe ten percent goes in our pot?"

"Oh no, Gabriella, our pot needs more than ten percent of the fee." Lily was adamant. "Ten percent is not nearly enough for our pot."

"How about splitting it fifty/fifty then?" asked Sophia. "I keep that in mind when I plant my garden. I plan on giving at least fifty percent of it away in addition to the amount I share through my bringing meals and 'gifts' to our meetings."

"Fifty percent seems okay to me," Diana added, "an even split. What do the rest of you think?" she asked turning to look at everyone. Laughing she turned back to Lily. "Well, I guess that's it then. Fifty-fifty, win-win. Just to double check. Does anyone feel the need to continue this discussion further?" Sobering for a moment, her gaze serious, Diana looked around the circle, meeting each woman's eyes. "By now you all know how important it is for each of us to have our say, to be heard, to have this place to speak out. So, know in your heart that the decision is not yet made. Not until everyone is heard and agreement reached."

Heads bobbed in agreement, every face wreathed in a smile.

"I guess this is the decision then," she said mirroring the smiling faces. "Fifty percent to the totem identifier and fifty percent to the Golden Cauldron fund. At least that's the name we've talked about for the fund when it was a dream of ours. What say you all now?"

"I move that we formally establish the Golden Cauldron fund and that those funds be used to support our highest good," announced Ashley.

"Blessed be." Echoed around the circle.

"I think we need some singing," Diana sang the words aloud.

"What song do you suggest?" Lily sang back.

"The River," shouted Gabriella and before she finished everyone joined their voices in song. They blessed the mother goddess, reveling in the joy that came from sharing such moments. After songs were sung and food consumed, they came together in a circle, holding on to one another, touching waists and hearts, shoulders and souls. With a soft out-flowing of breath they broke apart, each nourished in body and spirit, each with gladness in her heart, a spring in her step, and joy radiating from her soul.

As she drove home, Lily's mind was full of memories: the love and laughter she had shared with everyone tonight. With a sigh she recalled that Diana seemed to be the only person who understood why the pre-nuptial agreement was important to her.

~

THE NEXT DAY, Lily called and made arrangements to meet with Diana and Sophia for lunch. The conversation was long and thoughtful, about trust in oneself and one's intuition, as well as trust in others and the myth of independence in relationships. Diana shared a class exercise. The students pick an ordinary item such as an article of clothing, a food product, or even something like a newspaper, television show. They then chart out how many people in what parts of the world are involved in making the finished product. It was a powerful way to reinforce the reality of interdependence, the importance of relationships, and break through the myth of independence.

"Lots to think about," Lily said to Diana and Sophia as they left the restaurant. "Since Jackson will be out of town on Thursday, he's coming over tonight for dinner and talk. Hopefully I'll be able to express myself so he'll understand."

"Remember, Lily. He may understand, he may just not agree. Those apples and oranges you've mentioned? An apple doesn't become an orange and vice versa just because we talk about it. They are two different fruits forever to remain different." Diana gave her a hug and walked to her car.

"Consider talking without trying to convince Jackson or have him understand anything. You may find you get further that way, or then again, you may not," added Sophia, also giving her a hug before turning away. She waved at Diana as she also went to her car.

"In some ways this is more about trusting me than trusting Jackson. Trusting that I'm not making a mistake; trusting that I won't change in order to please him like I did with Paul; trusting that I can be independent from someone I love," Lily said to herself as she got in her car. "Without that trust in me, how can I ever hope to trust Jackson at the level I need in order to move through this?"

Lily's hands wrapped around the steering wheel, her bowed head resting on them. "After Paul left, I had so much to do to rebuild myself, to heal from the assault on my heart and soul even more than my body. I know it's my doubt of myself; my fear of being wrong; my need to protect myself that keeps me stuck, keeps me from moving forward," she whispered to herself.

Sighing, she leaned back, her head settled against the headrest, closing her eyes, she prayed. "Goddess, bring me peace and the right words so I can express my heart to this man I love. Blessed Be."

Jackson, who was waiting for her when she returned from her lunch with Diana and Sophia, rose and held out his arms as she came in the door. He looked tired, vulnerable, not like himself. She wrapped her arms around him and held him close.

"Something's come up on the job site," he spoke into her hair. "I have to take the first flight out in the morning." He shifted and she pressed against him, resting her head against his chest.

Goddess, be with me. In that moment, her way was clear. She hugged him to her and relaxed. "Jackson, would you mind terribly if we spent this evening together with no serious discussions, just enjoy being together?" Her heart pounded as she awaited his answer. His arms tightened a fraction before easing.

"No, I wouldn't mind at all." His hands roamed down her back, cupped her buttocks and pulled her against him.

His erection swelled against her abdomen. She smiled and wiggled so she could look up. The heat, the desire, the passion burned in his eyes, for her…just for her. She let out a shaky breath. "Do you have an idea of what you'd like to do first?" She wriggled against him. "Or do you need some suggestions from me?"

"Somehow, in this, I think we're in total agreement." His mouth claimed hers in a kiss so searing she was surprised she didn't burst into flames. He lifted her a foot in the air and then slowly, ever so slowly, let her slide down his body.

"Bed," she gasped as his mouth left hers and found her ear. "Jackson, bed," was all she could manage.

"Here. Now." He skillfully unbuttoned her top, unfastened her bra while maneuvering them to the couch. Sitting, he pulled her to straddle him. His hands grabbed the hem of her skirt, slipping beneath to rub her legs, caress the sensitive spot behind her knees before stroking her thighs. As his hands roamed up her legs, her skirt, caught on his arms, moved up too.

Lily reached between them, pulling his shirt from his trousers. She fumbled in her haste to get his shirt off. Her hands sought the buttons and zipper of his pants, her fingers curved around his burgeoning erection. *Now, now, now* pounded in her ears as she finally freed him from the confines of his briefs and moved him to her ready entrance.

Jackson grabbed her by the waist and guided her down. He slipped effortlessly into her wet heat. *Mine, mine, mine* echoed in his mind as he lost himself in her.

35 - BELTANE AND BEREAVEMENT

"Beltane…I absolutely love this time of year," Sophia said to no one in particular. She stood on the patio watching her circle sisters and their children weave and dip in a traditional Maypole dance.

"And, every year it's different," Lily said. "Even using the same ribbons the intricate pattern shifts. In some ways, it reminds me of us. We are still the same women who came together over seven years ago and yet we aren't."

"Philosophical musings?"

"Not really. Just trying to keep my thoughts flowing in a positive direction," Lily said. She watched the dancing, kept her breathing slow and even. Her heart was breaking into shards of sharp pain. Her stomach threatened to toss up her breakfast. This pain would not go away with a tiny white pill like it did after the accident. Her low voice trembled, "I looked up Charlie's high school website over Winter Break to see if there was a calendar. There is. I've known when he had a meet and I know the senior activities. This weekend is the Senior Prom," her voice broke. "I don't even know if he has a girlfriend, Soph. That's the hardest for me, the not knowing.

"I don't want to make things worse for him, but Graduation is the 31st. How am I...? After all the years ...,"she stopped.

"After all the years you've worked so hard to provide a home for him, it must feel like the worst sort of betrayal," Sophia said, resting her hand on Lily's arm. "I'm so proud of how you've handled his being gone this year."

"Thanks Soph, that means a lot coming from you. I have blessing in my life because he's been gone. My relationships with Eleanor and Jackson, the House Totems, the extra time to spend with you and the others...none of that would be as it is if Charlie was still home with me." She patted Sophia's hand, a smile on her lips. "They've finished."

The women sat on the patio while keeping an eye on the children playing in the yard.

"Logan is such a blessing," Ashley said watching Hunter's daughter laugh and play with her own much younger children. "Artie has a crush on her and Anthony too, if my eyes are telling me right." Her soft Southern voice ended in a sigh.

"I'm so glad she's been included today because there are times she feels left out. It means a lot to her to be here. When I see her playing with Ash's children, I know her child-like self is alive and well while she nurtures her older-self in growing and maturing." Hunter looked around at each of her friends with blue-green eyes bright with emotion, "It means a lot to me, too. Thank you."

"Beltane is about welcoming life, including children, remember? I don't know why we haven't done this before," Elizabeth said softly, a smile spreading across her face as she watched the antics on the lawn. "They're all such special children."

"You think all children are special, E.," Gabriella said, her bright grin aimed at her friend. "Beltane's about enjoying all the delicious delights of the Mother Goddess: flowers, food, children and how children are made." Groaning she continued, "Well, I can enjoy all but the last delight this Beltane."

"Next year you will," Lily said firmly. "If you want it, you shall have that special someone in your life next year. I can see him now," she said her voice lowering to a conspiratorial whisper, "tall, dark, handsome, a bit arrogant, gallant and ever so seductive."

"You've described Jackson's friend, Giovanni, Lily." Ashley's face was open and innocent but laughter lurked in her gray eyes. "They'd make a handsome couple and their children! Oh my, just think auburn haired little girls with their daddy's dark eyes."

"For shame! Ash, for shame! You're a married woman. You shouldn't have any idea what that man's eyes look like," Sophia said with a good-natured scold. "However, he is sinfully handsome with a naturally seductive look." She paused and winked. "And you're right about the babies."

"Why you'd want to see me with that arrogant man is beyond me," Gabriella sputtered. "Arrogant, seductive—just like a rake."

"Rake?" Elizabeth said trying to stifle her laugh. "That isn't the image that came to my mind—a garden implement?" she added with feigned innocence.

"You know exactly what I'm talking about, E. In Regency England, a rake was a man who seduces women."

"I think today they're called womanizers," added Diana.

"Well, they haven't always been called that," Gabriella rejoined with a bit of heat. Her eye caught the amused looks on everyone's face and she stopped. "Got me good, you all did, got me real good. But I have no intention of being involved with that kind of man, so you'll just have to forget it," she said with a haughty toss of her head.

"Before we got sidetracked with Gabby's love life," Sophia interjected ignoring the fake dagger-like look sent her way, "we were talking about Beltane. I don't think we've heard anything at all from Diana or Lily. Care to share?" she asked.

"I think Beltane is your favorite holiday, Sophia, because of the honoring of life through all that is growing," Diana stated, her violet eyes solemn. "My favorite is Samhain, the time of honoring those who came before. In ways they are alike because they honor the beginning and end of the circle of life and the veil between the worlds is thinnest at these two times of the year." She reached out for a sugar pea to nibble and laughed. "However, the best part of Beltane is it marks the beginning of the sharing of the bounty of your garden. What about you Lily?"

"You all know Winter Solstice is my favorite because it marks the return of the light. I like the dark cocooning feel of Fall deepening to Winter but by Solstice I'm ready for the return to light.

"Because I work with so many people who are at the end of their life's journey, Beltane reminds me of the importance to balance that with the celebration of life, the joy of creating both through the Goddess and within ourselves. Each of us in our own way is a creative person. E. creates families for children, Gabby creates stories, D. creates trainings that help people have more fulfillment in their lives, Ash creates a loving home for her children, Hunter creates a time and space where music and movement fill lives, and Soph creates her wonderful garden as well as opportunities for young minds to grow and learn. For me, it's the act of creation, however it manifests that brings me to Beltane each year with such gladness."

They sat in the semi-circle, comfortable in their silence. Some watched the children play, some were lost in their own thoughts, and some just enjoyed the budding and blooming flowers and the sweet scent of the evergreen clematis climbing one side of the patio, mingling with the dark purple lilac from a neighbor's yard.

Lily broke the silence by saying, "Eleanor is back. She got home Sunday. It was so good seeing her. She's much stronger and doesn't need a cane at all.

"And speaking of arrogant, yet charming men," Lily went on, "Jackson's friend Giovanni is in town for a few days. We're all invited to a big Italian dinner on Saturday…no business, just social time. The menu includes Jackson's spaghetti and salad along with Giovanni's lasagna and bread. Can everyone come?"

"Logan and I'll be there so she'll be able to keep an eye on your kids, Ash. So don't you dare think you won't be coming." Hunter stared at Ashley until she nodded.

"Remember, Jackson has that large entertainment center downstairs. Bring along some movies and if it's anything like last time, we won't even know children are in the house," Lily added.

~

THE THURSDAY after the Italian dinner, Lily added the bay shrimp to the tossed greens already in the bowl. Bread was warming, the table was set. She chuckled as a picture of Giovanni and Gabriella popped into mind. He enjoyed getting a rise out of her and teased until she sniped. Everyone noticed the fireworks crackling between them.

Over their dinner eaten at her small dining table, conversation covered every topic except an upcoming marriage. After clearing the table and cleaning up the kitchen, they moved into the living room and the couch.

"Well," Lily said licking her lips and chewing on her bot-tom lip, "we agreed to talk about things tonight. I want you to know how much it's meant to me to have these past couple of weeks to just be with each other without the pressure of trying to explain or talk about a wedding date." She spoke quietly; her eyes searching Jackson's face. "I know I've not been able to adequately explain why the pre-nuptial agreement is so important to me," she spoke calmly.

"I know it has something to do with your need to be independent and your inability to trust me, to love me enough, to know that we don't need this piece of paper for you to have what you need," Jackson replied just as quietly. "You know I love you, Lily. Why does there need to be more?"

"I have to know I am independent; that I don't need someone to support me. You know how hard it was for me when Paul left. He cleaned out the bank account but left the bills; sent sporadic child support payments; threatened to take Charlie if I couldn't manage alone.

"I struggled to survive month to month, worked hard to get what little I have: a house I'm buying, a little money in the bank. I just panic when I think of marrying without something in writing." Lily's voice broke. "Can't you see it isn't about how much I love you? Or how much you have? It's about what little I have. I'm too scared to risk it. I don't know what more to say. I'm sorry, Jackson. So very, very sorry," Lily choked out burying her head in her hands; her shoulders shaking from her deep racking sobs. "I'm sorry, Jackson," she whispered and turned away from him, curling into a ball.

Pain lanced through him as a waves of hopelessness crashed over him like ocean waves beating on rocks in a storm. Sprays of anguish throbbed through his body. Jackson sat immobilized with the reality of her words. There was nothing more to say. Nothing more to do. He only wished there was nothing more to feel. Standing, he walked the few steps to where Lily remained curled and sobbing on the corner of the couch. He ached with love for her. Reaching down he gently stroked her hair. "I love you, Lily. I'm sorry it isn't enough." He tore his gaze from her wracked form and walked out the door.

"I love you, too, Jackson," Lily whispered to the empty room. A wave of nausea wracked her. She stumbled up and dashed to the bathroom just making it before she heaved her dinner into the toilet. Her stomach empty, she rinsed out her mouth. Back in the living room, she pulled the dark blue coverlet from the back of the couch, and curling in a corner, tucked it under her chin. "Oh Goddess, what am I to do now? I've lost him because I can't trust myself enough for us to marry and he'll accept nothing less than my complete commitment and trust," she whispered to herself as a new wave of grief and tears swept through her.

Hours later when she woke it was dark. Drained, exhausted, beaten—emptiness seeped deep into the marrow of her bones. I've lost Eleanor too. "I don't think I'm strong enough to be with her, at her apartment, in Jackson's house with all those memories," she moaned. With a supreme effort, she dragged herself off the couch and shuffled to the bathroom thankful the dry heaves had ended.

Who was the woman looking at her from the mirror? That Lily had dull eyes red and puffy from crying, blotchy skin, tears streaming down her face and a nose that was red and running. "I don't think I can make it through the night without talking to someone," she whispered to the face in the mirror. "Will you do?" she asked. More tears escaped, her head slowly shook back and forth, back and forth, her whispered voice trembled, "No, I don't suppose you will."

Turning from the face in the mirror, she walked on leaden feet to her office. With the cordless phone in hand, she made her way back to the couch and curled up on the other end—his end. Her body sideways on the cushion, her head leaning on her arm, her shuddering breathing caught the citrus scent of his aftershave. Fresh waves of grief washed through her as she dialed the familiar number.

"Lily, what's wrong?"

"Can you come over, D?" tears choked Lily's voice.

"I'll be there in twenty minutes. Put the tea water on, Lily. I'm coming."

On wobbly legs, she tottered into the kitchen, put the tea kettle on to boil, and reached up for the Goddess mugs they'd each made as a project several years ago. Restlessness now consumed her and she paced through her small house; first turning on all the lights then reversing directions and turning them all off except two in the living room.

The tea was steeping in the pot when Lily saw a car's headlights pull into her driveway and another car pull to the curb across the street. Opening her door, a lump filled her throat and tears filled her eyes when she saw not only Diana, now out of her car in the driveway, but Sophia.

"Oh Goddess, You answered my unspoken prayer by having both D. and Soph come now. Thank You for Your wisdom," Lily softly prayed as her two friends came up the steps and onto her porch, wrapped her in a warm embrace, and held her close. Minutes passed. Without ever letting her go, Diana and Sophia withdrew.

"Guess it's time to go in, have that tea and talk," Diana said softly. "Let's go in and you can tell us all about it."

Sophia held her hand and whispered, "If you want me to leave, Lily, I will. No harm done. When D. called and asked for prayers, I decided to come too. I can't remember a time when you've ever called anyone in the middle of the night. I thought you might need more than prayers but I know you didn't call me," Sophia said gently.

"I didn't call you," the tears falling, her voice quavering, "because I know you have school in the morning. You'd...you'd be tired if you came," she stammered out. "I...I thought D's appointments and classes were later in the day." She clasped Sophia's hand. "I'm so grateful you are here, that both of you are here."

"Let's get our tea and you can tell us what's happening," Diana said slipping her arm around Lily's waist guiding her into the house.

Once mugs were in hand, they went into the living room where Sophia sat next to Lily and Diana pulled a chair close to the couch.

In a soft voice, tears streaming down her face, words stumbling and tumbling out, Lily spilled out what happened. Jackson had left. Forever. Instead of being with him forever, she was without him forever. Such a small word, in one context it signified immense joy and in the other immeasurable pain.

"It looks like you have some decisions to make," Sophia said when Lily'd been silent for a few minutes. Her voice was soft and encouraging as she reached out and took Lily's hand.

"What would they be?" Lily's ragged voice asked. She wiped her weeping eyes and blew her nose. "If I could get myself past my own issues I would have. I know what I should do. But when I think about marrying Jackson without a pre-nuptial agreement, I feel sick," she wrapped her arms around her middle. "My stomach churns and I feel like I'm going to vomit. I get so anxious I can't even sit down. My mind, my thoughts fly all over the place."

The tears that had briefly stopped flowed again. "I've thought about this until my mind is numb and I just can't think at all." She grabbed a new tissue and swiped at her eyes. Picking up the mug, she took a sip of her tea, the warm cup in her hand soothing, the chamomile tea calming. For long minutes, she gazed into her cup. The tears stopped. Finally she raised her head and looked at her friends. "It does come down to trust and commitment. As much as I love Jackson, it appears it isn't enough for me to trust him or us enough to say "yes" and know it'll all be okay in the end." The last words were no more than a whisper. Sobs engulfed her body and she bent around the closely held tea cup.

Diana reached out, took Lily's chin in her hand and slowly raised her head until she could see her face. She looked in her friend's eyes, her voice gentle, "That is the decision, Lily. To say "yes" or say "no.""

No one can make that decision for you. Making no decision leaves you in this space between." She looked calmly at Lily, held her gaze. "I think that's actually the most painful place. A decision one way or the other is movement. Movement at least has the possibility that things will get better. The space between does not."

They sat, sipping tea, words no longer needed. The warmth of friendship, the comfort of understanding took their place. As the light of day brightened the room, Lily said, "I don't think I could have made it through this night without you two." She reached out to take first Diana's hand and then Sophia's. "I don't know what I'll do right now except make it through the day.

"I remember you talking about some training you took, Soph, about a true conflict and the only thing you can do is nothing because in a true conflict no matter what you do, you lose something precious to you. That's where I feel I'm at. I know it's painful, but I think I need to be here, at least for a few days to see if a way becomes clear to me.

"In my heart I know I love Jackson more than I ever thought possible. I pray that the Goddess helps me find a way so I can move forward with him with joy in my heart." With a wry smile she added "or at least not feeling like I need to be only steps away from the toilet."

"I'll call you later to see how you're doing." Diana drew Lily into her arms and hugged her firmly. She stepped back and Sophia took her place.

"I'll call you this afternoon to check in also." Sophia wrapped her arms around Lily and held her close. "You do know we're all here for you however you need us."

"I know you are. I'm very blessed that you've both been here with me." Lily stepped back. She was still shaky, still drained, an acute pain still lanced her heart – but she was no longer alone with her despair.

They walked to the front door. Sophia put her hand on Lily's shoulder. "Thank you for the gift of asking us to come tonight. We all call and talk things over with each other, but I don't remember you ever calling like this before...especially in the middle of the night."

"No, I haven't," Lily said. "I've never felt this way before. Hopeless, helpless, vulnerable, sick, it'd be fine with me if I never felt this way again," she added in an ironic tone.

"And that's what makes your call such a gift. That you'd call me gladdens my heart," Diana said taking her hand and holding it.

Another long hug and Sophia and Diana left. Lily waited on the porch until they'd driven out of sight before she went back inside and curled up on the couch. She breathed in the citrus scent of Jackson's aftershave – a pang of heartache, a balm of comfort.

AFTER LEAVING LILY'S, Jackson drove home. The pain and frustration hadn't abated when he stormed into the house, grabbed a mug from the cupboard, and slammed it on the counter. The mug shattered. "Damn granite," he muttered. "Where's my aluminum cup," he demanded, jerking another cupboard door open and rummaging through it.

"What is the problem, Jackson?" Eleanor called from her doorway.

"Nothing to concern yourself about, Mother," he called back.

"Anything that upsets my son is something to concern myself about," Eleanor said walking briskly into the kitchen. She perched on a stool at the island watching her son bang around. "And, as much as I love and admire you, I must say you look like bloody hell right now."

"Thank you for sharing your thoughts with me," Jackson said his voice laced with sarcasm cleaning up the debris from the shattered mug.

"Does this have something to do with Lily?" Eleanor watched her son struggle to contain and control his emotions. "I know you were to have dinner with her. Indeed, I didn't expect you home tonight."

Jackson stopped, stood in his kitchen, hands on the counter, head down and sighed. "I didn't expect to be home either. It's over between us, Mother. She doesn't love me enough to trust me."

"Have you ever considered it may not be about you at all?" Eleanor asked, a droll tone to her brisk voice.

"I'm not sure I know what you mean, Mother," Jackson said resignation in his tone. "She wants a pre-nuptial agreement. A pre-nuptial agreement is about how to divide the assets when things don't work out. She refuses to marry me without having a plan for how to end it. How can you say this isn't about me?" The words came out like bullets from a machine gun. Staccato. Clipped. Short.

"Because it is another point of view," Eleanor said softly. "It is easy to think we are the reason for and are at the center of everything. But in reality, most of life is not about us at all. We are not the reason and we are not in the center of things." She slipped off the stool and came around the island to stand next to her son, her hand resting on his. "I do believe Lily loves you very much. And I also believe she trusts you and is committed to you. I also believe she wants to keep what is hers, what's she's built in the past separate from what she builds with you."

"She wants to keep what's hers separate from what she'll build with me? You think it isn't about me at all, but just about her?" he snorted in disbelief.

"I do," Eleanor replied firmly. "Lily has worked hard and long against formidable obstacles at least once in her life. I can appreciate she does not want to ever contemplate having to do that again. She has a son and while Charlie is graduating from high school and considered an adult, parents never really stop trying to protect their children. Really, Jackson, what she most wants is to keep what she has built as her own. She doesn't want you to pay off her house or any other debt. She wants the security of keeping what's hers while moving forward in her life with you. I do not think it is about what to do if your marriage ends at all."

"Well, I hope you're right, Mother. If it's that simple, if that's what it's all about, I can fix that. I don't care if she keeps everything that is hers in her own name. I'll even add to her bank account if that will help." Energy surged through him and ideas began to form.

"No, Jackson," Eleanor's voice was sharp. "You will not add to her bank account. You will not "fix" things." She reached up, grabbed his chin and turned his face so she could look him right in the eye. "Your marriage to Lily needs to be a partnership with you both being decision makers. Mark my words, Jackson. Do not take the arrogant, domineering, 'I can take care of the little woman' attitude with Lily. It will not work.

"And, Jackson," Eleanor continued. "I want you to think long and hard about why it has been so important to you to Not have a pre-nup. You have a part in all of this and while I love you, I'm equally sure you have not faced your own demons in this regard."

Jackson took his mother in his arms and hugged her. "I know. I want Lily to want me just as I am, to know I'm enough just as I am," he said, his voice breaking. "She isn't being unreasonable, is she?"

"No, she isn't."

"I'm not sure what to do. But I'll figure it out."

"No heavy-handed methods will work, Jackson," Eleanor said. "Remember Lily wants a partnership with you. Can you honestly partner with her?"

"Yes, I can." His mood lifted. A future with Lily shone before him.

36 - FINDING A WAY THROUGH

A week had passed since her world had fallen apart. He hadn't called but then she hadn't expected him to. She'd not called him because she had nothing new to say.

In the past when her life was bad, she'd buried herself in work. Caught in darkness now, even work was a challenge. She'd talked to Eleanor, who hadn't mentioned Jackson and she hadn't asked. They'd decided Lily would close her case. The plan was they'd stay in touch.

Multiple times a day her mind would snag on the idea of marrying Jackson without a pre-nuptial agreement. Moments later waves of nausea rolled through her. Sleep was restless, if at all. Food – even Sophia's invitations for dinner were turned down. Jackson was her last hope of finding the love she'd dreamed of having. And yet...and yet, the nausea always won.

A knock on her door grabbed her attention. Quickly saving the report she was working on, Lily hurried to the front door. A man in dark blue livery stood on her porch, a long white limousine parked at her curb.

"May I help you?" she asked, puzzled. "Are you lost?"

"I don't think so." A polite smile was on his face but she noted his eyes danced with amusement. "This is the address I was sent to. Are you Ms. Lily Hughes?"

"Yes. Yes, I'm she." Puzzlement was now joined by confusion. What was going on here?

"Then this is for you." The man held out a pristine white envelope; her name and address typed on the front.

Unlocking and opening her security screen door, Lily hesitated a moment before reaching out and taking the envelope from his outstretched hand. "I have no idea what this is all about." She turned the envelope over and over but other than her typed name and address there was no clue to its origin.

Hands shaking, she carefully opened the envelope and extracted the card.

"Trust Me". Nothing else. But she knew the handwriting.

"Are you supposed to take me somewhere?" Trembling started deep in her core as she stared at the man, searching for some sign to tell her what was going on.

"1425 SW 10th Avenue, Suite 2003," he said, his features still schooled in the same polite, professional look, laughter still dancing in his eyes.

The card gripped in her hand, she banded her arms around her waist to hold herself in. Lights flickered in the backs of her eyes. She thought she might faint. She had prayed to find a way through her fear to be with Jackson. "Trust Me." Two simple words that either held the answer or didn't. She loved him. Did she trust him? Trust him enough to see what this was all about. The lights faded, the trembling eased, her muscles relaxed. She did trust him.

"Oh, that's downtown. I can't go like this," she said reaching up and patting her sleep tousled hair. "I'm still in my robe."

"I was told to wait for you," the driver said simply.

"Give me ten minutes," Lily said over her shoulder as she raced to the stairs.

It was closer to fifteen when she came to the door dressed simply in a black pant suit with a blouse the same shade of blue as her eyes, black leather half-boots, hair styled and make up in place.

"I'm ready," she said breathlessly. Grabbing her purse, she stepped out the door.

The driver took her elbow escorting her to the limousine. Once she was settled in the back, he got in behind the wheel and slowly pulled away from the curb. Twenty agonizing minutes later, the limo pulled to a stop. It took some effort, but she stifled the urge to open the door and dash out on her own — that just wasn't done. It seemed to take forever for the driver to get out of the car, walk around the front, and open her door.

"Here we are ma'am," he said as he handed her out of the limo. "I believe the elevators are to the left once you're inside. Suite 2003."

"Thank you," Lily said reaching for her wallet.

"That isn't necessary, ma'am. It's all been taken care of."

"Oh, okay then. Thank you." She smiled and reached out to shake his hand.

Taking her hand in his, the driver bowed slightly before turning and walking with her to the door of the building keeping her hand on his arm. After opening the building's door, he smiled and gestured her in. "I believe you have someone waiting for you, ma'am. Good day."

Lily stood in the open doorway, watching as he turned, strode to the car, got in, and drove away. The car disappeared around the corner, before she turned into the building. The elevators were where the driver said they'd be. Pushing up, she stood, tapping her foot, waiting for one to arrive. When it did, she stepped inside and pushed the button for the twentieth floor. The doors closed and the elevator rose with a whisper.

Suite 2003 was the office of Thompson, Roberts and Associates, Business Services. "Hmm, that doesn't give me a clue at all," Lily mumbled, discreetly wiping her sweaty palms on her pants to better grasp the door handle.

"May I help you?" a man behind a desk said.

"Good Morning, I'm Lily Hughes," she said in her most prim and professional tone. "I was asked to come here this morning."

"They are expecting you, Ms. Hughes. Right through the door to your right." He turned to answer the ringing phone.

Lily walked firmly to the door, knocked once, and without waiting for a reply, opened it, and stepped inside. Stepped inside into a scene from an old movie: a kindly looking white haired gentleman behind a large desk; standing to his right, a younger man, looking less kindly and more formal. There the movie comparison ended because in front of the desk, dressed in a formal business suit and just getting to his feet was Jackson.

She stared, couldn't tear her eyes from the sight of him. Her breath caught in her lungs, her heart pounded so loud she knew the men could hear it. Standing with one hand on the door knob, she was frozen unable to step back or forward.

A warm yet cautious smile on his face, Jackson stepped toward her his hands outstretched in welcome. "I'm so glad you came," he said, clasping her elbow. "I'd like to introduce you to William Thompson, my attorney, and Benjamin Roberts, my CPA." He waved his free hand to indicate the two gentlemen behind the desk. He stood to the side and gestured for her to precede him into the room.

The feel of his hand, the sound of his voice brought Lily out of her trance. She needed her wits about her and struggled to appear composed.

On his feet now, Mr. Thompson rounded the desk his hand out to shake Lily's. "It's my pleasure to meet you, Ms. Hughes. My associate, Benjamin Roberts." He nodded toward the younger man who also approached his hand out in greeting.

"Gentlemen, I find myself at a disadvantage. I don't even know why I'm here or what this is all about," she stated, looking directly at each of them, pleased her voice sounded steady, confident. "Please enlighten me."

"By all means, Ms. Hughes," said Mr. Thompson, gesturing her to a chair at a conference table in front of windows that looked out over Fremont. "We have everything laid out here for your inspection."

"What exactly is it you want me to inspect, Mr. Thompson?" Lily sat in the chair Mr. Roberts held out for her and looked at the stack of legal papers in front of her.

"Let's start with this one." Mr. Thompson said taking the top document from the stack and putting it in front of her. "As you can see, these are papers incorporating The Golden Cauldron, drawing up an equal partnership with only the names of the signers entitled to any of the assets of the company. In other words, Ms. Hughes, the spouses, if any, of the women named in this document have no rights or claims to anything held by this corporation. As you can see, there are six signatures on this last page but seven names on the document. Should you agree, after reading the papers over, here is where you would sign," he said pointing to the 'sign here' sticky tag.

"How could they not tell me about this?" Lily sputtered indignantly. "I just ... ," her voice trailed off. Resigned to their subterfuge, she sat back to read. When she had finished, she looked up at Mr. Thompson who was still standing by her side. "Everything looks to be in order. Are you sure spouses will have no access to these assets?" Her thoughts flew to Dennis and Art, Diana and Ashley's husbands respectively relieved they'd receive nothing from The Circle's work.

"That's why Mr. Montgomery asked Benjamin and me to do this. It does take some expertise," Mr. Thompson said.

"Thank you very much," Lily said, looking in her bag for a pen.

"Here, Ms. Hughes." Mr. Roberts leaned across the table, a pen in his outstretched hand.

"Why, thank you Mr. Roberts. I'm sure a pen is in here somewhere, but it'll save time if I use yours."

"Next, is Mr. Montgomery's revised Last Will and Testament." Mr. Thompson said, bringing forth another set of papers. "The important provisions are that Mr. Montgomery's estate is to be divided equally between his mother, two sisters and you, Ms. Hughes. There is nothing for you to sign, but Mr. Montgomery wants you to have a copy for your records."

"Last but not least, we have a pre-nuptial agreement that simply states that whatever is in your possession prior to your wedding, remains your property. This paper would go into effect at the time of your marriage. The other papers go into effect upon filing with the proper authorities."

"Do you have any questions, Ms. Hughes?" Mr. Roberts sat quietly across the table from her.

Words failed her. Unshed tears brimmed in her eyes, emotions choked her throat. Butterflies flitted in her heart and lungs. Eyes closed she struggled to tame the worst of the shivers coursing through her, unaware tears now fell.

Jackson stayed still, not moving, not speaking, not reaching out for her, just watching, watching the emotions fly across her face, the tears, dear God let them be from joy, slip down her cheeks. When her eyes closed, he felt defeat start to creep over him. He closed his eyes calling upon all of his reserves to get him through this. Her voice.

"No, no, I don't have any questions." She turned in her chair and saw Jackson standing behind and slightly to her left. Her eyes shone with tears, her smile wobbled, her heart bursting with love, she took a shaky breath and turned back to the papers on the table.

Her hands clasped tightly in her lap, she looked from Mr. Thompson to Mr. Roberts and in a steady but emotion-filled voice said, "Where do I sign?"

"I do need to see some identification, Ms. Hughes. Your signatures need to be notarized." Mr. Roberts' previously formal expression had softened.

It took a minute for her trembling hands to retrieve her wallet, remove her driver's license and hand it to Mr. Roberts. Mr. Thompson went over the paperwork with her once more. First she signed the incorporation papers for the Golden Cauldron. He put her copy in a folder. A second folder with a copy of Jackson's Will joined the first.

Last was the pre-nuptial agreement consisting of these two sentences.

That which belongs to Lily Langdon Hughes on the day she marries Jackson Hubert Montgomery remains hers and hers alone.

That which belongs to Jackson Hubert Montgomery on the day he marries Lily Langdon Hughes remains his and his alone.

Tears quietly slid down her face as she picked up the pen and signed her name.

"Well, that takes care of that then, Ms. Hughes," Mr. Thompson said smiling. "Our firm hopes to do business with you in the future."

"We certainly do, Ms. Hughes," added Mr. Roberts as he completed the Notary Public record and returned her driver's license.

Standing, the chair pressed against the back of her legs, Lily saw the mountains and river out the window, saw Jackson's reflection superimposed over them. His presence filled the room. She turned and he was there—in front of her. He stood never moving a muscle, his eyes on her never wavered; his intense look consumed her.

Her arms slipped around his neck as her body pressed close. Her lips on his, her voice whispered his name – over and over.

Jackson held her close. His mouth raced over her face and found its mate, her lips, her mouth. Her, only her. Relief flooded through him. He held her tight, kissing her with a depth and intensity, with an energy that was palpable in the room.

Wrapped in his arms, Lily whispered, "Thank you Goddess for answering my prayers, for this man and this moment, for bringing my dreams to reality."

Clapping, cheering, chattering, and laughter finally seeped into their awareness. They broke apart: Lily's face pink with embarrassment, Jackson's face sporting a boyish, self-satisfied grin. All of her circle sisters and Eleanor were gathered around the conference table now laden with bottles of champagne, boxes of chocolate, and bowls of strawberries. The sound of champagne corks being popped had everyone's attention focused on the table as Mr. Roberts filled the glasses and the toasts began.

Gabriella made the first one: "To the Golden Cauldron, may the many blessings of the Goddess fill it to the brim with love and light, joy and happiness, grace and gratitude and peace. Blessed Be!"

"Hear hear," spilled forth as the champagne glasses were clinked and sips were taken.

"To House Totems." Ashley toasted.

"To House Totems," everyone chimed and lifted their glasses again.

"To Jackson," added Hunter.

And the chant "Jackson, Jackson, Jackson" filled the air until with laughter, glasses were touched and raised in the air in salute.

Jackson pulled Lily back into his arms and looked at her with unmasked desire flaming in his eyes. "Set a date, Lily. Damn it, set a date."

"Summer Solstice, Jackson. I'll marry you on Summer Solstice."

"Well, everyone, we've less than six weeks to put this wedding together. That shouldn't be a problem for the Sisters of the Golden Cauldron, should it?" Sophia asked.

A chorus of "no" was her answer.

Lily pulled Jackson's head down to within a fraction of an inch of her mouth. "No, it won't be a problem at all." Stretching up the last little bit, she kissed him with love and gratitude and a great deal of passion.

37 - THE WEDDING

The full-length mirror reflected the petite blond, her hair swept back in a simple but elegant style. The floor-length gown in a shade of blue that matched her eyes was trimmed with yards of intricate white lace. Love can change one in the most extraordinary ways. *I look so different. Not like me but at the same time, just like me.*

Sunlight shimmered through the lace curtains on the window creating wavering patterns on the bed's dark blue comforter. *I wish Charlie...* An overwhelming sadness cast darkness in her heart. He'd never responded to the long letter she'd written about Jackson, the House Totems, and getting married. Wishes aren't going to make anything different. The lacy patterns caught her attention. Intricate just like relationships. Weaves, patterns. After the papers were signed and the celebration ended, she and Jackson had sat on her couch. He'd told her how deeply wounded he'd been when Pamela left him, that his refusal to have a pre-nuptial agreement was his way of forcing her to accept him as he is...She blew out a breath and rubbed her heart. It hadn't been all about her.

At a soft knock on the door, Lily turned and called out, "Come in."

As her circle sisters walked into the room, she grinned. "I'm so glad to see you all."

"You didn't really think any of us would miss this day, did you Lily?" Hunter quipped as she came over and gave Lily a hug. "The spinsterish Lily marries the handsome hunk. Sounds like a title for your book, Gabby."

"Who knows, the title just might work," Gabriella rejoined as she too gave Lily a hug.

"Since we're all here and we've a little time, how 'bout a talking circle?" Ashley asked, standing just inside the door. "We've all been so busy the last few weeks. And with all the changes coming up, it'll be awhile before we're all together again."

"A talking circle is a great idea, Ash." Diana moved next to her. "Sophia, do you have something we can use?"

"I'm sure I can find something, D. Give me a few minutes to find the right something," Sophia said, scurrying out the door.

"Are we going to sit in here?" Elizabeth asked, gesturing around Sophia's bedroom. "Or are we going to go to another room?"

"Lily's choice," Sophia called out. "This is her day so it's her choice except she can't choose the backyard. Oh, and if she wants the family room, the drapes have to be closed."

"With those restrictions on the family room, I think I'd prefer the living room. On a day like today I want to be able to see flowers blooming and the sun shining in an-oh-so-blue sky. I feel like I could fly I'm so full of joy right now." Lily started out the bedroom door and down the hall toward the living room. Halfway along, she started laughing.

"What's so funny?" Hunter asked.

"I feel like a mother duck with ducklings or the Pied Piper of Hamlin with all of you following after me. Maybe the joy I feel right now will flow behind, above, before, and all around me. My prayer is that each and every one of you'll be filled with the abundance of joy that fills me now."

Her words were met with silence. Turning, she walked backwards. "Have I said something wrong?" Lily searched their faces for answers to her confusion. "I know I feel so very different, lighter really, like a huge weight's been lifted. That's what the joy I feel is like, like I'm floating, almost walking on air."

"There's nothing wrong with what you've said. I believe our silence is due to our being at a loss for words seeing how joy is manifested in you this day." Diana stepped forward, put her arm around Lily's waist, turning her around so they could continue on. She leaned closer and added, "I feel very blessed to be a witness to your happiness. You have a glow about you. A shining from within that radiates out and envelopes everything around you."

Sophia was waiting in the living room. "Come and sit everyone. I've our favorite piece of rose quartz as our talking stone as today is a day for love. Lily, do you want to start?"

"No, Soph, I'd like to be last."

"I'll start unless someone else really, really wants to," Elizabeth said as laughter bubbled out. "I've so much to talk to you all about. But first let's smudge and do prayers. This is a special day and a special time, a little ceremony feels right."

Within minutes the smudging was done and everyone stood together in a circle. Arms lifted in prayer, Elizabeth started: "Goddess, Spirit, Universal Source please be with us this day. Watch over, guide and protect us from all harm."

"Thank you for your many blessings most especially for a wonderfully bright and glorious day for this wedding," added Gabriella.

"Thank you for lighting the way for Jackson and Lily. May your light shine on each of us, lighting our path so we may find our own highest good," Diana said.

"Thank you Goddess for life. For our ability to stand here and bear witness to the love and happiness of Lily and Jackson," whispered Ashley.

"May your gifts be passed on through us to other generations. May your prayer be forever on our lips and those of women for generations to come," Hunter added.

"May we always be able to see our highest good served in the activities of our lives. May we experience grace and gratitude in abundance each day," Sophia remarked.

"May we never lose the connection with You and with each other no matter the future," Lily finished.

"Blessed Be." was the chorus.

They sat on the floor, knees touching. Sophia handed the stone to Elizabeth.

"My plane leaves tomorrow." Her face was alight with anticipation and joy. "I leave for Ireland tomorrow! I'm so excited I can hardly sit still. I know I'm repeating myself but it's as if I've all these words tumbling around inside and I'll explode if I don't get them out. I've worked it out so I'm taking five weeks off. I can scarcely believe I'll be able to visit all the special places I've wanted to see: The Cliffs of Mohr, the Connemara Mountains, the faerie hills, the sacred mounds." Her large blue eyes sparkled, her face animated with excitement and pleasure. "I've always wanted to visit the sacred places of power in Ireland and now I'm going to do it." With a shiver of delight she passed the stone to Gabriella.

With her hazel eyes flashing in delight, Gabriella turned to Elizabeth. "It makes no difference how many times you tell me about going; I'm always thrilled to hear your story. Your anticipation and delight surround more than just you, you know. It's like Lily said, the joy she feels radiates out and surrounds us all. Your anticipation and delight do the same. Take lots of pictures and keep a journal so we can all hear what happens. How the adoption agency will get along without you is beyond me, but I'm pleased you'll let them find out for themselves, so very pleased you are following your dream.

"As for me," she said her curly auburn hair bouncing as she turned toward the others. "I'm considering working half-time later this summer, just enough to keep my medical benefits and spend the rest of my time writing. If I live frugally through the next two months, I think I can go part-time for September and October. I feel such excitement at the idea of having time to write every day when I'm not so tired and haven't spent the entire day in front of a computer. If it works out, my plan is to go to the office in the afternoon so I'm fresh for my writing in the morning."

Lily's gaze drifted out the window to the clear, blue sky. The faint scent of honeysuckle wafting in through an open window teased her senses and brought her mind back to focus on her friends. Change was certainly stirring more lives than just hers.

Diana took the stone and looked around. "It struck me the other day that I'll be forty in less than six months. I'm thankful I've Lily's wedding and your trip, E, to distract me because it's daunting to think about being that age." Her gaze on Lily she cupped her hands at her heart and opened them as she reached out. "My prayers are for much joy and happiness to surround you." She added as her gaze took in the others, "I talked to William Thompson and Lily's tax person and am now a formal business with cards, tax id number and business plan. It feels good."

Ashley went next. "I go back in for another mammogram the end of July. Keep me in your prayers that the cancer is still gone." She looked at each of her friends with quiet intensity. "I don't know what I'll do if it comes back. Art's not real good with the kids or keeping things up around the house." She swallowed hard not wanting to say more about that and spoil Lily's wedding day. "Right now I feel good and the kids are all doing great." She held her pendant of an amethyst dragonfly tightly in her right hand and, turning toward Elizabeth, leaned forward, her direct gray gaze meeting bright blue eyes. "I'm so proud of you. You've talked about Ireland and the Holy places forever! Good for you that you're acting on your dream. My prayers and blessings go with you for a safe, memorable, wonderful trip." She straightened and handed the stone to Hunter.

"The studio continues to do well," she bubbled. "Thanks for your support of our Spring Program." She smiled and her eyes roved around the circle. "I'm keeping busy between the studio and Logan. Yes, she'll be a junior next year, thanks to Sophia's gentle mentoring and tutoring. You know she's a great young lady with basically a good head on her shoulders." She glanced out the window. "I truly do wish there was a maiden's circle for her to join. I know what having this circle and each of you in my life has meant to me. I wish as much for her.

"And Ireland! Oh, E you'll love it, love it, love it. I expect you'll meet Mr. Wonderful as the Irish men are a handsome, silver-tongued lot. I think I'll add that to my prayers for you," she said and laughed. "Ash, Logan and I have lots of flexibility so if you need something, just let us know." Her gaze shifted. "And, Diana, I'm so pleased you've formalized your business."

Sophia accepted the stone. Her eyes closed. A wave of sadness swept over her. "Weddings are wonderful moments in a life, when dreams are realized and hopes flourish." She breathed in the scent of smudge, opened her eyes and continued. "I remember so clearly the day Jonathan and I got married just as I remember so clearly the day I buried him. Three and a half years later, the pain is less but still there. Days like today bring him closer to me." She looked at Lily. "My prayers are that you and Jackson have as much happiness as Jonathan and I did. I doubt you could have more." She turned back to the circle. "Thank you for helping with the garden this month. You've given me the time to help my ailing friend with his affairs." A grin on her face she added, "Remember though, the harvest at the end of the summer will have enough zucchini for half the town.

"We're quite the impressive group here with trips to Ireland, writing books, teaching classes at the community college, popular and productive recitals, and getting married. I'm feeling a bit" she grinned mischievously, "inept in all of the 'eptness.'" Looking at Ashley, Sophia smiled softly saying, "I'll be stopping by to see what needs to be done," and then she handed the stone to Lily.

The warm rose quartz glowed in her hand. Around the circle sat the women who'd loved and supported her over the years. All of their lives had changed so much since that first meeting. Sophia's Jonathan had been killed in an auto accident and they'd all been there for her. Ashley'd had one bout of breast cancer and they'd stayed with her, helping with her children, cooking, and cleaning. All the children were growing up with the care and influence of The Circle, and some like her Charlie and Diana's Bill, were being let go as they came of age.

Her eyes filled with tears of wistful joy acknowledging today was another turning point for The Circle. She cleared her throat, swallowed the lump of emotions and smiled a radiant smile that blossomed from her soul.

"Thank you all for everything you've done for and with me these past eight months. At least I think it was eight months ago I called Diana for advice on working with Eleanor. Every time I needed anything, even when I didn't know I needed it, you were there individually or together. Without your love and support I don't know that Jackson and I would've made it through our challenges to this day.

"E, you've been a beacon of light while you've quietly and continuously moved toward your dream of being in Ireland. May your trip be safe. May you find your joy there.

"Gabby, thank you for asking me to be one of your readers. Your trust and faith in me to hold your dream safe and support you as it becomes your reality is a gift I shall always treasure.

"D. I don't have words to express all of the emotion I feel for you. No matter what time of the day or night, you were always there for me, encouraging me to find my way, shining a light when I felt trapped in darkness. May I be able to be that for you should you ever need it.

"And Ash, Jackson and I may be off somewhere but I do expect to get a phone call telling me about the test results. I don't want to hear it from anyone but you. I may not be here to hold you in my arms, but I'll hold you in my prayers. Regardless of the outcome, you're not and never will be alone. We'll all be with you through whatever is to come.

"Hunter, I must say that your first Spring Program was so much more than I'd expected. Jackson and I came expecting to find ourselves challenged to sit and pay attention. You excel as a teacher! Because you take each of your students and set things up so she can shine. Both Jackson and I were delighted to be in the audience and plan on attending and bringing friends to your next extravaganza! I know it isn't easy to raise a child and run a business but you make it seem effortless.

"Soph, I didn't even have to call you and you came to my aid.

However, the gift you've given me that I treasure above all is the gift of this circle. Without your invitation, I wouldn't know any of you and my life would be so much less than what it is. To me you all manifest the bounty of your garden: full of riches, full of health, full of love, full of life.

"May the Goddess be with each of us as we move forward on our paths. May She in her infinite wisdom see that our paths run true to our highest good. May we each find the joy and happiness that is ours because we are. Blessed be."

Lily took Elizabeth and Sophia's hands in hers and looked around at her Circle Sisters as they reached out to each other. Closing her eyes she raised her head and felt the energy, the love emanating, swirling, and surrounding them all. *I am so very blessed.* Gently squeezing Sophia's hand she opened her eyes. When she saw everyone else's eyes open, she smiled. Getting to her feet, she said, "Let's eat! I'm in need of sustenance if I'm going to be married in two hours!"

They all scrambled to their feet and headed toward the kitchen.

"I'm sure we can find something in the kitchen to nibble on. If my memory serves, you and Jackson have planned a feast at the reception later," Sophia commented.

"When I saw the menu, I was astounded," Hunter chimed in. "My goodness, Lily, you have everything, even shrimp!"

"Well, Jackson has contacts everywhere and he called in some of them to make sure this was special." Lily started to walk into the kitchen.

"Wait!" Sophia grabbed Lily and turned her around. "Someone check to make sure the drapes are closed. We've planned and plotted too much to have it spoiled this close to the wedding."

"What difference will it make if I see your garden now or in another hour or so?" Lily asked.

"You'll see soon enough," Diana replied her face lit with a grin. "Sophia is right. We've gone above and beyond to keep this from you, Lily, so don't spoil it and try peeking. We need your promise on this."

"My promise? Hmmm, I have the distinct feeling when I see Soph's backyard and garden it's going to look somewhat different than when

I last saw it. Right?" She looked around and spied Hunter, a smirk on her face, coming across the room from the drapes now tightly closed.

"I thought you were famished, starving, in need of sustenance?" Gabriella raised her hand putting its back to her forehead, feigning weakness; she sighed dramatically, "Soph, she may be too weak for the wedding if we don't get food into her quickly." Recovering with lightning like speed, she gave a cheeky grin saying, "Well, we all love you enough that one of us would be more than willing to stand in for you if you can't carry on."

"That's so very considerate of you, Gabby," Lily's voice was politeness personified. "I believe I'll be able to manage. But I do so appreciate your willingness to be of assistance should it be needed."

"Well, now that that's settled," Diana chimed in, "let's eat."

Within minutes every plate was filled and they were back in the living room because Lily wanted to see the sky. Time flew by as they ate and chatted. Hunter noticed a car pulling into the drive.

"Someone's here," she called out. "Let's get Lily back to Sophia's room. We don't want Jackson to see her before the ceremony!" She jumped up and helped Lily to her feet. "Out of here before it's too late and someone sees you," she ordered with a laugh.

"Do you believe in those old superstitions?" Lily asked.

"Why take any chances?" Hunter responded as she practically drug Lily down the hall to the bedroom. "I'll take first watch," she hollered over her shoulder to the others who were clearing the dishes up and putting leftovers away.

THE DOOR to the bedroom opened and Ashley popped in. "Are you ready?" she asked.

"Yes, I'm ready. Very, very, very ready," Lily said and laughed with delight. "I've been languishing away here in Soph's boudoir," she sighed dramatically, her eyes dancing with happiness.

"Well, come along then," Ashley said, opening the door and bowing her out. "Are you nervous?"

Ashley and Lily linked arms and started down the hall. "A little. It's much more anticipation nerves than anything else. To think I almost missed having this day. Oh, Ash, I'm ever so grateful to have a second chance. To have this wedding day." A quiet determination filled her and echoed in her voice.

Entering the family room, Lily saw her circle sisters looking like the proverbial Cheshire cat who'd just lapped up all the cream. Then she saw the seventh person.

"Eleanor!" Lily exclaimed as she rushed across the room. "I'm so thankful you're here now and not outside." She stopped a moment, "You look exquisite," she said before embracing Eleanor.

"Actually, you are the exquisite one." Eleanor's eyes filled with tears. "Just look at you, my dear...quite, quite lovely." Holding her in her arms, she whispered, "I am so very glad you are becoming my daughter."

"A sentiment I share, Eleanor. Thank you for all you've done to help Jackson and me get ready for this day."

"It has all been a pleasure, I can assure you," Eleanor replied. "Are you as ready for this ceremony as I believe my son is?"

"I most certainly am."

Looking around the room, Eleanor said, "Then, let us begin!"

"That does seem to be the next step in the process." Diana laughed and said, "Places everyone." Everyone moved into position. "Okay, on the count of three open the curtains. One. Two. Close your eyes Lily, no fair peeking. Three."

"When can I open my eyes? This isn't fair," Lily said petulantly.

"Now would be a good time," Gabriella whispered in her ear.

Lily opened her eyes, the breath whoosh out of her. "Oh my," she whispered. "Oh my! I've never ... I'd never dreamed ... This is wondrous...," her words rushed out. A few steps forward and she stood in the doorway.

Pots of flowers circled a raised platform that took up much of the grassy part of the yard. Over the platform was a canopy festooned with ribbons and banners. The two in front: a Dragon and a Great Horned Owl.

"Oh look, there's Badger and Fox peeking around the pots," Lily exclaimed, feathers fluttered in her stomach, laughter bubbled. "I can hardly believe my eyes; I think every House Totem I've ever sensed came here today." Turning around she looked at her friends whose eyes were filled with unshed tears. "Well, I'm at a loss for words. I never would have dreamed this, never expected anything so spectacular!"

Then she heard the music: the traditional wedding march playing softly in the background. She stepped out onto the patio and looked for Jackson. Where was he? She scanned the yard. As if by magic he was there, right before her!

With a smile of joy she started walking toward him.

"Mom, you're supposed to wait for me to escort you."

Her head whipped around at the sound of that voice. "Charlie?" exploded from her lips. She looked up at him in wonder. "I thought you couldn't make it?" He was so tall, his shoulders broader. "You couldn't...."

"Jackson fixed it so I could. I didn't want to miss this day, Mom. I just couldn't figure out how to do it," he said quietly, running his fingers through his brown hair in a familiar gesture. His voice was deep and serious, "I've missed you Mom, I really have missed you." His arms encircled her in a tentative hug.

"I've missed you too, Charlie. I'm so glad you're here," she whispered so only he heard. Keeping one arm around him, she turned back to the audience, "An already spectacular day made better!

"How many of you knew?" she asked with a mock show of fierceness. Every face was covered with a grin. "You all knew? Every one of you?" With a loud exhalation of breath, Lily looked over at Jackson indignation oozing from every pore. "You will get yours later, Jackson. You will pay dearly for this deception."

"I'm counting on it, Lily. Truly, I'm counting on it," he said with a wink. "I do think you mean I'll pay later rather than sooner – like after the ceremony and reception? Can we move forward so I can get my "just desserts"?"

The music began again, Daniel ushered Eleanor to her seat on the groom's side where she took her place next to Jackson's sisters and their families before he took his place as Jackson's best man. The chairs were not in rows as one might expect but were, instead, in a double crescent to make sure everyone was close.

Her circle sisters, acting as bridesmaids or matrons of honor, were next.

Charlie put his mother's hand in the crook of his arm, escorting her down the short aisle. After placing her hand in Jackson's, he stepped over to sit beside Logan.

Lily stood quietly by Jackson's side, her heart beating wildly, her face glowing with joy. The judge came forward to begin the ceremony. Before she could begin, Lily held her hand up, palm out. Turning to Jackson, her voice clear, she said, "I love you with all my heart, soul, and might. I don't know how we've come to be here in this time and space together, but I am so very grateful. The gift you've given me this day, seeing that Charlie was able to be here ... I have no words to express the emotions I feel. I am humbled by your continued presence in our relationship." Rising on her toes, she reached up and pulled him down into an embrace, a kiss of tenderness. "If we were on the couch, Jackson, I'd be in your lap right now," she murmured as the kiss ended.

"You are mine now and always," Jackson whispered fiercely, pulling her back into his arms for a passionate kiss.

Their breathing was ragged when he pulled back. "Let's finish this up. I've a honeymoon waiting with this woman."

When the ceremony concluded, there were few if any dry eyes. Before leaving for the reception, Lily found a little time to spend alone with Charlie. Jackson had arranged for him to fly in from Ohio on the red eye last night. Early this morning he'd picked him up at the airport, made sure his suit and shoes fit, seen that his hair was cut and taken him home where he'd designated one of the bedrooms as 'Charlie's room' to use whenever he wanted. His plane left at 7 p.m. which only left him a few hours.

"I know you'll be okay, Mom. He really loves you," Charlie said earnestly. "He'll take care of you and see you have anything you need."

"I know that, Charlie," Lily said hearing how important it was for her son to know she had someone to care for her. She reached up to brush back the lock of hair that fell onto his forehead. "I'm glad you like him."

"I don't know when I'll be back out though, Mom. Things are moving along in Ohio. I've got lots of offers for schools and will be making my selection soon." His head hung, he looked at his feet. "I'm sorry about graduation, Mom. I just didn't know what to do. If you'd come, it wouldn't have been a good thing. Dad, well, Dad isn't very understanding about you. I don't know what to say really other than I'm sorry. Maybe when I graduate from college, I'll have grown up enough to handle things better." Taking her hands and looking her in the eyes, he added, "I'm really sorry, Mom. I know it sounds lame."

"No, Charlie, not lame. It sounds like the truth. I'd rather know what's going on than wonder if maybe you just didn't want me in your life anymore."

"You're my mom, you'll always be my mom," he said resting an arm around her shoulders. "It isn't the same, but I've got something for you. Well, actually Jackson has it," he shifted to stand in front of her. "It's a DVD of the whole ceremony. My best friend, Jerry, well, his family was taking pictures and making a video of graduation. I talked to Jerry's dad about being able to use it to send to you. He did all kinds of close ups of me just like he did of Jerry. And, then he talked to me on camera at the end about things so you have that too. That part is just for you, Mom. He edited it out of all the other versions. I know it isn't the same. It's just all I could think of."

"I can hardly wait to see it," Lily reached up and touched his cheek. "You're not quite eighteen Charlie and I think you did a great job of figuring this out on your own." Her hand rested on his shoulder. "Always know I love you and no matter what happens, I will always love you. We've been through so much in the past, it's…well, it's hard for me to see you growing up and growing away from me. The reality is, whether you lived here with me or in Ohio, you are at that place in your life where you're growing up and growing away from me. That's just what our children do whether we like it or not."

"Do you remember telling me that Grandmother Moon looks down on us no matter where we are?" Charlie asked.

"Yes, I do remember telling you that when you so wanted to spend the night with friends but were worried I wouldn't be there," Lily said with a wistful smile. "I remember those times very well."

"Maybe that will help us now." Charlie took her hands, an earnest look on his face, his blue eyes serious. "Maybe we can look at Grandmother Moon and know that the other one is looking at her too. I always know on the full moon you're doing prayers, maybe drumming, putting your crystals out to be cleansed. I haven't forgotten those things, Mom."

"I think that's a fine idea, Charlie. I'll know you're looking at Grandmother Moon and on the full moon I'll know that you're thinking of me and I will send prayers to you through Grandmother."

"That's a deal, Mom," Charlie said hugging her tightly. "I've missed you, Mom." Taking a deep breath he added, "You still smell like lavender. Whenever I smell lavender, I think of you too."

"Thank you for talking to me. I miss that as much as anything, just hearing your voice. This time with you is a gift, something that has made my wedding day even more special." Lily's hand rested on his arm, her throat full of words she'd never speak. He'd given her bittersweet gifts of words and memories. They were gifts nonetheless.

"Well, Mom, people are getting restless. I think there's more to do before you and Jackson are off on your honeymoon. By the way, where are you going?"

"I don't know. He won't tell me. Can you imagine?" Lily sputtered looking up at Charlie. Seeing the delight in his eyes, she screeched, "You know! You know!"

He laughed and danced away.

"Jackson," Lily said with exasperation. "Does everyone but me know?"

"Know what, Lily," Jackson said with feigned innocence.

"About our honeymoon. Does everyone know where we're going except me?" She ground out, her jaw clenched in exasperation.

"Not for much longer, Lily love." He winked and drew her arm through his. "Shall we leave for the reception? People are probably starting to arrive and we're the guests of honor. It isn't seemly for us to be late." He chuckled, steered her into the house, and called over his shoulder as they disappeared inside, "We're on our way to the reception, see you all there."

〜

HER FEET HURT. Her legs hurt. Her hips hurt. That meant every joint that supported her in the upright position hurt. How did dignitaries ever do this? And she liked all these people and wanted to see them. Lily sighed. *I'd just like to do some of it sitting down.*

Mark Parker was here with Evan, the little boy he hoped to adopt. Most of her clients had come to the reception. She'd managed to arrange transportation no matter how challenging for everyone who wanted to attend.

Jackson's sisters and their families had flown in yesterday. They'd all had dinner last night but there wasn't enough time to visit beyond the superficial, to really get to know them. She hoped they could come back for Thanksgiving.

Daniel, handsome in his dark blue suit, had the jacket off and his tie loosened before he reached the reception. She'd never seen him in anything other than work or casual clothes. A squeal of laughing delight signaled Ashley's kids had found him. Charlie was catching up with Logan and visiting with those of her clients he knew. He circled around every fifteen minutes or so to check in and put his arm around her. His transportation to the airport was all arranged. "Don't worry, Mom. Jackson took care of it."

Moving to Eleanor's side, she smiled as someone else approached to wish her well and exchange pleasantries.

"I think Jackson is looking for you. Indeed, I am certain he is," Eleanor said beaming. "Oh, there he is." Spying her son, she waved discreetly drawing his attention.

"Thank you for finding her for me." Jackson leaned down to kiss Eleanor's cheek. "I believe you're staying with …"

"Yes, I am, Jackson," Eleanor interrupted him. "I'm all taken care of."

"Since you're settled, I'll take my bride and be off," he said with a flourish. Catching Lily around the waist, he brought her close to his side. "Now, my dear, we've an errand to run before we're off on our honeymoon."

"And what would that be?" Her irritation and frustration at being kept in the dark reflected in her voice, the set of her jaw, and her furrowed brow.

With a grin, Jackson took her hand, kissed her palm, and led her away. Outside Lily recognized the limousine driver as the one who'd taken her to the meeting with Jackson. She smiled and nodded in acknowledgement.

"Everything's as you requested, Mr. Montgomery," the driver said, opening the door.

Jackson handed Lily inside. His face split in a wide grin at her delighted squeal, "Charlie!"

The trip to the airport was smooth. Jackson lounged against the seat watching Lily's delighted animated face as she chatted with her son for the twenty minute ride. At the airport, he stood back while they said their goodbyes. Time was short and Charlie had to run to make his flight.

Lily turned away from the terminal entrance. "Thank you," she said reaching for Jackson's hand, letting him lead her back to the car. Inside, she curled up in his arms. He pressed soft kisses in her hair, felt as well as heard her deep sigh. She tilted her head to look at him, her eyes soft and glowing. He bent down, sealing their lips in a thorough, passionate, kiss. "Have you ever made love in the back of limousine?" he whispered in her ear as he nibbled her lobe and one-handed unfastened the buttons on her dress.

"Jackson, we can't. Someone might..." her words were silenced by a plundering kiss and her body arched up as his free hand found her breast, teased her nipple and pulled her even closer. When he felt her melt into him, he raised his head and smiled. "Why do you think the windows are tinted?"

~

"AND THAT MY SWEET," Jackson said in a pleased and sated tone of voice, "is the first of many adventures planned for our honeymoon. Care to guess what the second one might be?"

Lily curled against him as shock waves of orgasmic released rocketed on and on through her. "Just hold me, Jackson. Don't ever let me go."

"I'll never let you go, Lily. Never." Pushing the intercom, Jackson inquired as to where they were.

"About ten minutes away," the driver replied.

"If this limo stops and I'm found in this condition, I may become an instant widow," she grumbled wrestling her arms into the dress sleeves.

"Well, my dear, we have ten minutes to become somewhat respectable," he said while trying to straighten out his own clothing.

The limo came to a slow stop. Lily gave up trying to have everything back in place. At least my buttons are done. She looked down her front. Oops, not exactly. The door opened as she slipped the last button into its proper hole. Stepping out, her mouth gaped. They were at Jackson's.

"Thank you." Jackson pressed a folded bill into the driver's hand. He took Lily's hand and led her to the front door.

"What?" she sputtered.

"Sshh, you'll soon see my inquisitive one." Jackson smiled devilishly as he unlocked and opened the door. Quickly turning off the security alarm, he pulled Lily inside and into his arms.

Flowers were everywhere, their sweet scent perfuming the air. Champagne was chilling in a bucket and small trays of snacks were on the table. "We have two weeks Lily," Jackson whispered pulling her into his arms. "Two weeks with no telephones, no interruptions. Two weeks for us... ."

"But I don't understand," Lily said confusion and a note of disappointment in her voice. "We'll be here for two weeks?"

"Ah, Lily, our honeymoon will be an adventure," Jackson chuckled dancing her over to the couch. "Every day will be different. We'll be here, there, everywhere. You'll see," he added bending her over the back until she grabbed him to keep from falling. "I love to see surprise on your face. Your eyes get big; your mouth opens into a delightful 'o', your eyebrows raise. My plan is to see that expression at least once every day in the next two weeks." He finished tumbling them over the back of the couch maneuvering so he landed on the bottom. "See there it is again," he said as his lips found hers.

Sometime later, Lily snuggled closer, her head on Jackson's shoulder, a glass of champagne in her hand. "Well," she said enjoying him flinch when she rested the cold glass on his bare chest. "I don't think it fair for you to have all the fun. I'll have to think of some ways to surprise you." She giggled as she tipped the glass dribbling champagne down his naked chest. "Oh my, how clumsy of me," she smiled slyly, licking her lips. "Guess I need to clean this up myself."

And she did.

LEARN MORE ABOUT THESE BOOKS

Get the Latest News about New Releases, Special Events, Special pricing/sales

You have just finished reading *Lily: The Dragon and The Great Horned Owl* the first book in the Sacred Women's Circle series.

Be the first to learn about future releases, any pre-release pricing or sales and special events by signing up for my mailing list here. I do not spam and you are free to unsubscribe at any time.

For More Information on The Sacred Women's Circle series check out:
My website: www.JudithAshleyRomance.com
My blog: www.JudithAshley.blogspot.com

If you enjoyed reading about *Lily*, I'd be grateful if you would spread the word by telling friends and family, posting on social media and writing a review. Any and all of the above will be greatly appreciated and are a perfect way to support me.

ABOUT JUDITH

What do you do if you see visions and hear voices? If you're Judith Ashley, you write these stories down.

It helped that her visions and the voices were of seven women creating a sacred women's circle, a haven from whence they deal with the issues and struggles many of us face in everyday life.

It also helped that Judith experiences firsthand the healing power of supportive relationships and spiritual practices.

Judith's Prayer for you: *May your dreams manifest in "right time" and may you know the peace of unconditional acceptance, support and unconditional love.*

http://judithashleyromance.com

 facebook.com/JudithAshley.Romance

 twitter.com/JudithAshley19

 bookbub.com/authors/judith-ashley

WINDTREE PRESS

For more books from the heart in fiction and non-fiction please visit
Windtree Press

http://windtreepress.com